WINNER HARRIS

IAN ST JAMES, according to the press, was a millionaire at the age of thirty, when the merchant bank backing his enterprises suddenly collapsed and took his business with it. In the years afterwards he started a management consultancy and later turned it into a small investment house. In 1977 he retired to write full time. His earlier novels include *The Money Stones*, *The Balfour Conspiracy*, *The Killing Anniversary*, *Cold New Dawn* and *Justice*. He is married with three children.

D1471493

Available in Fontana by the same author

THE MONEY STONES
THE BALFOUR CONSPIRACY
THE KILLING ANNIVERSARY
COLD NEW DAWN
JUSTICE

IAN ST JAMES

WINNER HARRIS

FONTANA/Collins

First published by William Heinemann Ltd 1982
First issued in Fontana Paperbacks 1983
This reprint 1989

Copyright © Ian St James 1982

Printed and bound in Great Britain by
William Collins Sons & Co. Ltd, Glasgow

For my Mother

CHAPTER ONE

It was still raining when the cab turned into Holborn. Water streaked the windows soaking up dust as it ran down the glass, so that peering out was like looking through bars. Last time the bars had been real. My last glimpse of the Old Bailey had been through the rear window of a Black Maria, handcuffed to a policeman, with the words of the judge ringing in my ears. But that was two years ago.

I left the cab at the top of Chancery Lane and walked down towards the Strand, bending into the rain and side-stepping splashes thrown up by passing traffic. It had turned noon. The expense account trade – solicitors and their clients – gathered in Mario's entrance like fat cats sniffing a bowl of cream, while at the pub next door pasty-faced clerks washed their sandwiches down with half pints of bitter. A new wine bar had opened opposite Bream's Buildings – trendy *décor* and Chablis at eighty pence a glass – but apart from that the street looked much as I remembered it. Even the newspaper placards were vaguely familiar. Inflation was *down* to nineteen per cent, whereas it had been *up* to the same figure two years ago – and I was still working out if that was good or bad when I reached my solicitor's office on the corner.

The receptionist was new. Old Gladys would have given a yelp of welcome and rushed to hug me, whereas this girl finished painting a fingernail before she even deigned look up.

'I'd like to see Mr Collins.'

She focused on my unbuttoned raincoat, the creased suit and nondescript tie. I saw my face reflected in her spectacles – fair hair cut too short by the prison barber, watchful blue eyes, skin the colour of putty after two years' confinement. Her eyes blinked like the shutter of a camera while she catalogued my voice – London, not Cockney, but certainly London – and definitely not public school. She frowned at the desk diary in front of her. 'You have an appointment . . . Mr—?'

'Harris. Sam Harris. He'll see me.'

'There's nothing in the diary—' she began reproachfully, then faltered as she caught the look in my eye. Her unpainted hand reached for the telephone and I turned away to drop into a chair. Looking around I saw the other changes. The whole front office had been refurnished. Horsehair armchairs had given way to Mies Van der Rohe modernity. The carpet was new and a collection of sporting prints replaced the fly-blown calendars which had decorated the walls. Even the smell of the place was different. Once as musty as a museum, now as crisply scented as a new bank note.

'I have a Mr Harris asking for Mr Collins,' the girl said cautiously. She dried her fingernails on a nonexistent breeze, waving her hand limply from the wrist. Her eyes rounded and I smiled inwardly while imagining the reaction at the other end. Then she nodded once, said, 'Yes, Mr Collins,' twice, and a moment later ushered me along the carpeted corridor to the big back office.

'*Sam!*' Collins came out from behind an eight foot desk faster than a greyhound. 'You're looking great, Sam! Just great! D'you know that!' It was a statement, not a question. Goodwill radiated from his plump little body like steam from a grating. For a moment I felt almost warmed by it, but only for a moment. He advanced across the room like a bridegroom on a wedding night, a fat anticipatory smile spreading across his face, eyes shining, arms outstretched in welcome. I avoided the bear hug at the last moment by shrugging clear of my raincoat and tossing it for him to catch.

He clucked approval like a contented hen. 'I can't get over it. You look so *fit!* So goddamned fit!' He carried my coat to the wardrobe, throwing me admiring glances as he went. 'You've lost some weight though, Sam. A few pounds lighter maybe?' He peered at me like a doctor, then gave me a beaming smile, 'But you're looking as fit as a racehorse.'

'Clean living does wonders for the complexion.' I slumped into the chair opposite the desk. 'Or maybe it was the diet.'

He crossed to the sideboard and began to throw lumps of ice into cut-glass tumblers. 'Food was bad, eh?'

'Oh, I dunno – there was always a choice.'

'A choice?' He sounded pleasantly surprised, like someone from the Howard League.

'Take it or leave it.'

His interest evaporated. Gin was splashed over ice and he snapped the top off a bottle of tonic. 'Same old Sam – still a quick tongue.' He stirred the drinks with an ice-pick, and added lemon slices with enough dexterity to make me wonder if lemons came pre-sliced and cellophane-wrapped these days. 'Still, it's over now,' he said with a little sigh of satisfaction. 'It's behind you. Best to forget it. What happened to you could happen to half the men in London.'

'Especially the lawyers.' I sniffed the glass. Gin wasn't really my drink and alcohol was something I needed to work on after two years on the wagon.

He carried his own glass back to his side of the desk. 'Tell you what we're going to do. Have a snort or two here, then off to the White Towers for lunch. Table's booked and the champagne's already on ice. My treat, Sam – what d'you say?'

'Cancel it.'

'Cancel it? Are you kidding? It's a celebration for Christ's sake! It's not every day—'

'Sam Harris comes out of the nick.' I shook my head. 'What's to celebrate? Besides the White Towers is for impressing people. I'm impressed already.' I waved at the new furnishings. 'Business looks good these days.'

His shrug faked a look of disappointment. 'It's okay. Times change, that's all. The Law Society says to look more up-to-date – improve the image, all that crap.' He smiled self-consciously. 'Besides, we've got half a dozen American clients now – they don't go for quill pens and sealing wax. Know what I mean?'

I helped myself to a cigarette from a silver box. 'I know what *that* means. You've found a new gravy train. It didn't take long. You always did play a part well – you even talk like a Yank now – you know that?'

'It rubs off. I've been to New York five times in the last three months.' He grinned sheepishly, fidgeting in his chair, as if the talk was making him uncomfortable. I could almost see his mind search for a new topic of conversation. Then he stretched his smile another inch and said, 'Hell, Sam, let's go to lunch. I've already booked the table. It'll be just like old times. We can be there in ten minutes and—'

'Save the expense. I told you – I'm impressed enough for one day. All I want is an accounting – then I'll be on my way.'

'On your way? On your way where for Christ's sake? You got a train to catch or something? Do me a favour will you? Just relax for five minutes.'

He would have gone on like that for another half hour, but for the look on my face. So he shrugged, 'Well, at least let me send out for something. Smoked salmon from Mario's—'

'Just an accounting, Lewis.'

His face performed the predictable repertoire of expressions – surprise, doubt, disappointment – then he said, 'Well, if you're sure. Personally I think you're rushing things. A man needs time to adjust, time to think—'

'I've done time. Now I want to catch up on two years of living.'

He avoided my look and set his drink down before reaching for a buff folder. The practised smile faded to a memory and his face aged ten years in the process. He licked his lips. 'Catching up might be difficult. At least to start with. Like I said, things change—'

'That bad, eh?'

'Nothing's *that bad*,' he mimicked. 'It's not cancer, Sam.' He underlined the bad joke with a laugh, but it was a shaky, insubstantial sound in the quiet of the room. 'You've suffered a setback. A hell of a setback. That's all I'm saying. Of course you'll find your feet again – bound to – a man like you – but it's going to take time.'

'So tell me.'

'What's the hurry?' He flicked the corner of the folder with his thumbnail. 'Let's do the figure work next week. Give you a chance to—'

'*Now*, Lewis – I want to know how I stand.'

He sighed deeply and opened the folder. 'Well, to start with, the old Sam Harris bank account is like the old grey mare – it ain't what it used to be. I guess you know already but we spent a bundle on the case. Even a guilty plea costs more in legal fees these days than a full-scale musical at Drury Lane. And afterwards we had the investigations to pay for—'

'I paid. *You* advised – *I* paid – and *I* went to prison.'

He pretended not to hear. 'Private investigations cost money, Sam. It's not cheap hiring detectives in London these days – and our money hired the best available—'

'*My* money.'

'Okay, okay – *your* money! Stop needling, will you? What did they teach you in Brixton – acupuncture?'

He flushed and we swapped angry stares until he turned back to the folder. 'Then there was that settlement with Kay. Christ, Sam, she screwed us. I said at the time to offer her less. We should have gone to court. No judge would have stood for the settlement she bled out of you—'

'Lewis. You said no judge would send me to prison – but one did.'

'Davidson! *Judge* Davidson. We *had* to get him, didn't we? Everyone knows he's senile. Should have retired years ago. Why only last week—'

'Lewis! Just the money, eh? Like how much is left?'

His scowl etched deep lines in his face and tiny beads of sweat gathered at the edge of his hairline. He shuffled his papers and when he spoke it was to the desk, not to me.

'It's hard to understand how a fortune like yours can collapse. Of

10

course when the business went into receivership your entire investment was lost – but even outside the business you were a rich man. Property, cars, jewellery—'

'Kay had the jewellery. It was part of the settlement. Along with half the proceeds from the sale of Ashley Grange.'

'Sure, she got *her* half,' he said bitterly. 'Yours went on personal guarantees and legal costs, along with most of your bank account. Right now you don't even own a motor car.'

'What *do* I own?'

'Well—' he brought his eyes up to mine and managed to hold the look for a moment. 'You've still got the mews cottage. I had it valued a month ago. Thompson's reckon it would fetch sixty thousand on today's market – and that's excluding contents.' He looked pleased. 'If I remember right there're some nice pieces there – that William Kent writing desk would fetch five or six grand at Christies.'

'There's also a mortgage,' I pointed out.

'But paid up to date,' he announced triumphantly.

Part of his stewardship had been to make sure of that. Even so I breathed a sigh of relief. At least I had somewhere to sleep.

He ran a finger down a column of figures. 'I got a settlement figure at the end of last month – twenty-two thousand. So there's a slice of equity if you sell. And like I said, some of the furniture.'

'Cash, Lewis,' I said firmly. 'How much money is left to my account?'

Nervousness slid round his eyes like an animal looking for a bolt hole – but eventually he admitted, 'It's thin, Sam. It's earned interest of course. The money market's been hungry recently and we've added to—' he licked his lips, 'to what was left.'

I watched and waited in silence. I knew it would be like this. I discovered the weakness in Collins two years ago. The weakness and the greed. Discovered it just in time to be just too late. But even afterwards, when I was committed to prison, I had given him power of attorney over my affairs. I may as well have given the key of a safe to a burglar. But at the time I no longer cared. I was as tired as death and sick of life. Nothing seemed to matter any more. What with the business crashing, the police investigation, the accusations, the trial and committal. And Kay petitioning for divorce on top of everything else. There seemed nothing left to live for.

'I had the ledgers summarised last night – guessed you'd be in today,' Collins said softly. He dabbed the film of sweat on his upper lip with his handkerchief. Then he turned a page in his notes, took

11

a deep breath, and said, 'As of yesterday your balance stood at eight thousand, three hundred and twenty-eight pounds.'

Temper tore through me like a stab of pain. I almost snarled in outright protest. Even knowing Collins for what he was had failed to prepare me – like knowing someone is going to die, it's still a shock when it happens. I took a few deep breaths but when the telephone rang it was a relief for both of us.

'Sheila, I *told* you – no calls while Mr Harris is here.' Collins spoke sharply, mainly for my benefit, then he listened and covered the mouthpiece. 'The press are outside, Sam. Two reporters and a photographer. What do you want us to do?'

I swore. I had run the press gauntlet earlier, when I was released from Brixton. After that I had shaken them off, at least I thought I had, but here they were again – baying like hounds on the scent of a fox. I said, 'I'm not here, Lewis – and tell that girl of yours she's never seen me.'

He repeated the instructions into the telephone, listened for a moment, then said, 'No, I will not grant them an interview. I'm engaged with a client. No – Mr Harris has not authorised me to make a statement on his behalf.' He slammed the telephone into its cradle with a show of bad temper which just failed to mask his true feelings. Secretly he was pleased – pleased for a chance to act again – Lewis Collins protecting a client, showing his famous sense of concern. It was a good act. It had convinced me once. A long time ago.

'You've paid your own fees from my account?' I asked, stony-voiced.

His eyes rounded in a plea for belief. 'Cut them to the bone, Sam. Least I could do – but the expenses! Counsels' fees, research work, the sheer administration of running the action—'

'All of which you've itemised?'

'In detail, Sam – in detail! What else would you expect? It's being typed up now,' he glanced at his watch. 'Want to see if it's ready?'

'May as well. And Lewis – get your accounts people to write me a cheque for the balance, will you? Payable to cash.'

He was surprised and showed it, but accepted the instruction and passed it down the line via his secretary. After which he was at a bit of a loss so he went to the sideboard to replenish his drink, my glass was still full, and when he returned to his desk he asked, 'What will you do now, Sam?'

What ideas I had were pretty vague, but had they been crystal clear Collins was the last man in London to discuss them with. I

12

shrugged. 'Lick my wounds, I suppose – and start again from scratch.'

He shook his head. 'You'll need a lot more capital than you've got. Besides there's another complication.'

My eyebrows rose as I waited, watching him squirm in his chair like a stricken schoolboy.

'Sam, I figured I'd tell you this over lunch. But I've had the police onto me. They wrote a few weeks ago, and 'phoned yesterday to make sure I could read.'

'And?' Hair prickled on the back of my neck – whether from fear or foresight I'm not quite sure.

'I quote,' he extracted a letter from his file, 'Should Mr Harris endeavour to re-open a casino in the Metropolitan area, we feel it proper to warn you that we shall most strenuously oppose the granting of a gaming licence to him, on the grounds that he is not a fit and proper person to hold such a licence.'

That was bad enough but I was even more shocked when he added, 'And Davis 'phoned yesterday to make sure there were no misunderstandings. The police will oppose the granting of a licence to you, or any associate of yours, or any front company set up by you, or any organisation taken over by you.'

I knew who Davis was. Chief Inspector Davis, Club Squad, New Scotland Yard.

Collins went on: 'The same applies to restaurants, clubs, pubs or bars. Any application by you to obtain a licence to sell spirits will be opposed on identical grounds.' The fake transatlantic twang deserted him for a moment. 'I'm sorry, Sam,' he said softly. 'Sorry as hell.' And for a moment I believed him.

Then the girl came in with the cheque and half a dozen closely typed sheets of figures relating to the way Collins had spent my money. I took the cheque, examined it, and slipped it into my pocket. Collins sealed the sheets into an envelope which he handed to me. 'Any queries, give me a buzz, Sam. I'll be glad to answer them.' He stood up, relieved that the meeting was over, collecting my coat from the wardrobe and smiling sympathetically. 'Take it easy for a bit. Don't rush things. Have a rest. Then when you're ready to start again come and talk things over – just like old times, eh?'

But only a fool makes the same mistake twice. I accepted the coat and said, 'I'll go out the back way, Lewis, just in case.' He nodded his understanding and led the way to a door opening into one of those little alleyways which criss-cross Lincoln's Inn. As I stepped out I said, 'There's just one more thing you can do for me, Lewis. Those reporters – I bet they're still camped in your lobby.'

He brightened at the prospect of a press conference. There was even a photographer, which meant the chance of his face in tonight's *Standard*. 'Invite them in for a drink. Have a chat with them. Then say you no longer act for Sam Harris in any capacity whatsoever.'

'Sam!' he protested, but I was already walking away.

'Goodbye, Lewis,' I said as I turned the corner.

I walked through the back streets and into Fetter Lane, where I caught a cab outside the *Daily Mirror* building. The rain had stopped and the sun shone fitfully in the half-hearted way it does above London at the end of September. We trundled westwards; into Trafalgar Square, along Pall Mall, past Overton's in St. James's into Piccadilly and along past the Ritz. For a moment I was tempted to stop for a drink, or walk through Mayfair to look in at Annabelle's before lunch. But the moment passed. Meeting people, *some people*, might be difficult – either for them or for me. I wasn't ready to face that yet. The suit I wore felt uncomfortable and I knew it was important to look smart when I went back. When I went back! That was all I had thought about for months. Going back and taking the West End by storm the way I did before. But according to Collins it would be harder this time. Lack of money was bad enough, but a concerted effort by the police to keep me out of the gaming trade was worse. Hell, it was the only business I knew. Could they do that? Wasn't that restraint of trade or something? I remembered the sneer on Davis's face when he climbed out of that Black Maria. *Davis* could do it – one way or another.

We drove through Hyde Park, not the most direct route to Battersea but the way I wanted to go, and the cabby was ready to oblige a fare-paying customer. Then we turned east along Oxford Street and through Soho's back doubles into Piccadilly. For a while I forgot all about Davis. I just drank in the sights like a boggle-eyed tourist. Funny, but I've never wanted to travel. London has always been my place. When I was a kid all I ever wanted to be was someone important in London. Just that. Important at what never mattered – just as long as the place was London. Now every street is alive with memories. There's not a restaurant worth mentioning where I haven't eaten, not a bar where I haven't had a drink, or a decent nightclub I haven't owned – or had a share in – or been on the verge of buying at one time or another.

After a final lap around Leicester Square we drove across the river to the other world of Battersea. A grey, drab world by comparison. There I paid the cabby and went in search of Jack, who was where I expected him to be, propping up the bar in The Blue Posts. The lunchtime trade was thinning out and he was at the end of the counter beside an empty stool. His face split into a grin like a crescent moon as he eased his eighteen stone down from the stool. Then he gripped my hand until my bones ached. He didn't say anything, not even hello. He just stood there, looking me up and down, and grinning from ear to ear, until he raised his glass: 'Cheers, Sam,' he said, and stood aside to reveal a large scotch, the ice already melting and a water jug next to it on the bar. I might just have come back from the gents instead of two years in Brixton.

I could say a lot about Jack but he might read this one day and it would embarrass him. The truth is we are as close as two men can be without turning queer – and there's nothing like that about either of us. We grew up together in Battersea: same school, same girlfriends, same mob in the army, and when we came out we even went into the same line of business – restaurants and clubs and pubs. We were even partners for a while, but it never worked out. Our ambitions were different, Jack wanted to stay on the small side and I was out to conquer the world, so we split up. There were no hard feelings, well not for long anyway. I was a bit put out at the time but I got over it, and we were better pals than ever afterwards. In 1964 I gave Jack the money to start his restaurant – sixty thousand pounds, which was a lot of money in those days. But I had it then. I just wrote a cheque and said it was for old times' sake. Of course Jack insisted on repaying me and a year later he did, though he needn't have done – not as far as I was concerned – but his pride would never let him accept it as a gift. Odd, the way things work out. According to the papers I was worth over a million then, and all Jack had was his two little pubs in Battersea.

Now, all these years later, I was as good as broke and Jack owned The Blue Posts and The Golden Lion and his restaurant, plus a bit of property in the West End. He ran a Rolls-Royce and I didn't even have wheels. He had a beautiful wife and I was divorced.

'I expected you earlier,' he said.

'I stopped in to see Collins.'

He pulled a face, the kind people pull when they smell bad fish. 'Count your fingers, did you? After you shook hands. Hope you took a witness.'

'No need. Not this time. It doesn't take two people to listen to a catalogue of disasters.'

'Money?' he asked softly, watching a barman ring some into a till.

'Or the lack of it.'

'Cleaned you out, did he? He always was a little bastard. Always was and always will be.'

15

I smiled. Jack has never trusted lawyers, least of all Collins. More than once in the old days he called me a bloody fool for confiding in Collins the way I did. It's too late now to say I should have listened, but it boils down to that. I said, 'And worse, Davis 'phoned him. Apparently the police will oppose any application I make to get my licences back.'

Jack smiled sadly. 'That was always on the cards. But I knew Davis was spreading the word.'

'*You* knew?'

'He was in here last night. Five minutes before closing time. Full of himself. Asked if I expected to see you.'

I whistled. Spreading the word was right. If Davis had called on Jack, where else had he been?

Jack was still smiling his sad smile, watching the great British public spend its money up and down the counter while he talked to me. 'I told him my crystal ball was on the blink, so I couldn't say when I'd see you. But he left a message. Said you'd never run a casino again – not while he's on the force.' He cocked an eyebrow. 'Is that what Collins was on about?'

I nodded: 'Did Davis say anything else?'

'Never had a chance. It was closing time then so I saw him off the premises. Nothing personal, I said – just I've got my own licences to worry about.' He gazed back down the bar, a slow smile spreading across his face.

'Watch yourself, Jack – he's a spiteful devil.'

'Don't we know it,' he said. Suddenly his eyes narrowed. Then he leapt from the stool and shouldered his way through the crowd to the far end of the counter. As soon as I heard him speak I realised he had been waiting and watching for something. 'Excuse me, sir,' he said, 'but did you check your change just now?'

A small, sandy-haired fellow almost dropped his beer as Jack's hand fell upon his shoulder. 'Change?' the man said. 'Er – why? I mean I dunno – should I have checked?'

'Can't be too careful – not when it comes to money,' Jack smiled down at him.

The man glanced quickly at one of the barmen. It was a dead giveaway but he still tried to bluff it out. 'Oh, there's no need to check. I mean, not in here—'

'Anyone can make a mistake. Even in one of my pubs. Now then, sir – how much change did you get just now?'

The man put his pint and sandwiches down on the table and started to fumble through his pockets. His face turned pink as he eyed Jack nervously. I climbed down from my stool and ambled to the end of the counter – just in case the barman made a run for it.

16

'The other pocket,' Jack said. Nobody else was talking and every eye in the place was on the flushed-faced man with Jack. Every eye except mine. I was watching the barman. It was a very long counter manned by four men, all of whom cashed up into individual tills, It was all I could do not to laugh. Fancy them trying that old chestnut – especially on Jack. He would be furious. It's as old as the badger game – the barman pads the bills and short changes customers until he builds up a surplus in his till. Then just before closing his accomplice comes in, orders a beer or something, pays with a one pound note and gets the change of a tenner.

'Ah, *there* you are, sir,' Jack said triumphantly. 'You've got too much there, haven't you? All that change from a one pound note.'

'But it was—' the sandy-haired man began. Then his courage ran out. Not surprising really. Jack is six feet two tall and built like a Sherman tank. And the look on his face would have blistered paintwork.

The man nodded sadly. 'It must have been a mistake. I didn't notice, you see—'

'Of course you didn't,' Jack's face softened and but for the sarcasm he might have been conforting a baby. He scooped the notes and silver up from where the man had put them on the table, then turned back to the counter. The barman was a few yards from me, hemmed in by two other lads who had worked for Jack for years.

Jack said, 'We'd better check your till then, Ronny, hadn't we? You'll be a bit short after your mistake with this gentleman.'

Ronny went white. The cash till roll would tally with the till's contents. We all knew that. Jack scowled, then turned to the watching crowd. 'A little mistake, gentlemen,' he said with sudden cheerfulness. 'And we can't have that in a Jack Green pub, can we? So perhaps you'll all have a large whatever you're drinking – on the house, before you go.'

That started a buzz of conversation. One or two called out 'Cheers Jack' and 'Good old Jack'; that sort of nonsense. Jack smiled and returned to my end of the bar. When he saw where I was standing he said, 'All right, Sam – finish your drink. Ronny's leaving now anyway – Mick will see him safely off the premises.'

I eased away from the end of the counter and Mick took Ronny by the elbow, ushering him firmly through the door at the back of the bar.

Jack caught my eye and smiled sadly. 'Mugs. What do they take me for? Christ, I've been in this business twenty years and—' he broke off at the sight of the sandy-haired man leaving by the front door. 'Oi!' he shouted. 'You've left your beer – you daft what-name!' There was a roar of delighted laughter from the crowd at the bar and the incident was over.

'Come on, Sam,' Jack said, 'let's go home to lunch.'

On the way to the door he pulled Johnny Matthews, his manager, to one side and very quietly bawled him out. 'When I employ a watchdog, I don't expect to bark myself. You should have spotted that dodge a mile off. You're getting old, Johnny – or careless.'

Matthews flushed. He was a man of about fifty and as straight as a die. He worked for me at one time, before joining Jack, and I remember giving him a reference. 'I'm sorry, Jack,' he said, 'I've had my doubts about Ronny for a week now. I've been keeping an eye on him – off and on like—'

'More off than on. You'll be short-handed for a bit. It'll make more work for you. Serves you right. Get onto the agency for another barman and make sure this one is straight. Okay?'

'Okay, Jack – right away.' Matthews nodded, relieved it was over. Then he caught sight of me. 'Morning, Mr Harris, sir. It's good to see you—' he almost said 'out' – but stopped himself in time. It wasn't his day. He gave a half-hearted smile and said, 'It's good to see you again, Mr Harris.'

'And you,' I said, and we left.

Jack's car was outside. Not many in Battersea own a Rolls-Royce and it would have excited envy in most. But I never met anyone envious of Jack. Most of the locals are downright proud of him. They know he is rich, stinking rich by their standards, but they don't mind that. He is a character, larger than life and twice as colourful. Dozens of locals owe him a few bob and hundreds owe him a favour. Even that can cause resentment – but never with Jack. As far as Battersea is concerned Jack is 'local boy makes good' and unlike others they could name – which generally means me – Jack never grew too big for his boots when he made his money. He didn't move to a posh part of London – he just stayed in Battersea and turned The Dog's Home into an institution.

As restaurants go The Dog's Home is unique. Certainly in London and I should know. There's not much to it from the outside. It's on the corner of two rows of terraced houses – those tall, thin, four-storey town houses which sprang up in London a hundred years ago. Jack bought four of them with my money in 1964. Then he gutted them and made them into one building inside. People thought he was mad when he talked of opening a classy restaurant. *In a place like Battersea?* I was certain he would never make a go of it. That's why I told him to keep the money – I was sure it was lost anyway. But Jack just winked and said he knew what he was doing.

It took the builders months to finish to Jack's satisfaction, and he was away for weeks at a time while the work went on. Matthews was running The Blue Posts for him by then, and another manager looked after The Golden Lion – so his business ticked over during his absences. But where Jack went was a mystery. When he came home at weekends he avoided talking about it. Those who asked were given a grin and the answer that he was getting ready to open his restaurant. That's all he told anyone – including me.

Then it came to the sign going up. *The Dog's Home*. What a name! Classy restaurants should have classy names. How can you serve a *cordon bleu* meal in a place called The Dog's Home? But Jack just shrugged: 'Battersea Dog's Home is known the world over. It's almost the only famous thing in Battersea. So I'm paying a tribute to my old home town.' He grinned when he said it but not everyone shared his sense of humour. I shook my head and told him to see a psychiatrist.

Two weeks before the place opened, vans started to arrive from all over – Chester, Exeter, Norwich – everywhere it seemed but London. The joke at the time was that they were full of dog biscuits. But in fact they were stacked high with furniture – antique furniture. Hepplewhite sideboards, Pembroke tables, davenports, Victorian canterburies, Welsh dressers, all sorts of stuff. And not just furniture either. Bracket clocks, longcase clocks, oil paintings, sculptures, huge gilt mirrors, and silver and pewter bearing the crests of the oldest families in the country. The list seemed endless. Jack had raided sale rooms and auction houses far and wide for that lot. Some went into store but most went into The Dog's Home and became part of the reason for the phenomenal success of the place.

My way of opening a new restaurant was to call in Conran's Design Team or the boys from Knolle International and write them an open cheque. Certainly the furnishings became part of the place – fixtures and fittings to be depreciated on a balance sheet. But Jack's furnishings are all for sale. Not that anything is visibly priced, but if anyone admires something – a painting, or the silver on the table, or the decanters from which the house wine is served – Jack will appear, with the history of the piece – and its price. I thought his knowledge of antiques was a bit sketchy at first but over the years he has turned into a walking encyclopaedia, so that now collectors from all over dine with Jack when they are in London. I once saw a party of Americans finish dinner and take a table and chairs, and a dozen other pieces, away with them in a convoy of cabs. God knows what the Savoy said when that lot hit them at two in the morning.

The Dog's Home is like a series of *salons* inside – that's the only way I can describe it. Not a single room has more than six tables, but the rooms are inter-connected by tall double doors and the effect is amazingly graceful. Proper picture lights show off the paintings, but except for those the illumination is low and intimate. After dinner, people adjourn to the sitting rooms – full of *chaises longues* and stuffed ottomans – to play backgammon or chess using pornographic pieces carved from ivory, or just to sit around drinking. And talking of course. The talk is something you always remember after a night at The Dog's Home. Mainly because the people who frequent it are as individualistic in their lives as Jack is in his. Theatricals, artists splurging a commission, writers pretending to 'soak up atmosphere' when all they are doing is enjoying themselves. Jack treats them all as equals and wanders from room to room – joining uninvited into this or that conversation – pouring himself a glass of their wine – arguing with them, insulting them, joking – or sometimes, if a conversation is really interesting – he'll just slump into a chair and unashamedly eavesdrop.

Jack and Maria live in The Dog's Home. They have a couple of bedrooms on the top floor, but no other private rooms. That's the way they run the place – as their home. If Jack dislikes someone he'll tell them to their face, ask them to leave, never to darken his door again. It's a hell of a way to run a restaurant, but it certainly adds to the atmosphere. Makes it like a club, or a country house party with Jack as the host. It's more a way of life with him than a way of earning a living. The only thing he cares more about is Maria, his wife. She was in one of the sitting rooms when we came in from The Blue Posts. She took one look at me, gave a little cry of welcome, and threw herself into my arms. Her heart pumped against my chest and I could smell the fragrance of her hair. Then her arms reached up to pull my mouth down to hers.

Jack shouted, 'He's been without a woman for two years. Over excite him now and like as not he'll rape you on that bloody chesterfield.'

She pulled away, breathless from the kiss, her arms still about my shoulders. 'Oh *will* you Sam? Promise? *Promise* to rape me?'

I kissed her again and whispered something unrepeatable in her ear. She drew back, wide-eyed, blushing and laughing, and swearing softly in Italian.

Jack's got an eye for beautiful things, but Maria is the loveliest. Pale-skinned and raven-haired, black eyes that dance, and lips

20

which curve provocatively. That day she was dressed in a cotton shirt and black velvet trousers, and she wore nothing on her feet. She had the figure of a young girl which isn't bad for a woman I knew to be thirty-five.

'Oh, Sam – it's so *good* to see you.' She touched my face, tracing the line of my jaw with her fingertips, the way a sculptor might examine a subject before starting work.

'No scars,' I said, a shade self-consciously.

'None that show anyway.' Her eyes were moist when she spoke. Then she kissed me again and took my hand. 'Sam, come and meet my cousin, Lucia.'

Only then did I see the other girl. She sat watching us, grey eyes slightly amused, the shadow of a smile at the edge of her lips, light brown hair kept in place by a tortoiseshell comb. Her skin was bronzed that honey gold which people acquire on the Riviera and her simple white dress emphasised her tan. She sat with her legs crossed and one arm draped along the back of the Victorian sofa – like a glossy print in *Vogue*.

I said, 'Hello, Lucia.'

She shook hands with a cool, firm grip. 'Hello, Sam.' Her voice was low-pitched, almost husky, the sort of smoky timbre you sometimes hear in a nightclub singer.

'Well—' I said, foolishly awkward, 'this *is* a surprise. *Two* beautiful women to greet me.'

Jack grinned. 'Lucia's here on holiday. Been here a week and packs the place out – they dribble so much looking at her that their food gets cold.'

'Jack!' she scolded. 'Some of the dirty old men you get in here would dribble at a twelve-year-old schoolgirl.'

He was delighted. 'They do – they do!' he shouted. 'But only when they wear those kinky gymslips.'

Maria was laughing and scolding at the same time. 'Will you two *stop* it? Come on, let's eat. Sam, they're driving me mad – they tease each other from morning till night.'

At the door she stopped and looked up at me. 'Oh Sam, it's just so *good* to see you – so very good.' Then she hugged me again.

Jack roared: 'Will you stop kissing him. He'll get so bloody horny he won't be able to sit down – then we'll never get to eat.'

It was fun that lunch. Good food, chilled wine, crystal glasses – two beautiful women, Jack and me. Like coming alive again. Maybe animals feel that way after hibernating through the winter. Jack regaled us with stories about his clientele and we did a fair bit of reminiscing about the good old days. Apparently Lucia already knew something of my background but Jack insisted on recounting some of my past exploits, building up the successes and turning setbacks into hilarious anecdotes. The Dog's Home is closed during the day, so we had the place to ourselves. Maria had prepared the meal before I arrived, and afterwards we moved upstairs to the big sitting room for coffee and brandy.

'I was down at Rex Place yesterday, Sam,' Maria said. 'Gave the place a good airing and restocked your booze cupboard.'

Kay had left me and the mews cottage at the same time – while I was languishing in Brixton – after which she had sent the keys to The Dog's Home for safe keeping.

I said, 'Thanks – but you shouldn't have troubled.'

'No trouble. Matter of fact I was there last week. I took your suits to be cleaned. They're back now, hanging in your wardrobe. And I gave the place a tidy up – cleared out the closets and so on.' She picked at a loose thread in her trousers, and when she looked up she was blushing.

Her red cheeks startled me. 'What did you find? Skeletons in the cupboards?'

'Silly,' she said, and looked away.

I wasn't sure what to make of it, so I mumbled my thanks and said she ought not to have gone to so much trouble.

'I told you – it was no trouble. Anyway, Lucia gave me a hand. She did most of the cleaning.'

Lucia was sitting at my side, and when I turned I caught her staring at me. It startled me, looking into those level grey eyes, especially as she made no effort to conceal the fact that she had been watching me. Someone once wrote that the eyes indicate the antiquity of the soul. I remember being puzzled as to its meaning, but the look Lucia gave me was at least a clue. It suggested experience quite beyond her years. I marked her down as being in her middle twenties and I was sure I was right, but she had the poise of a much older woman. She sat there, confident and assured, waiting for me to thank her for cleaning my place, her eyes holding my look without rushing me, one arm along the back of the sofa, legs crossed and her body half turned towards me. The scooped neckline of her dress revealed the pale swelling of her breasts and I could just smell the light fragrance of her scent.

'You're very beautiful,' I said. Of course, it was a damn silly thing to say but I suppose the wine had got to me a bit – that, and the warm happiness of being back among friends.

She smiled faintly. 'Thank you – but I'm not sure that's a very great compliment. After all, you've not had much to look at for the past two years.'

Jack snorted. 'He did a hell of a lot of looking before.'

'So I hear,' she said, her eyes still holding mine. 'Maria's been telling me.'

'Oh?' Almost reluctantly I turned to Maria.

'It seemed only fair to warn her.' Maria looked shyly pleased with herself.

It had turned four, but we chatted away inconsequentially for a while longer, which was selfish of me because I knew Jack and Maria usually slept for an hour in the afternoons – most people do when they're up until three or four every morning. But eventually I summoned up the energy to leave.

Jack asked, 'Where now?'

'Back to Rex Place. An hour in the shower to get the smell of Brixton out of my pores.'

Maria went to fetch the keys and when she came back Jack was asking my plans for the evening.

I said I would look around town. 'Meet up with a few people. See what's changed – that kind of thing.'

'Take Lucia,' Maria suggested. 'She'd love to go. We haven't shown her the night life yet. It's difficult – dragging Jack away from this place—'

'*No!*' Jack startled us. '*Not* tonight,' he fairly snapped the words out. He must have caught our expressions, because he shrugged and looked away. 'I mean, not the *first* night. It'll be best for Sam to wander round by himself.'

It made an awkward moment. We were all standing, Jack with my old raincoat in his hands, obviously biting his tongue. I tried to make a joke of it by saying to Lucia, 'You've found a big brother. I'll persuade him I'm a reformed character if you'd like to come?'

She hesitated for a split second, then smiled. 'I'd love to – but not tonight, I'm washing my hair—'

Maria put her hand on my arm. 'Come to lunch tomorrow, Sam. Make the arrangements then.'

My disappointment must have shown because Lucia smiled as she touched my hand goodbye. 'Till tomorrow then,' she said, 'and I look forward to it.'

So I said goodbye, kissed Maria, and then followed Jack downstairs. He insisted on lending me his car and I was about to drive away when he said, 'Do me a favour, Sam. I'm worried about a place I've bought. Top end of Baker Street. I've got the ground floor and the basement. Big it is, eight or nine thousand square feet. Have a look at it for me, will you? It's empty at the moment, but I think it'll make a good club.' He smiled. 'That's if you're interested.'

23

I'm interested.'

He nodded. 'And about cash, Sam. Don't worry. When you're ready let me know. I've got the best part of a hundred grand not doing much at the moment.'

'Partners?'

'I'd like that,' he said solemnly. 'But I've got enough on my plate. If you can sort your licences out and if Baker Street appeals to you, why not use the money to get going again? Pay me back when you feel like it.'

What can you say to something like that? I got a bit choked up, punched him on the arm and promised to think about it. Then I drove back to the West End, full of warm thoughts about Jack and Maria, and cursing my clumsiness with Lucia. But I was quite right – she really *was* exceptionally good-looking.

Rex Place is just behind Park Lane. A hundred years ago the carriage trade stabled their horses there. Now all the little boxes have been converted into tiny dwellings, each with a glossy front door and a flower box window sill. Mine was standard size: a tiny entrance hall, sitting room, a kitchen-diner fit for a cabin cruiser, and an opening under the stairs euphemistically called 'a study'. Upstairs was a bedroom and a bathroom and that was the lot. The whole thing worth sixty thousand according to Collins – but that's inflation for you.

I was a bit wary about going back. The place held too many memories. Kay would fill every room, even though she had left months and months ago. The beginning of our married life had been spent at Rex Place, and it had been a happy time, despite what happened afterwards. But – memories or not – Rex Place was all I had left, so it had to be faced.

Once inside I knew why Maria had blushed. Everything was different – even the carpets and the paintings on the walls. Only the desk and the filing cabinet remained in their place in the alcove – nothing else was the same. Jack and Maria had furnished it originally – as their wedding present, although neither had liked Kay. Now they had *re-furnished* it, from top to bottom. A Klee sketch replaced Kay's portrait in the sitting room, and upstairs my suits and other clothes were in the wardrobes – but nothing there belonged to Kay. Her photograph had gone from the dressing table and not as much as an old scarf remained to remind me of her. Even the bath towels were new, and the crockery and kitchen things were all quite different. Kay might never have lived there.

I spent a long time in the shower and lay on the bed afterwards, thinking about all sorts but mainly my life and what I had made of it. Of where I had been and where I was going. I was forty-two. Ten years ago I had been rich and successful. Top of the heap. Now I had to start again from scratch, I wondered if I had the strength to do it all over again. But the shower relaxed me and the bed was luxuriously soft, so after a while I fell asleep.

The telephone woke me. 'Sam, are you cross with me?' Maria asked.

I was still muzzy-headed but I mumbled my thanks before adding, 'That's enough now, understand? No more surprises, no more handouts—'

'*Handouts!*' she yelped. 'You wait till you get my bill.'

'Okay – but you get the point?'

'I get the point.' Then she added softly, 'Sam, all the other stuff is in Jack's store – in case you ever want it – understand?'

'I understand – and thanks.'

'For nothing,' she snorted, 'and don't be late for lunch tomorrow.'

When she hung up I blessed her and went back under the shower. Good food and lovely women are not all you miss in jail. Apart from the loss of the big freedom, you miss all the little ones – simple things like enjoying a shower in privacy, the smell of decent soap, the feel of proper bath towels, and clothes that are softer than flour sacks.

I planned my evening as I dressed. The people I would meet, the places I would visit: restaurants, bars, clubs and casinos. Only when I fumbled with my cufflinks did I realise how nervous I was. Being accepted back was the most important thing left to me. And *of course* I had to do it as soon as possible. Like falling off a horse, you simply climbed back into the saddle.

Looking back I realise what a fool I was. Even Collins had tried to warn me – with all that guff about taking my time. And Jack had seen it coming, which was why Lucia had been kept out of things that first night. But right at that moment I was so full of the welcome Jack and Maria had given me that I was blinded to everything else. Of course they were my closest friends, but I told myself I had others. After all, who had I hurt when I was top dog? Nobody, at least no one I could think of. I had a stock of goodwill all over London – or so I thought – all ready to help me get going again. So by eight o'clock I was behind the wheel of the Corniche, dressed in a dinner jacket, with the evening ahead of me. And like a perfect fool I was looking forward to it.

It was disastrous. Even the memories are painful. I went to the Lucky Seven first. It's a club just off Bond Street. Not one of the bigger ones but I planned to work my way up during the evening.

And I knew Charlie Dyson from the old days. He had been my head waiter at Winston's before branching out on his own. But minutes after I arrived Charlie came into the bar and asked me to leave. I was astonished. 'Leave? But Charlie I only just got here—'

'Your membership expired,' he said, stony-faced. 'The doorman shouldn't have let you in.'

I didn't stay to argue. What was the point? Dammit, I only went to see how he was! I climbed back into the car, hot with temper, and drove away. Charlie Dyson was a *nothing*! Last I heard he was up to his ears in debt and barely making a living. The nerve of a man like that to throw *me* out!

I was still seething when I reached The Captain Morgan in Piccadilly. The doorman was new and we had never seen each other before, so he delayed me in the foyer while he sent for Ron Brown. But Ron was nowhere to be found and with no one to vouch for me I was refused admittance. Even then it never clicked. I tried the Grasshopper Club only to find that Terry Wickens had sold it the year before and the new people didn't know me from Adam – and then, at Gaston's, I was turned round in my tracks by two big fellows who appeared either side of me as I crossed the threshold.

'Sam Harris, isn't it?' one of them asked, peering into my face as he took my elbow.

'That's right – who are you?'

'Doesn't matter, Mr Harris. Membership's full. That's all that *matters*.' Six strides took us back to the Rolls. 'Nice motor you've got there, Mr Harris. Don't park it here and you'll keep it that way.'

His sneer infuriated me. He was inviting me to take a swing at him. I looked over his shoulder at his mate a yard away. Gaston's is in a cul-de-sac. The lighting is poor except for the blaze of neon around the club entrance, and we were clear of that and in the shadow. To take them both on was asking for trouble. I climbed back into the car and drove away trying to forget the contempt in their eyes.

I went to see Tony Fields at The Green Door. Tony owned Silver Bells as well and was in a big way of business. Not as big as I once was but big enough. He stood me a drink at the bar and seemed genuinely pleased to see me. He was sympathetic about the trial and went on to talk about some of the things that had happened while I was inside. A company called Tuskers had bought my club and restaurant chain from the receiver – for about ten per cent of what they were worth. I knew that of course. Even in prison you get to read the business pages. Besides Collins had been to see me once or twice, with the odd document which still required my signature. But who were Tuskers?

'Who's running the show, Tony? Anyone I know?'

He shook his head. 'They came from nowhere. Provincial crowd – started in Cardiff I think. Never thought they had the bread to buy half the West End – but that's what they're doing.'

We had another drink, but I sensed he was uncomfortable. Some people came in and threw odd looks in our direction, until eventually Tony asked me to step across to his office. He freshened my drink and set me on a studio couch, then he said, 'A lot's changed, Sam. Matter of fact I'm thinking of getting out myself.'

'If you're saying I'd be a fool to come back, I've heard it all evening – one way or the other.'

He sipped his drink and concentrated on avoiding my eye.

'Who's been to see you – Davis?'

He half smiled at that. 'Yes, Davis was in last week, he said you'd be out today.' He paused, as if wondering what to say next, then he asked, 'Bad inside, was it, Sam?'

'At least people talked to me. Tonight I've got the plague.'

He nodded thoughtfully. 'Word's out on you, Sam. It's as simple as that. Everyone's had a touch of the frighteners. Anyone helps you and he'll be in dead trouble.'

'Who says so? Davis?'

He shrugged. 'Davis ain't helping – but he's not the real pressure.'

'So who is?'

He finished his drink and refilled his glass at the sideboard. 'We're having a hard time right now. The money's not about any more. They buried the swinging sixties a long while back.'

'Come off it, Tony – the casinos are taking a fortune. Those Arabs still lose an oilwell a night.'

'Casinos are okay – not what they were, mind you, but still okay. But restaurant and club trade is down.'

'It'll come up again,' I said confidently. 'You can't break records every year.'

He shook his head. 'You don't understand. Taxation's changed – the police are more difficult – this Tusker crowd wants the bed to itself, and—' he hesitated for a long moment, and I was about to ask a question, when he said, 'and most of us are bled dry for protection just to open the door at night.'

I whistled. The club trade has never been easy. Every year or so some very rough people think it would be fun to run a nightclub – so they try to steal one. London has been lucky on the whole – compared to New York or even Paris – the police and professional club owners close ranks to keep the real villains out. At least they do for most of the time.

There was no point in beating around the bush so I asked how much he was paying.

He put his glass down and spread the fingers of both hands. 'Every week,' he said.

Ten thousand *a week*! I tried to imagine his cash flow. Even with clubs the size of The Green Door and Silver Bells the effect would be crippling. 'What about the police?' I asked. 'You said they were hopping about.'

'They stick us to the rule book, that's all. They're attentive – not protective.'

'Have they been asked?'

'Eric Blockley asked. And a week later he was killed.'

'I read about that. Wasn't he killed in a boating accident?'

'That's what the papers said. They also said you were guilty. I never believed that either.'

I was grateful for that and said so. He was getting a bit fidgety by this time, no doubt anxious to get back to his club and not quite sure what to do about me, but I pushed him to answer a couple more questions.

'Who's putting the bite on, Tony?'

He shook his head. 'We never see the same man twice. They're well organised.' *Then he said the most amazing thing.* He looked me straight in the eye and lowered his voice: 'Some say it's you, Sam. You must have heard that.'

I was astonished. I've never been more surprised in the whole of my life. 'For Christ's sake – why *me*? I've never been mixed up in anything like that—'

'You were convicted of a brutal crime,' he said simply.

I was stunned, I felt bitter and angry, and a little bit sick. I put the glass to one side, unable to finish my drink, and just stared at him.

He spread his hands, deflecting my attention from his embarrassed expression.

'If it's any consolation, I never believed it – and I've said as much.' He shrugged. 'Believe it or not.'

'I believe it,' I said, and I did. I took a deep breath and then asked, 'Were you serious, about selling?'

'I'd like to – that's the truth. It's no fun these days. Trouble is finding a buyer. It ain't easy. There's only one outfit buying—' he pulled a face, 'correction – prices they're paying – that's stealing.'

'Tuskers?' I guessed, and when he nodded I asked, 'Tony, would you sell to me? If I could raise a decent price?'

His eyes filled with a look of complete incredulity. 'You're not listening, Sam. Don't you understand? Did you hear what I said? Word's out on you. I'm not even supposed to sell you a *drink*. Sell you the clubs and we're both in the boneyard.' He paused long enough to let that sink in, and then his face slowly relaxed into a smile. 'Besides, what's the point? You've got other problems. From what Davis said the police will oppose a dog licence with your name on.'

I was too sick to smile. Two years ago a door had shut me in prison. Now another one was keeping me out of the West End. Was I really *that* bad? To be treated like a leper? And *who* was shutting the door anyway?

Tony cleared his throat. 'Sam, about membership of the club. I hope you'll understand – see it my way—'

I spared him the embarrassment. 'It's okay, Tony. I must be going anyway.'

Relief showed in his eyes and he put an arm across my shoulder as we walked to the door. 'Something will break for you, Sam. It's got to – a man like you—'

'Sure, Tony.' We shook hands inside the office so that nobody would see, then he opened the door and ushered me past the bar and into the foyer.

I drove around town for the next hour. Just round and round. I parked in Berkeley Square once, planning to call on Billy Rose at The Top Hat, but I lost my nerve at the last moment. If a friend like Tony Fields was worried about being seen with me, Billy Rose would have a coronary on the spot. So I cruised down Berkeley Street and into Piccadilly, across the Circus into Shaftesbury Avenue and then up into Soho. Miles and miles of flashing neon, dozens of clubs and bars and restaurants owned by friends of mine. I cursed them all and turned northwards into Euston Road.

I found the place Jack had spoken about quite easily. It was almost opposite Baker Street Station. A tired sign said it had been The White Rose Restaurant at one time. I had never heard of it. The place had obviously catered for the lunchtime trade, not the smart, free-spending night life I was after. I grunted. It was in the wrong part of town and looked as dingy and derelict and as broke as I was. I drove back to Rex Place, feeling sorry for myself and thinking it was a hell of a way to spend my first night of freedom.

Once back in the cottage I flung my jacket over a chair and poured myself a drink – and I was sitting in my shirtsleeves, staring moodily at the Klee sketch – when the doorbell made the most welcome sound of the evening. Cheerful and friendly. Somebody *wanted* to see me! I felt sure it would be Jack and Maria, and found myself hoping Lucia would be with them. But when I opened the door, Chief Inspector Davis stood on the step.

'Hello, Harris,' he said.

Disappointment flared to anger. 'It's *Mr* Harris to you! And what the hell do you want?'

'Can I come in?'

'Got a warrant?'

He smiled and shook his head. Davis is about my height, five foot ten, but heavier, say around fourteen stone. As always he was well dressed in a Savile Row suit and Gucci shoes which had only been inside a police quarter master's office when Davis was wearing them. A silk foulard tie spread across an Egyptian cotton shirt and I caught the glitter of diamond links on his cuffs. I stared at the sallow-skinned, dark-haired man who had helped send me to prison, noticing again that he wore the kind of permanent five o'clock shadow some men get when they shave twice a day. At some time in his history someone had broken his nose and whoever had set it had bodged the job because a blue kink showed half way down.

'Well?' he asked. 'Do I get asked inside?'

I couldn't trust myself to reply, so I turned back to the sitting room and he followed, leaving the front door slightly ajar. Without asking he sat on the chesterfield and let his gaze fall to the whisky next to my chair. 'You're not going to offer me a drink?'

'That's right – I'm not. What's all this about, Davis?'

'Inspector Davis,' he corrected. 'Chief Inspector Davis.'

I sat down and picked up my glass, looking at him the way I might a piece of bad cheese.

'You're a client of mine,' he smiled. 'I like to keep in touch. See how things are going.'

'Fine till I met you. And they'll go a damn sight better when you get off my back.'

When he smiled a gold tooth showed where his upper incisor had been. 'Oh, but I can't. This is my manor and I worry about it. Especially when a man comes out of jail.'

'A man sent there by a bent copper,' I snapped.

'I hope you won't say that in public,' he said quietly.

'I bet you do.'

He smiled again. 'Let me give you some advice, Harris. This town is closed to you. Why not make a fresh start somewhere else?' He waved a hand at the room. 'Sell up here and use the money for a new venture – somewhere a long way from London.'

'How many men have you got outside, Davis?'

'Men – outside?'

'Come off it – this is harassment. Provocation. You're hoping I'll poke your eye out. That's why you left the door open. Then your heavy mob will charge in here and—'

'My *dear* Mr Harris.' He threw his hands up in mock horror. 'What a lurid imagination. Things like that don't happen in London—'

'No? A bloody sight worse happens from what I've heard tonight.'

'Meaning?'

'It's your manor – you worry about it.' I finished the drink at a single gulp. 'Okay, Davis – I've got the message. Loud and clear. You want me out of town. Well that's your hard luck. I'll go or stay as I please – but I certainly won't be shoved by the likes of you. Now get out.'

He rose and took a couple of paces in my direction. For a moment I expected him to punch me. I looked up, tensed and ready to defend myself. But he got his temper under control, then scowled furiously and turned for the door. 'You've been warned, Harris. Step out of line and you'll be back inside so fast your feet won't touch the ground.'

'Do yourself a favour. Go and lean on the little girls in Shepherd's Market – they frighten more easily than me.' He was about to reply so I picked up the newspaper and pretended to read. 'And close the door after you,' I said over my shoulder. 'You can't trust the police in this town any more.'

He snorted like a stuck pig and slammed the door on his way out. I put the paper down and went out to the kitchen to make some coffee. My hands trembled slightly. I wondered whether from fear or from temper. A bit of both probably. I made the coffee strong and carried it back to the sitting room. I was too agitated for sleep and the night stretched ahead of me like an empty road. But I had plenty to think about.

I started in business when I came out of the army. Jack and I were demobbed on the same day and we travelled down on the train together from North Wales. We were both full of plans for the future. National Service had wasted two years of our lives and we were in a hurry to make up the lost time. Another pal, Bill Corcoran, the camp's light-heavyweight boxing champ was with us. The three of us had been almost inseparable during that time in the army.

We knew that train journey off by heart. Every six weeks we got a long weekend pass and we always went home to London. It took hours to reach Paddington and we played cards to pass the time. Anyway, on that particular day, two American soldiers got in at

Oswestry. We took no notice and carried on playing cards and telling stories, until after half an hour one of the Americans asked if we played poker? Jack looked at me and I looked at Jack, and I think Bill Corcoran looked out of the window. 'Poker?' Jack said, as if it were a foreign language.

'That's right,' the American nodded eagerly. 'Poker. Best card game in the world. You wanna learn?'

Jack said it was okay with him if we agreed. Bill turned back from the window and shrugged. 'What the hell – we've got three hours to kill – let's learn a new game.'

It was unfair really. We played poker all night long in camp. There's not much else to do half way up a Welsh mountain. So when it came to poker we were like fighters in training, and by the time we reached Paddington I had won fifty quid and Jack and Bill almost as much.

That was my first bank roll. Along with my savings of thirty-eight pounds I had a starting capital of nearly ninety pounds, and a week later I went into business. 'Sam's Place' I called it. It was nothing to look at – a crack in the wall at the cheaper end of Oxford Street, just before the junction with Tottenham Court Road. Still, Charlie Forte had started with a milk bar in Regent Street and he wasn't exactly starving to death.

Jack was astonished when he saw it. 'What are you going to sell in here – midgets?'

He had a point. Sam's Place measured twenty feet by six and a half. 'It's going to be a sandwich bar,' I said. 'Lunchtime trade only – take-away sandwiches for clerks and typists.'

'Take away where? Where are they going to eat them?'

'I dunno – anywhere they like, but they can't stay here – there's no room.'

He shook his head. 'If they're eating sandwiches they'll make them at home in the morning, and bring them with them.'

'We'll see.'

I did the place up myself. Laid lino on the floor and painted the walls and ceiling. Then I met a bloke who was in the demolition business. He was knocking down a bombed out pub in Bermondsey and he offered me the bar counter and one or two fittings – ten pounds the lot, including transport door to door. But ten pounds was too much capital going out for my liking, so I offered to work for him for a week instead, helping to knock this pub down. It was hard work but that's how I got my counter. Oak it was and as solid as a battleship; filthy dirty when I got it, but I scrubbed it down to the original wood and it looked really handsome in Sam's Place.

Funny how hard you'll work when you want something badly enough. My old Mum was alive then and I lived with her in Battersea. I used to get up at four in the morning and go straight to Smithfield. Not that I was buying in a big way, but the prices were better at the market, and at least my bits and pieces of ham were fresh. They had to be because there was no fridge in Sam's Place, at least not to start with. As well as ham I would buy joints of pork and beef, and take them home to Mum to cook. Then I went to Covent Garden and bought tomatoes and lettuce and cucumbers, and a few green peppers when I could get them. Butter and cheese came from a local wholesaler, and bread and doughnuts were delivered to Sam's Place at half past eight every morning. That was when the real work started. The idea was to get everything ready by eleven. Then I made a cup of coffee and waited for the rush. And rush they did. You would never believe how much food an eight stone typist can put away – even if it is brown bread and less fattening.

I used to finish at Sam's Place at about three o'clock. At least that's when I shut the door and hung up the closed sign. Then I scrubbed the counter and the floor, and made sure everything was clean and tidy for the morning. I cashed up then. It was the best part of the day, so I left it until last – to give me something to look forward to while I was scrubbing the floor.

Generally I got home to Battersea at about half past four. Mum would have cooked the roasts long before, so my first job was to slice the cold meat for the morning. Then I snoozed for an hour before going out again. I worked as a barman in the evening at The Jolly Friar in Buckley Street. It was a rough sort of pub – typical London backstreet place, but we sold a lot of beer and a few port and lemons to the local tarts before they went 'up West' for the night. Easy enough though, the occasional brawl on a Saturday night, but not much trouble apart from that. The wages paid my 'running costs', so that everything I made at Sam's Place was ploughed back into the business. And four years later I had nine of those little sandwich bars – all round the West End and into the City. I was twenty-four – and on my way.

It was 1961 then. London was changing fast – or so it seemed to me. There was more money about, and people's expectations were rising, my own included. I had done well with the sandwich shops, but I couldn't see a future for them. People with money in their pockets would want more than a cheese sandwich for lunch – at least I thought so. Luckily not everyone agreed. There was a chap I knew – Norman Higgins – who had half a dozen sandwich bars, mainly in the Edgware Road and Paddington area. His sites were well placed and he was doing nearly as much business as I was. We bumped into each other occasionally, at the markets and places like that, and we became quite pally, after all we were in the same line of business but hardly competitors – people don't cross London for a sandwich. Anyway Norman was looking for more outlets and one day he asked if I was interested in selling him my Oxford Street bar. I had a soft spot for Oxford Street, that's where it all started as far as I was concerned, and it was still my second best earner, even then. I thought it over for a week, then I turned him down – but I softened the blow by saying I would sell him the lot – at a price.

I suppose that deal got me started – on the road to the big time. It took Norman a month to raise the cash. I think every aunt and uncle in his family chipped in, so that what with their money and a loan from the bank he was able to come up with the hundred thousand I asked for. Then the accountants and lawyers took over and made a meal of it, but even so everything was finalised by the end of the year. I had saved a fair bit too, so at the beginning of 'sixty-two I was worth the best part of a hundred and thirty thousand, and all in cash.

I quit my job at The Jolly Friar then. I had kept it on more for the experience than the money; doing their ordering had taught me all about stock control and things like that – at least as far as the licensed trade was concerned. I could even read a balance sheet and write books up to trial balance, so all in all I was beginning to feel like a proper businessman.

Jack and I went to Paris to celebrate. Neither of us had been abroad before and we couldn't speak a word of French. But what a time we had! We didn't behave like proper businessmen in Paris – more like Proper Charlies looking back on it. The night life dazzled us. The Lido, the Crazy Horse, the Folies Bergères. We did the lot, night after night, club after club, and girl after girl. But hell, we were young, with money in our pockets; until, after ten days of it, our cash ran out and we just scraped enough to get back home.

Once in London I took a long hard look at the night life. I know it was changing, but compared with Paris it was as lively as a Sunday school. There were nude shows at the dear old Windmill of course, but none of the girls were allowed to move, so all you got for your money was a series of revolving tableaux of partly draped bodies. It suited the old colonels and the dirty mack brigade, but it never pretended to be a nightclub – not in the Parisian sense, nor even the American one. Hollywood was churning out all those tough guy movies then – Cagney and Bogart and Robert Taylor – and invariably some of the action took place in a nightclub. I reckoned MGM had gone overboard on a lavish set and to get their money back were staging a nightclub scene in every film they made. But whatever the reason, there was no doubt that films were spreading the idea of nightclubs.

It took me months to make my next move. My old Mum thought I would never work again, and worried herself sick about it. But I wanted to be *sure*. Something told me it was my big chance and I was afraid a mistake would ruin it. So I spread my risk in the end, and opened two places within six months of each other – and a third nine months after that.

Winston's was a club for businessmen. Of course London has always had its clubs – Boodles and Whites, the Athenaeum, places like that. But they were a different market from mine. I was aiming at the young businessmen, men like me in a way, who were making money and needed somewhere to take their clients for lunch. Most of the existing London clubs were too stuffy for my crowd, even if they could have obtained membership, and the food in some of them was pretty awful. So Winston's found a gap in the market.

I was lucky with the premises. A long lease on an old house in Belgrave Square. I spent forty thousand doing it up, put a ticker tape in the lobby and financial magazines in the reading room, hired my chef from Simpson's and commissionaire from Sandhurst – and went into business. Membership was ten pounds a year, payable in advance, and within a month I had two thousand members. And six weeks after that I had recovered my capital outlay and Winston's was a roaring success.

Jennifer's was very different. It was a disco at the bottom end of Carnaby Street. The youngest member of Winston's was probably about twenty-eight, but he would have been middle-aged at Jennifer's. Discos spread like a patch of weeds in the sixties but Jennifer's was among the very first. We had strobe lighting and hairy two-hundred-watt amplifiers, and a few dim corners for lovers. It's old hat now but it was as fresh as a daisy then. And being in Carnaby Street was just perfect.

Winston's was a lunchtime place and Jennifer's only opened in the evenings, so running the two of them was no real problem. But I was still gearing myself up for the big one. Both of my ventures were generating cash flow and I still had a chunk of capital to invest – but investing it was going to be the biggest decision of my life. Eventually I found what I was looking for. In Regent Street of all places. The location fell short of ideal. I would have preferred Soho or Shaftesbury Avenue, or even Piccadilly or Park Lane, but it was in Regent Street that I found a place big enough for what I wanted. It was a basement but the size was breathtaking – almost four thousand square feet and all on one level. I spent two days down there, watched over by a puzzled estate agent, pacing out what would be the kitchens and the restaurant, the dance floor and the bar, the lobby and the powder rooms – working my imagination overtime until I could see it. Until I could *hear* the band, *smell* the food, *see* the bare-shouldered women and the men in dinner jackets. It was just a dank and dirty basement then, but it came alive for me. I swear it was one of the most exciting moments of my life.

Of course, that was just the beginning. Months of work followed. Architects, building contractors, air-conditioning men, lawyers, accountants – meeting after meeting, talking, arguing, persuading. I would start at eight, lunch at Winston's and be back at Regent Street by two o'clock. Then at about nine every evening I went over to Jennifer's for a quick bite to eat before returning to my temporary office in the basement. The building contractors worked twenty-four hours a day because of a penalty clause in my contract, but despite the noise they made, more often than not I stayed in Regent Street overnight instead of returning to Battersea. People would ask: 'How do you sleep with that racket going on?' And I would grin, 'Who's sleeping? I'm dreaming.' And I was too.

It cost much more than I thought it would. All of my capital went and I was into the bank for another fifty thousand. Jack came over one evening – about a month before I opened – and we toured the place together. He was bug-eyed, astonished at the transformation, but worried sick about the cash I was spending. 'Sam, you'll over-reach yourself. Cut back for God's sake! Go on like this and you'll go broke.' But I just smiled and thanked him for his opinion. 'That's your point of view,' I said. Which is what I called the place.

The Point of View opened on New Year's Eve 1963, and the swinging sixties really roared into town. I gave a party for just about every celebrity in London and flew the girls over from the Crazy Horse in Paris. It was champagne and caviar all the way that night. My old Mum came up from Battersea and had a lovely time. She wore a new frock and had her hair fixed, and I gave her a rope of pearls to commemorate the occasion – so she wandered around smiling at people, just like the Queen Mum. Jack came too, of course, with his new girlfriend, a slim, dark-haired Italian beauty by the name of Maria.

We made the headlines in every gossip column bar one the next morning – even had pictures in a lot of them. Full of stories about Swinging Sam Harris and how the jet set was coming to London. I thought it was terrific. Mum started a scrap book of press cuttings and the future looked golden.

Funny how life comes apart in your hands, just when you think you've got everything you want. It started to go wrong in February. Thanks to the grand opening and all the publicity, The Point of View did middling to fair during January. More than a few people were willing to give it a try. But trade fell right away in February. I thought it was a bad week at first, but then it was a bad fortnight which stretched to a bad month. I went frantic. My outgoings were colossal. Big name singers, entertainers, dancers, the band – all that lot to pay for before I bought as much as a bottle of gin for the bar. I did everything I could think of – hired publicity agents, paid cabbies for the business they brought in, gave members of Winston's special prices, advertised, promoted – spent and spent and spent! In the end the bank put a stop to my overdraft and that near crippled me. If Winston's and Jennifer's had stopped earning I would have gone under for sure.

Then – half way through April – Mum died. She'd had this sniffling cold for weeks, and no matter how much I nagged she would never go to the doctor. 'It's just a stupid cold,' she said. 'It'll go away.' But it never did. I kept quiet about my worries but I think she guessed, because every day she told me how ill I looked. How ill *I* looked mind, not her – and me as strong as a horse, even if I was worried sick.

I used to get home to Battersea at about half past four most mornings – later sometimes – after Saturday nights for instance. Mum would snooze during the afternoons and evenings – she never slept properly anyway – and she waited up for me with a cup of tea. It was crazy really. I had more than fifty waiters working for me then, but Mum *had* to make me a cup of tea. I was never able to persuade her out of it, and I gave up trying in the end. We used to chat for half an hour, and then I would go to bed for a few hours' sleep.

Well, one morning in April, when I got home, she was dead. She was sitting in front of what was left of the fire, with my scrap book on her lap. Her head had dropped forward and I thought she had dozed off at first, but as soon as I touched her I knew she was dead. The shock hit me like a hammer. We had always been close – Mum and I. Dad was killed when we were bombed out in the war, and Mum brought me up single-handed – so life had never been easy.

I pulled myself together eventually. Then I went round the corner to 'phone the doctor. And Jack of course. He arrived ten minutes later, with a half bottle of brandy in his overcoat pocket. We sat drinking until the grey light of a Battersea morning crept into that tiny kitchen. The doctor came and went – and two days later I buried Mum at the little cemetery near Chelsea Football Ground.

It's all so long ago now. Looking back I'm glad she died when she did, which sounds pretty sick when you say it like that. But I was on my way up then. She had lunched at Winston's and been to Jennifer's, and had a few dinners at The Point of View. And she was so *proud* of it. I can remember her now, sitting in the kitchens in Regent Street, looking about her at the gleaming ovens and the serving dishes – and just sighing and cooing with wonder at it all. Thank God she never lived to see me charged with murder – or sat through the trial at the Oxford Assizes – or listened to the judge pass sentence on me. Any of that would have killed her for sure.

I saved The Point of View eventually, with Jack's help. He had bought a half share in his first pub by then – The Blue Posts – so he had his own problems, but nothing ever stopped him helping me. His pub closed at eleven and he was at my place by half past – all decked out in a dinner jacket and ready to lend a hand wherever he could. It was Jack who spotted the fiddles. Money lost to dishonest waiters and crooked barmen. Suppliers who padded their bills and paid a kick-back to the chef. Staff who stole the silver and others who walked out with the linen stuffed under their coats. Jack watched my back while bit by bit I got things under control. But it was touch and go for a time. The bank counted every penny and for weeks on end the profits from Winston's and Jennifer's were wiped out by the losses piled up by the nightclub. More than once suppliers were kept waiting for their money, and Fridays were a regular nightmare – waiting for enough cash to come in to meet the wages. But as the summer passed so did the crisis, and from early autumn business got steadily better, so that by the end of the year the battle was over. Even the bank relaxed – the overdraft had been halved and was moving down steadily – and The Point of View was established.

CHAPTER TWO

I slept badly that first night back at Rex Place. Absurd really, the soft bed and crisp sheets should have made me sleep like a baby. But I tossed and turned all night, troubled by old memories and fresh worries, until I awoke with a splitting headache. A couple of minutes passed before I even realised where I was – then it all flooded back – the cold shoulder around town last night, and a visit from Davis to cap it all. But just the simple act of making coffee cheered me up. After all, Rex Place was a sight better than Brixton Prison. If I had problems at least I was free to do something about them. So within the next hour I had shaved and dressed, and was ready to face the day.

The post surprised me. A letter from Maria. I recognised her handwriting on the envelope. But then it was a gesture typical of her. She would have posted it yesterday morning, to give me a surprise today. Except when I opened it, I found not so much a letter as the printed details of the place in Baker Street – and the keys to the premises. I grinned. Who could be down for long with friends like Maria? She and Jack were determined to help me start again. So I began to think seriously about the idea.

A prison record does not automatically disbar a man from holding a gaming licence, or even one to sell spirits – but it doesn't help. In both cases licences are issued by magistrates and the applicant has to prove himself a 'fit and proper person' to hold such a licence. Even in Brixton I knew the future would be difficult, and that was before learning that Davis was gunning for me.

My trial had left me disillusioned with lawyers. Courts are places for actors, not businessmen. Any *justice* resulting from the proceedings is quite accidental. It would be quicker and cheaper to spin a coin. At least I thought so then – and still do for that matter. But my application for licences would be heard by magistrates – so, like it or not, I was back in the business of hiring lawyers.

Tomlinson saw me at eleven o'clock. A tall, thin man of about sixty, as white and brittle as a stick of chalk. He kept licking his lips, and when he spoke he chose his words carefully, like an old-fashioned schoolmaster. Of course, he knew who I was. Every newspaper in the country had covered my trial, and lawyers follow court cases the way most men follow football. I told him my side of things and filled him in with the details. He listened attentively, his head half cocked as though he heard better through one ear than the other. Now and then he asked a question and noted my answers on a pad in front of him. His expression was neutral for most of the time, but there were enough flickers of doubt for me to wonder what kind of impression I was making. But eventually I had told him all there was to tell, and it was his turn to speak.

'How old are you, Mr Harris?'

'Forty-two.'

'You're still a young man. Full of energy. Experienced in life and in business. Why not try something else?'

'Because I know the casino business inside out. It's what I know best.'

He raised his eyebrows and peered at me from above his spectacles. 'Oh, come now. Business is business. A client of mine is a management consultant. He maintains the same rules apply whatever the business.'

'I'm not a management consultant.'

'But you follow my drift?'

'Are you saying I'll never get back?'

He hesitated at that, lawyers always do when you ask a direct question. 'I'm saying it's exceedingly unlikely. If the police lodge a strenuous objection, the magistrates are bound to take note of it.'

'But it's not the police – it's Davis.'

'Who happens to be a policeman – and a fairly senior one.'

'A fairly bent one!'

He steepled his fingers and looked at me severely. 'I really must caution you not to say that. Of course what you say here is privileged, but were you to say that outside—'

'I did. I said it to Davis – to his face last night.' I laughed, but without amusement.

That surprised him enough for him to want to know more, so I told him what had happened and he noted it down. Then he said, 'Let me tell you how this appears to me. You have just finished a term of imprisonment and Chief Inspector Davis was largely responsible for bringing the prosecution—'

'Not entirely *responsible*. But his manoeuvring had a lot to do—'

'That's as may be,' Tomlinson said with surprising forcefulness. 'But the fact is that you pleaded guilty. It's all very well for you to condemn the practice of plea-bargaining now – but now is far too late.'

I glowered but said nothing. So he went on, 'It seems to me that there is a good deal of personal animosity between you and Chief Inspector Davis—'

'Bloody right.'

'As a consequence of which,' he went on without pausing, 'you see your return to the world of nightclubs as a way of getting back at him. After all, you will no doubt say, I can't be such a *bad* chap if the magistrates have restored my licences. In a way it supports your present contention of being innocent—'

'Which I was,' I snorted.

He sighed, as if I was behaving like an obstinate schoolboy and in truth I was beginning to feel like one. Tomlinson was nobody's fool and if he was not exactly *right* about the way I felt, neither was he exactly *wrong*. He spent a moment or two watching me from over the top of his glasses, then he took another tack. 'You must realise by now that a plea of guilty means exactly what it says. An admission of guilt which lays you open to the full penalties of the law. There can be no question of re-opening the matter now. Put it behind you and forget about it – that's my advice.'

'What about my licences?' I asked doggedly.

His eyes betrayed a flicker of exasperation but he kept it from sounding in his voice. 'Unfortunately your own actions have made that even more difficult. You have, so to speak, added another few hundred feet to Everest. To have fought the prosecution and won would have been one thing – but to have *admitted guilt*! The police will make a meal of that, believe me. What more proof, they will ask, do the honourable magistrates require to find this man unsuitable?'

It was all very depressing but I was determined not to show it.

'So we're in for a fight – that's what it amounts to. I knew that anyway.'

'A fight you're unlikely to win,' he said gloomily.

'Well, I'll fight anyway. I want you to set up a meeting with the best QC you can get. After that—'

'I wonder if that's wise?' he asked thoughtfully. 'Cases in magistrates courts are generally dealt with by solicitors. For a barrister to appear is unusual – for a QC to appear?' His eyebrows climbed into his hairline. 'You follow my drift? It might be better to instruct a junior – play it low key. A QC will alert the magistrates to the unusual aspects of this case—'

'The police will do that anyway. No, I want the best QC available. Let's go in with all guns firing. The bigger the guns—'

'The more resounding the defeat,' he interrupted, and there was no doubt about whose defeat he meant. He looked at me steadily. 'Then you're quite determined to go ahead – whatever my advice?'

I nodded cheerfully, but in case I broke into a smile, he said, 'It will cost money. I don't wish to be indelicate, but—'

I took the cheque Collins had given me from my pocket. It was all the money I had in the world – apart from my share of Rex Place – but whoever said justice is cheap never fought battles in the Law Courts of London. 'A thousand should cover it, shouldn't it?' He thought for a moment, and then nodded. 'Take it out of this and give me a cheque for the balance.'

His eyes took in Collins's name printed on the cheque. 'May I ask why you are changing solicitors, Mr Harris? Collins and Waterman are a well respected firm.'

That was a lie and we both knew it. I never met Waterman but Collins had never enjoyed the respect of his peers in the legal profession – now he didn't even enjoy mine. Tomlinson blinked like an owl, and then added, 'After all, your former solicitors know the background so well—'

'There are two reasons for changing. First they lost the big one for me, and even worse, they never believed a word I said.'

'And you think I do?' he enquired mildly.

'It's no longer important. It would help if you did but it doesn't matter if you don't. You see, I understand the game now. Until my trial I believed in old-fashioned justice. That the truth, the whole truth and nothing but the truth would come out in court. All that kind of thing.' I grinned at him. 'Naive, wasn't it? Now I see it for what it is. An old style shoot out. The fastest gun wins. That's why I want the best shot in chambers.'

'It's not an analogy I entirely accept,' he said, steepling his fingers again. 'I'm more inclined to compare lawyers to tailors. Take some material to a tailor and he'll make you a suit. The better the material, the better the result.'

He came downstairs to say goodbye. 'All in all it will take five or six weeks. We'll be in touch with Collins and Waterman as a matter of courtesy and I'll make immediate enquiries about retaining a QC. Meanwhile, I'll apply for a hearing – which will get it on the lists.' He moistened his lips. 'Unfortunately that will also put the other side on notice of our intentions, so no doubt the police will take a special interest in your affairs. Discretion had better be your watchword. Keep out of trouble yourself and don't mix with any undesirable characters.' His severe look melted to a wintry smile.

'In the unlikely event of your obtaining licences, you'll have to put up with more than the usual amount of police scrutiny. Your new club will need the Archbishop of Canterbury as head waiter and the Queen of England on the cash desk.'

Tomlinson seemed a doubtful candidate for a sense of humour and when I looked at him I knew I was right. He was perfectly serious.

The Baker Street place looked just as bad in daylight. Of course I was still feeling depressed – after all, Tomlinson had been far from encouraging. But I let myself in and had a good look round. The basement had potential but that was about all. The ground floor was the wrong shape and the ceiling was too high. It would take all of Jack's hundred thousand to transform this place. And then there was the worry about location. It was too far from Curzon Street for my liking. Would the gamblers travel this far? But after pacing around for a while I began to feel more cheerful – or at least stopped feeling sorry for myself. So what if it was hard to start again? When had life been easy? Jack was willing to stake me and Maria was still fond of me, so I couldn't be *all bad* despite the cold shoulder around town last night. So after giving myself a good talking to, I looked at the place with a new eye – and it seemed very much better then.

Jack had left The Blue Posts by the time I arrived. Matthews said he had gone to The Golden Lion, so I followed on there. When I arrived he was at the bar talking racing with some cronies of his, arguing the merits of Piggott and Breasely as if they were personal friends of his. Knowing Jack they probably were – all sorts eat at The Dog's Home.

I waited until the others had drifted away, then I said, 'You might have warned me.'

He grinned. He knew what I meant all right. 'Last night? What difference would it have made? You'd have gone anyway – to see for yourself. Warning you wouldn't have stopped you.'

'You had any trouble?'

'From this protection mob?' he shook his head. 'Battersea's a bit out of the way for them. There's really only me down here, and the cash they'd take from me wouldn't be worth the fight they'd have taking it. Anyway, I'm small fry – those boys are catching bigger fish.'

'But you believe it? It's really happening?'

'It's happening all right. Eric Blockley didn't die in no accident. That business on the river was murder. Even the Old Bill know that.'

Jack had always been on good terms with the law. Publicans and restaurateurs often are, but at times I thought Jack's relationship with the police went a bit beyond the normal professional contact. It was his business and I never gave it much thought – but he often seemed to have some snippet of inside knowledge which couldn't have been gleaned from the newspapers.

'What else do they know?'

He grinned. 'They don't tell me and I don't ask. Why should I – it's none of my business.'

'But it could be – if it spreads. Things like that—'

'Never go looking for trouble. That's my motto. If it's got your name on it'll find you soon enough.'

'Some people are putting my name on it. Did you know that?'

'I heard,' he said softly. He gave me a long look, as if searching for the truth of something in my eyes. Then he chuckled. 'Silly buggers. Believe anything, some will. Sam Harris – the Al Capone of the West End! Come off it – where's your sense of humour?'

I laughed, but not enough to stop worrying. Mud sticks as I had reason to know. We finished our drinks and left The Golden Lion, and in the car I asked him about this new crowd – Tuskers.

'Welsh, I think. Leastways they've got some clubs and things down in Cardiff.' He pulled out to overtake a cyclist. 'Buying your lot from the receiver got them started in the West End. Since then they've gone from strength to strength. Must have plenty of cash behind them.'

Jack lacks curiosity to an extent which amazes me. By the sound of it Tuskers were getting bigger every day, yet as far as he was concerned they could be operating in Moscow.

'About the money,' I said. 'The hundred thousand. You were serious, weren't you?'

'Ever know me joke about cash?'

'Thanks.' Then I told him about my meeting with Tomlinson, and my visit to Baker Street. And about what I planned to do. He pulled up outside The Dog's Home just as I finished. 'And this Tomlinson?' he asked. 'He reckons you're wasting time and money, does he?'

I nodded, knowing I had to ask if he thought so too, even though I might not like his answer, but someone lending you a hundred thousand is at least entitled to an opinion. He climbed out of the car and locked the door. 'What I think doesn't matter,' he said, leading the way into The Dog's Home. 'The money's yours anyway. Sam Harris will come again – whatever the odds. But it seems you're going the hard way about it. Why not operate from behind a front?'

I shook my head. 'Davis would get behind it. He'll know I'm involved because I'll have to work night and day to make a go of that place. If Davis queered things afterwards your money could be in danger. It's better this way. If I fight now and win, there can't be complications later.'

'And if you lose?'

'You keep your money.'

Maria and Lucia were in the big sitting room upstairs. Two porters were with them; big beefy types with sweaty hands and red faces twisted into expressions of exhaustion. The room had been *completely* refurnished. A Chinese washed carpet graced the floor, all pale blues instead of the strong reds of the kashan which had been there yesterday. Even the paintings had been changed, or at least most of them had.

'Finished?' Jack asked cheerfully.

Maria pulled a face in a pretence of indignation. 'Wouldn't you believe it? Your timing's perfect. You're out boozing while Lucia and I are lugging furniture about.'

Jack's grin widened as he looked round the room. 'You've done a good job, I'll say that. That goes well,' he pointed to a Victorian bookcase made of tulipwood and satinwood. 'And those oval medallions are good – they pick up the blue of the carpet perfectly.' He turned to the porters. 'And you've been supervising I suppose – letting the ladies do all the work?' He grinned and thrust a fiver at them. 'Go on – get yourselves a beer at The Posts – looks like you've earned it.'

Maria kissed me as the porters left and Lucia smiled hello from across the room.

Jack said, 'There was a feller in here last night who swore blind that the *chaise longue* – the one we had against the wall – was genuine eighteenth century. *Swore blind!* Said it was Georges Jacob. I told him it was a copy but he wouldn't believe me. Would he Maria?' She was on his arm, smiling up at him. Jack shrugged. 'In the end I *had* to let him have it – just *had* to. Twelve hundred quid – cash this morning.' He shook his head sadly. 'Beats me where they get the money. Wasn't worth six hundred that – even at today's prices.'

'And what did it cost you?' Maria chuckled.

Jack looked shy enough to blush. 'Oh, I dunno. Forget – hundred and eighty I think. Mind, it's been in stock for a while.'

Maria laughed. 'At least three months.'

'And you do all this,' Lucia asked, part amused, part puzzled. She waved a hand at the room, 'whenever you sell something? Change a whole room?'

'No,' Maria admitted. 'Not *every* time. But sometimes when a major piece goes it alters the whole balance of the place.' She nodded thoughtfully, convincing herself. 'It's all a question of balance, isn't it Jack?'

'That's right – bank balance mainly,' he said happily. 'Come on, let's have a drink before lunch.'

Nobody can be depressed when Jack's in a good mood – especially when Maria is sharing it with him, and Lucia added glitter, like tinsel on a Christmas tree. I had been worried sick when I left Tomlinson, even though I had tried to hide it – but after half an hour at The Dog's Home, all my troubles were forgotten. I was laughing as much as anyone. And when I wasn't laughing I was watching Lucia – and trying not to show that either. She was as delicate as – as – I don't know what? As lace, as delicate as a fresh rose, or Dresden china. Yet she had this *sureness* about her. Whenever she looked at me I sensed some hidden knowledge – some secret – some private awareness of what was going on which she was withholding from me. Beautiful eyes as clear as springwater, yet with a curious depth to them. Enigmatic – but not off-putting – in fact just the opposite.

So I spent a happy hour, laughing at Jack's stories and looking at Lucia; talking to her, admiring, smelling and occasionally touching her – while all the time warning myself against her. She was not for me. My old Mum used to say there was a time and a place for everything. Like when I got married. I was thirty-two then and top of the heap. Fit, young, wealthy and carefree. Running around with every chorus girl in town. It was fun for a while, but when you can't remember their names – not even when they are in bed beside you – it's time for something else. Like getting married. It was the *time* for it.

But that was ten years ago. Now I was nearly broke. Struggling for survival. Magistrates courts – Davis – the heavy mob. It was time to fight – not a time to be distracted by someone like Lucia. And I was just resigning myself to that when she turned and asked, 'Where are we going tonight?'

I thought she was talking to all of us for a moment, then I realised she meant just me. 'Tonight?' I repeated stupidly.

'I washed my hair *last* night – remember? Especially.'

Her hair looked like Vidal Sassoon had combed it out an hour before, but that was beside the point. Especially when she added, 'Didn't you say something about showing me the town?' She looked away. 'But of course, if you've made other arrangements—'

'No,' I said quickly. 'No – I haven't made other arrangements.' She looked back at me and I was drowning in those clear grey eyes. I laughed shakily – unsure of what to say: 'It's just that – well London is closed as far as I'm concerned. Off limits. I've been warned off – that sort of thing.'

She was sending me up because her eyes opened a mile wide and she said: 'The *whole* of London is closed? You must be a very wicked man, *Mr Harris*.'

The *Mr Harris* broke the ice. She had called me Sam ever since we met and *Mr Harris* sounded absurd. Anyway we all laughed and it gave me a chance to think of where I might take her. Eventually we settled on a show and supper afterwards, and despite my earlier reservations I looked forward to it. Then, just as we were about to leave the table, Maria reached across to grab my lapel. 'Listen, Sam,' she picked up a fruit knife and held it between her teeth like a pirate. 'You treat my cousin but good, huh? Because she knows some very big men in the Mafia. So you give little Lucia—' she pronounced 'leetle' like a Mexican bandit, 'a good time, eh?'

I was nodding, laughing and wondering what Tomlinson would say to my squiring a Capo's girlfriend around the West End. Of course it was a joke, even though Maria followed it with a funny look and Lucia blushed furiously.

I said, 'I try to give my girls a good time,' and Jack said, 'That's what worries us.'

I left The Dog's Home at about half past three, still driving Jack's car. Keith Prowse have a theatre booking office in the Hilton so I went there first, to see what tickets I could get at short notice. Luckily they had two cancelled stalls for a revue at the Garrick, and with the tickets safely in my pocket I returned to Rex Place.

Once back in the little sitting room I got to thinking about what Tomlinson had said about providing lawyers with good material. It was an obvious enough point perhaps, but it concentrated my mind on the case we had to present to the magistrates. No doubt Davis would paint me as the biggest rogue ever to walk the streets of London, using my trial and prison sentence as evidence against me – whereas we had to show those events as being quite unrepresentative of my life as a whole. Of course when I met the QC in chambers I would explain the background, but I wondered if I couldn't do better than that? Meetings in chambers are all very well, but at best they are question and answer sessions, with counsel asking the questions which occur to him at the time. *But suppose he never asks the right questions?*

I brewed a pot of tea, collected a scrap pad from the desk, and settled into an armchair. Remembering back over the years is difficult at times, but my restlessness the previous night had started the process – and Tomlinson's request for material was the only stimulant needed. So I began to search my mind for anything which might help them to see things from my point of view – until those very words – point of view, opened a floodgate of memories. After all, so much sprang from there.

Running a nightclub is an education. At least it was for me. The Point of View was my university, much more than the army ever was. Oh, we met all sorts in the camp in North Wales, but that was different. People were playing soldiers there – the professionals willingly, and the National Service bods like reluctant schoolboys – and there was a great deal of resistance to what the sociologists call class mobility. If you were ex-public school you got a commission – if you went to Battersea Secondary you were in the ranks with me. Not that I cared – neither Jack nor I ever saw ourselves on the General Staff – but it meant that although you met all sorts, you never actually *mixed* with them, not socially anyway.

Whereas all types mix at a nightclub. All types and all sexes, and if you think there are just two you've never run a nightclub. And of course *I* was different. I was nobody in the army, whereas I was the owner of The Point of View. I had grown up, matured, smoothed enough of the rough edges to acquire a certain amount of what they call polish. I was never Valentino, mind you, but neither was I a kid from Battersea any more. I said 'Harris' instead of ''arris' and could tell good wine from bad. And I had become a fair businessman, even though I say it myself. So I suppose I was turning into what I always wanted to be – 'someone important in London'.

On the other hand Jack wanted a quieter life. He needed to make money, of course, but *his* way. 'Bigger and better doesn't always mean best,' he would say and although I tried to persuade him to stay he decided not to, and half way through 'sixty-four he stopped coming up to the West End. A few months later I gave him the money for The Dog's Home and I was on my own again – but not for long, because shortly afterwards I was invited to invest in the casino business.

Legitimate gambling arrived in London with the Gaming Act of 1961, after which casinos became part of the scene – part of the night life, a tourist attraction, a stimulant in the lives of some people – and big business. *Very* big business.

I'm not really a gambler – unless you count being a businessman – but a hell of a lot of rubbish gets talked about it. Later, when I was running the casinos, I came in for stick from all sorts of quarters. Of course some weak people do become gambling addicts – but I'm damned if I'll accept it's criminal to run a casino because it encourages the habit. You may as well say anyone who serves a pint of bitter encourages alcoholism, or a chemist dispensing aspirin encourages drug addiction – or the pill encourages prostitution. Hell, where does it end? It's all beside the point now but it used to get me steamed up angry at that time.

Anyway, four years after The Point of View opened its doors for the very first time, it was established as the best club in town. Winston's was flourishing and Jennifer's had given birth to daughters – Pamela's Place in Chelsea and Josephine's in Fulham – so with everything nicely under control, I was looking for my next step forward. And then one day I had a 'phone call from a man named Weston – Charlie Weston. I knew him slightly – he was a member of Winston's among other things, and an occasional visitor to The Point of View. He said he had some business to talk about so we fixed a meeting, and I thought no more of it until he arrived at eleven the next morning.

He brought a whole team of people with him. Five altogether. I've forgotten their names now but I remember their occupations. One was Weston's lawyer, another was an architect, the third was a merchant banker – complete with assistant – and then there was Weston himself. After shaking hands we indulged in the usual pleasantries, then I arranged them on chairs around my office and asked Weston what was on his mind.

He was older than me, but not by much. I was twenty-eight then and he was maybe thirty-six. I knew he was fairly big in the haulage business – he never stopped boasting about it at Winston's – but apart from that I knew little of his background. He was a well built man about six feet two and broad with it – black hair and blue eyes, looked a bit Welsh but spoke without an accent. A rough diamond, who had started as a long distance driver and never looked back. Strong and rough, with a handshake like a coal crusher.

He said, 'I'd like to make a suggestion before we begin. We think this will be an important meeting – for all of us. So it might be helpful if your secretary took notes – sort of leave you with something to think about.'

I was a bit surprised and irritated – after all it was *my* office and she was *my* secretary – but I was more intrigued than anything, so I asked Brenda to join us and bring her pad.

That meeting lasted six hours! I had sandwiches and drinks sent in from the club – and innumerable pots of coffee and extra packs of cigarettes – until, at about five o'clock, we had talked ourselves to a standstill. What it amounted to was this: Charlie had just bought into two casinos – The Chequers Club in Curzon Street and The Derby in Brook Street – and had obtained the necessary licences to open a third, at the bottom end of Park Lane. The Park Lane project was huge – Las Vegas style. The architect unveiled plans and elevations like the president of the Royal Academy presenting the Summer Exhibition. It was a hell of a place – incorporating a new hotel, service flats, indoor swimming pool, squash courts, everything. The capital outlay was enormous but Charlie's accountant was there to talk about the subsequent profits. I failed to see how it concerned me but it was fascinating stuff which captured my interest.

When the accountant finished, Charlie took over. He showed me copies of the latest accounts – all fully audited – to prove what a viable business he had acquired, and although the casinos were making good profits I was pleased to realise I was making better ones. But as he said, The Derby was in its first year, the capital outlay had been enormous, and interest charged on borrowed money had dug deep into his margins. I remembered my first year with The Point of View and sympathised.

Then the merchant banker took over. His bank had been making a study of the leisure industry – and here were the figures. So I waded through a lot more detail which merely confirmed my gut feeling – that the casino business had growth written all over it. I listened, nodded, looked suitably impressed – and asked myself why the hell they were telling me this? Then the lawyer explained. The Park Lane project – while hugely profitable – was too big for Charlie to finance himself. So they were looking for a partner. But that was just the beginning. The idea was that Charlie and I merge our businesses, then float a public company and sell a chunk of our stock to the investing public. That would give us the cash to finance the Park Lane venture and after that everything would come up roses. Hell, we'd even be millionaires – at least Charlie and I would.

They had certainly done their homework. When they finished I realised they knew almost as much about my business as I did. But what impressed me most was the proposed new board of directors. Lord Hardman was to be chairman, and the others would be the Earl of Darlington, Lew Douglas (who owned a string of hotels), Charlie and me. Hardman was blue-blooded business, owning outright the oldest firm of wine merchants in the country, and Darlington was on the board of the merchant bank. But it was more than that. They wanted me – a boy from Battersea – to run the whole show as managing director.

We discussed a whole lot of things. The merchant bank's hand was obvious in choosing the team, but I was surprised to learn that Charlie Weston actually knew Hardman quite well. Their backgrounds were so totally different that I couldn't imagine how their paths crossed – but apparently Charlie ran a special fleet of road tankers to transport Hardman's wine in bulk, and the two had come to know each other through business. Anyway we talked and talked; how many shares each would own in the new set-up and things like that – and at the end of the meeting I promised to think about it.

Jack brought Maria over to dinner that night, and my current girlfriend made up the foursome. Jack thought I was mad to even consider it. 'What's in it for you?' he wanted to know. 'You've already got everything you want. Your own business – money – the good life. What more do you want?'

'I dunno – but I've got to think about it. This could be big – the biggest there is.'

'You're out of your mind,' he sounded disgusted. 'Those guys will give you so much aggro you'll wish you were back in Oxford Street making sandwiches.'

'It's his life,' my girlfriend said protectively.

Maria smiled. 'But his friends worry about him.'

I remembered that afterwards – Maria sitting at that table,

watching me with her dark, liquid eyes, concerned and anxious. I smiled and patted her hand, telling her there was nothing to worry about. 'I'm a big boy now. I can look after myself,' I said – and you can't get more complacent than that.

We floated Apex Holdings on the second of April, 1967. The shares were over-subscribed three or four times, so the under-writers made a killing and I was officially a millionaire – at least on paper. I was thirty years old and life had never been sweeter.

The freehold of the Curzon Street premises was owned by Charlie Weston, or to be more accurate by Apex Holdings, since he and I had put everything we owned into the business in return for shares. It was a fine building with enough room on the upper floors for our head office, so from then on I worked there. I had long since moved from Battersea to a flat in Mount Street just round the corner and so – unless it was raining – I walked to the office every morning. If it was wet Tom, my driver, fetched me in the Rolls.

And after that I was given my head. Board meetings were a formality. Hardman presided with a light touch and was invariably the first to propose the acceptance of my report each month. There was rarely any dissension. They were all experienced businessmen and as long as the figures were coming out right they were happy to see me every four weeks and then rush back to their individual enterprises. I was left to get on with it – and running Apex proved to be little different from running my own venture. Just the scale was bigger, that's all.

Mind you, I worked all hours God sent. I organised the business into three divisions – casinos, restaurants and discotheques – and put a man in charge of each. The first year was murder – meetings, planning, decisions; but bit by bit I assembled a strong team of people. Of course I made mistakes, who doesn't? Luckily none were too serious though because we prospered overall, and oddly enough, the Park Lane project, the reason for us getting together in the first place, was postponed – on my recommendation. We did open a casino there, but it was a scaled down version of the original project. Caution on my part really. I felt we had enough on our plate; best to let the new team settle down before embarking upon such a massive venture. Anyway, that was my feeling and the others went along with it.

It was at the end of those very busy twelve months or so, that I met Kay. During Ascot week. Apex were sponsoring a number of races – principally the Apex Gold Cup – and we had a permanent box for entertaining VIPs. The usual sort of thing – champagne and caviar and smoked salmon sandwiches – lots of social chatter with the occasional look at the races. And Edgar Hardman – *Lord*

Hardman – came down for the third day of the meeting – and brought his daughter Kay.

Truthfully I wasn't immediately attracted to her. Of course at the time I was being faithfully – if that's the right word – serviced by some of the prettiest showgirls in London, so I was hardly looking for spare crumpet. And besides I was working when we met, being host at these business things demands concentration, or at least I find it does. Diplomacy is not second nature to me and any charm I may have isn't natural – I have to work at it.

When we shook hands she said, 'So we meet at last. I was beginning to think you only existed in newspaper photographs.' She stepped back to eye me up and down. 'Like the centre spread in *Playboy*.'

'I'll see if my navel's turned to a paper clip when I go to bed tonight.'

'Do better than that,' she smiled into my eyes. 'Come over to my place and I'll see for you.'

It was the kind of provocative remark typical of Kay. She wore her sexuality like an aura and was the most *feminine* woman I ever met. Men swarmed round her like bees at a honey pot. Yet the strange thing was she was neither pretty nor beautiful – at least not in the accepted sense. Of course she had a superb figure and I suppose an expensive finishing school had taught her to make the most of it, but although her face was striking, it was certainly not beautiful. She had inherited her father's square jaw for one thing – and his bold way of looking at people, so that a glance from her could turn the most mundane conversation into an argument. She had a look which bestowed a judgement, as though she was evaluating you, weighing your worth. If you passed inspection her eyebrows arched almost imperceptibly and she gave a nod of approval, and when she smiled the sun shone. I've seen men spend an evening trying to win her smile and go home happy if they did so, and I've seen others leave with murder in their hearts because of a cross word.

But none of that was known to me when we met at Ascot. All I saw then was a girl of medium height, with golden hair and blue eyes, who turned to smile at me as she reached the other side of the box. She raised her glass and said something – but the words were lost in the general chatter, and all I remember is her smile making me feel better than I had felt all day.

After the last race was over people began to gather their things for the journey to town. We were a party of twenty and a fleet of cars waited to convoy us back up the M3. I had just sent a message to Tom to bring the cars round, when Kay excused herself from the people she was with and came over to join me. 'Still giving orders, Mr Harris – doesn't the boss ever relax?'

'The name's Sam. And I *never* give orders. It's more polite to ask people.'

'Even when they have no choice but to obey?'

'Everyone gets a choice in life,' I said gently, but already felt an indefinable challenge.

'People only do what they want to do? Is that what you're saying?' She cocked her head to one side and watched me quizzically.

'Something like that. Leastways I've never known anyone act against his best interests.'

'And attending to your – your *requests*. That's invariably in their own best interests?'

'That's for them to judge.'

I wondered why I sounded defensive? There was nothing aggressive in her manner, but her directness was unusual. As though she went through life taking whatever she wanted as a matter of course – as if it was hers *by right*.

Then, quite unexpectedly, she announced: 'It's my birthday today. Did you know?'

'Well no – no I didn't know. Many happy returns.'

She thanked me and looked down at the racecourse. The crowds were still milling around, saying goodbyes or making arrangements to meet again later. Bookies were packing their satchels and a patch of white cloud momentarily obscured the sun. She turned back to me and put one hand on my lapel: 'I'm having a party tonight – will you come?'

I tried to imagine her kind of party. Ten years separated our ages and our backgrounds were light years apart. I had called at the Hardman family home once and nobody left there without being impressed. Wyndham Hall was drenched in history. Hardmans through the ages looked down from the walls and their ghosts paced the terrace at night.

'I'm afraid I'm working,' I said, then added more diplomatically, 'My business plays havoc with my social life.'

'Don't you have managers? People like that – to look after things?'

I smiled, 'It helps if I show an interest.'

'But you don't have to lock up – balance the books at the end of the night – that sort of thing?'

'No, not these days.'

'Then come when you finish. I'll expect you,' she said simply. 'Will you have eaten or shall I see you for dinner?'

There seemed no way of avoiding it without seeming boorish. A meeting elsewhere might have enabled me to refuse with conviction, but I had nothing planned and her smile weakened my powers of resistance.

'I won't be finished until about ten—' I began, but she cut me short by saying, 'Dinner will be waiting for you.' She thrust a card into my hand just as her father came over to join us. 'Hello, Father,' she grinned up at him. 'Lost a fortune?'

'Had quite a good day as a matter of fact,' he linked his arm through hers. 'Won seven hundred I think – er I say – is that Hutchinson waving to us?' Hutchinson was my assistant, and he was indeed waving. The cars were ready and waiting.

'*Au revoir*, Mr Harris,' Kay said. She smiled brilliantly with just a hint of mockery in her eyes. 'It's been a perfect day—' she lowered her voice, 'and it's not over yet.'

Back in the West End I said goodbye to my guests and went home to change for the evening. Kay's parting look stayed in my mind. It defied analysis. Amusement perhaps? Mockery? Provocation – challenge? But a challenge to what? To go to a party – a birthday party? Finally I gave up trying to work it out and went to The Chequers Club to make my first call of the evening.

I had developed a routine by then – though routine is probably the wrong word for something which varied so much – but I would call on each of our clubs and restaurants between eight and midnight, stay for a drink, answer any queries, gauge the night's takings – and then move on. I tended to leave the discotheques to Smithers who was my man running that division, but I did the clubs every night, though never in the same order. During the evening I took dinner along the way and then went home, sometimes alone but more often than not with a current girlfriend. Which is what I would have done that night except, according to the card Kay had given me, I was expected at an address in Chelsea.

I left for her place at nine forty-five, expecting the worst and cursing myself for being talked into going. The meal would be one of those scrambled buffet affairs (how else could she keep dinner for me at a party?), the wine would be undistinguished and the guests the crowd of chinless wonders who make up the upper class party set. I promised myself to stay an hour and then flee to The Point of View.

But when the cab drew up outside the address she had given me the place was in darkness. No loud music split the silence, no shafts of light lit the darkened pavements, no shouts of laughter disturbed the neighbours. In fact there were no signs of a party at all. Puzzled, I checked the address and asked the cabby to wait while I rang the bell. Perhaps it was a joke? Was that why she had mocked me?

Invent a nonexistent party – just to see if I was mug enough to turn up? It seemed a bloody silly thing to do and my temper was rising when the door 'phone squawked in my ear: 'Come up, Sam – I'm on the first floor.' The automatic lock buzzed and the door moved open an inch – so I paid the cabby and went in, closing the door behind me.

It was a well appointed house. Thick carpet drifted upwards from the wide hall onto the sweep of the staircase. Hessian-covered walls were decorated with modern paintings – all originals and properly lit. And Kay was waiting for me on the landing – in a dress which took my breath away.

That fact alone needs explaining. After all, the most glamorous chorus line in London worked for me then. Apart from the *other* girls – vocalists, entertainers, hat check girls, receptionists – even secretaries and typists. All were good-looking. Nightclubs and casinos draw beautiful girls like moths to a flame. I was no stranger to attractive women – fully dressed, partly clad, in the nude or in my bed. So what was so *special* about Kay – after all, I have admitted already that she was not beautiful.

Sensuality I think. I found out later that if she as much as brushed a speck of dust from my sleeve the gesture became a caress. Her fingers paused as if to linger, go further, explore, excite, tempt and seduce. I thought it was an act to begin with. No woman arouses a man and remains unaware of it; coquetry is not a reflex action – but if that is true Kay was the exception to prove the rule. Her sensuous acts were quite unplanned. She behaved the way she did *because* of her sensuality. It was quite unconscious. In her case she would have to act to appear otherwise – and she never showed the slightest inclination to do that.

Her dress was grey satin. She liked satin. She liked the *feel* of it on her skin. The neckline plunged deeply, caught itself, flattened and then reached down to the floor. It was only held together at the waist and any movement revealed a long leg up to the thigh. She wore silver slippers and I guessed – correctly as it turned out – nothing else.

She kissed me lightly on the cheek. 'How like you to be exactly on time.'

Taking my arm she led me into a large room, graciously furnished to serve as combined sitting and dining room. A huge alcove at one end revealed the bedroom.

'Downstairs belongs to Father,' she explained. 'But up here's all mine.'

I sat on a sofa and watched her pour me a drink. 'Why is it so like me to be punctual?' I asked. 'And how did you know I drank scotch?'

She laughed, low in the throat, a muted chuckle of amusement. 'You're hardly unpredictable, Sam Harris. Or do you think you are? Tall, fair and mysterious – is that how you see yourself?' She handed me my glass, smiling radiantly.

'I'm not sure I see *myself* at all,' I raised the glass. 'Happy birthday.'

'It is, isn't it?' she said curiously. 'I've prepared Chinese by the way – I hope you like it.'

'That's fine.' I looked round the room, vaguely puzzled. 'Where are the others? Am I the first?'

She seemed surprised. 'What others? There's only you and me. Do you mind?'

'No – I don't *mind*. But I thought you said a party—'

'We're having it. Relax. Enjoy yourself.' She sat beside me and the dress opened obligingly to reveal the perfect cup of her breasts to the nipples.

'But—'

She giggled. 'You see! Predictable. What would you have said had I asked you to dinner? Just like that. The first time we met. Either you'd have wriggled out of it entirely, or you would have insisted on taking *me* out to dinner.' Her smile seemed even more radiant and she sat close enough for me to feel her heart beat. 'Isn't that right?'

'Well, I suppose—'

'There's no *suppose*. That's exactly what would have happened. And I much prefer this – don't you?'

'This is fine.'

'You'd have taken me to one of your clubs where we would have been interrupted every five minutes by people you know. Then we would have had the business of waiters taking orders—' she stopped long enough to pull a face. 'Sorry – attending to our requests – and we'd never have a moment to ourselves all evening. This is much better.'

'This is fine,' I said again, like a stuck record.

'Question,' she said. 'How did I know Sam Harris would be on time? Answer – because dynamic businessmen are *always* on time. How did I know Sam Harris drank scotch? Because it's turned six o'clock and English businessmen *always* drink scotch in the evenings.' Again the vivid smile. 'You see, quite simple.'

'I'm flattered by the dynamic bit.'

'Why? That's what the papers call you, isn't it?'

'Newspapers print a load of rubbish.'

'Not about you. You *are* dynamic. My father says so.'

I felt the vague stir of an idea. 'Is this anything to do with your father? I mean – this quiet evening – drinks by candlelight—'

'Good God, *no!*' she laughed. 'Did he put me up to it, you mean? For some business reason? How Machiavellian.' She shook her head, still laughing. 'No, he's half way to Derbyshire by now—'

I laughed with her. 'It's absurd of course.'

'Positively. If he as much as saw me in this frock he'd have a fit. Bellow at me to put some clothes on or something.'

'Well it is a bit—'

'Revealing? Because you can see my tits?' Then as a horrified afterthought, 'You do *like* tits, don't you?'

'Very much.'

'Thank God for that. Not all men do you know.'

'No?'

She shook her head, then said, 'Have another drink before I fix dinner.'

Dinner was superb. Whatever her faults, Kay was a brilliant cook. I was to find out later that she could do anything – soufflés, crêpes suzettes, vichyssoise – anything and everything. We drank sake with the meal and as the evening passed, the talk became more personal. It always did with Kay.

'Why aren't you married?' she asked at one stage.

'Oh, I don't know. I've been too busy I suppose. Besides I've never wanted to get married.'

'And you always do what you want?'

'Don't most people?' I remembered our conversation at Ascot.

'Didn't we cover this earlier?'

'You expressed your views on it.'

'Which you don't share?'

'Certainly not.' She poured the last of the wine into my glass. 'You mustn't dismiss something because it comes easily to you. You *are* dynamic, and positive, so you do *do* exactly as you want. But most people don't. They lack that kind of courage.'

It was all very flattering. I asked, 'And what kind of courage do you have?'

She grinned, 'Oh, yours of course – but a lot more of it.'

I laughed and conceded the point. But it must be easy to be *dynamic and positive* if you are born as rich and as vivacious as she was.

'But seriously,' she said, 'you ought to get married.'

'What on earth for?'

'You're a man in a hurry, Sam. A winner. And you need a wife for the next steps. And a house – with your wife presiding over dinner parties – guiding the conversation, impressing, persuading, cajoling. An elegant background to impress the fat cats – prove you're here to stay, not a flash in the pan.'

I wondered how much of this had been gleaned from her father. Edgar Hardman was a blue-blooded old bastard, but he was also the shrewdest businessman I knew. And he *was* my chairman. I asked: 'Is that what people say about me?'

She grinned. 'People *say* you're screwing every chorus girl in London. They're jealous as hell but it's not helping your reputation.'

'I like screwing.'

'Doesn't everyone? But none of the positions in the Kama Sutra stimulate the mental processes.'

'So I should settle down? Buy a pipe and carpet slippers? Get a dog?'

'Not all on the same day. But I still want you to get married.'

'And you always get what you want?'

She smiled her simply radiant smile and leant across to kiss me lightly on the lips. 'That's already been established. Shall we take our drinks across to the fire?'

After that the talk became steadily more intimate and of course we ended up in bed, where I discovered that cooking was Kay's *second* most polished accomplishment. I awoke at around six the following morning to the realisation that, once again, she was moving gently in my arms.

'By the way,' I murmured, holding her off for a moment. 'Just how old were you yesterday?'

She took ages to reply, but eventually she said: 'Twenty-two years, four months and seventeen days.'

'Funny kind of birthday.'

'I thought it was lovely,' she nibbled my ear. 'Besides, some things should be celebrated more than once a year.'

And they were. We 'celebrated' every night for the next three weeks – *every* night and *most* mornings and *some* afternoons. I was younger then – and a good deal fitter – but it never occurred to me that there was anything abnormal about Kay's sexual appetite. She was the earthiest, most inventive, most demanding sexual partner I've ever encountered – but that wasn't a complaint. I was too busy enjoying her, and anyway – as she said – 'none of the positions in the Kama Sutra stimulate the mental processes'.

Three weeks after we met she went to Antibes where her father maintained a yacht. I was invited to join their party for a month's cruising along the Mediterranean coast, but I was too busy to go. Anyway, I've always had this thing about London – so much happens there that I'm afraid to leave in case I miss something. Kay was furious and we had a hell of a row about it.

'Dammit, Sam!' she stormed. 'You're not indispensable. The business won't collapse because you take a few days off.'

'A month is not a few days.'

'Then come for a fortnight! Come for a week! Placate your bloody working class morality that way.'

'I'd just get bored, honestly. I'd put a damper on things for everybody. I don't *want* to come.'

'And Sam Harris always gets what he wants?'

'It's not a matter of—'

'It damn well is! Of course it is. What else is it a matter of? Well, I always get what I want too!'

The argument ended in tears and we went to bed to make up. But I never went to Antibes with her. Something warned me not to go. It was important to establish some priorities at the outset. For weeks the chemistry had been working between us and even then I think I knew we would end up together. It wasn't just the sex, though that was part of it, but she was *different* from any girl I had ever known. Outrageous at times, but generous, funny and provocative at others.

I missed her when she went to Antibes, even more than I thought. But I filled the hours by working hard and the weeks slipped by. She came back a day ahead of the rest of the party, catching a flight from Nice and arriving back at Heathrow early one afternoon. She telephoned the night before to ask me to meet her. She looked tanned and vibrant and more alive than ever.

'How are you?' I asked after we had kissed hello.

'Numb.'

I blinked in bewilderment. Then she said: 'Not all over you crazy bastard. Just the top of my legs. You'll have to prise me open with a can opener.'

I sent Tom back to town with the car and Kay and I took a cab to The Glades, which is a motel ten minutes from Heathrow. She hammered on the glass to the cabby. 'Can't you go faster? Can't you *see* I'm going to have a baby?' He broke his neck looking at her trim figure: 'You don't look it. Shall I go straight to a hospital?' Kay shook her head, 'No, I'm having the real thing – not artificial insemination.' And by the time he worked that out we were there.

We married five months later. I bought Rex Place and while Kay and I honeymooned in the Bahamas, Jack and Maria furnished it for us.

We were very happy to begin with – ecstatically so during the early months. I was busy at Apex, negotiating to open some provincial clubs, while Kay was looking for 'our place in the country'. The mews cottage suited me but Kay wanted something larger – something grand – somewhere she could entertain, give weekend parties, dance on the lawn in the summer, crowd a log fire in the winter. Eventually she found Ashley Grange, not far from Oxford.

'But when am I going to be here?' I asked, when we drove down to see it.

She stroked my neck. 'It's only an hour down the motorway. Less if you hurry. And I'll be waiting for you.'

It was an impressive house, or at least it *had* been. When I first saw it the slate roof needed replacing and that was just for starters. It had stood empty for two years and been used as a girls' school before that. Not for twenty years had it been used as a private residence – people just don't *live* in houses like that any more.

Kay said, 'We are *not* people. We're special. You're a tycoon, Sam – for heaven's sake act like one!'

The house cost a hundred and seventy thousand as it stood, or fell, which seemed much more likely. But that did include sixty acres of farmland. Jack came down when the builders were fixing it up. We looked across the gardens to the fields beyond and a line of elms on the skyline. 'How much is yours?' he asked.

'Far as the eye can see.' I did my Texan accent for him.

'What are you planning to do? Make hay?'

Kay did with my money. She spent two hundred thousand doing it up and another eighty furnishing it. It looked very grand when she finished, but then so does half a million in the bank. I funded the operation by selling some Apex stock and running a big mortgage to suit my tax position. At the time I told myself it was all for the best, that I was putting down roots – but I suppose I had fallen for Kay's sales pitch by then – the tycoon bit, and living life on the grand scale. Of course Kay was wealthy in her own right – Edgar had already divested himself of some of his loot to minimise death duties – but even so I insisted on paying for everything: the doubtful benefit of a working class upbringing I think.

Kay planned the first party even before the builders finished. I remember asking who was to be invited. 'Winners,' she said simply. 'People like you. Don't worry, darling – you'll love them.'

And so the pattern was established. Anyone who made headlines came to Ashley Grange. Tennis players, racing drivers, pop singers, actors – the whole circus beat its way down the M4 to our place. It was open house to everyone – *when they were winning*. If they lost, or had bad notices, or took a fall in the ratings – their names were quietly removed from the invitation lists. It wasn't as cold-blooded as it sounds. Kay was very upset about some of them. She pulled strings behind the scenes where she could and if someone was *really* down she even sent money through indirect channels.

'Maybe you'd help more by inviting him down here again?' I suggested once, about a television actor who had been resting six months. 'Give him a chance to meet people, make contact—'

'Darling, we're not an *employment exchange*! You *don't* understand. You're a winner. You can't afford to be associated with losers – it's that simple.'

After Kay 'opened' Ashley Grange, which is more or less what it amounted to, the early hours of most mornings found me driving down the motorway to Oxford. But after about a year it became too much – especially when I'd had a few drinks, and drinking was a business necessity in a job like mine. I had a chauffeur of course but I used him during the day and to have another seemed too pretentious for words, so I scrubbed round it and arranged for Kay to spend two nights a week at Rex Place to save me the drive. But as time passed people were always staying at Ashley Grange and it was increasingly difficult for her to get up to town – so I grew accustomed to spending a couple of nights a week alone in Rex Place.

I was too busy to ask if I was happy. What is happiness anyway? I was building Apex into the biggest company of its kind in Europe, and that was immensely satisfying. My working day was a long one but I enjoyed every minute of it. And as for life with Kay, well, we adapted. My absences for two or three nights a week bothered her at first, but after about eighteen months she accepted it. Nothing else changed, as far as I could see. When we were together our love-making was as explosive as ever. If our acts of union ever lacked tenderness they never lacked passion. We *owned* each other's bodies, no intimate part was left unexplored, no privacy was tolerated, no holding back permitted. We made love like animals, groaning and panting, and urging each other on until our exhausted, abused bodies were satiated and glutted. I used to think we made love that way because we had so little time to ourselves, but I was wrong. The real reason was Kay's provocative sensuality. It filled my nostrils, guided my hands, led my eyes, plucked at every nerve in my body. My body would harden just at the sight of her. Even thinking about her has the same effect. If she came through the door now it would be the same – even after what happened.

But it was true about us having little time to ourselves. Dinner at Ashley Grange was rarely for less than ten, and most of them would be house guests. Kay arranged their comings and goings without reference to me. They did their best to amuse me when I was at home, but they were her friends, not mine. Their allegiance was to her. It showed itself in little ways. They were more *comfortable* with her, they shared 'in' jokes which rarely seemed funny to me, even when explained. Kay teased me by saying that responsibility was making me middle-aged before my time – and I believed her for a while.

I remember going home once. It was a Friday evening and Kay was giving a special dinner party, so I had promised to be early. As it happened it was an easier day than most and I left the West End before the rush hour, arriving at Ashley Grange at about five thirty. Four strangers were using the tennis court and screams of excitement came from the swimming pool. I parked the Rolls next to half a dozen other cars and crunched across the drive and into the house. Kay was in the drawing room, pouring a drink for a dark-haired Frenchman.

'Hi, Winner,' she kissed me and turned to make the introductions. 'Come and meet Marcelle.'

That was when I met Marcelle Faberge for the very first time. He was tanned and athletic looking, dressed in casual clothes decorated with a lot of personal jewellery. A songwriter with a hit in the charts – already very well off according to Kay, who could make me feel quite poor at times.

'Marcelle can't stay for the party,' she pouted. 'I've spent the afternoon trying to change his mind, but he insists on leaving in half an hour's time.'

The Frenchman murmured something about an early morning recording session in Hamburg and having to be at Heathrow for a seven o'clock flight. I said it was a shame, and we chatted for a while until his taxi arrived. His case was already packed in the hall and we went to the door to say our goodbyes.

He kissed her hand. 'Kay, what can I say about the past two days? It's been an experience to treasure. One day I'll write a song about it.'

After he had gone I finished my drink and then went up to change for the evening. Kay joined me in the shower.

'What about your guests?' I asked after she had kissed me properly.

'Fuck the guests,' she said, and for the very first time I wondered if she did. Something in the Frenchman's manner had raised a doubt in my mind. A glitter of triumph in his eyes, a dismissive, almost contemptuous handshake when he said goodbye to me. But the doubt faded as Kay soaped my body. Then, with our limbs still damp, we fell upon the bed to consume each other with our usual hungry thoroughness. Except this time I held back, at least for the first few moments. Part of me stood aside and looked down at her lovely white body, watched it writhe under my touch, watched and looked with a voyeur's searching eye. Looked for marks – scratches – bites. Looked and found nothing. Then the blood pounded my temples, my body ached and throbbed under her fingers and everything was forgotten – as it always was with Kay.

The bell should have startled me. Instead it sounded far enough away to belong to somebody else – in another room, another house, another world. I was lost in my memories, until the shrill, persistent ringing snagged at my consciousness. I thought it was the door at first and it took a few seconds to realise it was the telephone. When I answered Lucia said, 'Have we still got a date tonight?'

'*Oh Christ!*' My notes lay scattered over the sitting room carpet and I still had to change for the evening. 'Are you ready *now*? Ready *already*?'

'And have been for the last half hour,' she said in a crisp, cool voice. 'Where's this good time you promised?'

It was half past seven! I had arranged to collect her from The Dog's Home at seven. The show at the Garrick started at eight! *Damn and blast it!*

'Look Lucia – I've been working on something – hadn't realised – look, I'm *very* sorry.' It sounded so inadequate. I tried again. 'It'll take me ten minutes to wash and change, but by the time I get there—'

'I'll get a cab to your place,' she said. Then she paused. The tone of her voice changed. 'Unless you'd rather not bother—'

'I've got the tickets. And booked a table at Oliver's.' The latter wasn't quite true but it would be by the time she reached Rex Place. 'And I'm looking forward to it.'

'Obviously,' she said acidly. 'Well then – if you're quite *sure*—'

'Positive.'

'Then I'm on my way.'

'You've got the address?'

'I was there last week, remember? *Cleaning the place.*'

She hung up. I felt a perfect fool but there was nothing I could do about it. Except get washed and changed in record time and try to make amends during the evening. So I 'phoned Oliver's, booked a table, and dashed upstairs.

As it happened Lucia had trouble in getting a cab, so it was almost eight thirty when she arrived. Had there been more time perhaps memories of Kay might have inhibited me in welcoming another woman to Rex Place, but the rush to get ready put Kay out of my mind. Besides I was excited by the prospect of feminine company and the sight of Lucia settled any doubts I might have had. She had looked beautiful earlier but dressed to go out she was sensational. Her eyes conspired to look mischievous and wise, her hair shone, she was fragrant with stephanotis, and when she removed her evening cape she revealed a black sheath dress which hugged her figure right up to her throat.

'Look, I've made a bit of a mess of things—' I began, but she interrupted. 'I can see that,' she said, looking at the scraps of paper littering the floor.

I began to collect them up. 'I booked for a show at the Garrick,' I began, then we both said together – 'but it's a bit late now.' *We said it together, word for word.* We both laughed, and I relaxed. 'Let's have a drink here and re-plan the evening.'

'Fine.' She handed me a few sheets of paper which had found their way onto the chesterfield. 'Is this what you were working on?'

'Yes – sort of. I had an idea earlier and got a bit carried away with it.'

'Is it important?'

'God knows. It's probably a waste of time but at least I feel I'm *doing* something.'

I mixed her a Bloody Mary, while telling her a bit about the magistrate's court and the kind of case I would have to present. When I finished she said, 'Sam, that's *terribly* important. And urgent by the sound of it. May I read what you've written?'

I hesitated. Not everything remembered had been set down but there was enough to indicate what I felt about Kay. It was too private, too revealing. I shrugged. 'It's just so much scribble – you'll never read it.'

'I can read this.' She glanced at the last sheet in her hand. Then she smiled as she handed it to me: 'I'm sorry, Sam – I didn't mean to pry.'

Prison robs you of the social graces. Not just by the denial of feminine company but with monosyllable conversation. You lose the art of nimble speech, the ability to turn an enquiry aside, the knack of re-arranging a person's question to suit your answer. But there was another reason for hesitating – the warmth in her eyes might be damaged by a snub – and no matter what the future I felt in urgent need of friends. So I mumbled clumsily, 'Well if you're really interested—'

'Of course I'm *really* interested.' Her voice conveyed that last bit of reassurance and her eyes told me to trust her. So I managed a wry sort of smile, handed her the rest of the notes, and went off to the kitchen in search of more tomato juice. When I returned I settled in the chair opposite and watched her decipher my scrawl. She frowned now and then, and turned back once to check something on a previous page. When she finished she looked up and smiled. 'You sound very human – for a business tycoon.'

'Perhaps I never was one – a real tycoon, I mean.'

She tapped the notes. 'When have these to be finished?'

I shrugged. 'Tomlinson is making an appointment with counsel as soon as possible. Which probably means next week or the week after.'

She turned to the last page. 'You're only as far as the end of the sixties. You've a long way to go. Perhaps you should stay in tonight and write some more?'

'You sound like a schoolmistress. Besides I'm taking you out to dinner – and looking forward to it.'

She looked serious, as if considering it, or thinking about something else. Then she surprised me by asking, 'Do you have a typewriter?'

'There's a portable in the desk. I'm not sure—'

'Well, let's do both,' she smiled eagerly. 'Go out to dinner and come back here afterwards. I'll take everything down in shorthand and type it up later.'

Of course I protested, but she was determined to do things her way, and after a while I gave in. It was flattering to have a good-looking woman take such an interest, and prolonging the evening was fine by me. And she was so obviously relaxed that the initial awkwardness was forgotten. Some of my old confidence returned and we chatted away happily for another half hour before leaving for Oliver's.

I was in two minds about taking Jack's car. Parking is a problem in the West End, even in the evenings. But the air was wet with a fine drizzle which might have spoiled Lucia's hair, so we took the Rolls – and just as I edged out into Mount Street another car pulled out behind us. Cars come and go at all hours in Rex Place so I had no reason to pay particular attention, and what with Lucia chattering happily beside me I forgot about it. Or at least, I did until later.

Oliver's is in Dover Street, on the corner. The ground floor entrance leads into the bar and beyond that to the restaurant, with a tiny dance floor in the middle. Above is an open gallery, which turns the dance floor into a central courtyard. It's quieter up in the gallery. Our table overlooked the dance floor on one side and Dover Street on the other. Through a chink in the velvet curtains I could see Jack's car where I had parked it on the other side of the road.

Of course I had used the restaurant before but not often, so I felt there was a good chance of the evening passing without me being recognised. The food was good, the wine excellent, the music soft and tender, and Lucia looked ravishing. Brixton Prison seemed a lifetime away.

During the meal I tried to get to know her. After all she knew a lot about me, whereas I knew next to nothing about her – only that she was Maria's cousin. She told me some things quite easily. For example she had been educated in Geneva and New York, as well as Milan, which explained why she had no discernible Italian accent. She had travelled extensively – Europe, the States, one trip to Canada: 'I've never been so *cold*!' She shivered at the memory. But she was more reticent about others. She was expensively dressed but she gave no hint as to where the money came from, and she casually mentioned a man's name when talking about Geneva, and another when talking about New York – but the impression given was they were just friends, nothing more. I was glad about that, despite my determination not to become involved.

'You're another beautiful mystery,' I said at one stage. 'Just like Maria.'

'Is Maria a mystery?'

'In a way. At least I've never understood everything about her, so it amounts to the same thing.'

She smiled faintly but her expression was encouraging enough for me to tell her the story, even though she must have heard at least part of it before. But I was trying to draw her out and felt that talking about Maria might be a way of opening doors.

Jack met Maria a month or so before I opened The Point of View. He says he picked her up in the slums of Naples, but that's just to tease her. He's never been to Naples – not even now. Anyway I know the truth – or at least in part.

They met in some auctioneer's shop. Even in those days Jack was fascinated by antiques and most of his free time was spent browsing around sale rooms. Not that he had spare cash to buy anything but I suppose he was soaking up knowledge for the day when he could. On this particular day he was in a place in Sloane Street: I've forgotten the name but I know they specialise in silver. Jack was just looking around when this girl came in. She wore a charcoal grey suit and from the way she walked Jack felt sure she was a model. A brown paper parcel was tucked under one arm and she barely hesitated on her way to the counter.

'I'd like your professional valuation on a piece of silver,' she said to the clerk. 'Is that possible?'

'Certainly,' said the clerk and waited patiently while she untied the string.

Quite by chance Jack was standing a few feet away, so he edged a bit closer to see what was in the parcel – and to take another look at the girl. Finally the string was unfastened to reveal a silver candlestick. Jack could hardly take his eyes off the girl but when he did the clerk was examining the candlestick with considerable interest. 'It's a very fine piece. Very fine. Early eighteenth century I'd say – magnificent workmanship.'

'Seventeen forty,' the girl said.

The clerk was surprised. 'Oh? You know its history, Madam?'

'Yes,' she said. Then for some unaccountable reason she blushed. Jack said she looked lovelier than ever.

The clerk was still absorbed with the candlestick. 'French I'd say. Yes, definitely French – look at that mark there.'

'It *is* French,' the girl confirmed. 'It was made in 1740 by the French court silversmith, Thomas Germain.'

'Germain!' The clerk was enthralled. He hesitated for a second. 'May I ask you to take a seat, Madam? The Senior Partner is in today and I'd like the benefit of his opinion.' He smiled appealingly. '*Germain* by Jove! It really is an excellent piece – quite excellent.' He curbed his enthusiasm long enough to say, 'Of course its value would be enhanced if it were accompanied by the rest of the set.'

'They are all available,' said the girl. 'There are twelve altogether.'

'*Twelve!*' The clerk fairly quivered. 'That is interesting.' He waved the girl into a chair and left for a back room, carrying the candlestick like an Olympic torch.

'Now's the time to run for it – if it's stolen,' Jack murmured. 'That's what he's doing you know – checking the police wanted list.'

She would have stamped her foot had she been standing. As it was her nostrils flared like a startled racehorse. She aimed a ferocious glare at Jack. 'Do you think you are looking at a thief?'

'I'm looking at the most beautiful girl in the world,' Jack said. 'And I was only joking.'

That mollified her a bit but only a fraction. Jack said she was throwing off body heat like a frigidaire with the door open. But he can be a determined devil when he sets his mind to it and what he was looking at then excited him more than a free pass to the stock-rooms at Sotheby's. So he said, 'My name's Jack Green. And I'd very much like to buy you dinner tonight.'

'That's *quite* impossible.'

'Purely business,' Jack lowered his voice and whispered. 'If you really *do* have twelve of those candlesticks I'll double the price they offer you here.'

The girl's eyes rounded with surprise. She looked him up and down, then said, 'Those candlesticks are *very* valuable, I'm expecting a considerable sum for them.'

'And I'm expecting to pay it,' Jack said confidently, though at the time he would have been hard pressed to find the price of one, let alone a dozen.

Just then the clerk came back, accompanied by his boss, a big florid-complexioned man in a check suit, who beamed and told her his name. He hinted for her to respond with hers but she ignored it and prompted him to talk about the candlesticks. Jack was standing a yard away while this was going on and the boss kept throwing sideways looks, trying to decide if Jack and the girl were together.

'Were you wanting to auction these pieces?' the boss asked. 'Or would you prefer us to make an offer on our own behalf?'

The girl frowned, and in the pause which followed Jack made his move. Very politely he explained how dealers worked, careful to praise the boss's establishment in the process, so that when he finished all four of them were standing in a cosy little group.

The girl looked worried. 'The matter is *very* urgent. Does auctioning take more time?'

'Oh, considerably,' the boss said, sensing a bargain. 'There's the catalogue to prepare and circulate, advertisements in the press, all that sort of thing. Couldn't do a proper job inside six weeks – two months preferably.'

'Perhaps we should discuss it over dinner?' Jack suggested to the girl helpfully. Which is what happened. The girl was no fool though. She asked the boss to keep the candlestick overnight – she said while she made her mind up, but the real reason was she wouldn't risk walking out with Jack on one arm and the candlestick under the other. The boss agreed and the clerk made out a receipt.

'What name shall I put?' he asked, looking up at the girl.

She hesitated. She had evaded the issue earlier but there was no escaping it now. Then, in a firm clear voice, she said, 'My name is Maria Serracino-Torregianni.'

Which is how Jack met Maria. Jack sold the candlesticks for her, to a private collector who in fact did pay twice the price offered by the dealer. After which Maria returned to Italy. But she turned up in London again a month later – this time with some very fine pieces of jewellery. She telephoned Jack when she arrived and again he helped find a buyer – and this procedure was repeated four or five times during the course of that year. The sums of money were quite sizeable, I think, but where Maria fitted into the scheme of things – whether the items were hers, or whether she was an agent, where the money went – I never found out. Jack never told me so I never asked. After all it was none of my business. All that concerned me was that my best pal was marrying a beautiful Italian girl – who went on to make him very happy.

Lucia had tears in her eyes when I finished. I was *astonished*. I had told the story in a jokey kind of way, indulging my curiosity perhaps, but mainly trying to amuse her and get her to talk about herself. Instead she looked sad enough to cry. 'Poor Maria,' she said, her voice huskier than ever.

'They lived happily ever after,' I pointed out.

'Yes,' she brightened but her smile was a shadow of the radiant look she had given me earlier. 'It's nice when a story has a happy ending.'

I wondered why she was so upset, and I was trying to think of a way to change the subject when she said, 'So you know our family name?'

'Serracino-Torregianni? Did I mispronounce it?'

'A little,' she nodded.

'It's not an easy name to say.'

'Or to live with,' she said, almost under her breath.

Suddenly – astonishingly – someone banged into my shoulder so hard that I was almost knocked out of my chair. I grabbed the table to steady myself but the tablecloth gave way under my weight, jerking the wine bottle into a glass and then onto the floor with an enormous clatter. My chair tilted alarmingly until I got a hand to the floor to push myself upright.

'What the hell?'

A man staggered drunkenly, lurching into the table as he pointed at me. 'Harris, isn't it?' He shouted, slurring the words, '*Winner* Harris.'

'What the devil do you think you're doing?' I snapped, conscious of Lucia's startled expression.

'It *is* Harris!' the man roared. 'Don't bloody pretend it isn't! So they've let you loose again, have they?'

He was well built, in his mid-forties, smartly dressed but for the loosened tie and unbuttoned shirt collar. A red-faced, angry man, who was quite obviously the worse for drink. I had never seen him before in my life.

'Get up, damn you,' he shouted.

Two waiters rushed over and tried to restrain him, but he shook them off contemptuously. 'You owe me fifty thousand quid, Harris.

That's what I lost when Apex went up the chute. *Fifty thousand –* and I want paying!'

One of the waiters grabbed the man's arm and tried to pull him away from the wreckage of our table, but the man knocked him away and shouted, 'You're a swindler, Harris. *A bloody swindler!* A crook. A filthy damn crook and a murderer! MURDERER!' He sent the other waiter spinning and came at me with fists flying.

Whoever he was, he was no fighter. His left arm looped wide and I stepped inside and hit him twice, once below the heart and again on the point of his jaw as his knees buckled. It was done instinctively, to protect myself. A woman screamed at a nearby table and a moment later others joined in. The head waiter arrived and the whole place erupted into pandemonium. The man at my feet never moved. Flash bulbs popped like champagne corks and the gloom of the restaurant cracked open with the flashes of light. Lucia watched with terrified eyes.

'Come on, let's get out of here.' I reached across to her with one hand. She tried to squeeze between the bodies separating us. A man got in the way, I shoved him aside, the head waiter tried to stop me, I shouted: 'Dammit man – it wasn't my fault – ask your staff.' I saw the waiters nodding from the corner of my eye, then I pushed through the crush of bodies, drawing Lucia along behind me. I shouted: 'I'll settle my bill downstairs.' I could feel Lucia trembling but it would have been madness to comfort her there. I just wanted to get out, the sooner the better. People came up from the dance floor and we fought our way through the mob at the top of the stairs.

Down in the bar someone went to fetch Lucia's wrap while I settled my bill. Restaurant staff crowded round in a swarm, some apologising, others chattering with excitement. A woman 'tut-tutted' while the man with her muttered 'disgraceful exhibition'. The head waiter was in doubt about letting me leave, until the look on my face convinced him. Lucia's wrap arrived and we made our way to the lobby, trailing people, some making half-hearted attempts to catch my arm as if to delay my departure. Then – *suddenly* – there was the most *colossal* explosion. For a split second the ground seemed to shake. The walls *did* shake. Then there was a 'whump' and a rush of wind – *and the front of the restaurant blew in*.

It was a miracle nobody was killed. The heavy drapes inside the front doors caught most of the flying glass, but the force of the explosion rocked the place. Plaster showered from the ceilings: a chandelier broke away from its fastenings and fell with a sickening crash: bottles were smashed and a tray of crockery fell from the hands of a startled waiter. Women screamed – and the whole scene shuddered like the segments of a kaleidoscope.

I was nearer the door than anyone and after pushing Lucia into the arms of a waiter I pushed past the velvet drapes into the street.

Dover Street is a quiet place at ten o'clock at night. It lacks the bright lights of nearby Piccadilly and has never rivalled Park Lane's plushness. Oliver's is almost its only restaurant. During the day the street comes alive with the advertising men who work in the offices, and the fine art dealers who can't quite afford the rents in nearby Bond Street. But at night it is quiet – as a rule.

That night was different. I stood in the wrecked doorway and looked about me. Windows were smashed for forty yards in every direction. Behind and above me came the shouts and screams of hysterical people. Dust hung in thick grey clouds in the pale light cast by the street lamps. The acrid smell of explosives caught in my nostrils. Opposite, on the other side of the road, I saw the cause of the explosion. Jack's Rolls-Royce was a gutted, smoking mess of twisted steel and gaping windows.

The next half hour was a nightmare. Police cars arrived within minutes but I was back in the restaurant by then, trying to quieten the general hysteria. The Italian head waiter went completely to pieces, babbling away and waving his arms like a windmill – until Lucia took over. She was magnificent. She delivered some very sharp-sounding Italian to the staff in general, then helped usher people back to their tables, where they were encouraged to remain until the police had finished outside. Lucia arranged for large brandies to be served all round, compliments of the management, and shortly after that she even persuaded the band to play again – softly and jerkily, like a dirge of off key notes, but music nonetheless. Waiters cleared some of the debris and after a while people's voices lost the raw edge of panic. It was like a scene from the blitz, and I had just finished explaining to the Bomb Squad that I had been the driver of the Rolls, though not its owner, when Chief Inspector Davis stepped through the wreckage of the entrance. He gave me a sour look but refrained from speaking immediately. Instead he directed the three men with him to begin taking statements and interviewing people.

Of course, the story of the punch-up came out. It had occurred almost immediately before the explosion, so the two events were linked in most people's minds. People pointed at me and I heard whispers behind my back. The odd thing was that the man who attacked me was not to be found. I was quite sure he had not left by the front door, which meant he had gone out the back way – but nobody remembered seeing him go. And the waiters said he was a stranger, they had never seen him before. He had arrived ten minutes before the incident and gone straight to the bar to have a drink until some friends joined him. After which nobody took any notice until he appeared on the gallery with me.

Eventually Davis came across to where I was standing. 'I ought to run you in, Harris,' he growled.

'For what?'

'Assault. Causing a disturbance. Any number of things.'

'Really? Well this time I've got witnesses – so just you try.'

He flushed angrily. I thought he *would* arrest me for a moment – witnesses or otherwise. Then he leant forward so that only I could hear him. 'You're trouble, Harris. Out thirty-six hours and in the middle of a punch-up *and* a bombing. Do us a favour and go and play somewhere else.'

'Someone should straighten you out, Davis. You're supposed to protect the public – not persecute them.'

'Take my advice,' he growled back. 'Get out of town.'

'When I'm ready. Right now I'm ready to take this young lady home. If you've quite finished?'

He turned and walked away. I looked across to the inspector from the Bomb Squad who had been doing his best to eavesdrop. 'Okay if we go now?'

He nodded. 'Don't leave town without letting us know.'

That was rich. Davis wanted me to go and this joker wanted me to stay – how's that for teamwork? I took Lucia's arm and led her into the street. She gave a little gasp when she saw Jack's car. I can't say I blame her. It lurched drunkenly on a broken axle, with its doors blown out and without a square inch of glass in its windscreen. The police had rigged up arc lamps and were taking photographs. I turned Lucia away and steered her towards Piccadilly. The street had been roped off and a few young constables were doing their best to restrain the usual crowd of morons who gravitate to disasters like vultures round a corpse. Someone grabbed my arm, 'Anyone killed, Mister?' I pushed him away and shielded Lucia as best I could.

We caught a cab outside the Ritz. I gave Jack's address and Lucia sat back in the seat with a sigh of relief. Strain showed as dark bruises beneath her eyes. We had barely spoken since our dinner table had been knocked over. I wondered how much of the evening she blamed me for? It had been a disaster from start to finish – except for a couple of hours in the middle, when we were getting to know each other. We travelled in silence while I tried to think of something to say. Then she reached over and took my hand, clutching it tightly, the way a child might grasp the hand of a parent.

'Quite an evening, Sam. Do you always go to so much trouble to impress a girl?' Then she kissed me briefly and the moon glinted on the river as we crossed Chelsea Bridge.

CHAPTER THREE

I overslept the following morning. After taking Lucia back to The Dog's Home Jack and I had talked half the night away. He took the news of his car without batting an eyelid. 'Time I had a new one anyway – let the insurance boys worry about it.' But he had been worried sick about Lucia and me, and as soon as the girls went to bed he came right out with it. 'That was a warning, Sam. You'd be a fool to ignore it.'

'So what the hell do I do? Run away and hide?'

He shrugged and poured himself more coffee.

When he remained silent, I said, 'What I can't understand is *why* – and *who*?'

We sat there until five in the morning trying to fathom that out. Then we admitted defeat and I caught a cab back to Rex Place, where I went straight to bed. But not to sleep. The events of the evening were too vivid in my mind for that. The car which had pulled out when we left Rex Place – the man who had attacked me in the restaurant – the smoking wreckage of Jack's Rolls-Royce. Even Jack himself. Funny to be disturbed by Jack, but his manner had been odd somehow. He was shocked of course, but at one point I formed the distinct impression that he *knew* something, that he was holding something back, not telling me. Then I forgot about him and thought of Lucia. Lucia Serracino-Torregianni. The family name – hard to say and hard to live with – or so she had whispered, so softly that I had almost missed it. Finally I dozed off, until the telephone woke me at ten o'clock.

'Harris?'

It took me a moment to recognise his voice: 'Tomlinson?'

'You've seen the newspapers, I suppose? What the *devil* are you playing at?'

I shifted the 'phone to the other ear and swung my feet onto the floor. I was still only half awake. Not that Tomlinson cared. He was barking, 'You'd better get across here straight away. I'll expect you in half an hour.'

It took me forty minutes and he was still simmering when I

arrived. His secretary left a pile of press cuttings on his desk, gave me a funny look and then scuttled off to make some coffee.

Tomlinson was even whiter than usual; not from shock but temper. 'I never gave much for your chances to begin with,' he snapped, 'but what on earth possessed you to get mixed up with that?'

That was the pile of press clippings. I picked up the top one. It was the front page of the *Express*. A photograph of what was left of Jack's car appeared beneath a stock one of me taken years ago. But the picture below that was even more startling. It showed me with raised fists, standing over the man in the restaurant. Two waiters looked on, while in the background Lucia's lovely features were caught in an expression of alarm. The headline read: *Winner Harris is back in town!*

All the papers carried the same story. Most of them even had the same pictures. The *Mail* broke the pattern with a shot of Lucia descending the staircase from the gallery, and a story speculating on the identity of 'Winner Harris's lovely new girlfriend'.

Tomlinson barely gave me time to read them. 'Well?' he demanded. 'I'm waiting for an explanation.'

'Don't treat me like a bloody schoolboy, Tomlinson. I'm the client – remember? And it seems to me the papers give a pretty full account of what happened.'

'You undertook to stay out of trouble. Only *yesterday* for heaven's sake! And now – *now this*!'

His girl arrived with a tray of coffee and reduced us both to a state of smouldering silence. Tomlinson's attitude sparked my own temper. It took self-control not to have a go at him, but something told me I would need him before this mess was cleared up.

I waited until the girl closed the door behind her. 'All right – let's calm down. Any undertaking given by me was abided by. Trouble is we didn't get an undertaking from the other side.'

'What *other* side?'

'The other side who attacked me in a restaurant. The other side who blew up my car! *That* other side, Tomlinson! Would you feel any better if I had been knocked cold in Oliver's? Or blown up in Dover Street? It was a put-up job – can't you see that?'

Temper made dagger points of his eyes. '*Mr Harris*' he said sharply. 'You claimed it was a put-up job when you were last in trouble. Now you're in trouble again – and *again* it's a put-up job. Is that what you're asking me to believe?'

'One.' I ticked the points off on my fingers. 'A man attacks *me* in a restaurant. He attacked me – not the other way about. Witnesses will testify to that. Two – he came there for that *express purpose*. He arrived, had a drink until the staff forgot about him, then he came looking for me. Three—'

'That's supposition!' Tomlinson said sharply.

'Like hell it is. He wasn't *led* upstairs. He wasn't *shown* to a table by a waiter. He came *looking* for me. What's more he knew exactly where to find me.' I glared, but Tomlinson's blank stare might have meant anything, so I continued: '*Three*. At least two people in that restaurant had cameras and flash guns. When was the last time you took your camera out to dinner? *Think about it!* Two people there expected to photograph something. And when they did they delivered prints to every paper in Fleet Street.'

I was ticking points off like a fighter throwing punches. '*Four* – the man who attacked me vanishes afterwards. He's a mystery. Even the photographs don't show his face, just his body crumpled on the floor. And *five* – the car I was using gets blown to pieces.' I ran out of arguments but that seemed enough to go on with, so I said, 'If you think I organised *that* to draw attention to myself you're out of your bloody mind.'

Some of the anger faded from his face. 'Well ... put like that—'

'Put like *that*? For God's sake! What other way can you put it? That's what happened. Even the papers say that.'

He nodded thoughtfully, hesitantly. 'Yes ... yes they do ... don't they?'

I gulped some coffee and tried to define the look he was giving me. Certainly it was less angry. Even the doubt was beginning to fade. Finally he cleared his throat and said, 'I may have been wrong about you, Mr Harris. In which case I apologise.'

I sighed. An apology was irrelevant. I said, 'Forget it. You were angry because it makes your job harder. This won't help our case with the magistrates one little bit, will it?'

'I'm afraid not.' He steepled his fingers and moistened his lips in that characteristic way of his. Then he spoke slowly and carefully. 'In fact, I think it probably destroys what slender chance we had.'

'Even though it was a put-up job?'

He barely hesitated. 'Even though it appears not to have been your fault. Violence seems to follow you around, Mr Harris. That fact alone will worry the magistrates.'

I stood up and walked to the window. I knew what he was saying. Pull out now. Avoid the expense of counsel's fees. Take my money back. Use it more profitably. Start again, somewhere else. Exactly what Davis had said. Even Jack was beginning to gauge the odds.

'Would it be such a blow?' Tomlinson asked softly.

Tony Fields's words came back to me: '*I'd like to get out, Sam –
it's no fun these days.*' Would I feel that if I got my licences back?
Maybe all I was doing was trying to recapture the past? That would
be stupid – times had changed, I no longer had someone to share
things with.

I sighed and walked back to my chair. 'I don't know – that's the
truth of it – at least about the licences. I'd like them back because
I think it proves something – though don't ask me what. But this
pressure – harassment, intimidation if you like – from the police and
other people – that's something else. Whatever I do next is for *me*
to decide. Dammit, I *won't* be pushed!'

'Stubborn pride can be an expensive commodity in a court of
law.'

'Stubborn pride, rubbish! A sense of justice might be nearer the
mark.'

He let that pass. 'So we go on?'

'Yes.'

The word was out before I could stop it. I glared defiance across
the desk, half expecting him to say I was wasting time and money.
But instead he gave his wintry smile and said he had arranged to
see counsel at the end of the following week. 'And yesterday I sent
off our application for a court hearing. They'll get it this morning,'
he tapped the newspapers, 'after reading these over breakfast.'

I shrugged. 'Who's the QC?'

'Tim Hastings,' he said quietly, and watched for my reaction.
Even *I* had heard of Hastings. His reputation for cross-examination
scared most people rigid even before they took the stand. I grinned
spitefully at an imagined vision of Davis being hammered
unmercifully. It would be worth the thousand – just to see that.

Tomlinson looked at his diary. 'Ten thirty on the twelfth at his
chambers. Perhaps you'd call here first, say at ten, and we'll go
round together.'

I nodded. Then I told him about the stuff I was writing at Rex
Place. He listened politely, but when I finished he said, 'Do you
think it's really *necessary* for Hastings to read your *memoirs* before
appearing on your behalf?'

'Material. That's what you said yesterday. How can he show me
a "fit and proper person" if he doesn't know me?'

'He'll make his mind up as to that when he meets you.'

'Judge my life on an hour's interview?' I shook my head. 'Sorry,
that's not good enough – not this time.'

He met my look with a shrewd one of his own. 'There can be no
question of re-opening the matter of your trial. You do realise that?
If that's your purpose you're wasting your time.'

'Stop complaining. You asked for material and you'll damn well get it.'

'I don't guarantee he'll read it.'

'No? Well you get it onto his desk before we meet and say I'll be bloody angry if he doesn't know it off by heart.'

He gave a tiny smile of acceptance. 'I'll put it more tactfully than that – for your sake.'

The meeting was over and I was about to leave when I remembered the other matter. 'There's something else you could do for me. I want a company search on an outfit called Tuskers. Usual stuff – directors, share capital, copies of balance sheets.'

He made a note of it and said it would take about a week to get the information from Companies House – then he took me downstairs. 'I know,' I said, as we shook hands. 'Stay out of trouble.'

He smiled with unusual warmth. 'I'm beginning to suspect that is impossible – but try your best. It's awfully important.'

The telephone was ringing when I returned to Rex Place. It was Lucia, reaffirming her willingness to play secretary. I looked at the pile of notes and breathed a sigh of relief. Time was short if Tomlinson was to read them before passing them to Hastings. But I hesitated about involving Lucia further.

'Have you seen the newspapers?'

She giggled. 'Sam Harris's lovely new girlfriend? Don't worry, I'll come in disguise.'

'Maybe you shouldn't come at all?'

'I won't, unless you want me to,' she said quickly. The husky voice lost some of its warmth.

A better man would have stopped her there; someone less selfish would have turned her away rather than risk her getting hurt. But I felt in need of company and the prospect of *her* company was especially appealing. In some ways it would be embarrassing to work on the notes with her. There were parts of my life I would prefer her not to know – but if that was the price of having her around I knew I would pay it. So I said, 'Of course I want you to come.'

'Good. I'll have lunch and be straight over. Oh, and Sam – let's eat in tonight, shall we? It might be easier on the nerves.'

Afterwards I made coffee and sandwiches, and then settled down to work on the notes. I fiddled about for a while, numbering sheets, wondering where to start, what to leave out and what to put in.

But reviewing my life had taken on a new urgency. Only *part* of it was to provide Tomlinson with what he called material. Now there was another reason. I felt like a running man, looking back over his shoulder. Jack had said it – *the car bomb was a warning*! But from whom? And why? Who was trying to push me out of the West End? Questions gnawed at my brain and all I could do was to try to remember.

Casinos are machines for making money and we made a packet at the end of the sixties. I raided our cash flow to buy amusement arcades and more restaurants, and before 'sixty-nine was over we moved into betting shops by acquiring a chain of forty from a company called Winwright. It was a heady time and hardly a week passed without mention of Apex Holdings in the financial press. And while I made news in the 'heavies' Kay became the darling of the gossip columnists. It was inevitable really. She was England's number one party-giver by then and it seemed that not even a Labour Government could stifle people's curiosity about the lives of the rich – even the moderately rich like us. So Kay became a willing target. She was articulate, outspoken, and very photogenic if not beautiful. Her heavy-lidded eyes promised seduction to every camera pointed at her. She became an up-to-date composite of Mae West and Elsa Maxwell, with the same gift of answering a simple question with a quotable headline. 'Winner's Wife' they called her, and the chat shows loved her.

Business continued to flourish well into the seventies – at least for Apex Holdings. Others were less fortunate. First the London property market collapsed, then the energy crisis tore great gaps in the country's economy, carrying off gamblers like the victims of a 'flu epidemic. But others took their place. Iranians, Saudis, Libyans – the Arab invasion of London gathered the momentum of a caravan descending upon an oasis. And at the very centre of the watering hole lay the casinos. Arabs lost fortunes. The money passing across the green baize tables around the West End made London the gambling capital of the world. By comparison, gamblers in Vegas were playing for matchsticks in a school yard. And at the very centre of the casinos lay Apex Holdings. It was the classic case of being in the *right* business in the *right* place at the *right* time. Winner Harris had it made. I was what I always wanted to be – someone important in London.

But the take-over attempt in 'seventy-five caught me napping. True, we were making huge profits but Apex stock had never been the most sought after in the City. So when somebody started to buy our shares in a big way it caught me off guard. Of course the shares of all public companies are bought and sold – that's what the Stock Exchange is for – but generally the value of a share remains fairly stable. The market assesses its worth and unless something dramatic happens its value alters very little. It reflects interest rates and anticipates profits, but exceptional circumstances are needed for the value of a share to alter by much. So when our shares opened at a pound seventy-five on the morning of the second of May, the price was more or less the same as it had been for months past. But six hours later the price had risen to *two pounds twenty*! Somebody *big* was buying – and buying in large enough blocks to send the price through the ceiling.

I spent the whole of the following morning telephoning our brokers, while Edgar Hardman called up half of the City. But all to no avail. The shares were being bought by nominees, and try though we did, we failed to discover the identity of the bidder.

The following day was even worse. Another bout of heavy buying took the price through the two pound fifty barrier. We estimated that enough of our shareholders had swapped their shares for cash for ten per cent of our company to be in the hands of someone not known to us.

The next day was a Saturday, so mercifully the market was closed. I had stayed in town overnight and was drinking a solitary cup of coffee for breakfast when the telephone rang. 'My name is Corrao,' he said after I confirmed I was speaking, 'I would very much like to meet you. Rather urgently if possible.'

'In connection with what?' I asked brusquely, still worrying about the report in the *Financial Times* open in front of me.

'A proposition of interest to you.'

I was like a bear with a sore head already, and his approach made me snarl. 'No thanks, I'm loaded with life assurance and—'

'It concerns Apex Holdings, Mr Harris,' he interrupted just quickly enough to stop me hanging up. 'And the events of the past forty-eight hours.'

That cleared my brain faster than the scalding hot coffee. 'Who are you?'

'I told you. My name is Corrao. Pietro Corrao.'

'Representing?'

He laughed softly. 'An interested party.'

Stalemate. His name meant nothing to me and if he wanted to play games there seemed nothing I could do about it. His attitude irritated me, but I knew I had to meet him. I *had* to find out who was buying our shares. But I tried to sound unconcerned in an effort to diminish his importance. 'I suppose that *might* be possible – a meeting I mean. Say towards the end of next week. Perhaps if you called me on Tuesday or Wednesday—'

He laughed again. 'Better make it sooner than that. After all, a few more days trading on the Stock Exchange could change the circumstances of our meeting dramatically.'

It was an open threat. They would continue to buy until they obtained control. I said, 'That could cost a lot of money.'

'Money is like sex, Mr Harris. It's all you think about if you're not getting enough. I never think about either.'

I sighed. I knew when I was beaten. 'When had you in mind for a meeting?'

'Why not now? Join me for breakfast. I'm at the Hilton. The Kennedy Suite.'

We met half an hour later. He was a trim little man, dressed in black mohair and a pyjama striped shirt. Dark hair was pasted across the crown of his head as neatly as a bathing cap, and he sported a thin Ronald Colman moustache. Smoked glasses hid his eyes and his way of jerking his head added something birdlike to his manner. Birdlike – as in vulture.

He pointed to the covered dishes on a side table. 'Bacon and eggs – kedgeree – what will you have, Mr Harris?'

'Just coffee. I'm pushed for time as it is.'

He smiled and poured the coffee, while giving me a lot of old guff about the benefits of a good breakfast. But finally he got to the point. 'People I represent are interested in acquiring control of Apex Holdings, Mr Harris. I am authorised to make a very generous offer for your shares.'

'Are you going to tell me who is behind all this?'

He jerked his head. 'I'm afraid not. That would exceed my brief.'

'You can't hide behind nominees forever.'

His head barely moved this time, but his shoulders hunched into a shrug. 'That is not my decision. I am merely a messenger.'

'The Stock Exchange have issued a recommendation on take-overs,' I said carefully. 'Anyone holding more than ten per cent should declare their interest – and their intention.'

He smiled. 'You just said it all, Mr Harris – a recommendation.'

'Likely to become compulsory.'

'Perhaps,' he sounded doubtful. 'But I'm sure we'll have finished our business together long before that.'

I gave up. 'So what are they offering?'

'Two forty-five. It's a very good offer.'

It was. Two forty-five was less than the inflated price on the Exchange but that was just for mopping up smaller interests. The price was inevitably lower for a big block of shares. And lower still if you got locked in.

Corrao let me digest that information before adding: 'The same offer is open to your fellow directors, Mr Harris.'

'Naturally,' I said. I thought about the others. Between us we controlled a third of the voting shares – Hardman, Charlie Weston, Lew Douglas, Darlington and myself. When we put the merger together and floated the public issue we had signed an agreement saying that none of us could dispose of any shares without the consent of the others. Approval had been generously given for me to sell some shares when I was ploughing cash into Ashley Grange, but apart from those not a share had been sold since we started. I wondered how the others would feel now? Hardman and Darlington would be with me. We would reject almost any offer because of the growth potential, but I was not so sure about Douglas. And Charlie Weston might be tempted. But the agreement still had a year to run – so we could block them if we wanted. I reached a decision and decided to bluff: 'I'm sorry but my shares are not for sale. Neither are those of my co-directors.'

He drummed the fingers of his right hand on the table: 'I *said* it was a very good offer, Mr Harris.'

'I didn't say it wasn't. But I don't want to sell.'

His head jerked: 'My people spent a lot of money on Apex stock last week. They won't like being stuck with a minority holding.' The change in his voice was unmistakable. His tone had been conversational before – now it was hard and threatening.

'Then tell them to sell.'

'On a falling market? They'd take a loss. A very big loss. They won't like that either, Mr Harris.'

'Tough tit,' I said cheerfully.

He was obviously watching me because his face was turned towards me, but his eyes were hidden behind the dark glasses, so it was like looking at a blind man. He paused, then said, 'We haven't time to bargain. I'll go to two fifty-five but not a penny more. I suggest you accept our offer and tell your colleagues to do the same.'

I would have laughed outright but for the way he said it. His arrogance was astonishing. As it was his blatant threat made me see red and I snapped, 'You can suggest whatever you damn well like. The answer remains the same.'

'You have until Monday to change your mind,' he growled, 'I suggest you consult your colleagues before giving me your final answer.'

'I'll do that, but don't hold your breath – you've had our *final* answer.'

He literally trembled with temper. Never have I seen a man fly into a rage so quickly. 'You're making a big mistake,' he snapped. 'This thing of ours is too strong for you. We shall take Apex, Mr Harris – *one way or another*!'

I had listened to all the threats I could take for one morning, so I left – and I never saw Corrao again. Nor did I find out who he was working for, though I spent a deal of time thinking about it. I felt sure nobody in the City would hire him. I suppose if I suspected anyone it was the Arabs. After all, they were buying into property and businesses in London generally, so buying Apex would at least be one way to safeguard their gambling losses. It made a certain kind of sense, but it was all so much supposition. I never collected a scrap of evidence which connected them with Corrao in any way.

We had a board meeting the next day. They were all there – Edgar Hardman, Darlington, Lew Douglas and Charlie Weston. It was a Sunday but the emergency demanded that we met before the market re-opened. I outlined the details of my meeting with Corrao, and I knew I had a fight on my hands as soon as I finished.

'It's a bloody good offer.' Lew Douglas waved his cigar with excitement. 'Take the money and run, eh? Two fifty-five can't be bad.' He was already working out his profit on a scratch pad.

Darlington was inclined to agree. 'Certainly justifies the initial investment. It's an excellent return, very good indeed.'

I never mentioned the way I had treated Corrao, nor what I thought of the man. Personal likes and dislikes are irrelevant in business, especially with a matter like that. Too much money was involved. Corrao had said he would 'phone for an answer on Monday, *after* I had taken the views of my colleagues, so that was the extent of my report.

'Wonder who he's acting for?' Darlington speculated.

'Who gives a damn,' Douglas said happily, 'as long as he's got the cash.'

'Sam?' Edgar Hardman cocked his head, inviting my opinion. He was a tough old bird, Edgar. Carried himself like a soldier, dead straight back and all the rest of it. Strong square jaw, blue eyes, brusque upper class voice – but never any *side* to him. He and I had always got on, even before I married his daughter. 'Sam,' he said, 'what do you make of it?'

So I began my argument – how two fifty-five was a good price *now* but that Apex would be worth a lot more by the end of the year. This was 'seventy-five remember – before the scandals and all the rumours. Arabs were still flooding into London like pilgrims to Mecca. Individual gamblers could lose two hundred thousand in an evening. The drop at The Chequers Club was three times that most nights. I could see no end to it. Casinos were like geese laying golden eggs – and only fools sold those.

After listening for half an hour, Darlington began to shift his ground. 'Defer this profit for a bigger one next year? That's what you're saying?'

'Why sell at all? We're earning good dividends—'

'Never turn your back on a certain profit,' Douglas was adamant. 'Cash in the hand, Sam – can't beat it. What you're saying is all very well, but it's only a forecast. Take the money and run I say – it's always the best policy.'

It went on like that for another hour – Darlington wavering, Douglas for accepting, Edgar Hardman prodding for ideas. Perhaps it was inevitable that Lew Douglas and I were on opposite sides. He and I had never got on. He was too flashy for my liking, and a loudmouth to boot. Whatever anyone had, Lew had a bigger one – or a better one. I always thought him the odd one out in our board room. Hardman and Darlington were old school money, polished, urbane men of impeccable family backgrounds. Charlie Weston and I were the young thrusters, men who made it on their own account – but Lew Douglas was second generation money. His father had built up the string of hotels which provided Douglas with his fortune, and Lew himself had been over-indulged, over-fed and over-valued ever since he was born. There was a streak of greediness in him which I found offensive. He was about five years older than me, and patronised me at every opportunity.

Charlie Weston kept quiet for a long time, but when he finally joined in he voiced the question at the back of most people's minds. 'What about the agreement?' he asked. He meant the one about us not selling our shares.

'What about it?' Douglas demanded. 'We gave Sam permission to sell some of his. We can do the same again, surely?'

But Edgar Hardman was unsure about that. 'We were all *agreed* about Sam. Unanimous policy. This might be different.'

Douglas went red in the face. 'Are you saying you'll *enforce* the agreement? If one of us wants to sell?'

Edgar tried to smooth him over. 'Oh, come on Lew – it just needs talking about. We've never had a split vote on *anything*. I'm sure it won't come to that.'

But it damn near did – despite Edgar's efforts to play the role of conciliatory chairman. I remember him saying to Douglas, 'Look at it this way, old boy – when we put this thing together we backed a man as well as a business. And Sam's done damn well for us, proved his judgement every time. Why quit now? We work well together, none of us *need* quick cash – and Sam says the future is golden—'

'That's not the point,' Douglas snapped.

But it was, very much so. An exception had been made for me, so why not for him? That's what he *meant* though he stopped short of saying it. Instead he tried another tack. 'What about the other shareholders?' he demanded, 'our public responsibility?'

'Some shareholders are selling now,' Edgar pointed out. 'It's only us who are restricted.'

Selling some of my shares had compromised my position, which made it awkward to argue as strongly as I would have liked – and I was just thinking things could go either way when Edgar put forward his astonishing suggestion. 'Look, I'm sorry you feel this way, Lew,' he said, 'so I'll make you an offer. Not to buy your shares now, but I'll guarantee they'll be worth much more than two fifty-five in a year's time.'

Douglas was caught off guard. We all were, come to that.

'Guarantee *how*?' he asked.

Edgar shrugged. 'Sign a note if you like – guaranteeing you three pounds say – in twelve months' time.'

It was a gigantic vote of confidence in me – but a hell of a way to buy peace in the board room. Perhaps Edgar thought the gesture would be enough – that Douglas would refuse to take him up on it – but he was wrong if he did. Douglas damn near snatched his arm off.

Then Charlie Weston asked, 'Does that offer stand for the rest of us?'

He spoke quietly but it was like a bomb going off. Edgar underwriting Douglas's corner was one thing – Douglas only owned fifty thousand shares. Charlie Weston owned *ten times as many*. Charlie was the biggest single shareholder in the business, ever since financing Ashley Grange had forced me to sell some of my holdings. Underwriting Charlie's end could cost Edgar *one and a half million pounds*!

Edgar stiffened and tiny spots of colour appeared on his cheeks. 'Do I take it that you'd like it to?'

Charlie grinned, 'It's just I can't bear to see Lew get the better of me. He's getting a hell of a good deal – I'd like it too.'

I immediately protested and to his credit Darlington supported me. We said Edgar would be mad even to consider it. It was a ludicrous risk. He was on a hiding to nothing, and it was all so damned *unnecessary*. But our words fell on deaf ears. Edgar sat bolt upright and stared coldly at Charlie Weston, who grinned back in a taunting kind of way, as if daring the old man to back down. That's what did it I think. The implication was there, innuendo if you like, that Edgar would be breaking his word if he failed to carry Charlie's risk. It was all so much nonsense of course, but Charlie made it *sound* that way.

'Very well then,' Edgar said frostily. 'You've got the same deal as Lew.' He turned to Darlington. 'How about you?'

'Don't be a bloody fool, Edgar. You know me better than that. If you and Sam want to reject this offer, I'll go along with you – but I'll have nothing to do with this other business. It's lunacy – sheer, damn lunacy.'

Edgar barely acknowledged him. I think he was pleased with Darlington's reaction, but there was nothing in his manner to show it. And there was no doubt Darlington would have been given the same cover had he asked for it.

I was very unhappy about the whole business. I tried to pursue it there and then, but Edgar declared the meeting closed and left immediately afterwards. And when I 'phoned the next day he just laughed about it – dismissed it – told me not to worry, forget it and concentrate on running Apex. Of course I never *forgot* it – but after that so much was happening at Apex that it slipped my mind at times, along with everything else.

The only thing which gave me any pleasure was in giving Corrao his answer – and after that the take-over battle *really* started. We did all the usual things – full-page advertisements in the financial press; profit forecasts, anticipated growth, that kind of thing – all advising our shareholders not to sell. And then we announced an increased dividend which pushed the price of our shares still higher. They hovered at around three pounds for a while, at least until trading slowed down.

I suppose the actual battle only lasted a month. By then most shareholders decided to hang onto their shares and the price stabilised – and some weeks after that Corrao's nominees started to sell. The price slipped back a bit then, and Edgar reckoned Corrao and Co. must have lost the best part of half a million pounds – maybe more. Not that we cared. We were jubilant. Like the survivors of a *real* battle, basking in the joy of victory as life returned to normal. Except we got it wrong. Life never *ever* returned to normal after that. It was merely the lull before the storm.

I was still thinking about Corrao when the doorbell rang. Lucia had said to give her an hour or so and a quick look at my watch said it was about her time. I turned my notes face down on the desk and hurried to greet her. But I faced a man when I opened the door.

'Mr Harris, Mr Sam Harris?'

A cab was parked at the kerbside, empty of passengers and driver.

'Yes.'

'Letter for you, Mr Harris.' He thrust a slim manilla envelope into my hand and turned to go. I noticed my name and address typewritten on the envelope, and when I looked up he was already climbing back behind the wheel of the cab.

I followed him across the pavement. 'Who sent this?'

'Search me, guv. I took a fare to Paddington and when I dropped him he asked me to deliver it. He paid, I delivered, you got your letter.' He twisted the ignition key and the cab shook itself like a black shaggy dog.

'What was he like? Your fare?'

'Business type. Black coat and rolled umbrella. Solicitor perhaps?'

'Is that all? Can you remember anything else about him?'

Fifty yards away a man stood on the corner of Mount Street and waved a rolled umbrella above his head to attract attention. An electric milk float whined to a halt nearby. The milkman jumped down and walked to the back of the float, whistling in the manner of milkmen everywhere. He gave the cabby a quick look and then began to restack a crate of empty bottles. I repeated my question, but the cabby's attention had already shifted to the man waving on the corner. 'I told you, solicitor-looking type. It's *your* letter. Open it and see.'

The man on the corner turned to go and the cabby eased quickly away from the kerb. 'Perhaps you've won the pools,' he shouted, then his head jerked forward and he chugged down the road in pursuit of his fare.

I was still staring after him when a flame red mini turned into Rex Place. It paused to negotiate the cab, dodged the milk float, and scampered towards me like a playful puppy. The driver's window was down and Lucia smiled up at me as she drew alongside. I opened the door and she unwound onto the pavement – five foot eight of curves knitted into a black sweater and ski pants. The casual brush of her lips on mine suggested a relationship established months instead of hours. She ducked back into the car and collected a wicker basket from the back seat. 'Dinner,' she announced, slipping an arm through mine and turning towards the front door.

'Where did the car come from?' I asked.

'Rented. Who cares if that gets blown up? Avis have got thousands.'

The joke jangled my nerves. I had been so busy remembering the past that I had almost forgotten the present. A picture of Jack's car flashed through my mind. I shuddered as I imagined Lucia's broken body in the debris. Then I closed the door and watched her carry the basket into the kitchen.

'Important letter?' she asked, when she came back.

'It must be. Someone paid a cabby to deliver it.'

I stared at the manilla envelope in my hand. Suddenly I was *afraid* to open it. Anyone capable of blowing a car to smithereens would have no difficulty with a letter bomb. Especially one delivered without being mangled by GPO sorting machines.

From the look on her face I guessed Lucia thought the same. She stared at the envelope, then back at me. 'Steam it open, Sam. Just in case.'

I would never have thought of that. God knows what I would have done, but once she said 'Steam it open' it seemed such a logical thing to do. In the kitchen I set a saucepan on to boil and Lucia arranged a toast rack across the brim. Then she slipped the envelope into one of the slots, took my hand and led me back to the sitting room, closing the door behind us.

'What do we do now? Sit under the table?' I said it too sharply but I was confused. Part of me was scared stiff but another part said we were behaving stupidly – too damned melodramatic by half. Besides, the way she had taken over touched a nerve. I still cast myself as the dynamic leader and for a pretty girl to take charge was bad for my ego. Male chauvinistic piggery – but so what? Then she made amends by shuddering and saying, 'You *could* comfort me. Things like this may be everyday occurrences for you, but they scare me stiff.'

I drew her down onto the sofa and if her kiss lacked passion it was at least warm with friendship. I was reminded of our dinner talk at Oliver's. She had been responsive to a point – but she had shied away from some of my more personal questions. As if she wanted friendship to ripen before committing herself – prepared to go so far at a time. Don't rush it – take your time – *que sera sera*.

She drew away, holding one of my hands between both of hers. 'Sorry – that was silly of me. Last night must have shaken me more than I thought.'

'Last night shook everyone.'

'Have you heard any more about it?'

'Not directly. Old Tomlinson got all uptight this morning. Said me being attacked would prejudice the magistrates against me.'

'But that's absurd. It wasn't your fault.'

It was nice when she defended me. I thought about taking her to see Hastings; her big grey eyes would convince anyone. I said,

'Tomlinson thinks I'm a walking disaster area. Putting me back into a casino would be like putting a bull in a china shop.'

She frowned at that and I wondered if they put bulls in china shops in Italy. But then she said, 'That man Davis said something like that this morning.'

'You've seen *Davis*? *This morning*?'

She nodded. 'He wanted me to sign a statement. More or less what I said last night but all typed up on police forms.' She saw the flash of concern in my eyes because she squeezed my hand. 'Don't worry – Jack read it and took a copy before letting me sign.'

'Bloody Davis,' I said softly.

'He had another man with him. Please don't fret, Sam – Jack was with me all the time, standing guard like a bulldog.'

I nodded. Poor old Jack. Looking after my interests was turning into a full-time job for him. Then I remembered the saucepan boiling in the kitchen. The wall hadn't blown in so I guessed it was safe to go back. I opened the door to a two inch crack while Lucia told me to be careful. The kitchen was full of steam but through it I could see the envelope with its mouth wide open. Lucia had positioned it at exactly the right angle, which was clever of her. I turned the stove off and carried the letter back to the sitting room like a fisherman handling a slippery catch.

Three pieces of paper were in the envelope. If you count an airline ticket as a piece of paper. British Airways, first class to Sydney. *One way*. The other two were press cuttings, one from the *Telegraph* and the second from Sydney's *Morning Star*. All the papers were limp and damp, and the biro entries on the airline ticket had smudged slightly. The story from the *Telegraph* was eight months old and carried the headline: 'London Club Owner dies in river accident.' Eric Blockley smiled up at me, next to a photograph of his wrecked cabin cruiser. The Sydney story was more recent. 'Gambling booms down under' it said, and along the bottom had been typed 'Go Winner – before your luck runs out.'

Lucia and I each smoked most of a cigarette before we spoke. Then she buried her head in her hands and whispered, 'Mary Mother of Christ, please help us.'

I was on the telephone to Tomlinson a minute later: 'Can you get over here? I've got some—' I struggled for the right expression. 'I've got some new material which you ought to see.' I expected him to protest, claim other appointments or pressing engagements, but he agreed to come with barely a moment's hesitation. He checked my address and promised to leave within ten minutes.

Lucia asked, 'Sam, aren't you frightened?' The tan had faded from her face and I could hear the strain in her voice.

'Thirsty,' I said. 'Can you make coffee?'

She tossed her head as she went towards the door. 'I *am* Italian,' she said, which explained everything.

I telephoned British Airways. 'Some friends of mine promised to book me a flight to Sydney. On—' I examined the ticket. 'On the second.' *The second was Saturday!* They really were in a hurry! The girl repeated 'Sydney' and 'the second', and I said, 'That's right. Look, I'm sorry to be a pest but they've probably forgotten all about it and it's vital I catch that flight. I would book myself, but now I'm worried about causing a duplication.'

They employ bright girls at BA because she said, 'May I have your name, sir, and I'll check with reservations.'

I told her and waited. A minute later she said, 'Mr *Sam* Harris? You have a reservation on our flight KL629, Mr Harris. Departure 0900 from Heathrow on Saturday the second.'

I sighed with mock relief and then said, 'Look, I must pay them for the ticket. Can you tell me how much it cost – and where it was booked?'

'Hold the line please, sir.' The telephone clicked and the cool voice vanished. It was back a moment later: 'First class single to Sydney costs eight hundred and forty pounds, Mr Harris.'

'Eight forty. And do you know where it was booked?'

'Our tickets are the same price at all outlets, Mr Harris.' Her voice was cooler now. I was becoming a nuisance.

'But if I knew where the ticket was booked I would know who to thank,' I persisted. 'I mean, it would be one guy in Manchester, but a different one in Birmingham.'

'Hold the line.' She *was* irritated. Perhaps it was the end of her shift? My hand was sweating and I tightened my grip on the telephone until she returned. 'Your reservation was made at our office in Victoria this morning.'

'Victoria? Victoria, *London*? This morning?'

'Right on all counts,' she said wearily.

'Did they – did *he* – pay by cheque? You see, if I had his name—'

'Your ticket was bought for cash, Mr Harris.'

'*Cash?* Isn't that unusual? I mean, eight hundred and forty pounds—'

'You must have some very rich friends – who think a lot of you.'

'You can say that again,' I said, but she didn't. Instead she said, 'Goodbye, Mr Harris,' and hung up.

I was about to go into the kitchen to tell Lucia about my detective work, when the doorbell rang. It was Chief Inspector Davis – with a friend.

'Come in,' I said, 'I was just about to send for you.'

'An invitation from Winner Harris,' Davis murmured, 'that *is* an honour.'

Lucia came in with the coffeepot just as they were about to sit down. They bobbed up and Davis said, 'Good afternoon, Miss Serracino-Torregianni.' His accent was pretty good. He even pronounced Serracino with a 'ch' sound as in china – instead of 'seeno' the way I did.

Lucia put the coffeepot on a low table and seemed uncertain about what to do next. 'I'll fetch some more cups,' she said, and fled to the kitchen.

'Keep her out of this, Davis,' I said with a hard edge to my voice.

'Out of what?' he enquired mildly.

The other man said, 'We've already taken her statement. We have no further business with the lady.'

He was taller than Davis. Not so wide across the shoulders but he looked just as strong. Like Davis he was dressed in an expensive dark suit, with a silk tie and handmade shoes. What with index-linked pensions and all the other perks, a policeman's lot has changed a bit since Gilbert wrote *The Pirates of Penzance*. We were still staring at each other when Lucia returned with the cups. She must have heard what was said because she said, 'Sam, if you don't need me perhaps I could start typing the notes?' She turned to the desk. 'Are these them?'

I flushed. I had intended to edit some of the things I had written – especially about Kay. But Lucia was already collecting the sheets of paper and I could feel Davis watching me. The little Olivetti was in its case next to the desk. Lucia picked it up. 'Okay to work upstairs? It will be more comfortable than the kitchen.'

We watched her go and Davis asked, 'Writing a book, Mr Harris?'

'Rogues I have known. You've got the star part.'

The other man said, 'That could be construed as an offensive remark. We could arrest you for that.'

'What's your name?' I asked coldly.

'Evans – Detective Sergeant Evans.'

'Listen, Evans. Someone took a swipe at me yesterday. The car I was using got blown to pieces. *Now* I'm getting threatening letters – and all you talk about is arresting *me* for offensive remarks. You get your priorities into the right bloody order or I shall be shouting offensive remarks at the Chief Commissioner. Understand that?'

They understood. They swayed back on the sofa as if I had halitosis. Davis blinked. 'Threatening letters?'

The envelope and press cuttings were still on the coffee table. 'Read them yourself,' I said, and went across to the telephone to retrieve the airline ticket. 'And this came with them.'

They were still huddled over the press cuttings when Tomlinson arrived. I relieved him of his coat and took him in to make the introductions. 'The police go around in pairs in this town,' I explained. 'Battersea gets constables but we get the top brass.'

The effect of the introductions was quite startling. Tomlinson looked downright angry and Davis and Evans seemed vaguely apprehensive, as if they had been caught in the act. Certainly Davis moderated his attitude towards me. He would never invite me home to meet the wife, but his normal hostility diminished. Mind, we had a good old flare up before he left, but Tomlinson blamed me for that afterwards. In fact Tomlinson blamed me for a good deal.

The flare up started when Davis asked, 'Have you any idea who might have sent this?'

'How about you?'

When he just stared I added, 'You're always telling me to get out of town.'

He flushed and cast an anxious glance at Tomlinson. 'My attitude about licences does not include the condoning of threats.'

I said, 'That's very commendable – if it's true.'

Tomlinson broke it up by asking Evans, 'The question is what are you *doing* about it? My client has suffered three threats to his safety within twenty-four hours. I cannot stress too strongly—'

'Are you asking for police protection?' Evans interrupted, looking at me.

Hell, what *was* I asking for? I certainly could live without the law on my doorstep. I said, 'I want you to find the source of this intimidation—'

Davis snorted. 'Intimidation! We've nothing to go on, have we? You could have fabricated this stuff yourself—'

'You're crazy! Dammit Davis, I even had a witness. Lucia was—'

'Not *here* when the letter arrived. You said that yourself. You said she came just afterwards—'

'For Christ's sake!'

'You never even took the number of the cab. Did you?'

'No, but at the time—'

'You didn't think? But you thought enough to *steam* the letter open. Destroying any clues there might have been—'

'You're mad, Davis. Stark, staring bloody mad!'

'You've even got a typewriter in the house. You could have typed that message yourself.'

I threw my hands into the air and looked at Tomlinson for support. He was furious. He sat bolt upright, his face even whiter than usual and his expression very, very angry. I almost expected to see frost on his breath when he spoke, 'May I ask why you called here today, Inspector?'

'To get a statement signed about last night,' Davis snapped, then he remembered he was speaking to Tomlinson so he moderated his tone. 'But if it's inconvenient I suppose we could make an appointment.'

'Mr Harris's written statement will be with you tomorrow,' Tomlinson said crisply. 'I shall attend to that. Now unless you have any other query?'

Davis and Evans swapped glances, but they knew they were beaten. I was sure it was bluff but Tomlinson gave the impression they either had to arrest me or play it his way. So they contented themselves by making a few notes and asking additional questions. Then they asked to take the press cuttings and the airline ticket, plus the envelope of course – and after collecting a receipt Tomlinson showed them out. When he came back he was blazing angry.

'Being your solicitor means I represent you at law. *At law* Mr Harris! Which includes the police. If I ever find you talking to that man Davis again without me being present I shall resign at once.'

'What if they call—'

'You *refuse* to answer any questions without me being present. That's your right and by Heavens you are going to insist on it.'

It took him ten minutes to cool down. What he said was fair enough, which is why I took it, but a couple of things struck me. The first was that working with Tomlinson was going to be a damn sight different from working with Lewis Collins. And the second was that meeting Davis had been a good thing for Tomlinson. It brought him into the fight somehow – pushed him into my corner.

When we finished working on my statement, Tomlinson asked me to call at his office in the morning to sign it. Then he said, 'I think I might try for an earlier meeting with Hastings. If he can spare the time, could you make Monday at eleven?'

'Yes, I think so.'

'What about the notes you are working on – will they be ready?'

I thought of Lucia upstairs. We were supposed to be working on them *now*! I calculated quickly. If we did a couple of hours' work this evening, and some more tomorrow? 'I'll have them ready by Friday morning – just about.'

'Good,' he nodded. 'Get them round to me on Friday then, will you? I'll have a look at them before sending them round to Hastings. He can read them over the weekend.'

At the front door, he said, 'These Tusker people? You asked for a company search. They are restaurateurs, aren't they?'

'Among other things. They bought the wreckage of Apex from the receiver.'

'Is your enquiry urgent?'

I stood there, trying to decide what the hell was urgent and what was not. Then he explained. 'I happened to have a clerk in Cardiff today on another matter, so I asked him to call at Companies House to look up the files. We'll have the information you asked for by tomorrow.'

I thanked him and after letting him out I went upstairs. Lucia was standing at the window, looking out into Rex Place. It was dusk outside and the room was grey with shadow, but I saw the typewriter on the dressing table beside a neat pile of paper.

Lucia turned as I entered the room. 'Everyone gone?'

I nodded.

'I've been reading the life and times of Sam Harris. It's very impressive.'

'Yes,' I said stupidly.

'Larger than life. Glamorous – like your wife. Maria says she was quite beautiful.'

I ought to have said Lucia was lovelier. That she was a better person. Worth ten of Kay any day of the week. But I was still mixed up about Kay and the words wouldn't come. So I stood there, feeling awkward and tongue-tied, until she smiled and held out her hands. 'Come on, Sam, let's go for a walk. Just to clear our heads. Then I'll cook dinner while you do some more remembering.'

We crossed Park Lane into Hyde Park and ambled towards the Serpentine. My hands were thrust deep into my pockets and as we walked she linked her arm through mine. It was comforting, her being with me. I wondered who I would have turned to had she not been there? That's what got me down more than anything. This business of being ostracised. *Why?* There had been *so many friends* in the old days. Dozens, hundreds of friends. But none had even 'phoned since I came out. Just to ask how I was. Not one had offered to help. Just for old times' sake. *Not one!* Except Jack and Maria, and this girl Lucia.

'Penny for them?'

I shrugged. It would be ungrateful to tell her, so instead I said,

'Tomlinson seems to think the notes we're working on might be useful after all.'

'Sam, they're vital! *Absolutely vital!* You must remember *everything*. Everything you possibly can.'

Her forcefulness surprised me. After all, my problems could mean little to her. We had only just met. It was kind of her to become involved but the outcome could only be of passing interest to her.

'What's that expression of Jack's?' she asked, just as strongly. 'Don't let the bastards grind you down. Don't let them, Sam – you mustn't.'

I laughed. Typical of Jack to say the right thing – even if it was through a third party. And what was that saying of Kay's? 'The surest way to be a loser is to act like one.' It was time to pull myself together. We walked on for a bit, then I said, 'Look, you are supposed to be on holiday. I'll tell you what. We'll finish this thing of ours, then spend the weekend in the country somewhere. We could go—' I broke off as she stiffened on my arm. Her stride faltered and she took a half pace instead of a full one, so that we bumped into each other. 'What's the matter?'

'What – what you just said?'

'A weekend in the country?' I laughed as I caught the expression on her face. 'Look here – I didn't mean – well, I suppose we could have separate bedrooms. I just meant to show you the countryside—'

She shook her head. 'No. You said – "*this thing of ours*".' She stopped abruptly and stared at me.

'So? Those notes for Tomlinson. You were the one who said they were vital.'

I could see the questions in her eyes even in that dim light. She searched my face for such a long time that it was embarrassing. But eventually she smiled, uncertainly at first, then with more confidence. She relaxed her grip on my arm and said, 'Yes, that would be nice. A weekend in the country. Sam, it sounds a lovely idea – just what we need.'

After which she became so enthusiastic that I forgot how startled she had been. What did it matter anyway? A misunderstanding obviously. I imagine it is easily done when you are not speaking your natural language, however fluent you may be in another. When she asked where we would go I suggested the Wye Valley, and we were still talking about it when we returned to Rex Place.

'Let's have a drink before I start dinner,' she suggested. 'You fix them while I fetch your notes.'

So I did as I was told and a moment later she came back downstairs, frowning over the last sheet of paper.

'This man Corrao?' she said, taking the chair at the hearth. 'What did he look like?'

I cast my mind back over the years. 'Short and thin, about five six, weighing a lot less than me. Black hair, dark glasses.'

'Anything else?'

I shrugged. 'That's not bad is it? I only met the guy once.'

'Think, Sam – it is *important*.'

'Why?' I asked, thinking instead of Tomlinson. 'The lawyers won't be interested in—'

'Forget the lawyers,' she said sharply. 'Concentrate on Corrao.'

'But I told you—'

She shook her head. 'Try, Sam – was there *anything else* about him?'

I stared at her, wondering what on earth she meant. Then she prompted me. 'What about his hands, Sam? Was there anything special about his hands?'

Suddenly I went cold. I knew what she meant. I saw Corrao back in that hotel room, sitting at the breakfast table. Buttering a slice of toast *with one hand*. His right hand. The toast slid around the plate a bit, but instead of holding it with his other hand he just pushed it around with his butter knife. Then he did the same with the marmalade. He poured the coffee with his right hand, put the pot down, picked up the cup and passed it to me – *all with his right hand*. And when he finished he opened a pack of cigarettes with his right hand, just as if his left hand were paralysed or something.

Remembering that surprised me, but it was nothing to the shock I felt as I looked at Lucia's excited expression. How had she known? And what the hell did she mean – 'forget the lawyers'? Dammit, that's *why* we were working on the notes, wasn't it? *Wasn't it?*

I went back to the sideboard to collect my drink.

'His hands, Sam. Do you remember them?'

I was as cold as the grave. Cold with a sudden fear. Fear of betrayal. Betrayal by another woman! I swallowed the scotch neat and refilled my glass, this time adding a dash of water. Then I turned to face her. 'Yes, I remember. And I remember something else. Thinking about Corrao reminded me. He said this thing of ours is too strong. *This thing of ours*. When I used the same words in the park you almost seized up. And I remember something else. How calm you were at Oliver's after the explosion. Calm, like a nurse, like a – a professional. And I remember you saying these notes are vital, "absolutely vital". But not for the lawyers, apparently?'

I looked at her coldly, hating myself for distrusting her, trying again to decipher the look in her eyes. My image of her shattered. Hair prickled on the back of my neck. I forced the words out, made myself ask, 'Who are you, Lucia?'

She sat perfectly still, but even from across the room I sensed the tension in her body. Like a cat ready to pounce. But before she could move I heard a step in the hall and a moment later the sitting room door opened.

'Good evening, Mr Harris. No, don't move – please remain exactly as you are.'

It was the man from the restaurant! *The man who had attacked me!* I watched in amazement as he opened the door wider to admit another man. They were both so calm. Unhurried, casual. I swung back to Lucia, suddenly frightened for her despite my doubts of a moment ago. But I need not have worried on her account. She knew them! From the look on her face they were friends of hers.

'You heard?' she asked the man who had attacked me.

He nodded, without taking his eyes away from me. 'Sorry about last night, Mr Harris – but I had to get you away from that window.'

I heard what he said but it barely registered. The world, *my world* was going mad. I no longer understood it. I took a deep breath and asked, 'Who the hell are you?'

'My name's Henderson. Attached to the Home Office.' He produced a wallet from an inside pocket and flicked a plastic identity card in front of me. I saw the name Henderson and a passport photo which resembled him.

Lucia asked, 'What happens now?' *She spoke to him, not me.*

The man called Henderson said, 'Headquarters.' He shrugged, dismissing the questions in her eyes. 'It had to happen, sooner or later.' He looked at me. 'You're coming with us, Mr Harris. Don't be alarmed. You'll be quite safe, well looked after. My colleague will help you pack an overnight bag.'

'Am I being arrested?'

He smiled, faintly amused, then he shook his head. 'You'll be back here within a day or two.'

Lucia said, 'Sam, it's all for the best – please believe me.'

But I was incapable of believing anyone by then. 'I'm *not* going.' I said, panicking, 'I don't *want* to go. I'm not going anywhere, d'you hear me?' I swung back to the two men as they crossed the room towards me. 'Look, what the hell is this all about? How did you get in here anyway?'

The man from the restaurant smiled. 'I said there was no cause for alarm, Mr Harris. You must accept that.' He moved a pace nearer, reaching out to take hold of my elbow.

I stepped backwards. 'Get out. Get the hell out of here. *Get out – d'you hear?*'

But everything was happening at once. Lucia was pleading, 'Sam, it's all for the best. Really it is.' And the man from the restaurant was boring in on me. 'Let's be sensible, Mr Harris. There are two of us and only one of you.'

I lashed out but he must have been in training overnight because he rode the punch like a professional fighter. Then his mate wrapped himself over my back like an overcoat. I struggled and shouted, but I was no match for both of them – besides there was no space to manoeuvre in that little room – and a minute later I was being forced into a chair as my sleeve was pushed up above the elbow.

'Sorry about this,' said the man called Henderson. 'Believe me, it's for your own protection.'

I was telling them to go to hell, get out, leave me alone – but it made no difference. The needle went in just the same. Suddenly my body felt heavy and the lights went dim in the room. Lucia was watching me, white-faced and anxious, one hand at her mouth while she repeated 'It's all for the best' over and over again like a chant. Then her face turned upwards and all I could see was the ceiling, reducing in size, as big as a tablecloth one minute, then a pocket handkerchief, then as small as a postage stamp. A grey mist enveloped the room, fogging everything. My mind grabbed passing thoughts, trying to hang on, make sense, understand. Lucia asking the men if they heard? *Heard how? Heard what?* Us, talking together in that little sitting room. Heard? How? Lucia had helped refurnish the cottage. Refurnished it with hidden microphones? How stupid. *Bugs?* Ridiculous to think of Lucia doing a thing like that. Lucia Serracino-Torregianni. A hard name to say and a hard name to live with. And then I blacked out.

CHAPTER FOUR

I do remember *some* things after that. It's not a *complete* blank. For instance I know I was in a moving vehicle. It was too big for a car, because I was stretched full length on something like a camp-bed. And somebody was sitting close by. I remember that because I felt the jab of a needle afterwards and I went back to sleep. And then

– later – I had this most peculiar dream. I was in a room, talking to people. God knows who. It was pitch dark, but once or twice I felt a light on my eyes. I couldn't see, I think my eyes were closed – but I sensed a light turning on and off. And all the time talking – answering questions – people telling me to remember this, or tell them that. And me not wanting to, feeling sick and tired, just wanting to sleep – or to die.

Lucia was in the dream. Not that I could see her, but I knew her voice. And there were other voices – men's voices. One with a cut-glass accent, like Edgar Hardman's. (Edgar, is that you? After all this time?) And an American, but an American accent softened by years of travel, time spent in Europe perhaps? And a voice which sounded like the man called Henderson. Then another voice. So many voices. So many questions.

'Describe Corrao?' 'Are you sure you only met him once?' 'So what happened when you rejected his offer?' 'Yeah, yeah – the take-over battle – we know all about that – *but what happened afterwards?*' 'Afterwards is important – that's what we want to know about.' 'So okay – you told Corrao no dice – then what happened?' 'Sam, you must tell us.' 'How did they put the skids under Apex – that's what we want to know about?'

It was like the lull before the storm – that summer in 'seventy-five. Not that it began as a storm. Occasional squalls perhaps, but not a storm. There was a fight at Pam's Place on a Saturday night, then a spot of bother at Winston's a few days later. And some kids were caught smoking pot at Jennifer's the following week. None of the incidents were big in themselves, but they seemed to mount up – so that after a while there was some kind of trouble every week, then twice a week, and then almost every night. I thought it was a run of bad luck at first. There seemed no pattern to the events. But when we lost our licence at The Derby I was *really* worried, and I think I guessed what was happening then.

The law is an ass when it comes to gambling – full of hypocrisy and double standards. Gambling is venal but permissible if the Government gets a cut – and as long as certain proprieties are observed. Such as the forty-eight-hour rule – which was invented to placate the Holy Joes. Nobody can play the tables unless he has been a member of the gaming club for forty-eight hours. It's supposed to give the unwary time to repent before taking the plunge. In practice it's a pain in the neck. Gamblers arrive at a club and bribe the reception staff to backdate a membership card. Nothing happens to them if they get caught, and all that happens to the reception staff is that they stand to lose their jobs. The one who really gets hurt is the casino operator – and he can lose his licence.

Well, one night the police raided The Derby and found gamblers who were neither members nor guests of members. About twenty of them. They all swore blind they had just walked in off the street and gained admittance without question. It was absolute rubbish of course, but it was their word against ours – and they lied their heads off. Afterwards we found two emergency exits wide open. That's the way they came in – in fact some of the police arrived through the very same doors.

Even the business of the emergency exits was fixed. The doors were fitted with crash bars on the inside, to comply with local fire regulations, and a member of staff guarded each door every night. But that night one man had been called to the telephone urgently, and the other was trying to quieten a drunk. Both the telephone call and the drunk were bogus – and the doors were mysteriously opened within minutes of the men leaving their posts. Not that Chief Inspector Davis believed a word of it. Nor did the magistrates subsequently – though faced with the *evidence* of twenty men perjuring themselves it is difficult to see how the magistrates could have believed otherwise. And so The Derby was closed.

That was a hell of a blow. The Derby was our biggest club and accounted for almost ten per cent of our profits – and all this came about when we were committed to pay an increased dividend because of the take-over battle. But we could have weathered even that had it not been for all the other things. Fights which broke out for no reason. A bad case of food poisoning at Winston's. And then the whispering campaign started – rumours that Apex was going broke.

Start rumours in a business like ours and it's like a run on the bank. No gambler likes to think the kitty will be empty when his win comes up. So our business suffered – especially the betting shops which took a real beating. Apex had been financially healthy to begin with but after six months of that ... well, I suppose the writing was on the wall. Even though I refused to read it.

Then I was having this dream again. One minute I was remembering The Derby – and the next minute I was dreaming. *Except was it a dream?* The light seemed to be stronger and the people's voices were growing louder.

A voice – *a woman's voice* – said, 'He's resisting. He's rejecting—'

'Ask him about Edgar Hardman.'

'Ask him about his *wife* for Chrissakes!'

'He's resisting I tell you. It's no good. For heaven's sake – you'll kill him!'

'That's enough,' another voice said firmly. 'More than enough. It was a mistake. He needs to be conscious. It will require a conscious effort for him to remember.'

'Just get him going about his wife. Please, just for another few minutes.'

'No! That's an end to it. Put him back under.'

Then the needle again. Deep black waves rolling over me like a velvet curtain. And rest, blessed rest. But the voices? Fading – going away – going far away.

It was morning when I awoke. The curtains were drawn back and the light from the window was strong enough to reveal the furniture. I propped myself up in the strange bed and looked about me. It was a large room, larger than average, comfortably furnished with a dressing table and a chest of drawers, two armchairs and a wardrobe. A handbasin mounted on the far wall was surrounded by splash tiles, with a mirror above. Wall-to-wall carpet followed the shape of the old-fashioned bay windows. A single door was set into the wall on my right. Regency striped wallpaper rose to a high ceiling. No pictures decorated the walls. No flowers dropped their heads in vases, no bric-a-brac cluttered the surfaces. It was a masculine room – a comfortable, old-fashioned, country house kind of room.

A cock crowed in the far distance. That was the only sound. No traffic noise broke the stillness, no transistor relayed the breakfast show to all and sundry – and when the cock exhausted itself silence descended again like a cloak.

Seven o'clock. I had been 'out' for almost twelve hours. A dull hangover buzzed at the back of my eyes but apart from that I felt well enough. My legs supported me across to the handbasin and my face looked normal in the mirror. Normal! What the hell was *normal* now? The word had lost its meaning. Normal was to be a businessman, a restaurateur, a casino operator. Normal even meant being in Brixton Prison. Normal implied the predictable, a busy life, the daily round. *But this?*

The windows overlooked a kitchen garden; neat rows of bean sticks and cabbages. Thirty yards away a small shed nestled against a high brick wall and beyond that ploughed fields were criss-crossed with hedgerows and the occasional tree. Flat land, like East Anglia.

The door was locked but I expected that. People had taken a lot of trouble to bring me to this house. Doors would stay locked until they told me why. Until *they* told me. They! They included Lucia. I saw her face in my mind's eye; heard her voice; 'Sam, it's for your own good.' Like hell! For my own good, like two years in the army. Like two years in Brixton! Bullshit! I decided what's for my own good. Not them. Not Lucia. She sat there and let them do it! Watched while they held me down and stuck a needle in my arm. Bitch! Treacherous rotten bitch!

I examined my arm and saw the puncture marks. Three – not one. No, four, five even. I shuddered. I had been injected *five* times. It made me feel sick. Just the thought of a syringe brought back memories. Memories which were better left dead and buried. Then I stiffened as I remembered the dream. Those voices? Asking questions – me not wanting to answer. Suddenly I was sweating all over. Sweating with alarm as I remembered a voice saying, 'He's resisting I tell you. It's no good. For heaven's sake – you'll kill him.' God, what had I told them? And who in Christ's name were they anyway?

My clothes were in the wardrobe – shirt and tie, socks and shoes. I washed. Shaved with an electric razor. Dressed and combed my hair. Puffed on the first cigarette of the day. I felt no fear, which surprised me at first. Then I realised why. I was too angry to be afraid. Not blazing come outside and say that angry – but a tight, concentrated burning temper – so that when the door opened I was ready for anything.

'Morning, old boy,' said the man called Henderson. 'Found everything you want?'

'Next time get me a room with a private bath, will you? And I like a cup of tea before I get up.'

'Don't we all.' He sat on the bed and watched me finish knotting my tie. 'Glad you're an early riser though. We've a busy day ahead of us.'

'Doing what? Knocking people cold in restaurants? Jabbing them with needles?'

He smiled. 'Nothing so exciting, I'm afraid. Talk, mainly, and a few film shows. But you'll meet some interesting people.'

My nerve cracked. 'Where the devil are we?' I waved at the window.

'Headquarters,' he said simply. He stood up. 'Does it matter where it is? Really it's better if you don't know – better for you I mean.'

I remembered Lucia and said, 'For my own good?'

'Precisely,' he smiled again. 'Shall we go down to breakfast? One of the benefits of this place is the food is bloody good.'

'I'll tell Egon Ronay.'

101

I was right about the country house bit. We crossed a wide landing to a sweeping staircase grand enough for Fred Astaire to dance down. Wood panelled walls were decorated with military crests, and two suits of armour stood to attention in the hall below. Everywhere smelt of deep shine wax and metal polish. It was a bit like Edgar Hardman's pile at Wyndham Hall, but more institution-alised. More like a club than a home. A club, or an officers' mess – especially the dining room.

Three men were already eating at the end of a long table when we arrived. Heads turned and conversation stopped as Henderson ushered me in. I just had time to notice silver serving dishes on the sideboard, and french windows which opened onto a terrace, when the man at the head of the table rose to greet me.

'Mr Harris,' he shook my hand warmly. 'My name's Llewellyn. It's a pleasure to meet you.'

He was a tall, straight-backed man of about sixty, dressed in the kind of tweeds which old English families reserve for the country. Thinning grey hair, strong blue eyes, a clipped military moustache, a very firm handshake – and a voice like Edgar Hardman's.

'Let me introduce two of my colleagues – Bill Kaufman and Enrico Bonello.'

'Glad to know you,' Kaufman rose briefly, and waved a hand. Then he settled back in his chair and continued eating.

Bonello said, 'Mr Harris,' and shook hands with stiff formality.

The man called Llewellyn steered me to the sideboard. 'Have some breakfast. Ham, eggs, bacon, it's all there. Or smoked haddock if you prefer? Coffee and tea – just help yourself, eh? Make yourself at home.'

Henderson grinned and passed me a plate. Make yourself at home seemed odd words for a kidnapper, but it seemed best to go along with them – at least for the time being. I carried a heaped plate back to the table and sat opposite Kaufman. I wondered if Lucia was in the house? But it was only a passing thought – mainly I was memorising their names – Llewellyn, Kaufman, Bonello.

Kaufman speared an egg with a forkful of sausage and munched happily while staring at me. Judging by the food on his plate he would have a weight problem in a year or two, but the prospect appeared not to worry him. He was a pleasant-faced man in his early forties, sandy-haired and green-eyed. He even had freckles. A knitted tie was buttoned under his shirt collar and he wore a casual woollen suit. 'You ever shoot craps in those casinos of yours?' he asked.

I recognised another voice from my 'dream' but kept my nerves under tight control. 'Some,' I said, 'but blackjack and roulette were more popular.'

He chewed the last mouthful and loaded his fork with another: 'French roulette or American?'

'French.'

He shook his head. 'House gets better odds with American.'

'You in the business?'

He looked surprised. 'Me?' he said, pointing his knife at his chest. 'Hell, no, just a punter. Craps is okay though – it's the only game I can win. Can't understand some of them. That *chem de fleur*—'

'*Chemin de fer*,' Bonello corrected.

'That's right,' Kaufman nodded. 'Can't understand it.'

The door opened and two other men came in. Llewellyn bobbed up and made the introductions in the same cordial manner as before: 'Tony Hewit and Bob Richardson – meet Sam Harris.'

'Hi, Sam.'

'Glad to know you.'

They smiled and turned to the sideboard with happy anticipation. Holy Christ, it was like a golf weekend! After breakfast we would all troop down to the locker room for a few practice swings! I nodded and concentrated on my food – repeating their names over and over again – Hewit and Richardson – Bonello and Kaufman – Llewellyn and Henderson. I tried to establish a common denominator, some characteristic shared by them all – but without success. For a start at least three different nationalities were involved – British, American and Italian – and their conversation was of no help. What talk there was confined itself to the weather or food – 'pass the coffee' and 'have some more toast', and except for Kaufman's opening enquiry about the casino business, my presence went largely ignored. I wondered if it were deliberate? Perhaps they expected me to jump up and demand an explanation. Maybe it was designed to get on my nerves? Whatever it was I steeled myself and ignored them right back – and just got on with finishing my breakfast.

Eventually, when even Kaufman pushed his plate away, Llewellyn suggested I join him for a stroll on the terrace – 'before we get down to business'. The perfect bloody host! But at least it gave me a breath of fresh air and a chance to look round. The house was Edwardian, I think, maybe Victorian – mostly red brick and a lot of high gables. Large but not exactly impressive, though certainly bigger than Ashley Grange. Formal gardens stretched down from the terrace and fifty yards away met the same high wall I had seen from the bedroom window. Llewellyn and I strolled up and down,

. niffing the air like pointer. on a lea. h. I watched a jet fighter trail vapour as it climbed high in the sky. Perhaps we were close to an airfield? A military base? Gloucestershire? No – the countryside was too flat – it had to be East Anglia.

Llewellyn watched my face. 'Worked out where we are?'

I shrugged. 'Hadn't thought about it.' I gave him the best smile I could manage. 'I'm sure you'll tell me – when it's good for me to know.'

Either he was being polite or the answer appealed to his sense of humour, because it delighted him. 'Exactly! That's quite the right attitude.' He turned back to the house. 'Shall we start?'

I wondered what would happen if I said no? But I was more nervous than I was letting on, and I was curious about where this was all leading. Besides, I was struck by another thought. Tomlinson was expecting me at ten thirty. If I missed that appointment he was likely to have every policeman in the country looking for me. It was a comforting thought, so I hung onto it.

We assembled in the room next to the dining room. It was almost as large and laid out for a conference. A top table butted onto a longer one to form a T shape. Water jugs and glasses flanked pads and pencils. A small cinema screen was set into one wall. The other men from the breakfast room were already taking their places at the tables.

'Perhaps you'd care to sit here?' Llewellyn stood behind a single chair at the end of the longer table. 'As you're by way of being guest of honour.' He smiled as he pulled the chair out. 'It will give us a chance of a good look at you – and to hear what you think of our little scheme.'

I sat down and Llewellyn walked to the other end of the room. He took the central place at the top table, flanked by Kaufman and Bonello, exactly opposite me, separated by ten feet of mahogany and an avenue of curious eyes. Perhaps it was Llewellyn's bearing, but the atmosphere reminded me distinctly of a court martial.

'Make yourselves comfortable,' Llewellyn said. 'It's going to be a long session and I'm not quite sure where to begin.'

I snapped: 'Why not start by introducing yourselves? You've told me the name's Llewellyn, but not *who* you are. Or *what* you are?'

I cursed under my breath. I had meant to remain silent. Let them make the running – but the whole thing was playing on my nerves too much for that. Shock I suppose – Lucia's treachery, being kidnapped, a meeting in a house located God knew where. My hand trembled as I reached for my cigarettes.

Kaufman said, 'Relax, Sam. Nothing's going to happen to you. You're our guest, that's all.'

'Perhaps I don't like the way I was invited?'

'Okay, okay—' he patted the air, as if to say calm down. 'We're sorry about last night. We did it that way—'

'For my own good?'

'Right,' he smiled. 'As to who we are that can come later.'

I remembered Henderson saying 'Home Office' and flashing an identity card, but that made no sense at all and I was about to say later wasn't good enough when Kaufman added, 'Sam, this is going to be hard for you. We've a lot to tell you and mostly we're only going to say it once. When we finish you're going to have to make a big decision. A very big decision. So listen real good, huh?' He smiled again. I was too far away to see the freckles but I knew they were there, hiding in the creases around his eyes. He finished by saying, 'After that you'll be taken back to that elegant little pad of yours – all safe and sound. Okay?'

'What happens then?'

'That depends on your decision,' he said, still smiling.

I was reminded of the time Charlie Weston came to see me to discuss the casino business. When he brought his team of advisors. But it was no comparison really. Charlie was a businessman. His people had been bankers, accountants, other professional men. Whoever – whatever – these people were, they certainly were not bankers. Bill Kaufman might be doing his friendly downtown salesman bit but it was faked. Freckles or not, something in his expression worried me. Then I realised what it was. However far that smile spread across his face it would never reach his eyes. They remained as cold as ice.

I cleared my throat. 'So I'm to be given a choice?'

Kaufman chuckled: 'Everyone gets a choice in life. Isn't that your philosophy – *Winner*?'

He dropped the old nickname in so softly that I thought he was being sarcastic. But I was being too sensitive. It was just his way of saying he knew all about me – *everything* about me. He turned and looked across Llewellyn to Bonello. 'Enrico, why don't you start? After all, it all began at your end.'

Bonello nodded sadly. Watching him, I was reminded of Charles Aznavour. The same wiry frame, brooding, unhappy eyes, quick mobile face. Perhaps he was French or Armenian, not Italian as I imagined? But his opening words proved me wrong.

'I am a Sicilian, Mr Harris,' he said. He smiled shyly, as if worried about how I would take it. When I sat blank-faced and silent he continued, 'Most people only know of my homeland because of the Mafia. It is our curse, a stain on our ancestry. The Honoured Society. I suppose you've heard it called that? You've heard the words? *Omerta* – manliness, the code of secrecy unto death. *Ripeittu* – the Mafia law of keeping hands off one another's property.' He sneered. 'Viciousness disguised as chivalry, that's all – folktales for peasants. We almost stamped it out before the war. Caesare Mori fought the Mafia to a standstill in the twenties. Mussolini trampled them underfoot in the thirties. But then the war came and afterwards—' he shrugged. 'The Mafia was back in Sicily, stronger than at any time in its history.'

Why tell me, I thought? But I remained silent. He screwed a cigarette into a black holder and sat playing with it, rolling it in his fingers, looking at it with brooding eyes. Then again the brief, shy smile. 'No offence is meant to my American friends when I say they helped the Mafia regain power in Sicily. When the Allies invaded, the Mafia facilitated their advance. One *capo-mafia* in particular, Don Calogero Vizzini, was of such great help that in the immediate post-war years he became the American advisor. He even persuaded them to appoint former *mafiusi* as mayors in many towns in Sicily. Oh, I don't blame the Americans – they never knew the histories of the men they appointed. How could Americans be expected to sort the goats from the sheep on our little island?'

He smiled forgiveness at Kaufman who shrugged and made no effort to reply. I glanced quickly at the other faces. They expressed polite interest, but nothing more than that. As if they had heard the story before and were faintly bored by it.

Not that Bonello was discouraged. 'After the war, democracy made things even worse,' he said. 'One man, one vote, was new to Italy. Many Italians – many Sicilians – were unsure about it. But the Mafia caught on. They realised that voters could be organised. Soon it became known that the Mafia could deliver the vote at election times. After that no political candidate had a chance in Sicily, unless he bought his votes from the local Mafia chief. And the price, Mr Harris?' Bonello raised his solemn eyes to mine. 'Political connivance in Mafia dealings.'

He put a light to his cigarette and puffed in silence. Then he said, 'Old style Mafia like Vizzini ran Sicily until the early sixties—'

Suddenly Kaufman interrupted. 'Fix that date in your mind, will you, Sam? The early sixties, right. You're in London laying the foundations of your business empire, while in Sicily—'

'Vizzini was still in power,' Bonello said quickly. I threw Kaufman a look of surprise but before I could say anything Bonello was continuing. 'Vizzini worked in the shadows – dispensing favours – granting protection, wielding political influence. But then came a new generation – young *mafiusi* who flaunted their wealth and importance – men who drove flashy Alfas and who lived a more open, café society style of life. And when the young *mafiusi* clashed with the old, the streets of Sicily ran with blood. For example, in 1962, fifty-six people were shot dead over two months in Palermo alone.'

'1962, Sam,' Kaufman said with strange emphasis.

'That's got nothing to do with me!' I said sharply.

'Oh, but it has,' Kaufman insisted softly. 'This is *your* story, Sam. Believe me. There are men in this room from all over the world – Milan, New York, Palermo – and for why? Because of *your* story.' He smiled, and stifled my astonished denial by saying, 'Oh, not that crap you've been handing Lucia. That's only a part of it. The rest is where your life crossed other people's – that's a lot more fascinating.'

I stared at him in complete bewilderment. Blank astonishment. There *had* to be a mistake. Whoever – whatever – these men were, they had confused me with somebody else. But Bonello was already continuing, 'Other things were happening in Italy. For instance, there was a great migration of Sicilians to the north. Industry was hungry for labour. More than a quarter of a million Sicilians exchanged their dirt patch in the south for a job at Fiat's in the north. But wherever the Sicilians went, they took the ways of the Mafia with them. Disrespect for law and order, this conspiracy of silence – ah—' he waved a hand. 'Only when you've spent a lifetime fighting it can you really understand.'

I was understanding nothing.

Kaufman met my astonished gaze for a second, then turned back to Bonello. 'Tell him about the family, Enrico.'

'I was just about to,' Bonello said, faintly irritated. He looked at me. 'A man named Vito lived in Milan. A northerner, important, successful – a business from an old family. When he was young he studied in Rome and became friendly with people who owned land in Sicily. One summer his friends invited him to stay in Sicily, and during his visit he met the daughter of one of their neighbours. The two young people fell in love and wanted to marry. But marriage in Italy is a complicated affair – less so today of course, but then—' he waved a hand into the distance. 'Many things had to be taken into account. But both families were wealthy and the two young people persevered – so in the end they were married. Gifts were exchanged and, as was the custom then, the name of the newly-weds was linked to incorporate the names of both families.'

He paused to sip some water. For the tenth time in as many moments I asked myself *why* I was being told all this? What had Kaufman meant about it being my story? How could it be? I had never been to Italy, let alone Sicily.

107

Bonello swallowed his drink. 'Vito qualified as an engineer and took his young bride back to Milan to live. There he inherited the family construction business. They survived the war and even prospered from it. Afterwards they had a child and seemed set to live happily ever after. The wife, Franka, kept in touch with her parents, but less so than most Italian daughters.' Bonello shrugged. 'Palermo and Milan are far apart and the lives of the people quite different – and besides, the wife had kept something secret from her husband. That her family was Mafia – and she kept this from Vito for twelve long years.'

'Until when exactly?' Kaufman asked, with one eye on me.

'June, 1952. She had to tell him then. There was a power struggle in Palermo between the two largest Mafia families. Many people were killed, among them Franka's parents and her sister-in-law. Her eldest brother, Guiseppe, fled to the hills with his two small children – a boy and a baby girl who was just a few months old. Somehow Guiseppe got a message to the Sicilian colony in Milan, who passed it to Franka. Would she take the baby girl and bring it up as her own? Of course Franka had to tell Vito everything. He listened, forgave her, and agreed to take the child – which is what happened.'

Kaufman interrupted again. 'How old was the other child when this happened? Vito and Franka's own child?'

'About seven.'

Kaufman nodded, looking at me but still speaking to Bonello. 'Who was also a girl?'

'Yes,' Bonello agreed. 'Luckily she took to the new baby and Vito and Franka grew to love the child as their own. Whatever one child had, the other also had—'

'Two young girls, growing up in a wealthy household,' Kaufman summarised, looking at me. 'An enlightened household, would you say, Enrico?'

Bonello nodded. 'Yes. The children were well educated, privately—'

'Taught several languages,' Kaufman said.

'That too,' Bonello agreed.

Kaufman threw me another look. The *emphasis* of his interruptions, combined with the looks he was giving me, somehow stirred my memory. But Bonello mistook my look of concentration for one of understanding because he said, 'I see you are ahead of me, Mr Harris. But let me fill in the missing years.'

'Just the important ones, Enrico.' Kaufman cautioned.

'Nineteen-sixty-one was the most important of all,' Bonello looked at me. 'I'll remind you of what I said earlier, Mr Harris. The early sixties in Palermo were a bloodbath. Franka's eldest brother had long since returned from the hills to establish himself as *capo-mafiusi*. God knows he was vicious enough – but his son!' Bonello threw up his hands. 'His son was the wildest of all. Fiore he was called – Fury in English. Fiore was involved in every killing in Palermo. He was a *butcher*! A sadist, who tortured his victims before killing them. He terrorised the whole of Western Sicily until finally he went too far. Some of the other families turned against him. They fought back, and with the carabinieri hounding his every move, Palermo got too hot for Fiore – so he fled to Milan.'

'Nineteen-sixty-one, Sam,' Kaufman said sharply.

Bonello continued swiftly. 'In Milan Fiore made no effort to contact Vito and Franka. After all, he barely knew them, and the child they loved as their own – Fiore's own sister – had been a baby when he last saw her.' Bonello shook his head: 'No, Fiore submerged into the underworld. Smuggling currency across the Swiss border, running prostitution, trafficking drugs, and bleeding club owners for protection money.'

'Nineteen-sixty-one,' Kaufman said again.

Suddenly I knew what he was saying! Pieces fell into place. He was wrong about it being my story – quite wrong – but I knew whose it was. Two girls. Italian, well educated, speaking several languages. And what was it Bonello said about the marriage? The names of both families were linked – as was the custom. A hyphenated name! *Serracino-Torregianni!* A hard name to say – and a hard name to live with.

Bonello caught the sudden interest in my eye. 'Within a year,' he was saying, 'Fiore's protection rackets spread to cafés and shops and the construction industry. Building sites are very vulnerable – especially at night. As I said – Milan was booming – new construction projects were starting every day – and Vito was the biggest builder in Milan. And he *refused* to pay protection money. Vito was a brave man, Mr Harris. He fought like a tiger. He even formed his own security corps to guard his properties. He toured his sites every night. Some of the carabinieri helped, but some—' Bonello spread his hands, 'some were already on Fiore's payroll. The fight lasted a year. Every week one of Vito's sites was hit. Fires would break out, work would be wrecked, materials looted. But *still* Vito fought. Until, on the fourteenth of December 1962, he went to a site on the outskirts of the city. It was night time. Two of his security guards travelled with him, and the site was supposedly guarded by twenty of his own people. But when he arrived none of his staff could be found – and Fiore was waiting for him.'

Bonello paused to eject the half-smoked cigarette from its holder.

He stubbed it into an ashtray and his voice took on a harsh new note as he finished his story. 'I arrived on that site the following morning. Of course I was younger then – not in charge, you understand – but *I* was the one who cut Vito's body down from the scaffolding. His eyes had been gouged out, his testicles cut away, and – and every inch of his body had been mutilated. He was barely recognisable as a man – as a human being – a thing of dignity—'

His voice tailed off. Nobody moved. We sat in silence, watching the play of muscles in Bonello's white face as he struggled with his emotions. I risked a glance at the others. They were all the same, perhaps not displaying the same degree of personal misery as Bonello but grimly tense and determined. The common denominator was there now – in their faces. And Bonello had said he wasn't in charge. What did that mean? That he was a policeman of some kind? Were they all policemen of some kind?

My imagination struggled with the picture of Bonello handling that terrible corpse. I shuddered – at the exact moment the cigarette holder snapped in Bonello's hands. It broke the spell. He looked up at me and said, 'Terrible though that was, it was not the end of the story. Vito had fought with the courage of a tiger, but his wife was to fight with the demented fury of a wounded tigress. She insisted on identifying Vito's mutilated body. She had it photographed. She sent copies to every paper in Italy. Many published it, some on their front pages, and then Franka took over Vito's business and ran it herself,' he paused, shaking his head. 'Franka was unique, Mr Harris. Never was there a woman like her. Proud, beautiful, determined and—' a smile played briefly at the corners of his mouth, 'and stubborn. People wanted to help, believe me – not all Italians are cowards or scum like Fiore. But Franka would have none of it. It was her fight and she fought it. She went broke fighting it. She sold her home, her jewellery, everything she possessed. Her daughter sold many of the more valuable pieces in London – *and for why?*' He sneered in sudden anger, 'For why? Because many Italian dealers were afraid to buy in case the Mafia burned their shops to the ground.'

He sat with an expression of disgust on his face, fumbling through his pockets for a cigarette until Kaufman passed him a pack. I was leaning forward, watching intently, but at the back of my mind I saw another face. Lucia's face. Her eyes brimming with tears as I told her how Maria met Jack. Selling the family heirlooms in Sloane Street!

Bonello puffed on a new cigarette. 'Finally Franka had only one property left. An apartment building. Vito's staunchest workers fought the world to finish that project. Completing it might have saved Franka from ruin. Day by day it drew nearer completion. Week by week it inched up above the city skyline. Even Milan's cowards watched its progress with admiration. Franka Serracino-Torregianni was spitting in the eye of her husband's murderers. It was something to be proud of – to make men walk tall again – the defiant courage of one woman and a loyal band of workers. But it was too much for Fiore – the humiliation was too much. A week before the apartment block was due to be opened, Franka was kidnapped and – and taken to a basement.'

His voice dropped to a whisper. I strained to catch his words. 'And what they did there was, was—' Finally words failed him. His head shook from side to side, as if denying some terrible knowledge. His hands clasped and unclasped in front of him.

'Enrico,' Llewellyn said so gently that I looked at him. His soldier's brusqueness had slipped, now there was only sympathy in his voice. 'Enrico,' he said, 'I want to show the film. Why not get yourself a breath of fresh air—'

'No!' Bonello sat bolt upright. 'No. I'll stay. As Kaufman said – it's my end of things. Mr Harris – Sam – may ask a question which only I can answer. I have to be here.'

Kaufman shook his head sadly, raising his shoulders in a faint shrug. He went to the windows to close the drapes. 'This isn't very pleasant, Sam,' he said, 'but I want you to see it. The can's through the door if you need it.'

The room turned grey as the natural light was shut out. Grey and stuffy, like the inside of a tomb. Even the silence was oppressive. Then the screen in the far wall flickered and drew my attention like a magnet. I sensed Kaufman walk behind my chair.

'That's the entrance to the basement,' Bonello said as a narrow doorway appeared. 'Franka was taken down there and stripped naked. A proud, handsome woman of forty-seven years of age. Then she was spreadeagled across a table, tied securely – and raped by twelve men. At the end of it she was revived with a glass of wine, and asked if she had a last request before they killed her.'

His voice shook – then he astonished me by sounding close to laughter. 'Do you know what she said? Yes, she said, she did have a last request. She would like sexual intercourse with a *real* man – if they could find one.'

He laughed outright then, a thin crackle of sound which drove a shiver up my spine.

The camera was going down the steps and along a passage. Blue paint peeled in strips from the walls. The lighting was dim and the picture lost definition, then an arc lamp blazed directly into the lens

111

and shattered the image into a million fragments. The light turned aside and the camera focused on a crude wooden table.

'That was the table, Mr Harris. After they raped her they applied electric shock treatment, and after that—'

The arc lamp probed slowly along one wall. The bricks had been painted blue, but time and damp had stripped the colour, so that the splashes of bright red stood out vividly. Then the camera began to dip towards the floor.

Bonello said, 'They shaved her head first – and removed hair from all over her body. They, they—'

'That's enough! FOR CHRIST'S SAKE – *that's enough!*' I had seen what was on the screen. I had seen it! 'For God's sake!' I shouted. I shut my eyes and raised my hands to my ears to blot out Bonello's commentary. I tried to rise in my chair but Kaufman's hands were on my shoulders.

Kaufman's shouts rose above mine. 'Look at it, Sam. Damn you, look at it. Another week and you'll say something like that never happened.'

'Get off! For pity's sake, get off!' I struggled to break his grip. I felt sick. Sick to the pit of my stomach. Sick that someone could have done *that* to another human being.

'It took eight hours for her to die,' Bonello was saying.

Kaufman snapped, 'Shut up. It's enough that he sees it.'

I was fighting Kaufman and shouting at Bonello at the same time. 'You can't know! You can't *know* these things. How long it took – how they did—'

'There was a witness,' Bonello lashed back angrily.

The camera was moving away. Thank God! The camera was moving away from *that* – that terrible corpse. But then it found another one – smaller, less disfigured, still recognisable as a human being. A young girl, face down, her back mutilated as if cut by a thousand lashes, strips of skin and flesh hanging like ribbons. The gorge rose in my throat as I watched a figure lean over and gently turn the body onto one side.

'She was made to watch,' Bonello was saying. 'For eight hours they made her watch. Then Fiore did – did that—'

It was the face of death itself. Except it was so beautiful. The face of a lovely child. No more than twelve years old. A girl with the promise of vivid beauty still visible on her white skin. Cheek bones that I recognised. Then her eyelids flickered and opened. Wild staring eyes. Grey eyes that had seen hell. Lucia's eyes!

Bonello said, 'Fiore did that – to his own sister.'

Then, mercifully, I broke free of Kaufman's grasp and was

stumbling towards the door, holding the hot vomit in my mouth as I struggled to reach the lavatory in time.

I returned to find Kaufman had opened the french windows and was about to follow Llewellyn out onto the terrace. They were both looking out at the garden and as I joined them I saw Bonello pacing a path by the rosebeds, his hands clasped behind him and his eyes cast down, as if searching for something lost a long time ago.

'Ah, Harris,' Llewellyn said through his pipe. 'Feeling better?'

Kaufman smiled. 'Waste of a good breakfast, eh?'

I was still angry. 'Why was I shown that filth?'

'My idea really,' Llewellyn said mildly. 'Bit of a shock to the nervous system, of course, but – well, there were reasons.' He pointed the stem of his pipe at a garden bench. 'Let's sit down, shall we? It's warm enough now, and I daresay you could use a breath of fresh air.'

So we sat, Llewellyn in the middle and Kaufman reaching across to offer me a cigarette, which I declined. I sniffed at the clean air, faintly scented by flowers growing nearby. A thrush sang. The sun shone in a washed out sky. It was a perfect morning. An English morning as opposed to an Italian night. A country garden, instead of a cellar. Life, not death.

'This is by way of being a second career for me,' Llewellyn observed. 'I was in the army for thirty years,' he smiled at the memory. 'Overseas mainly, but once upon a time I had to deal with chaps like you. Like you were, I mean, when you were doing National Service. Of course, they mostly hated it. Called it a bloody waste of time. Uprooted from their homes and families, with only the NAAFI girls for comfort. So I used to pack them off to the camp cinema and show them war films. The real war. War Office material, not the diluted stuff shown to the general public. All the atrocities and concentration camp bits. Made them think a bit I can tell you. Gave them a reason for being there – stopped them feeling sorry for themselves.'

'And you thought I needed that?'

He smiled. 'It did seem appropriate – don't you think?'

I was about to tell him exactly what I thought when I saw Lucia walking along the side of the house. She carried a basket of cut flowers over the crook of her arm and made such a perfect picture that she might have belonged there – as if the setting had been designed for her. Thin sunshine turned her hair a lighter shade of brown and the yellow dress matched her golden skin. Even from thirty yards away she looked beautiful.

Bonello had seen her too. He hurried across the garden, raising his head as he called her name. She turned, startled at first, then glowing with a smile when she saw who it was. Then they were in each other's arms.

'He's her uncle,' Llewellyn said, following my gaze. 'Franka's brother.'

'Franka's brother? And he watched that film?' The horror of what I had seen filled my mind.

'He shot it actually,' Llewellyn said. 'When they first went into that basement they thought Lucia was dead as well. Took her pulse of course, but it was so weak they missed it. It was only when she opened her eyes that they realised she was alive.'

I was stunned by the nightmare.

'Interesting chap,' Llewellyn said in the same dry voice, nodding at Bonello. 'He was fourteen when Franka left home to get married. Like her he had seen the Mafia from the inside and hated it. But he could never escape it in Sicily – he knew that – so he ran away, and a month afterwards he turned up in Milan. He waited for Vito to go out, then he called on Franka – and begged her not to send him back.'

'And did she?'

'How could she? She had run away herself, in a sense, to seek her own happiness. She could hardly deny Enrico his. Luckily she had a maid, a woman called Rosana Bonello, who agreed to look after the boy. Of course Franka paid for his keep so it suited everyone. As a result Enrico grew up under his sister's eye, and when he was old enough he joined the police force.'

'And nobody ever found out? What about – Vito? Did they never tell him?'

Llewellyn knocked his pipe out on the heel of his shoe, scattering strings of charred tobacco over the flagstones. 'Franka couldn't tell him – not without revealing her secret. Of course she made a clean breast of everything eventually – when the Sicilian gun battle broke out in the fifties, and she took charge of Lucia. But Enrico was a young man by then, and away at police college. Meanwhile Rosana Bonello had adopted him – to give him a new name along with his new life.'

I shook my head and said, 'Remarkable,' without even realising it.

'They're a remarkable family,' Kaufman said.

Lucia and her uncle strolled towards us, arm in arm, their heads close together as they talked in low, soft voices. Suddenly she looked up and saw me watching her. She halted at the bottom of the terrace, confused for a moment, then she unlinked her arm from his and slowly climbed the steps. She stopped a yard away, stretching her

114

hands towards me, her face anxious as her eyes met mine. I understood that expression now. All that suffering. Her subsequent life haunted by those terrible memories.

'Please forgive me, Sam,' she said as our hands touched. 'For – for deceiving you.'

I rose and drew her into my arms. The gaps in my understanding were enormous. What was going on? How was I involved? But I suppose I would have forgiven her anything after watching that film. She saw it in my face because when she drew away she simply said, 'Thank you.'

Llewellyn stood up. 'We've a lot to talk about. If you've had enough fresh air we ought to resume.'

He looked at Lucia. 'Perhaps you'd care to join us?'

As we turned for the doors Henderson came out carrying an envelope. Kaufman opened the flap with his thumb, read the letter quickly and passed it to me. It's from Tomlinson,' he said casually. 'That statement for Davis. Better sign it, and we'll get it back to him.'

Tomlinson! An hour ago he had been my ace in the hole. The one man who might get me out of here. Now I was so confused that even leaving would worry me – until I found out what was going on.

'Is Tomlinson in on this?' I asked. 'Is he – one of you?'

'Hell no,' Kaufman shook his head. 'But we couldn't have him all steamed up about your appointment, so we 'phoned his secretary. Said you couldn't make it but you'd send a messenger.' He shrugged. 'Sign it, Sam – we've other things to talk about.'

But I wasn't buying that. Not that easily. 'How did you know I was meeting him?'

Kaufman smiled. 'Rex Place. You made the arrangements there, remember? The whole place is wired. We can even hear you brush your teeth.'

Tiny spots of colour appeared on Lucia's cheeks. So I had been right! What had seemed preposterous last night, was perfectly true. No wonder she had wanted to discuss the notes there – Kaufman had heard every word we said.

His lack of apology infuriated me. I snapped: 'Just who the hell are you, Kaufman?'

'William Kaufman. United States Bureau of Narcotics,' he said, his manner still cool and unconcerned.

Narcotics? Even that surprise failed to stem my temper. 'And *that* gives you the right to pry – to eavesdrop – to abduct—'

'With a little help from my friends,' he waved a hand at Llewellyn and Bonello. 'Sam,' he said, 'we'll explain *everything* – if you give us a chance.'

'Explain,' I sneered. I wondered what Kaufman's explanations were worth. I looked at Bonello. 'And what do I call you? Bonello? Serracino? Torregianni?'

He smiled sadly. 'So you know my secret as well? It's quite a chapter of revelations, isn't it? But Bonello will do. I've lived with the name for most of my life and tried not to dishonour it.'

'Please, Sam,' Lucia squeezed my hand. 'Please hear us out.'

I never even bothered to read Tomlinson's statement – just scrawled my signature and handed it back to Kaufman. Then we all went back into the conference room.

Lucia sat next to me at the table. I was in the same place as before but she set a chair on the corner close by. I could feel her trying to reassure me. I suppose she did in a way. But the others worried me sick. Llewellyn and Bonello were courteous enough, and Kaufman proved what an old buddy he was by calling me Sam every five minutes. But the whole thing frightened me. Hewit and Richardson had yet to speak but the look in their eyes was enough. I was to be used when it suited them – made to do what they wanted – to be manipulated. They were positioning me for something – I could feel it.

Kaufman resumed by saying, 'We'll go back to Enrico's story later. Meanwhile remember the dates, will you, Sam? They're important. Franka was murdered in 1963, right? The same year you opened The Point of View. A critical year for the Mafia. Police were moving against them in Italy like never before. We were hounding them in the States.' He paused, as if struck by a sudden thought. 'By the way, the name Joe Valachi mean anything to you?'

'No.'

He smiled briefly. 'That proves you're not an American. Valachi was a convicted trafficker in heroin. In June 'sixty-two he was doing a stretch in the Atlanta Penitentiary when he suddenly went berserk and killed a guy. He said the guy was planning to kill him and he got in first. Anyway, afterwards he realised he killed the wrong man – got into a hell of a state about it, and sang his heart out to the FBI in exchange for State protection. Kennedy called it the biggest breakthrough ever made in combating organised crime in the States.'

'Senator *Robert* Kennedy,' Hewit spoke for the first time, to add a word of explanation. 'He was Attorney General at the time.'

Kaufman nodded impatiently. 'Kennedy was going after the mobs in a big way. He clashed with Hoover about it. When Kennedy started, the FBI had only four agents fighting organised crime in the whole of New York – while four hundred were tied up

116

watching domestic communists. Well, Kennedy reversed the emphasis, understand?'

I nodded, which meant I heard what he said. Understanding was another matter entirely.

Hewit said, 'Valachi's information helped us hit scores of Mafia activities. But mostly the Mafia pulled out when we arrived. Take drug trafficking – when we hit the pushers, the Mafia faded. Sure, they still control heroin imports into the States, but now they let the blacks and Puerto Ricans run the wholesale market. The Mafia took a step backwards. Get the picture?'

I fidgeted uneasily. 'Look, this has nothing to do with me. Nothing whatsoever. I have never ever been involved.'

'Sam!' Kaufman shouted: 'Will you let us finish, for Chrissakes?'

'What's the point – when it's nothing to do with me. I don't—'

'Just wait a minute, will you?' Kaufman snapped.

We glared angrily at each other, but it seemed time I put my foot down. He had called it *my* story earlier. That was rubbish!

Llewellyn scraped his pipe into an ashtray. 'Bill's just anxious to give you the background to what happened in the sixties,' he said slowly. 'The main point is that for the first time in history the Mafia came under simultaneous pressure in the United States and Italy. Mafia families reacted differently. Some changed their ways, adopted new tactics, switched their activities – some even emigrated. In particular, some emigrated to the United Kingdom, and eventually to London.'

'The Mafia in *London*?'

Bonello answered, 'Yes, Mr Harris. For example, Milan was too small to hide Fiore Serracino. I had been given a squad of five hundred men to fight the Mafia and, in particular, to catch the man who murdered my sister and her husband. But Fiore got away. We found out how later. How he slipped through our net and returned to Sicily, and how from there he was smuggled to Malta aboard a fishing boat. How he acquired Maltese papers, a passport, a new name, new identity – and how after that he went to live in Cardiff.'

Cardiff? A note of warning jangled in the back of my mind, but before I could pursue it Llewellyn said, 'Of course we never knew that until much later.'

'Pieces of jigsaw,' Richardson said softly.

Llewellyn barely paused. 'Fiore Serracino was a rich man. He had enough money in Swiss banks to retire. The pity is men like him never do. He fitted into the sleazier parts of Cardiff like a hand in a glove. Of course, the Maltese have controlled the vice trade in

Cardiff for years – we knew that. Prostitution, the café clearing houses on Bute Street, protection rackets – but we were gradually cleaning them up. Until Serracino arrived, in the late sixties. We never knew it was him then, but suddenly the vice trade became a lot better organised. The men running it had more money. They were buying greater influence, gaining more protection from authority. The rackets started to grow bigger.'

'That's an understatement,' Kaufman interrupted. 'We found out later that Serracino organised some sort of conference in Cardiff in 'sixty-eight or 'sixty-nine. Not just Mafia either. Certainly the mobs from New York were represented, but other known criminals attended as well. An organisation called the Pipeline was set up there – and believe me, the Pipeline is some organisation.'

Richardson nodded. 'By the early seventies the Pipeline was operating illegal activities in various parts of the country. Mainly at ports – Portsmouth, Harwich, Southampton – suddenly the Pipeline was everywhere. Except we never recognised it – we just put it down to a general increase in criminal activity.'

Hewit cleared his throat and broke in with a sudden question. 'Mr Harris, have you ever heard the expression – "this thing of ours"?'

This thing of ours! I swung round to Lucia – remembering her startled face in the park. What the hell did it mean?

Hewit watched me closely, waiting for an answer. When I failed to provide one he said, 'Strictly translated it means "our thing". Strictly translated from the Italian that is. In that language the words are *cosa nostra.*'

Cosa Nostra! The Mafia! Is that what they thought? That I was connected with the Mafia, simply because of an expression I used?

'You've heard it then?' Llewellyn asked quickly.

'What does it mean, Sam?' Kaufman snapped.

'You know bloody well what it means. Why ask me? Am I being accused of—'

'We never knew what it meant until 'sixty-two. Valachi told us. Who told you, Sam?'

'I don't know – books – films—'

'Have you had any dealings with the Mafia, Sam?'

'For Christ's sake! What are you saying?'

'You've had contact with the Mafia.'

'You're out of your bloody mind!'

'Corrao was Mafia, Sam. Remember Corrao? The man who tried to buy Apex Holdings?'

'Corrao?' I puffed nervously on a cigarette, hiding behind a smokescreen. 'So what?' I struggled to sound normal. 'I mean, I never did business with him. I only met him once. You must know.'

'What do you think of the West End now?' Kaufman changed course unexpectedly.

'What do you mean – "what do I think of it"? Dammit, I've hardly had a chance to go back. I've only been out—'

'But you *have* been back. Looked up old friends – that sort of thing, you have been back haven't you, Sam?'

'I—' words dried up as I caught the knowing look on Henderson's face. Henderson had created that scene at Oliver's. He knew I had been back. And he knew how the West End had reacted. He knew – it was in his eyes. They all knew!

'A lot has changed, hasn't it, Sam,' Kaufman said. 'And I'll tell you why. Because the Pipeline has started to take over.'

I remembered Tony Fields – 'A lot's changed, Sam'. Why was I sweating? My mouth was as dry as a bone and I reached for a glass of water.

Kaufman said, 'It's big, Sam. This thing of theirs. And getting bigger.'

'So why tell me? You're the law. Or you say you are. Break it up. It's *not* my story, Kaufman. It's nothing to do with me—'

'You became involved when they tried to buy Apex.'

'I never became involved.'

Kaufman suddenly lost his temper. 'They know you. Corrao's orders were to take Apex without hurting you. *Without hurting you, Sam.* Why?'

'How the hell do I know? You've got it wrong. You're trying to implicate me in something I know nothing about—'

'The men running the Pipeline know you,' Kaufman insisted. 'We're certain.'

'You said that man Fiore – Fiore Serracino runs it. I never met—'

'I never said that. Serracino helped set it up, but he's not the top man – at most he's three or four in the chain—'

'Chain?'

'That's how they work. Especially at the lower levels. One man reports to another – the only contact is the man above and the man below him. That's the chain—'

'How do you know?'

'How in hell's name do you think we know?' Kaufman snarled. 'We've been trying to break the Pipeline for seven years now. Seven long years. And the nearest we ever got is the tenth man in the chain.

119

And we made him talk. He told us Corrao was part of the Pipeline. And he told us Corrao's orders as far as you were concerned.'

I was sweating badly now. Sweating and frightened. 'So ask Corrao – don't ask me.'

'Corrao was nine in the chain. He disappeared.'

'Well, what about number eleven?'

'Gone. They've all gone. It's part of the system. If we pick a man up the contacts on either side of him vanish within hours.'

I shook my head. 'I still don't understand. This has nothing to do with me. Nothing.'

'Why did they try to take Apex without hurting you?'

'I don't know!'

'The top man knows you. He's a friend of yours. He's been to Ashley Grange, gambled at The Derby, seen the show at The Point of View—'

'You're wrong! Wrong! I'm not involved and by Christ you'll not get me involved!'

Kaufman snapped back, 'We'll see about that. Take a look at this film, buddy boy.' He leapt from his chair and crossed to the windows. He shouted over his shoulder at me as he drew the drapes. 'Take a good look. Then say you're not involved.'

Before I could answer a disembodied voice came from the loudspeakers. 'Sam Harris? *Winner* Harris you mean? Yeah, I knew him. We did bird together in Brixton.'

I was still trying to place the voice when his image appeared on the screen. Out of focus to begin with, then it jerked until the definition improved. A middle-aged man sat in an armchair. The camera moved to a head and shoulders shot and I recognised him. I mean I knew his face – placing him, putting a name to him, was something else.

The man said, 'Hard bastard, Harris. Most of us stayed clear of him. He got special treatment in Brixton. Worked in the library, nothing manual, know what I mean? But a real hard case. One night the feller in the next cell to him got worked over – real bad, hospital job. Never found out who did it, but most of us reckoned it was Harris.'

The film changed to a thin-faced, foxy-looking man, balancing a cup and saucer in his lap as he fumbled through his pockets for a light for his cigarette. 'None of us knew Harris well,' he said. 'Not really *well* – kept himself apart too much for that. But those rumours about losing all his money were rubbish. I mean they had to be. Harris was looked after in the nick. Any trouble and the screws closed ranks round him like a private bloody army – and that costs money, take it from me. Harris ain't broke and he ain't alone neither. He had some sort of set-up working for him on the outside. He ran it from Brixton, passing messages through the screws like they were messenger boys. The West End's not my scene, mate, but I'll tell you this – Harris will be back, he ain't called Winner for nothing, is he?' The man smiled his thin crafty grin and put a light to his cigarette. 'Best bloke to talk to is Micky Blisset. He got closer to Harris than anyone.'

I watched in amazement. *None of it was true*. Memories of people met in prison flickered through my mind. I *had* worked in the library, but apart from that it was a pack of lies. But Micky Blisset rang a bell. I shared a cell with him once, for about eight weeks. Then he was there – up on the screen – larger than life and seeming to look right at me.

'People could never make head nor tail of Harris,' he said. 'Never knew which way to take him. Well, he was never your average villain, was he? In fact he once told me he never knocked that feller off – the one he got sent down for.' Blisset shrugged, as if sceptical about the whole thing. 'But Harris is still big time, and it's true about people working for him. And about the list of names. Buggered if I know who's on it or where it gets kept – but he's got it all right. I asked him about it once. "Insurance," he says, "anything happens to me and that list gets published. There're names on there to blow this thing of theirs right open." So I asked him outright if that's what he's going to do – spill the beans when he gets out? Know what he said? "Mickey," he said, "you don't understand business. That list is collateral. I don't want to bust these boys, I want to join them. That list is my way of buying my way back in".'

Then the screen darkened and went blank. Kaufman swished the drapes open and the sweet normality of daylight flooded back into the room. It all registered, but only just. I felt bewildered, like a backward child trying to grasp a difficult lesson.

'Still say you're not involved?' Kaufman sneered.

'It's a bloody pack of lies. Who were those men? Why were they saying those things?'

I looked round the table for an explanation. Llewellyn avoided my eye, just sat there puffing his old briar and filling the room with the scent of Dutch tobacco. And when I looked at Henderson he looked away. Richardson was examining something in a pocket-book. Hewit was looking out of the window. Lucia was staring at the floor next to me. Bonello was looking at the ceiling. Nobody would look at me.

Kaufman said softly, 'There are ten of those men, Sam. They all did time in Brixton. They started coming out three months ago. At staggered intervals. The last man was released a couple of weeks ago. They're all spreading the same story.'

'Spreading it? *That story?*' I gestured at the screen.

Kaufman nodded comfortably, 'To anyone who will listen.'

'But why? Jesus Christ, no wonder I'm treated as a leper. They've got to be stopped.'

Kaufman shook his head: 'We can't do that. You see – they are *our* men. Undercover agents. They are spreading that story on our say so.'

I could hardly believe my ears! None of it made sense.

Then Kaufman added, 'You've been set up, Sam. For the second time round.'

I gripped the arms of the chair, half rising to my feet, shock waves bursting like shells through a red mist blurring my vision. 'You bastards! BASTARDS! Who the hell are you anyway?'

'I told you. My name is Kaufman. We'll go into the details later.'

'We'll go into the details now!' I shouted. Then I realised what he had said. 'You've been set up, Sam. For the *second* time round.' My blurred eyes found Henderson across the room. 'You said you were Home Office. Is that true?'

He nodded. His lips were set in a grim line and most of the colour had drained from his face.

I sat down again, very slowly. 'So you're Home Office,' I said softly, still looking at Henderson. 'And you know I was innocent. You knew all along and you let them send me—'

'*Sam!*' Kaufman shouted. 'We didn't know. Not to begin with. But we do now. Grab hold of that, will you? It'll help you understand—'

'BASTARDS!' I buried my head in my hands, interlacing my fingers in an effort to stop trembling. They knew! Knew I was innocent. Suddenly I was shaking like a leaf, bewilderment, anxiety. I took a few deep breaths and shuddered as if someone had walked over my grave. Then I just felt drained – drained and empty, and as limp as a rag. Somebody touched my elbow and when I looked up Henderson was next to me with a glass in his hand. 'It's whisky,' he said. 'Ice and water are already in – just the way you like it. Drink up, you'll feel better.'

I slopped some of the drink down. Two of the others were serving coffee. Hewit was pouring from a percolator at a side table. Richardson carried cups around the table. Sugar and cream arrived. I shovelled in some sugar and pushed the cream away.

The hot coffee helped – even though my hand shook when I lifted a cup. They say hot drinks are good for shock. Kaufman was mad.

They were all mad. But the insane don't sit around country houses pretending to be Home Office and narcotics men – do they? *Do they?*

'You bastards,' I said softly. 'Why wasn't I released immediately? Why—'

'Why does an innocent man plead guilty?' Kaufman snapped back.

'I – we – there was no way of proving it. No way of clearing myself—'

'Yeah? That's what you say. Where I come from there's only one way a guy takes a rap like that. And proof doesn't come into it.'

I stared at him, only partly understanding.

'*Omerta*' Bonello said: 'The conspiracy of silence. We had to be sure—'

'You thought I was—'

'You bet we thought,' Kaufman growled. 'Especially as you pleaded guilty—'

'When you could have told the truth,' Bonello said.

I looked from face to face and wondered just how much they knew? How much of what had really happened on that night three years ago.

Kaufman shrugged. 'You had your reasons, we had ours. You are the best chance we've ever had. Our best hope of breaking the Pipeline is to nail the top man. And he knows you. Which means you know him—'

'You're wrong. Completely wrong. I would know someone—'

'Not for what he is,' Kaufman interrupted. 'He's too clever for that. Get it into your head, will you? This isn't some tin pot outfit. It's vast. As big as your top companies here – Shell, ICI, Unilever – bigger than them and growing twice as fast—'

'Rubbish! The casino business is big, but—'

'Crap, Sam! Wake up, will you? Forget restaurants and casinos – discos and clubs, they're a nothing. A front that's all. Good meeting places – channels to launder the Pipeline's money—'

'Then what the hell are we talking about?'

'Narcotics – and the whole ragbag of rackets that goes with it. You got any idea how big that is? Like fifty billion dollars a year in the States. Like as much again across Europe—'

'It's *not* my story,' I said stonily, retreating to my earlier position.

'Those men made it your story,' Kaufman pointed to the screen. 'Those men reckon you've got a list of names, Sam. Men in the Pipeline. Men in the—'

'But I haven't—'

'Yeah, well the Pipeline don't believe that – they've already taken the bait.'

I remembered the looks around town – the expressions. Fear? Hostility?

Kaufman kept at me. 'They misunderstood to begin with. Thought they could frighten you off. Bombing your car, sending you flight tickets. But you're staying, Sam – and we've sent them a message to prove it.'

He fumbled into a folder and produced three photographs, sliding the first one down the table to me. 'Tony Carmello. Ran the prostitution and drug trafficking for the Pipeline in South Wales. Until yesterday. Last night his body was fished out of the Cardiff docks.' He skimmed another photograph down the table. 'Larry Hopkins – the Pipeline's man in Liverpool until the early hours of yesterday morning – when he was killed by a hit and run car. Third – Benny James – worked Birmingham, until midday yesterday when he was found knifed to death in a back alley.'

Kaufman nodded grimly. 'That's the new message the organisation got this morning.'

'You mean – they'll think I was responsible—'

'Who else?'

'But—' I struggled to grasp the implications. 'You killed those men—'

'They were all killers. We had files an inch thick—'

'You killed them. Without benefit of trial or—'

'You had a trial, Sam! What fucking benefit was that? Will you stop crapping about it. Get your head together and listen. We're dealing with animals at that level. We're dealing with narcotics pouring into London like water through a sieve. This country can't build drug dependency clinics fast enough – you know that? A kid here gets hooked and he can't get treatment for three months. Three months for Chrissakes – he's a hardened addict by then, into prostitution, crime, anything – just to get the price of a fix.'

'A heroin addict reduces his life expectancy to five years,' Llewellyn said mildly.

'If he's lucky,' Richardson interrupted. 'Some of the stuff on the streets now has been cut with brick dust, detergent or even strychnine, for Christ's sake. You shoot that shit in your arm and you will die even more quickly.'

Henderson said, 'The Home Office daren't publish the true figures. Hard drug addiction is growing at the rate of at least twenty per cent *per annum*. And it's the same in Germany and most other European countries. Drug-related crime is rising in the West at an annual rate of ten per cent—'

'And I'll tell you something else,' Kaufman said, pointing a finger at me. 'This country is being used as a clearing house for heroin on its way to the States. And the man running it is a friend of yours.'

Llewellyn said, 'The Pipeline is by far the biggest and the most dangerous drug-smuggling operation ever encountered anywhere—'

'You ever had any experience of heroin?' Kaufman shot at me suddenly. I felt the blood rush to my face and I had a great deal of trouble in meeting his eye. 'Yeah, well,' he growled, 'we'll talk about that later. Meanwhile have a look at this morning's papers.' He slid copies of the *Telegraph* and the *Mirror* down the table and Richardson passed them on to me.

Gangland Killings was typeset in letters an inch high. Three men were pictured at the head of the story. I knew who they were without reading their names. The same mug shots were on the table next to them. But as I stared at the newsprint other pieces of the jigsaw fell into place. Henderson's act at Oliver's. The photographers! They had been Kaufman's men – they had to be. Yesterday the papers were full of me, now they were dealing with a gangland killing. The connection was obvious.

Kaufman read my mind. 'That's right – we're talking to the Pipeline on the front pages. Beats the shit out of the personal columns.'

He watched me carefully, then said, 'The top man knows you, Sam. Knows you've served your time, knows you're out – and he thinks you've got a list of names. So now what's he going to do?'

I remembered that film, the cellar, and shuddered.

Kaufman smiled. 'He ain't going to damage you – not until he's sure about the list. And while he's making up his mind, we'll move in.'

'You're mad. You've no right—'

'They've got to negotiate, Sam. They can't risk anything else – not before they talk to you about the list—'

'Which I don't have.'

'Neither do we. Not a complete list. But we've got bits and pieces. Cells of the organisation. We could wrap Southampton up tomorrow. But what's the point? They'd duplicate it within a couple of weeks and the new set-up would take months to penetrate.'

Llewellyn added, 'We could do the same in Hull and several other places. But they are merely distribution centres for narcotics. Raiding them would not cut the Pipeline—'

'They'll make contact, Sam,' Kaufman said confidently. 'All you got to do is insist on meeting the top man.'

'Just like that,' I said sarcastically.

'Sure, just like that. They'll pass you up the line. Shall I tell you why? Because you'll threaten them. Tell them that for every day they delay you'll blow one of their operations. Starting with Southampton. Anonymous tip-off to the police—'

'Every day? How long will this last for God's sake?'

He shrugged. 'Ten, twelve days – a couple of weeks maybe.'

'You're monitoring that many of their operations?'

Llewellyn nodded. 'But it's the Pipeline itself we're after. We know it starts in the Middle East and North Africa – we think it runs through Sicily—'

Kaufman interrupted. 'And we know a big shipment is planned for a couple of weeks' time.'

'And big is very big,' Henderson said, 'maybe as much as two hundred million pounds worth at street prices.'

'What we don't know,' Kaufman said, 'is how in God's name they land the stuff here and tranship some to the States.'

When I stopped grappling with the thought of two hundred million pounds worth of drugs something else occurred to me. 'Nor do you know the name of the top man.'

'Oh, but we do, Sam,' Kaufman smiled. 'That's just it. But knowing and nailing the bastard are two different things.'

I looked at the faces around the table. Grim, tense, expectant – hard, calculating eyes following my every reaction.

'So I'm to be used as bait?' I said in a harsh, strained voice. 'Staked out – like a tethered goat.'

'Yeah, well,' Kaufman growled, 'there's going to be a lot of white hunters waiting for the tiger.'

'And if I say no?' I said coldly.

Kaufman's eyes flashed with temper. 'What's the matter with you? Don't you want to know who framed you? Who ruined you?'

'That's not the point—'

'So what is the point?' he snapped. He leapt from his chair and strode down the room to where I was sitting. 'You want to see the point of all this? To see what we're really up against?' He reached for Lucia next to me, pulling her to her feet. 'Turn round,' he snapped, brushing her hair from her shoulders to get at the zip of her dress – then he tugged it down to her waist. 'See that! *Look at it!* You can only do so much with skin grafting. Like when there's no skin left you're fucked! That's what they did ten years ago. She'll carry that to her grave. And she's one of the lucky ones. Look at it – then maybe you'll see the point! Understand the animals we're dealing with.'

Lucia's back was corrugated! The sweet curve of her body was ridged from just below her neck to the gaping V of her dress above her buttocks. Puckered skin, ugly with discoloration – alternate stripes, some white as bone, others which looked red raw and calloused.

I growled, 'There was no need for that.' I pushed Kaufman to one side and gently drew the zip up Lucia's back. Her face was crimson as she turned away.

'Yeah? Well maybe I thought it was time you stopped being so damned pious.' Kaufman turned on his heel and went back to his chair. 'You say no any time you want, buddy boy. But let me tell you something. Ever since you left Brixton we've had a team of men covering you. Sixteen of them. Plus Lucia. We've watched over you like a baby. If you're with us that team stays put. If you're not—' he shrugged and sat down.

Nobody moved. They were all watching me. The chimes of a distant clock made me look at my watch. Eleven o'clock. Holy Christ, was that all? Had I only been in this room a few short hours? I sat down wearily and reached for my cigarettes.

'Like the book said, Sam,' Kaufman murmured softly. 'We had to make you an offer you couldn't refuse.'

CHAPTER FIVE

So much happened that day. Kaufman kept after me, hour after hour, using a carrot and stick technique which made my head spin. It was supposed to be an interchange of information, and it was for some of the time – but if I was suspected of shading the truth or evading an issue Kaufman erupted into a furious temper. Most of it was simulated, I felt sure of that, but knowing that was of little consolation. Arguing with Kaufman was a wearing business and on the odd occasion he was lost for words Bonello and the others were ready to pounce. They were obsessed by a sense of urgency – there was information they had to tell me and information I had to tell them – but all within the space of a few hours. It was essential for me to be in position tomorrow, back at Rex Place, waiting to hear from the Pipeline. At one point Llewellyn even admitted that I had been right about my 'dream'.

'Mr Harris,' he said gravely, 'when you arrived last night we administered certain drugs. A doctor was present and you were in no danger. We apologise for our action, but it was necessary because of time – time is of the utmost importance. You told us various

127

things while you were semi-conscious – some we knew, others we guessed at – but it is imperative that we know the whole of your story as quickly as possible.'

I swore at him. It was a mockery of an apology. He was only sorry because they had not found out what they had wanted to know – and I was beginning to have a shrewd idea of what that was. Not that I said anything – at least, not until later. But I found out a few things – principally about the scale of the operation – because at one stage Henderson said, 'Your release date was planned months ago. More than two hundred operatives are in position now – in London, New York, Milan—'

'And all because of your story, Sam,' Kaufman interrupted. He was transferring various items from a briefcase onto the table in front of him. Even from where I sat I recognised the Apex Minute Book, and I saw a file marked 'Transcript of Trial' with various other files which bore the crest of the Home Office.

'Your story,' Kaufman repeated with a smile. He waved a hand at the paperwork in front of him. 'I've got most of it here. I've read it a hundred times – discussed it with dozens of people – checked a million details – and you know something? One item still puzzles me.'

I shifted in the chair and said nothing.

'Or perhaps I should say one person puzzles me,' he said. He opened a large brown envelope and slid a glossy photograph onto the table. I was too far away to see what it was – but I sensed an immediate reaction from the others. They knew what it was, and were watching Kaufman to see what use he would make of it. 'Sam,' he said, 'we committed a burglary early this year. Oh, not us personally. None of the people in this room. But members of our staff. We burgled a private house in London. Cracked a safe and took some valuables, just to make it look good. What we were really looking for escaped us, but in the process we came across a photograph.'

He picked it up and held it at an angle so I couldn't see it. Then he walked slowly down the room and sat on the edge of the table near me. I expected him to hand me the photograph, but instead he placed it face down on the table and rested a hand on it, just in case I reached for it.

'But to go back to what puzzles me,' he smiled, 'in this story of yours. I've thought about it a lot. Imagined you – fighting to save your business – day after day and night after night. You never knew it but you were fighting the Pipeline, and you gave them a hell of a battle. But what puzzles me, Sam, is what your wife was doing while all this was going on?'

'Why?' I puffed on my cigarette and looked up at him, keeping my voice neutral and my face expressionless.

Kaufman's eyes narrowed. 'Your story, Sam – remember? That's why we're all here. She's part of it—'

'Not part of Apex – of what went wrong—' I waved a hand, 'of any of this.'

'Remember the deal, Sam,' Kaufman persisted. 'Your story. Don't dry on me now, baby.'

'Kay is not relevant—'

'Dammit! I'll decide that. Will you get that into your head? You can't hold back on anything.'

He was driving me down a path I wanted to avoid – and we both knew it. I scowled at him, biting my lip, holding onto my words in case he turned them against me.

'Don't give me that mule-eyed look,' he snapped, 'it cuts no ice with me. I'm not your defence counsel.'

'What's that supposed to mean?'

'As if you don't know. Like I spent a day grilling the bastard. Getting the inside story of how you instructed him. Trying to find out why in God's name you pleaded guilty.'

'You had no right—'

'Shove it! It's over and done with. I did it, that's all that matters. Want to know what he told me?' Kaufman lowered his angry face to within inches of mine, 'That you clammed up tight whenever his questions got within a mile of that precious wife of yours! Well, you clam up on me, buddy boy, and I'll break every bone in your body!'

Then he slammed the photograph face up on the table in front of me. It was a picture of Kay. Naked. On a bed. She was not alone, but I wasn't there. I closed my eyes. Oh God, would the nightmare never end? Never go away? The look on Kay's face. *That look*. Even before I opened my eyes I turned the photograph over, face down, hiding it.

'Where – where did you get that?' I asked in a curiously thick-sounding voice. But Kaufman walked away without answering.

Henderson leaned forward slightly. 'We'll tell you later. I promise – but meanwhile we must get the rest of your story. It's vitally important. In fact the man whose safe we took the photograph from is the man we suspect of running the Pipeline.'

'We know!' Kaufman shouted. 'We don't suspect. We know he's running the Pipeline.'

I hardly heard him. I was wondering who had seen the

photograph. Gloated over it. I imagined the snide comments, the dirty jokes, the sick remarks.

'Okay, Sam,' Kaufman sighed, 'you sent Corrao away with a flea in his ear. Then all the problems start. Fights break out in the clubs, food poisoning, things like that. We get the picture. But what happened then?'

They said I killed a man in 'seventy-six. It was a lie, of course, but I damn near killed Sam Harris. Apex was in a hell of a mess. I lived like a fireman for months on end – putting out one blaze before rushing off to another – quite literally once when someone put a match to Pamela's Place in Chelsea. We spent ten weeks renovating it, but it was never the same; when we re-opened the kids were frightened to go there, just as the punters were afraid of our betting shops. And the press gave me hell. I remember one photograph, taken when I was leaving The Point of View at two in the morning. I had rushed over there to hold an inquest on a brawl which had broken out for no apparent reason – and this photographer caught me as I was leaving. It was in the papers next day – 'Winner Harris' – with a big question mark after my name. And no wonder. My shoulders were slumped and my face bore that haunted expression I get when I'm tired. I looked deadbeat, like a fighter who won't make the bell.

Running Apex turned into a nightmare. So much happened, so many things at the same time. Key men had accidents or fell ill – or just resigned to take jobs elsewhere; and training their replacements took more time than I could spare. Every day brought a conflict of priorities, a new crisis, a fresh source of anxieties. And board meetings became a farce. Only Edgar Hardman gave me unqualified support, the others seemed to lose interest – as if I had got them into this, so it was up to me to get them out. We had a hell of a row about it one day. Lew Douglas did the smooth bit about his lack of interest being merely an expression of confidence in me, but Charlie Weston got a lot more pointed. 'You were happy enough to make the decisions before,' he said, 'it's too bloody late to complain now.' It brought home to me how much the take-over battle had unsettled things. Charlie wanted that deal, and I had blocked it. And Lew Douglas felt the same. He had latched onto Edgar's offer as second best, to cover himself – but from that day on he was always criticising and finding fault – so that board meetings turned into slanging matches without much chance of constructive work. I got on with it as best I could but it all added to my sense of isolation.

I hadn't seen Kay in weeks. By then I was working a sixteen hour day, often seven days a week. Constant emergencies kept me in town. Even when I grabbed a few hours' rest at Rex Place the telephone shrieked with a fresh crisis. But despite that – despite the worry and the strain and the long exhausting hours – I always thought we would win in the end. At least I did until my problems started with Kay – and then life came apart at the seams.

The troubles at Apex were about nine months old then, and all the time Kay and I continued to live our funny sort of lives – married but living more apart than together. That fifty mile stretch down the M4 looked as wide as the Atlantic at three in the morning – and on the few occasions I did get home Ashley Grange was too noisy for my liking. It was like trying to sleep at a carnival. Of course Kay never saw it that way. To her mind she was playing her part in the 'war effort'. Winner Harris was as solvent as the Bank of England to listen to her – and as long as Winner was all right Apex had to be. At least that's how she explained it to me – but then she was to explain a good many things over the next few weeks.

One night, one early morning, I did go home. It was a Friday and I was on my knees with tiredness. I 'phoned Kay during the day to let her know, but it was very late when I arrived, four in the morning I think, though it may have been later. She was asleep in bed and I undressed in darkness to avoid waking her, but she switched on the light as I rolled into bed. Her expression was warning enough – a truculent, petulant look which suggested that the row we had avoided on the telephone might break out now we were face to face. I tried to head it off with an apology for disturbing her.

She shook her head. 'You didn't. I was awake anyway. Maybe that's the trouble – you don't disturb me any more, you don't disturb me at all.'

'Knock it off, Kay, tell me tomorrow. Right now I'm ready for bed.'

'Ready for sleep, you mean. Bed used to mean something very different.'

'Tomorrow, eh? We'll talk about it.' I slid between the sheets and hoped that was the end of it.

'That bloody office,' she said softly, but I could hear the bitterness. 'Those damn clubs. They're all you think about—'

'It won't last forever—'

'Oh, come on! How much longer are you going to say that? It's all I've heard for months. Well, maybe forever means different things to us? Everything else does – so why not that?'

'That's crazy,' I turned over and drew her towards me, 'we'll soon be back to normal, you'll see.'

131

I held her close and kissed her. She resisted for a moment, but finally gave in. It was the best way of stopping an argument I knew. God knows I'd used it often enough. After that she lay there, stroking my face, watching me. I smiled and closed my eyes. Christ I was tired! Neither of us wanted a row – not really – that was the good thing about it – but there were things she wanted to say.

'Sam, is it worth it? Why not sell out now?'

Something gave me strength to answer. A spark of temper maybe. Not temper with her, but with the situation, with them, frustration with things in general. 'Because the bastards are pushing me, that's why. God dammit, why the hell should I? All the plans for Apex, the projections for next year, the things we could do in Europe—'

'We? Since when was I included?'

'You know what I mean. Look, we'll talk in the morning. I promise—'

'Are you going up to town?'

I took a deep breath. 'No, not tomorrow.'

'Not even tomorrow night?'

'No,' I agreed wearily, 'not even tomorrow night.'

'Promise?'

'Promise.'

She let me sleep. I would have slept the clock round had she not woken me. As it was she left me until noon before appearing with some breakfast. She put the tray on the bedside table and went to the windows to open the curtains. The strong light of a summer's day painted the room yellow. Holiday sounds floated up from the garden – the phut of tennis balls intermingled with an occasional shout – 'good shot' – 'your point' – that kind of thing. And I felt rested and strong again, for the first time in days.

I blinked in the sunlight and looked at Kay. Her face was freshly made-up and her expression showed none of the petulance of the night before. Instead her eyes flashed with a hint of the old devilment, and when she looked at me her smile was as sunny as the day. She wore a frothy lemon negligée which opened invitingly as she plumped my pillow. I put a hand to her breast.

She kissed my cheek. 'All the comforts of home, darling. I was beginning to think you'd forgotten.'

I tried to slip an arm round her waist but she ducked away. 'Eat your breakfast – I don't want your strength failing at a critical moment.'

She sat on the bed watching me, her legs tucked under her, one shoulder almost bare as the negligée slipped down slightly. I was hungry for food, hungry for her – God, suddenly I felt so much better! We talked as I ate, and I prayed that the 'phone would remain silent. That no crisis in the West End would demand my attention, that I could have twenty-four hours' peace and quiet – a chance to recharge my batteries and to mend my fences with Kay. Then my heart sank at the thought of a houseful of guests.

'Who's staying at the moment?'

'The usual crowd – nobody terribly amusing,' she shrugged, and the negligée slid another inch, revealing the plump curve of one breast to the nipple.

'So what's the programme?' I tried to sound enthusiastic, but amusing Kay's friends was a chore as far as I was concerned.

'Any programme they like. Mrs Jones will feed them, and there's all the booze they can drink in the drawing room. They've got the run of the house – let them amuse themselves for once.' She smiled at the empty tray, 'I'll get you some more if you like?'

'No, that was fine, but we ought to—'

'Winner, don't fuss,' she removed the tray to a table. 'I've already told them about your condition. They all understand—'

'My condition?'

She slipped free of the negligée and stood at the foot of the bed, flicking her hair loose, both hands rising to the nape of her neck, her breasts rounded, pink tipped, nipples hard and erect. Sunlight washed over her body, whitening tiny blonde hairs and adding a soft glow to her silhouette. The inside of one thigh turned dusty pink with shadow as she pulled back the bed covers, and when she moved the light dipped across the flat plane of her stomach, then lost itself in the golden curls of pubic hair.

'My condition?' I reminded her as we reached for each other.

She giggled. 'That you'd love to go down to see them – but with me impaled between your legs you'd have trouble walking.'

Neither of us walked far that day. We made love and talked, and talked and made love. Outside the sun moved across the sky and lengthened the shadows, but inside we lived in a rosy glow. The pity was I had no way of knowing that we would never spend so much time together again. Yet the clues were there, if I had listened. God knows we tried to reach each other. Each tried to explain priorities, needs, requirements for living. Each tried to convince the other without hurting. And when language failed our bodies took over.

She clung to me. 'Oh Christ, Sam, that's so good. Sam – do you know how long it's been?'

'Too long.'

'Four weeks for God's sake! I can't last that long. I really can't. You don't understand, darling, you really don't. It's like being a diabetic or something – I end up gasping for it – Sam, I need it—'

133

'I know ... I know—'

'Oh Sam, that feels so good. Oh God! Harder, Sam ... *harder* ...'

In between we rested and slept, laughed and talked. Her moods changed like quicksilver, so that one minute's laughter would dissolve into tears at the next. But there were other moments when we just talked about what was happening to us.

'Kay, I've got to sort this thing out at Apex. It won't take much longer. I'm beating it now—'

'Charlie Weston doesn't think so. He says it's beating you.'

'He talks a load of rubbish. Anyway, how do you know?'

'He was over here the other day. Said he was passing, so he called to take me out to lunch.'

'Kind of him,' I said drily.

She giggled. 'We all went. Brooksy and Marcelle – and Annie Crawford was down for the day so she came too. We went to The Fisherman and had quite a party.'

The Fisherman was an hotel on the river near Didcot. Lew Douglas owned it. It was a watering place for the smart set, weekends in the summer, longer if the weather was good.

'Quite a party,' I said bitterly, 'listening to Charlie shoot his mouth off.'

'Oh Sam, no,' she put both hands to my face and kissed me. 'Darling, it wasn't like that. Don't be angry – don't spoil today for us.'

'So what did Charlie say?'

'Nothing. At least not in front of the others. But when we were leaving he took me aside. Winner, he's worried about you. Truly he is. He says we should sell out now. We'll all get a good price and you wouldn't have to work so hard—'

'Damn Charlie Weston,' I went hot with temper. I felt betrayed, angry, hurt that they should talk behind my back.

'Winner – no! I said it wasn't like that. Of course I listened – but then I told him – you run Apex, not me. If that's good enough for the shareholders and the rest of the board, it ought to be good enough for him.'

She kissed me and traced patterns over my body with her fingertips. I relaxed, reassured of her loyalty and ashamed of my earlier doubts. Then she moved closer and her hands reached down for me. 'But it won't be long now, will it Sam? No more months like the last one? Or the one before and the one before that? Promise me Sam – promise.'

'Soon. I'll promise soon. Another few weeks – then things will get back to normal.'

'No, Sam, not a few weeks, please no.' Small-voiced, like a child, with a hint of tears again. Then her hands and body moved more urgently, as if the gift of physical pleasure would convince me, clinch the argument for her. And moments later her body was locked under mine, her back arching upwards, her nails raking my back. 'Oh Sam – that's good – so very good. Never stop, Sam – never stop winning.'

Even that was a clue – that business about never stop winning. Getting laid – getting laid by a 'winner' – summed up at least some of Kay's demands on life. An analyst might have explained it. Her need to belong to 'a winner'. Her need for the world to pay homage to her as 'Winner's Woman'. It made her extra special, forced people to acknowledge her uniqueness. Maybe it stemmed from growing up without a mother, worshipping a dominant father – basking in his success, enjoying the reflected glory – it was all there, had I realised it. But it took me two years in Brixton to work it out – and I had lost everything by then.

Needless to say, the troubles at Apex were not resolved within a few weeks – or even a few months. The battle seemed to rage forever. I fought desperately. I was facing ruin, and if the unthinkable happened – if Apex collapsed – Edgar might be ruined as well. That weighed with me as much as anything. He and I had become very close. Like soldiers in the trenches. He always supported me, whatever I did. I think I only ever had two real friends in the whole of my life – Jack was one of course, but the other was Edgar Hardman.

There came a stage when I would have sold out – just to cut our losses – but Corrao never appeared again, and no other party showed even the slightest interest in acquiring Apex Holdings. I put out a few feelers – had meetings with a couple of restaurant groups, testing the possibility of a merger – but the response was cold and discouraging. Too many people knew something odd was happening at Apex – and that was enough to frighten them off. And so the fight went on. I continued to work around the clock, grabbing sleep when I could at Rex Place, rarely getting home to Ashley Grange, and as the weeks passed so the rift grew between Kay and I. I think we both tried to avoid it. Our explosive rows were punctuated by some pretty torrid bouts of love-making, and we managed the occasional half-civilised conversation – but it became more and more obvious that we were drifting apart. As if we were being drawn down separate paths, not of our choosing perhaps but we seemed powerless to prevent it.

When Kay put on 'the party of the year' at Ashley Grange, the papers were full of it. And full of speculation about my absence. But

135

she and I had argued bitterly two days before, so I sulked in my tent at Rex Place and let her get on with it. Others took my place. Half London was there, or so it seemed – and it felt that way when I got the bill. And after the party she started to hit the town a bit. Perhaps the novelty of being a grand hostess had finally worn off, or perhaps Ashley Grange was becoming claustrophobic. But whatever the reason Kay began to accept invitations back – to this party – or that opening – so that within a short while she became one of the leading lights of the celebrity circuit.

Some of the 'celebrities' worried me. That French songwriter, Marcelle Faberge, was always hanging around, along with a couple of acolytes – Archie Brooks, a black American, and a Corsican called Pipo Martinez. Faberge, Brooks and Martinez. They had collaborated in writing a musical which was enough the rage then to make them instantly newsworthy wherever they went. And where they went, Kay went too. That's what threw me. It was always the four of them. No other woman ever accompanied them, there was never the slightest suggestion of couples – and Kay seemed equally fond of each of them, so I suppose I stopped worrying. I rationalised it. After all, Kay couldn't spend the whole of her life cooped up at Ashley Grange. She had to go out – and if she went out, she had to have an escort – and three escorts seemed safer than one. So I put up with it – but I never liked it.

One night they came to the casino on Park Lane. They had been to the opening of a new show, then on to a party afterwards, and they were all a bit high. I was at The Point of View when they arrived, but I was sent for an hour later – when the trouble started. Faberge was a gambler. We knew that. Not that he gambled at our clubs often, but we had our spies around the place and made it our business to know every gambler in town. Anyway, that night his luck was out. He lost a few hundred at baccarat and the other two fared little better – and when their cash ran out they asked to change a cheque – for five thousand pounds. Cashing cheques is a tricky matter for people in my business. Gambling debts are not recoverable at law. Giving credit is forbidden under the terms of the Gaming Act, and cashing cheques is frowned upon. But despite that we did both for people we trusted. Of course Paul Hammand – my man running the club – knew who they were, partly because of their reputations and partly because Kay was with them – so he cashed the cheque. After which they gambled like drunken sailors and lost the lot within an hour. Then they went back to Paul for more.

Paul had sent for me by then, but as I was still en route he had to make the decision. He was a good operator and his technique was invariably successful. 'Gentlemen,' he beamed, 'it's just not your night. Lady Luck is riding against you – why not leave it until tomorrow?'

'Are you refusing us?' Faberge asked bluntly.

'I know when to look after my friends,' Paul said smoothly, 'you'll wake up in the morning and thank me.'

'I'll thank you for more chips and less chat.'

Paul smiled at him, parrying the insult like a fighter riding a punch. 'I've just had an idea,' he said, 'why not come again tomorrow night? Be my guests for dinner – then your luck might change and—'

'We wanna play tonight,' Martinez whined like a sulky child, hopping from foot to foot at the prospect of a scene.

I learned afterwards that Kay had watched these goings on with amusement, but had taken no part – until that moment. 'Give them their chips, Paul,' she said quietly as she joined them. She stood barely as high as Paul's shoulder but there was no doubting her air of authority. When Kay asked, it was a command.

Paul lied smoothly. 'It's beyond my limit. Only Mr Harris can sanction—'

'That's not true, Paul,' she said coldly, 'anyway what goes for Winner goes for me too. These people came here with me. You're embarrassing me in front of my friends.'

'Not just them,' Paul murmured, glancing around the gaming salon. Various people had stopped playing and were drifting closer, sensing scandal. Paul made another despairing effort. 'Come and have a drink in the bar. Knock off for a while. Maybe the cards will run your way after a break.'

'We don't wanna break,' Martinez said querulously, 'we wanna gamble, man—'

Kay interrupted, 'Put the chips to my account,' she said crisply. 'I want ten thousand pounds worth immediately. Stop this silly nonsense, Paul, and let the boys get back to their game.'

Paul squirmed with embarrassment. No member of the staff was allowed to play, let alone take credit. No member of the staff, or the management, or even their families. Which included me – and certainly Kay. Paul took her elbow to steer her away towards the office – aware of the curious looks and the rising buzz of conversation. He tried to turn it into a joke by laughing loudly and using his free hand to slap Martinez on the back.

Kay tore herself away. 'Are you refusing *me* as well?'

'Please—' Paul began, but Faberge swung him round angrily. 'The lady asked for some chips,' he hissed into Paul's face. 'We came here to gamble, not to stand round gabbing all night. You do like she says or I'll start believing what I've heard about this place.'

Paul went white as a sheet. 'And just what *have* you heard about this place?' he asked softly. His face should have been warning enough. Casino managers are smooth as silk as a rule. Paul was bristling like a dog.

Faberge mimicked him in a high falsetto voice. '"And just what have you heard about this place?" Sam Harris is a crook. The tables are rigged. Apex is on the rocks . . .'

I had arrived by this time. It took a moment to get rid of my coat and to spot Kay amid the crowd of people gathering in the salon. I heard Faberge's shrill comments – I saw Paul bump into him – then Paul's shoulders hunched as the punch went in. Nobody saw the actual punch. All they saw was the look of concern on Paul's face as he held Faberge upright. Faberge went green at the gills and gasped for breath, then Paul got him pointed in the direction of the office.

Nobody saw the punch, but Kay guessed. 'Bastard,' she hissed at Paul. Then she arranged Faberge's arm across her shoulders and took some of the weight of his sagging body. 'Marcelle, are you all right? Darling—'

'He'll be fine in a minute, Kay. He needs a breath of fresh air, that's all. Don't crowd him too much.'

She jumped at the sound of my voice, and again as I touched her arm. Jumped, as if she was afraid of me. Brooks and Martinez were edging away, but by this time three of Paul's people were shepherding the entire party across to the office. One of them murmured 'heart attack' which added authenticity to the look of concern on Paul's face – and a moment later we were mercifully out of the salon and into the office.

Martinez realised what had happened because he thrust a finger under Paul's nose. 'Jesus! You *hit* him, man. Out there, in front of all those people—'

Paul dropped Faberge like a sack of potatoes and sank his fist so far into Martinez's midriff that it almost came out the other side. Martinez buckled as he clutched himself. Paul turned an enquiring glance at Brooks, but the negro pretended to be busy helping Faberge into a chair. I grabbed Kay's arm and hurried her into the next room, closing the door after us.

She was white and frightened. 'What's happening to my friends?'

I was blazing angry. 'Forget your bloody friends. What's happening to your husband?'

'You're asking me?' she demanded, pointing to herself, trembling like a leaf. Her voice shrilled, 'Why ask me? I don't have a *husband*. I have an empty bed. I have 'phone calls. I have spare suits in the closets. That's what *I* have – not a husband, a man, not someone who shares, who cares. He's in the papers more often than in my bed, so don't ask me. I just read about him, same as everyone else—'

'At least you know where I am. You know I'm working.'

'Working! I know you're at the clubs. And clubs have hostesses don't they? You did all right before. So don't hand me that lonely little Winner bit—'

'That's bloody ridiculous and you know it. You're being hysterical.'

'Hysterical! That's rich from you. If anyone's hysterical it's Sam Harris. Strutting round his kingdom like a little Caesar. Like Nero! Proving what for God's sake? That you can save it? Well you can't. It's going, collapsing, falling down, breaking up. Everyone knows it but you. And you'll sacrifice everything to prove them wrong, won't you? Your name, money, us, me—'

'That's unfair.'

'I'm sick of it, Sam!' she shrieked. 'Hear me. *Sick of it!* Sick of waiting, sick of worrying, sick of pretending that being Winner's wife is the best thing since—'

'For God's sake! Will you listen to me? Sit down a minute and—'

'I don't *want* to listen!' She was quivering, shaking with nerves, temper, fear. 'Why in God's name should I listen? You never listen to me—'

'Do you think I like the way things are? I've no choice. I've *got* to go on—'

'Until you drop! Have you looked at yourself lately? Seen how tired you look. Like a beaten old man. A whipped dog! You're down, Sam, but by Christ I won't be dragged down with you. I won't! Won't, won't . . .' she collapsed into a flood of tears. I tried to take her into my arms but she shook herself free. 'No! NO! It's no good. No fun any more. Dammit, it's not what I *want*! I won't be sacrificed on the altar of your bloody ego—'

Suddenly an explosion of sound next door rocked the place. The partition wall shivered as something smashed into it. There was a shout of pain, followed by the sound of a chair being knocked over.

Kay screamed. 'What are they *doing* in there? For God's sake – is this what you do? Beat people up when they come out for a little fun?'

'Fun? *That* was fun? Attacking my reputation—'

139

'Reputation? Oh you poor, blind, stupid bastard! Blind, deaf—'

Another shattering thump drowned the rest of her words. The noise from the other room was deafening. There was a hell of a crash. Kay set off for the door but I pulled her back. 'Kay, will you sit down! Stay here a minute. Give me a chance to see what the hell's happening in there – then we'll talk.'

'I don't want to talk. Can't you understand that—'

Suddenly the door opened and Paul poked his head round the corner. 'Boss, can you spare a minute?' He stopped at the sight of us struggling, resting his eyes on Kay's tear-stained face. Then he mumbled, 'I'm sorry, but—'

'For Christ's sake, Paul! Can't I have a minute's peace?'

He flushed and withdrew just as another terrible crash rocked the place. I cursed aloud and turned back to Kay. I was trembling as much as she was by now. 'We've got to talk—'

'There's nothing to talk about.' She was crying, her hands to her face, shaking her head. 'Nothing left any more. Me – you – I just can't take any more ...'

I've never known such emptiness. All the hours of worry – the late nights – the endless cigarettes – the strain – now this? But even as I made one last despairing attempt to reach her, the shouts next door rose to a new pitch. I was across to the door, and wrenching it open before I realised it.

The room was full of people. Martinez was backed up against the far wall, struggling helplessly in the clutches of two uniformed policemen. Faberge and Brooks were on a sofa, flanked by two other policemen. And Paul was arguing with Chief Inspector Davis. Two of Paul's assistants stood shoulder to shoulder with him but despite their efforts he was clearly getting the worst of it.

I shouted, 'What the bloody hell goes on here?'

The room went suddenly still. Martinez was in an armlock which forced him to his knees and kept him there. Paul stopped talking in mid-sentence. Brooks threw me a frightened look as a policeman next to him tightened his grip. And Chief Inspector Davis turned slowly to face me. 'Ah, Mr Harris.'

Martinez giggled. 'Mr *Winner* Harris.'

Paul ironed the creases in his face with the back of his hand. 'Martinez has been caught in possession, Boss. He claims he got the stuff here.'

Davis opened his hand to show me three badly made reefers. 'This club is a pick up point for drugs.'

I took a deep breath and looked at Martinez. One glance said he was lying. God in heaven, a blind man could see that! He was causing trouble, any way he could. I got a tight grip on my nerves and tried to steady my voice. 'One man's word, Inspector,' I threw a withering glance at Martinez, 'the word of a junky. You'll have to do better than that.'

Martinez sniggered, 'Pick up point's in the shit house, man. Third one along. Up in the cistern. Everyone knows that.'

I glanced at Paul who shook his head. We'd had that trick before – at Josephine's. Ever since then every public lavatory on our premises came with its own attendant – *and* our security boys inspected them every hour. If Paul said we were clean, I believed him.

'You've checked?' I asked Davis.

He shrugged. 'I've got the evidence here.' His fingers closed over the reefers and he tapped my chest with his closed fist. 'All I need to close this place down,' he gloated.

'Your evidence is against him,' I nodded at Martinez, 'not against the club.'

'We'll see about that,' Davis said grimly.

There was a knock on the door from the salon and another uniformed policeman came in. He looked at Davis and shook his head. I shuddered at the thought of the search going on outside. Well heeled gamblers hate the police watching them enjoy themselves. It would kill our business and be another nail in the Apex coffin.

It took half an hour to get rid of Davis and the boys in blue. They took Martinez away with them, and Faberge and Brooks left at the same time, muttering assurances about bail to Martinez while threatening action against the club, Apex Holdings and Winner Harris in particular. Paul poured me a stiff drink. I noticed his hand tremble slightly. The strain was getting to all of us, shredding our nerves to pieces. I swallowed the whisky, then went back to the other office, wondering how on earth to deal with Kay in her present mood. But she had left, by the other door. I was stunned. I know I wasn't thinking straight, but I had expected her to wait. Dammit, we needed to talk. We had to sort things out!

I went to Rex Place, telling Paul where to contact me in emergency, and to pass the word round the other clubs. But there was no sign of Kay at the cottage. I telephoned Ashley Grange and after five minutes Mrs Jones, our housekeeper, answered. No, Kay had not returned home. Nor had her guests (Faberge, Brooks and Martinez – all of whom were house guests at the time). I told Mrs Jones to ask Kay to call me the minute she got in – and after that I hit the bottle fairly hard until about five in the morning. I suppose I dozed off then – I must have done because the post startled me when it fell through the letter box two hours later. I 'phoned Mrs Jones again, but the answer was still the same. Kay had not been home all night.

I was worried sick until the papers arrived – then I read all about it. The more sensational of them ran the story on the front page. There was even a picture of Martinez leaving the club, flanked by policemen, with Davis in the background. And a photograph of Kay leaving the police station an hour later. It was a toss-up which was the bigger story – 'Martinez on drugs charge' or 'Winner's wife puts up bail'. The Winner's wife bit got the edge because two of the three papers led with that, and a gossip columnist dripped acid over an inside page.

APEX BOSS LOOKS A LOSER

Sam Harris – better known as Winner to intimates of the West End club scene – looked a loser all the way tonight. First there was trouble at The Park Lane Club when England's Hostess with the Mostess – Sam's own quotable wife Kay – arrived for a spot of late night gambling with her live-in pets, Faberge, Brooks & Martinez of Tin Pan Alley fame. Observers say that after dropping a bundle at the tables FB & M were on the point of leaving (one way or another, if you take our meaning) when their departure was interrupted by Scotland Yard's Drug Squad. Pipo Martinez, later charged at Wells Street with possession of the dreaded weed, spent the night in the cells – despite a sporting offer from Winner's Wife to stand bail.

Breakfast with Winner might have made an amusing meal this morning but Cool Cat Kay showed aristocratic disdain (Daddy is Lord Hardman, Chairman of Apex) by deciding to give it a miss. Instead she booked into the Connaught with – no prizes for guessing – Faberge and Brooks. All three are expected to show at Wells Street Court this morning when Pipo Martinez makes his unscheduled appearance. After that, who knows? Lunch at Winston's perhaps? With Winner?

I 'phoned the Connaught but there was no answer from her room. Not even half an hour later when I tried again. I was tempted to go round there but the thought of the newspapers dissuaded me – we had all the publicity we could handle for one day. So I washed and shaved, and got ready for work. I was at the office by eight thirty and on the 'phone to Lewis Collins an hour later. He sent one of his people to the court for me and 'phoned back afterwards to tell me about it.

He sounded disgusted. He always did when he spoke about people who incurred my displeasure. As if he really cared about my problems. It was why I trusted him I suppose. 'Martinez got a suspended sentence,' he growled, 'plus a Mickey Mouse fine and costs. That's all. If you ask me magistrates are far too lenient—'

'Was Kay there?'

'You bet! Kay was there – Fleet Street was there – and you couldn't move outside the court for TV cameras. I just hope to Christ she didn't say anything, that's all.'

So did I. It was the end of the morning by this time. For once I had no luncheon appointment and I was glad of it. I fidgeted through the paperwork on my desk, waiting in vain for Kay to call. When I 'phoned the Connaught they said she had booked out – and when I tried Ashley Grange there was no answer at all. That worried me until I realised it was Wednesday. Mrs Jones went to her sister's on a Wednesday. I tried to work out where Kay would go. Eventually I was too tired and worried to think straight so I decided to call it a day and go home. Home to Ashley Grange. Kay would have to return there some time, and I planned to be there when she did.

But first I spent an hour on the 'phone to the clubs, speaking to the managers; then I called Tom, my chauffeur, and asked him to collect me. We stopped at Rex Place first, but there was still no sign of Kay, so twenty minutes later we were on the motorway, heading for Oxford.

It was five past five when we arrived. Funny remembering that now, but I suppose those next few minutes will live with me until I die. I remember a great sense of relief at the sight of Kay's blue Jaguar by the front door, slung carelessly across the drive, as if she had parked in a hurry. Tom asked what time I wanted him in the morning. I said to 'phone me before leaving town, then I sent him on his way. I walked across the drive to the front doors. The Jaguar's engine was cold, I felt the bonnet as I walked past. Then I went up the steps and into the house.

The smell of pot was everywhere. Unmistakably. Enough of the stuff is around the club scene for me to be quite sure. The drawing room was drenched in it. I flung open the windows and looked round the room. Kay's mink was thrown across the back of a sofa and her shoes were kicked under a chair. I checked the other rooms: dining room, music room, Kay's private snug, the kitchen, even my study. They were all empty. Then I went upstairs.

I heard the sounds as I reached the half-landing. A long moan –

143

'Oh my God – my God!' A man's voice, Brooks I think. Then there was a sort of muffled groan.

I sprinted up the stairs two at a time. I think I called Kay's name but I'm not sure. I heard Faberge's rasping voice cry out, 'Baby, that's sensational!' Then I was through the doors and into the master bedroom.

A man should never see some sights. Shock etches the details into his brain for the rest of his life. Seeing Kay like that – on the bed with the three of them – *servicing the three of them* – was that kind of experience. I couldn't believe it. My mind rejected the picture of all those intertwined limbs. My ears tried to blot out the noises. Then the realisation drilled every tiny detail into sharp focus. Sounds crashed around in my brain. One of Kay's arms was turned towards me. Her small white hand obscenely around Brooks's black penis. But even as I turned my eyes away I saw the blue bruising on her inner arm. The kind of bruising which comes with a needle.

Emotion overrides judgement at such moments. Disgust. Anger. Pity. Self-pity? You react without knowing it. I was pulling bodies apart, then my hands closed round Faberge's throat, forcing his head back, trying to snap his neck. Martinez was screaming like a woman. Brooks rolled off the bed and onto the floor: then he was upright, one black arm encircling my head while his knee slammed hard into my back. But my fingers remained locked around that scrawny throat. I would not let go. For some reason Faberge was the worst, he was my most vicious enemy. The man I hated most! Brooks got both hands to my face, pink palms pressed over my nose, stifling air. I slipped his grip and smashed Faberge backwards against the headboard. His face was turning black, mottled and bruised, his eyes widening, pleading, pleading for his life. Then, suddenly, pain exploded behind my ears as something hard crashed down on my head. Another blow, a taste like iron in my mouth, a red mist, and then unconsciousness.

By the time I came round the local doctor had sewn nine stitches into my scalp. Mrs Jones stood at the foot of the bed, her hands busy screwing a handkerchief into a tight little ball. I got her outline first, then her face, and after that the colours and complicated floral design of her dress.

'Oh, thank heavens,' she said, 'I thought you was dead, sir. I got back at six. The front doors were wide open, things all over the place. I was that frightened I can't tell you.'

But she was about to try when the local doctor came in from the bathroom. We had met once, when I watched him play cricket for the village, but I had never consulted him professionally. He was a gentle giant of a man with soft hands and a booming voice.

I got the rest of the story while he checked me out for concussion, waving fingers in front of my eyes and looking into them with a little torch. Apparently the signs elsewhere were of burglary. Some of Kay's clothes were missing and a good deal of her jewellery – cupboards had been ransacked downstairs, some silver had gone, that sort of thing.

'Amateurs,' said the doctor, 'that's what the police think. There's a sergeant downstairs now, but you've no need to see him until the morning if you don't want to.'

I lay there thinking of Kay. Not of the scene I had witnessed earlier. I tried to blot that out of my mind. Tried and failed. So I superimposed others over it. I remembered how happy we were when first we married. Both so sure it would last forever. And now – now this? Christ, she had to be sick – sick to do – do what I had seen. With those – those animals. Why? What sort of gratification – what sort of kicks – what would drive her to something like that? My absences? My apparent indifference? Boredom? Drink? Drugs? Jesus, I had been blind. Those marks on her arm! Blind and stupid. Hadn't she called me that – last night at the club. 'You *blind* stupid bastard!' Injections. Heroin? That shit? Mainlining? Was that it? Most of her crowd were into the occasional joint, sniffing, cocaine – *but mainline heroin*?

I groaned and the doctor looked at me carefully. 'Head ache? I'm afraid it will for a while.' He smiled sympathetically, 'They must have been worried about you though. They put a pillow under your head after they busted you.'

Kay did that. I nearly said it. Kay put the pillow there. Dammit, there was still a spark – a spark of something left. Wasn't there? I smiled and thanked the doctor for his help. After that they let me doze for a while, until about an hour later when Mrs Jones came back with a bowl of hot soup.

'Lord Hardman is downstairs,' she said, 'he's asking to see you if you're up to it.' She sniffed with disapproval as she shook her head, 'I told him the morning would be better, but he's very insistent.'

I was up to it but I didn't want to see Edgar. He would ask questions about Kay, where she was, with whom, why and all the rest of it.

'I'll tell him the morning then shall I?' Mrs Jones nodded. 'That's the best. He said he'll stay overnight if need be, and—'

'No!' I snapped. Edgar staying in the house was the last thing I wanted.

It would be better to face him now. Make up some story. Get it over and done with, then send him on his way. I said, 'Dammit, Mrs Jones, I only had a bump on the head. I'll live, don't worry. You'd better send him up.'

I was too sharp with her. I cursed my clumsiness, and as she turned to go, I added, 'Oh, and Mrs Jones, you did very well – very well indeed. I really am most grateful.'

Her disapproval melted to blushing confusion and she went off to fetch Edgar. I looked around the room. It was fairly tidy. There were even clean sheets on the bed. I wondered who put them there? Kay, before she left? I hoped the smell of marijuana had cleared from the drawing room.

Edgar arrived in a mood of embarrassed agitation. 'Ought to be carrying a bunch of grapes,' he grumbled, 'but all the damn shops were closed.'

Typical of him to be surprised by something like that. When Edgar wanted something he expected Fortnum and Mason on hand to provide it. But he never arrived anywhere empty-handed and Mrs Jones followed him in carrying a bottle of champagne in an ice bucket.

'Doctor says you can have half a glass,' she sniffed her disapproval at Edgar's back, 'persuaded against his better judgement if you ask me.'

But neither of us did. When she left Edgar said, 'Doc says you'll be all right by the morning. Bit shaken up, eh?'

'I'm okay.'

His blue eyes searched my expression. 'Bad business though – one damn thing after another, eh?'

I sipped champagne and nodded.

'Burgled. Knocked on the head. Man should have a wife around at a time like this.' He looked at me carefully. 'The local CID asked where she was by the way. Dunno why, but I said the first thing that came to my head – said she was at my place in town. Damn silly of me really,' he shrugged, 'still said now, can't be mended.'

I wondered how much he knew? What did he expect me to say to something like that? I could think of no way of answering, so I sipped champagne and said nothing.

He stood up and crossed to the window. It was almost dark outside, the fag end of twilight. He peered out while he talked to me over his shoulder. 'Mind you, daresay the police read the papers, just like the rest of us.'

Edgar was fishing. I was determined not to bite, but clearly he was as worried as I was.

'Tried the Connaught,' he growled, still with his back turned to me, 'but she booked out this morning.'

'I know.'

He swung round with enough agitation to spill his drink. 'God in heaven, Sam, she's in some sort of trouble isn't she? What the devil's going on? You're here with stitches in your head. Papers are full of nonsense. One blasted thing after another. She ought to be here – now – looking after things.'

I couldn't think of a thing to say. Edgar worshipped his daughter. Of course he had spoiled her rotten, but a good many fathers do that to an only child. It's thoroughly bad for all concerned, but it's not criminal.

He positively grunted with embarrassment. 'I don't want to pry, Sam. Not my style, you know that. You and I – well, we've always got on. But between you and Kay. What I mean is – well something's gone wrong, hasn't it?'

'It's just the hours I work. The abnormal life I lead—'

'You lead! You weren't the one racing round town last night, making a fool of yourself. You weren't offering bail for some damn fool idiot who's causing trouble for all of us—'

'He was a friend. A guest here—'

'For God's sake, Sam! That's enough. Friends, guests – spongers and troublemakers more like it. What I want to know is where the devil is she?'

'I – she's out – she'll be back later—'

'Then I'll wait. It's high bloody time I had a word with my daughter—'

'There's no need—'

'There's every damn need! Should have done it years ago. It's time—'

'I'd rather you didn't. Wait I mean. Really. Best for me to—'

'You don't want me hanging around because you've no idea when she'll turn up!' He banged his empty glass down onto a table. 'You've no bloody idea where she is either. But I'll find out – by God I will! And I'll tan the backside off her when I get my hands on her. She's not too old for that you know—'

'For Christ's sake, Edgar—'

But he slammed the door shut as he went out. I could hear him stamping down the stairs. It was too late in the day for Edgar to play the heavy Victorian father bit, but he wasn't hanging around to hear it from me. I did a funny walk to the door and collapsed into a chair half way there. And by the time my legs worked Edgar's car was crunching ripples in the driveway. I swore aloud and went back to sit on the bed. That was all I needed – Edgar rushing round the West End brandishing a horsewhip.

I wrapped myself into a dressing gown and went downstairs. I'm not sure why I did. Just that I was too agitated to get back into bed I think. Besides it was that bed and I knew I would never sleep in it again.

Mrs Jones made me a pot of coffee and I sent her off to her flat at the other end of the house. I carried the coffee into the study and sat down. The study was my room – the only room in the house barred to visitors. I might have included my bedroom in that category before that night, but now that was enemy territory too. So I camped down in the study – with coffee and a bottle of scotch and a head full of worries. I collected a carton of two hundred cigarettes from the store cupboard and settled down to smoke them. It was going to be a long night, waiting for news of Kay – and wondering what the hell to do about her when I got it.

Kaufman came down the room to where I was sitting. He picked up the photograph from the table and turned it over. I saw Kay again, on that bed with Brooks and Faberge. My face burned and I was about to reach for the photograph when Kaufman stopped me. He slid it back into the large brown envelope and handed it to me. 'It's yours anyway, Sam. To destroy or do with what you want.'

It was such an unexpected gesture that it took me by surprise. But before I could say anything he returned to his chair at the other end of the room. 'Faberge was a pusher, Sam,' he said. 'We know that now. He got out of his depth with his gambling losses and had to make a quick buck. Then he got hooked himself.'

Llewellyn said, 'You haven't told us when this, er, this incident took place, but I imagine we can guess. Would I be right in saying that some hours later you were found in circumstances which eventually led to you being charged with murder?'

I nodded.

Lucia touched my arm. When I turned round she handed me one of those sachets they give you on airlines – the sort you wipe your face with when you are sweating.

'I know this is painful,' Hewit said, 'but we really are all on the same side you know.'

'Yeah?' I growled at him. 'Well you sit in this chair, Hewit, and we'll pump questions at you for a while.'

He smirked, 'I haven't a past worth talking about.'

'You won't have a future either unless you wipe that look off your face.'

Surprisingly Kaufman grinned and said, 'Attaboy, Sam, you tell him.'

Llewellyn cleared his throat. 'Of course, you realise where this is all leading don't you, Mr Harris?'

'I don't need a diagram if that's what you mean.'

'But this time we want the truth, the whole truth, and nothing but the truth.'

'Now where have I heard that before?'

'Okay, Sam,' Kaufman said soothingly. 'But remember this. The man running the Pipeline ruined you. Indirectly he ruined your wife too, because the stuff Faberge was hawking was Pipeline material. Directly or indirectly the Pipeline cripples a thousand lives a day. And the man running it is a friend of yours.'

'But you're not going to tell me his name?'

'Oh, Sam – but we are. That's why we're all here, remember? We tell you what we know, and you tell us what you know. Like, for example, all the things you forgot to tell the police.'

'I didn't forget anything.'

He smiled. 'Well now that's just peachy, isn't it? We've not got a thing to worry about in that case, have we?'

I drank some coffee and thought about it. Whether he knew it or not, Kaufman's remarks about the supply of drugs to Faberge touched just the right nerve. The clock can never be put back – but if ever I laid hands on the man who put heroin within reach of an animal like Faberge!

'You know him, Sam,' Kaufman persisted with sly emphasis, 'and we took that photograph from his safe.'

I knew then that I would tell them everything. But I still wanted reassurance about what I would get in return. 'You promise to give me his name?'

Kaufman raised his eyebrows. 'The name of the Ferryman? That's what they call him. We'll give you his name all right. We'll do better than that. We'll prove he is the Ferryman. And remember this – we set this whole deal up so that he has to come to you. And when he does . . .' Kaufman opened and closed his hand, 'we'll put him away for the rest of his life.'

Lucia cleared her throat, 'And Fiore Serracino with him.'

There was a long silence after that. I wiped my hands with the tissue – hating the thought of having to re-live old nightmares, not wanting to, but knowing I would – that I had to.

Kaufman settled back in his chair. 'Now where were we, Sam?' he asked softly. 'Ah yes – you're sitting in that study that night at Ashley Grange remember? You've had a crack on the head. You've sent the housekeeper back to her room – what happened then?'

I took a deep breath and then told them the rest of the story.

CHAPTER SIX

I sat in the study for hours. Or to be more accurate, I stayed in the study. Not all of the time was spent sitting down – I was on my feet as often as not, pacing up and down until I threatened to wear furrows in the carpet. My head throbbed from the crack it had taken and my nerves felt as raw as an open wound. I chain-smoked and drank a gallon of black coffee – and chased the coffee with a whisky or two.

I didn't know what to do. I've always gone my own way, made my own decisions and built my own life. Rightly or wrongly I've never felt the need for advice. But I felt the need then – especially when Edgar telephoned.

'She turned up yet?'

I almost said yes. I nearly said she was at home and in bed asleep. But Edgar in his present mood would have demanded to speak to her. And failing that he would have arrived – breathing fire and brimstone.

'No,' I said, 'not yet.'

'It's two o'clock! *Two o'clock!* Sam – where the devil is she?'

'Two isn't late. She's probably on her way home – trouble with living in the country is it takes hours—'

'Don't give me that. Something's happened. I don't know what but I know something has. We ought to call the police.'

'Edgar, nothing's happened. You're getting into a state for no—'

'She's not at the Connaught. I tried there just now.'

'For God's sake—'

'Listen, Sam – I may be an old fool, but I know my daughter. And I know you. I know when you're not telling the truth.'

'What's got into you? All this fuss—'

'Over a burglary? Nonsense. I don't believe that story for a minute. I hope the police do, that's all – for your sake. Otherwise there'll be hell to pay—'

'I don't know what you're talking about—'

'Come off it. Something happened there earlier but I'll lay money no burglar was involved. More like those precious house guests—'

'Rubbish—'

'Who ever heard of a burglar overlooking a mink coat? I was there – remember – when what's her name, that woman of yours, Mrs Jones – was tidying up. Kay's coat was in the drawing room of all places. A mink for heaven's sake! Easiest thing to dispose of—'

'Maybe they were interrupted—'

'They? A gang now is it? They all forgot the mink? And you never got a look at one of them?'

'Oh, for Christ's sake—'

'It got out of and hand you know it. Can't you see that? Whatever's been going on with this crowd Kay's fallen in with – came to some sort of head—'

'Edgar—'

'If you won't tell me, I'll have to tell you. Sam, I'm not blaming you. You're ambitious – always have been—'

'Blaming me!'

'Listen a minute. I know what you've been going through with Apex. Working every minute—'

'Well—'

'And don't think I'm not grateful – but you can't sacrifice everything for the business. Don't you see that? You had a good marriage once. The best. You and Kay – I used to think you were made for each other – dammit, I still do – but she's bored, been left alone too much, been neglected—'

'Now hang on a minute—'

'She's in with the wrong crowd. That's all, Sam. I don't know what happened earlier – don't want to know – I'm prepared to believe it was Kay's fault. But it's no good blaming her now.'

I very nearly told him what his daughter was doing earlier – but I shut my mouth in time. Besides he was talking twenty to the dozen – just getting the odd word in was difficult enough.

'It's my fault,' he said, 'should have spoken out before. Wish to God I had now – but I didn't want to seem an interfering old busy-body. Hoped the pair of you would sort it out between you—'

'Edgar—'

'But you're a fighter. By heavens you're that all right. I thought you'd take steps. Look – whatever Kay has done – you're still her husband. You're still my son-in-law and I've been damn proud of you, don't mind saying so. But this isn't you – letting people walk all over you—'

'For Christ's sake! I can't be everywhere at once—'

'Stop feeling sorry for yourself! That's not you either. I'm worried sick about my daughter and so should you be. She's still the girl you married – underneath, she still loves you – but she needs

151

our help right now, both of us, and Sam, these people she's with, they frighten me to death and I don't mind admitting it.'

It took me a long time to get rid of him. At least twenty minutes. He kept going on about Kay still being in love with me, and how he should have interfered months ago. I had been fairly strung up to begin with, but after dealing with Edgar my nerves were completely wrecked. He was so convinced that Kay was in danger – positively convinced – as if some parent's intuition gave him the right to be certain about such a thing. I might have dismissed it in anyone but Edgar, but I had known him have a hunch before – and he was always right. Just as he had shrewdly seen through the burglary.

So I sweated it out – driving myself sick with worry and fear. I even thought about calling the police. But the situation was already too complicated for that. What with the faked burglary and Edgar's lie about Kay's whereabouts – plus the possibility of the police finding them in possession of drugs ... then they would all be charged. Kay in court ... more headlines ... more trouble and even more heartache.

I got in a right bloody stew. Then, at three thirty, the telephone rang. I answered, half expecting it to be Edgar. But all I could hear was the sound of someone crying. It was an eerie, weird sound. Not just because of the late hour and the state I was in – but because of the quality of the sound itself. Not tears of grief, or fear or pain – but of utter hopelessness. It wasn't even clear who was crying. It might have been a child or a girl or a woman. The sound just went on and on. Nothing I said seemed able to stop it. Endless sobbing, moans of despair.

I kept shouting, 'Kay – Kay, is that you?' But there was no answer. Nothing intelligible anyway. Just this crying. A relentless, forlorn, deserted sound – interrupted now and then by a split second pause, as if whoever it was was struggling to regain control, then the attempt was abandoned and after a sort of shuddering noise the sobbing was more hopeless than ever. It was unrecognisable as Kay. She had cried before, when we had fights, but she always sounded like her. It had always been her voice, pauses taken in accordance with her speech patterns, her temper had never been far from the surface. But this? This whipped dog sound, this whimpering, this sound of such utter despair and total defeat?

My own nerves were shot to pieces. My hands were shaking badly – and, and I just put the 'phone down. I'm not sure if it was deliberate or accidental. Certainly I wasn't thinking straight. I reached for a fresh pack of cigarettes but my fingers couldn't even open the cellophane wrapping. I swore and hurled the pack to the floor. Then the 'phone rang again and when I answered – again, there was this terrible sound of crying.

'Kay? Kay? For Christ's sake! Is that you?'

'Don't ... don't hang up ... *please* don't ...'

It was Kay! Still sobbing, but making a desperate attempt to talk through her tears. It's hard to remember how I felt. I was so mixed up. Part of me was angry, but part of me was so relieved that I nearly cried with her.

'Kay, pull yourself together! Where the hell are you?'

'Oh, Sam – you're all right! Thank God ... you're all right ...' Her voice shook and tailed off, racked by sobs until the words became unintelligible whispers. She said my name over and over again – I recognised that much – but none of the rest made sense. Eventually my frustration overwhelmed every other emotion, and frustration made me angry. How could I help unless she told me where she was and what had happened?

I shouted, 'Kay – where are you for God's sake?'

'Don't ... don't shout ... don't hang up, Sam ... *please* ...'

'Okay, okay – I am *not* hanging up. But you've got to tell me ...'

'Just ... just talk ... talk to me, Sam ... please. Oh thank God you're all right. I thought ... I thought ...'

'Kay, will you listen to me? It's four in the morning. I've got a splitting headache. I've had nine stitches sewn in the back of my skull. The local police are buzzing round like blue-arsed flies – your father thinks I'm a useless husband – my wife's turned into some kind of sex freak – and you're glad I'm *all right*!'

'Just ... just don't hang up ... that's all ...'

I was gripping the telephone so hard that I damn near crushed it.

She said: 'Sam, you're *alive* ...'

Then the sobs subsided and she started to laugh – once started it seemed she would never stop. Hysterical, out of control, over the edge. It was even more horrible than before. I wanted to reach out, grab her shoulders, shake her, slap her face, put a hand over her mouth. I remember shouting at her, telling her to get a grip of herself, pull herself together, tell me where she was, what was happening. I felt so bloody impotent on the end of that 'phone! I think she tried to answer, but she was so incoherent that none of it made sense. One minute she was laughing hysterically, the next she was sobbing uncontrollably. I shouted – she screamed back – I shouted again, until eventually I was almost as hysterical as she was.

Finally I calmed down. I don't say I was normal – I was

trembling, bathed in sweat, my heart was pounding – but at least I stopped shouting. Maybe her tears got through to me. Some of the fog lifted from my brain. Nothing was solved by shouting. Blame, anger, outrage, jealousy – all were a waste of time. At least part of the responsibility for what had happened to our lives rested with me. Edgar was right. Kay was crying for help.

My free hand groped for a cigarette. I cursed as I knocked my glass of whisky all over the desk. I tried to recover the pack of cigarettes from the floor. I was as jumpy as hell but at least I calmed down enough to talk in a level voice – and bit by bit I began to get through to her.

'Kay, where are you?'

'Sam . . . I'm so frightened . . . and so ashamed . . . sick . . .'

I spoke slowly and carefully, trying hard not to raise my voice. 'Just tell me where you are—'

'God, I'm miserable, so miserable . . . I could kill myself . . . I will kill myself . . . now I know you're all right—'

'Kay – *where* are you?'

'I'm lost . . . I'm lost forever . . .'

It was crazy talk, but at least it was talk. She cried occasionally but with a sniffing sound, not the body-racking sobs of earlier. As if her emotions had burned out and left her exhausted. But her voice sounded unnatural – flat sometimes, and tinged with fear at others – but the fear aspect made no sense – not until later. I was concentrating too hard at that moment – trying to find out where she was, and what had happened.

Then the pips sounded on the line.

I panicked. 'Kay – quick – what's your number? I'll 'phone you back.'

'I . . . I don't know . . . it's so dark . . . I can't see . . .'

'Quick Kay, what's the number?'

'It's too dark . . .'

Then the line went dead.

Oh, sweet merciful Jesus Christ! I rattled the receiver, then slammed it down. What would she do? Suppose she had no more coins? What would she do then? Reverse the charges? Would she? Would an operator answer at this time of night? Please – come on Kay – please 'phone back.

I retrieved the pack of cigarettes from the floor – tore the cellophane open with my teeth – and tried to stop trembling. Then I stood the glass upright, splashed in some scotch, topped it up with water – and almost choked when the telephone rang.

'Kay?'

She was crying again, but the words came through in gulps. 'Sam,

I'm so frightened . . . everything got out of hand . . . they're insane . . . really insane.'

'Where – are – you?'

'I . . . I don't want to tell you . . . not after what happened . . . what I did . . . and . . . and then leaving you there, like—'

'Kay! *Where are you?*'

'Don't shout . . . please . . . don't shout . . . you promised not to shout.'

I bit my tongue.

Then she said, 'I'm at . . . at the boat-house. You know the 'phone box? Up the lane? I'm there. Oh Sam, it's so dark and . . . and—'

'What the hell? Why – why there for God's sake?'

'It's near where they wanted to go. Marcelle wanted to see someone—'

'Where are the others?'

'Brooksy went over to The Fisherman . . . he 'phoned someone when we got here. They said we were going to have a party . . . launch the boat . . . breakfast . . . breakfast on the river . . . except something's gone wrong . . . Brooksy went off threatening to kill someone . . . and Sam . . . I'm scared out of my mind! Marcelle is hopped up to the eyeballs and . . .'

'Get out of there, Kay,' I panicked again, and started to shout, 'Get out. D'you hear me?'

'I . . . I can't . . .'

'Can you drive? Are you okay to drive?'

'The car . . . it's round by the boat-house . . . Marcelle would see me. He'll stop me. Oh, Sam, he said he'll kill me if I run out now. Sam, I'm so afraid—'

I tried to visualise the 'phone box. It was up the lane from the boat-house. About fifty yards from the river. A deserted, country lane. Didcot was at least three miles away, five probably. Were any cottages nearby? A door she could knock at – a sanctuary? Think man – *think*!

'Calm down, Kay,' I said, 'calm down.' I repeated the words over and over again, while I tried to get my brain in gear. 'Can you see any houses from there?'

'No . . . it's too dark to see anything . . . trees . . . the lane . . . the boat-houses down by the river. Oh, Sam – what shall I do? Marcelle will miss me any minute and . . . and come looking for me—'

'Look – I can be there in twenty minutes – thirty at the most—'

'Oh God! They're calling me. I think I can see Marcelle searching around down by the river . . . Marcelle will kill me if—'

'Kay, listen to me. Get out of there. Get through the nearest hedge. Stay off the road – get across the fields. Understand? I'll be there as soon as I can – twenty minutes – fifteen—'

'Can't I stay here? Wait for—'

'They'll find you there. Get out of there. You said they made a call earlier – and Brooks may be coming back from The Fisherman – you'll run into him on the lane. Use the fields – Kay, I'm on my way—'

'Hurry, Sam – for God's sake hurry . . .' a muffled sob, then she said, 'Oh, Sam – I'm so sorry. Can things ever be the same again? Will you ever forgive me? You, me—'

'We'll sort it out – don't worry – just do as I say—'

Then the pips sounded again. I still lacked the number of the 'phone box! I heard her say, 'I love you, Winner . . . forgive me—'

Then the line went dead.

It took me three minutes to dress. Three minutes! Not that I dressed properly. Just pulled a pair of trousers over my pyjamas, grabbed a sweater and an old jacket, socks and shoes. God why did every pair of shoes have laces? Then I was back downstairs, heading for the kitchen, trying to think of what to take with me. A gun? I hadn't got a gun. Not even an old twelve bore for keeping the rabbits down. Put a kid from Battersea into the country and he's still a towny. No obvious weapon presented itself in the kitchen, and a moment later I was through the scullery and out of the back door, running across to the garage, holding the back of my head to stop it throbbing. Then my knees buckled with the shock of realisation. Just grappling with the thought was like being beaten over the head. I skidded to a halt, cursing my stupidity, propped myself up against the garage doors, gasping for breath, almost whimpering with worry and fear and frustration. Kay had taken the Jaguar. The Rolls was in London. How was I going to get to the boat-house? It was such a blinding revelation that I almost fell over.

The mini! We had an old mini! Kay used it sometimes for the odd bit of shopping in the village. But not for ages – unless Mrs Jones used it? I had never driven it. But where were the keys? Those for the Rolls and the Jaguar were on my key ring. But they were the only car keys I had. I switched on the light in the garage, and saw the mini in the corner, covered in dust, grimy, neglected and abandoned.

The key was in the ignition! The engine turned once – then coughed and died on me. I took a deep breath and counted to ten. My brain raced to find an alternative. Call the police – 'phone Edgar at Chelsea – Jack in Battersea? Could I hire a car? Borrow one? Steal one? I pumped the accelerator, took my foot away, checked that the gear stick was in neutral, tried the ignition again. A splutter – prolonged by my foot back on the accelerator and my hand on the choke. Don't flood it, for heaven's sake, don't flood it! The engine faded and died. Oh God! How long had I been? Count to ten again. Try the lights. They worked – the electrics were all right. But the needle on the petrol gauge barely moved. Try the ignition again. She started! Oh, blessed, sweet, beloved Jesus Christ! She started! But what about the petrol? She was almost empty – just a spot in the bottom of the tank by the look of the gauge. The garage in the village would be closed. Oh Jesus!

I switched off, ran out of the garage and across to the gardener's shed. Opened the doors and found what I was looking for – the sit-on lawnmower looked as big as the mini in the poor light. Petrol! *Petrol!* Where would the man keep it? Then I found a jerry can behind a breeze block partition at the back of the shed. Cap off, smell it – yes, it was petrol. A gallon? More perhaps – a gallon and a half – two gallons even? Kay was about fifteen miles away – not more than twenty. Twenty miles in a mini – on two gallons of petrol? Thank God it wasn't the Rolls. A funnel – find a funnel. How long had I been? Tools on the wall. A heavy spanner. A weapon? I staggered back to the garage – grazed my knuckles on the jerry can – threw the spanner onto the back seat of the mini. Filled up with petrol. Counted, switched on, waited, stabbed the accelerator – and, miracle of miracles, she started! I did a racing start down the drive, bouncing gravel as high as the windscreen lights blazing full beam, wipers going, heater blasting cold air into my face.

I lost my way twice! Would you bloody believe it? I lost my way! Country lanes look all alike in the pitch black of night. And the mini was so low on the road it was like driving on the seat of my pants. I skidded a couple of times but the roads were dry, so the tyre pressure must have been faulty. And all the time I kept asking myself – how long had I been?

That bloody boat! I had bought it the summer before. Hardly used the damn thing! But Lew Douglas owned one and after spending a convivial day on his Kay said what fun it would be to have one of our own. 'Darling, it seems such a waste not to make more use of the river – and we could have such parties in the summer.' Even then nothing would have come of it if Douglas hadn't poked his nose in. He 'phoned me a week later – he had this friend of his who was going abroad. 'Got a smashing boat, old boy. And a boat-house, just down river from The Fisherman.' So Kay went over and Douglas spent a whole day taking her out in the damn thing – and I heard all about it that night. 'Darling, it's an investment. Lew says they appreciate like mad. So we could have a lot of fun without it costing a penny.'

I had been out in it twice since we'd had it. Twice, that's all. It was all right, I suppose. If you could stand those boating types – all dressed up in white flannels and yachting caps – slinging nautical terms about as if they'd been round the Horn with Chichester. Floating gin palaces, that's all they were.

Oh God – how long had I been? I promised Kay twenty minutes. I must have been longer than that already. Half an hour at least. At least! And I still wasn't there. Was it left or right at Didcot? It must be right. And they had put one-way streets in since I was last here! One-way streets in a one horse place like Didcot. Bloody madness! Through the town and out again. Not far now. There was the road sign. Take the little lane on the left. About five miles to the river. All twists and turns. Not a house in sight because sometimes the river bursts its banks in winter and floods the fields for miles around.

I clipped a grass verge with the back wheels and zig-zagged across the road. The mini righted itself. A wind whipped low clouds across the sky, scudding the face of the moon. I was too low to see above the hedgerows. Not that it was light enough to see much – but it was lighter than when I started. Or had my eyes become adjusted to the darkness? Christ, how long had I been?

Another mile. The lane straightened. Go faster. No! Slow down. Kay might be in the fields near here. The 'phone box would be soon – round the next bend perhaps? Steady – slow down – Jesus, there's *something* in the road! In the middle of the road! Eyes – looking at me – a bump as the wheels went over a rabbit. Oh God – Kay, where are you?

Around the curve at the bottom of the straight. Nothing – no 'phone box. Damn and blast – the 'phone box should be here! I could see the boat-houses – black blobs on the blacker skyline, above the hedges, next to the dark trees. Another bend. The 'phone box! There – on the left. Dark, no light inside. But Kay had told me that – too dark to see the number. Slow down – slower – stop. The box was empty. Get out of the car, look inside, stupid waste of time – back into the car – hurry! Go to the boat-houses. Hit the horn in case Kay can hear. Make a noise. Attract attention. Attention? From whom? In this dark and deserted place. It looked like the end of the world.

Three boat-houses. Mine was the middle one. Big, barn-like buildings, made of creosoted clapperboards, lapped one over the other. A scruffy track led up to the 'back doors' – the front ones opened onto the river itself.

I stopped the mini. Switched off, sat listening. Nothing – not a bloody thing. Except the sounds of the night. I got out – shivered in the cold. A door creaked on rusty hinges. The night was as black as pitch. There was the sound of the river running a few yards away. Nothing more – no sign of the Jaguar. No sign of anything.

'Kay,' I shouted.

Wind hurled my voice back into my face. A bird screeched and crashed its wings against the upper branches of a tree. It started to rain. The river sounded faster running than I had ever known it. The night shifted and rustled all round me.

'Kay,' I shouted again, at the top of my voice.

A door creaked, then banged violently shut. I jumped. Hairs bristled on the back of my neck. I turned back to the car and collected the heavy spanner from the back seat. Then I walked slowly towards the boat-house.

I was a yard away when the door moved. Further away than that and I wouldn't have seen it. But the door slowly opened outwards, an inch at a time – as if someone had heard my shouts and was coming to investigate. I hefted the spanner into my right hand, and reached for the door with my left. Then – suddenly – it slammed back with a crack loud enough to rouse the dead!

I shall never forget standing outside that boat-house. The wind whistling and rattling through the clapperboards – the rain beating down in gusts. I cursed my stupidity for not bringing a torch. I wondered about going back to the mini – I could reposition it – switch the headlights full on – they might be of some help. But I was making excuses. I was afraid. Afraid to open that door – afraid of what, who, might be hiding in there – afraid of what I might find. Then I took a deep breath and gritted my teeth – reached for the latch – and pulled the door towards me.

The force of the wind bowled me over. I was lifted off my feet. Like being in a wind tunnel. It was a wind tunnel. The river doors were wide open. Wind hurled through the gap behind me and sent me sprawling in the dirt. The door cracked shut and I was in almost total darkness. I looked up, caught the glitter of black water a yard ahead, and saw the grey light at the other end of the boat-house. Then I heard the laughter. High-pitched like a woman's, but not a woman's. Hysterical, maniacal, screams of laughter.

'Shit man! See who just came in? The Winner Man himself. What d'you want, Winner Man? Nutting here belongs to you.'

It was Martinez. I would have recognised that whining sing-song voice anywhere. But I was damned if I could see him. The light was too poor. I had dropped the spanner when I fell over, so I rolled over on my hands and knees in search of it. Martinez whooped with

159

laughter. He sounded so close I expected to feel his hands at my throat at any moment. The wind howled, the door creaked and rattled behind me. Then my hand found the spanner and closed around it. I was gasping for breath, winded by the fall, but somehow I raised myself into a half crouch and edged backwards towards the door. Wherever Martinez was, he could not be behind me. If I could only shut that sodding door – at least I would feel secure from that direction. I edged slowly along the wall and fumbled for the latch with my free hand.

'Go home, Winner Man,' Martinez taunted, 'ain't nothing for you here.'

My hand was on the latch. I held the door against the wind – and the latch dropped home. Then there was a tremendous explosion of noise! The sudden blast of sound hit me with physical force. A deep, booming roar – so loud that I dropped the spanner and clapped my hands to my ears to save my eardrums. I rolled over and over on the ground, trying to avoid the sound – as if it were a weapon of some kind. Only when it stopped did I realise what it was. The fog horn on the boat. Magnified by the confined space, sound waves bouncing off the water and the walls and roof of the boat-house. Even when I took my hands away my ears were still buzzing. And when they stopped I could hear the shriek of the wind again, and the howl of Martinez's laughter.

'What's the matter, Winner Man? Lost your tongue?'

My foot knocked against the spanner. I stooped to retrieve it. Martinez must be on the boat? There is not much room in a boat-house. Certainly not much in mine. An oblong, about thirty feet by sixty, with doors at each of the narrow ends. I was standing on the jetty, which was about eight feet wide and which extended down one side in the shape of an L. The rest was water – except for the boat, which was tied up lengthways, the prow facing me less than twelve feet away. Not that I could *see* twelve feet. I moved away from the door, sliding crabwise into the corner of the L. Slowly my eyes adjusted to the darkness. The grey light coming off the river helped. I could just make out the shape of the boat rising above the jetty. I even identified the cockpit. If I could edge down the side of the jetty I might even be able to see into the cockpit.

'Stop fooling around, Winner Man. Go home, before you get hurt.'

I wondered if he could see me? Surely not. The wall was behind me, whereas the light of the river was behind him – what light there was. I had the advantage. Even so I hesitated. I wiped the sweaty palm of my left hand against my trousers and transferred my grip on the spanner. Every step I took down the long wall took me further into the misty light coming off the river. I halted – trying to think of a way to distract him – to make him think I was still at the door. Then I retreated, moving as quietly as possible. Not that noise was a problem. The wind howled incessantly, shaking every loose board in the building, rattling and clanking the lifting chains hanging from the roof – the river hissed and gurgled past the open doors at the far end – and Martinez jeered and catcalled without let up.

I reached the door and shouted, 'I've come for my wife, Martinez. Send her out and—'

'You ain't got no wife, Winner Man. What you had was a share in the best piece of tail in town.'

Suddenly Kay's screams rose above everything – above Martinez's sneers, above the wind and the clinking chains and the slapping, rushing water – and above the sound of my running feet as I dashed back to the corner and started down the long side. Then my foot caught a coiled rope and I stretched my length in the dust alongside the boat. I saw Kay struggling in the cockpit, fighting Faberge, clawing at his face and kicking his shins. Then I was on one knee, shouting to her, stretching out my left arm, trying to reach her, my right hand never letting go of the spanner for a moment.

Faberge turned at the sound of my shout. It was enough for Kay to scramble free.

'Jump, Kay – for God's sake *jump*!'

She threw herself across the gap between the boat and the jetty, landing a yard from me, her knees buckling awkwardly as she fell. But I was up by then, swinging the spanner in a wide arc, shouting, roaring, screaming – completely out of control. Fear perhaps, the shocks of the night, hatred of Faberge – wanting revenge, wanting blood, wanting to kill him. The heavy steel spanner cracked against bone and he screamed with pain – then my free hand found Kay's arm and I was dragging her back to the corner.

Then that blasted searchlight came on. The one on the boat. It blinded me for a moment. I stopped dead in my tracks, throwing Kay off balance, so that we both sprawled into a heap in the corner. Martinez whooped with triumph. His shadow fell between us and the lamp as he scuttled forward on the boat. I did the only thing I could think of. I threw the wrench at the searchlight. It must have hit the side because the lamp spun giddily as it smashed. We were in darkness again, but something registered as the light went out. Martinez springing forward, clearing the prow of the boat and landing on the jetty. He had reached the door ahead of us. We were cut off – and I had lost our only weapon.

I backed Kay into the corner, pushing her behind me – expecting an attack from two directions at once. She was trembling violently. I doubt I was much better. Falling over had opened the cut on my head. The neck of my sweater was sticky with blood. My strength was beginning to fail.

'Where's Brooks?' I panted.

'Not back . . . he went to The Fisherman—'

Martinez shouted, 'Hey – Marcelle. We got 'em trapped, man. In the corner. They ain't going nowhere.'

Faberge shouted some kind of reply. I saw his silhouette in the cockpit. He was hugging his right shoulder with his left hand, twisting his body like a hunchback. I knew what he was going to do as soon as I saw him. I knew I had to act fast, before he recovered. I cupped my hand to Kay's ear, pitching my voice against the wind, but not wanting it to carry to Martinez.

'The mini's outside – key in the ignition – take it and go—'

'No, Sam . . . *NO!*'

I smacked her face hard. Every split second counted. Martinez would rush me any moment. Already Faberge was hunting for a boat-hook in the stern of the boat. I grabbed Kay's hand and started to run, pulling her along behind me. 'Go, Kay – *GO!*'

I was at the door before Martinez launched himself at me. His knee thumped upwards into my groin, but he was at the wrong angle to get any force behind it. Not that he had any real chance anyway. I was fighting like a mad man – screaming and shouting – kicking wildly, lashing out with both fists – forcing him backwards, making him scream to Faberge for help. And by the time Faberge arrived with that boat-hook Martinez and I were rolling over and over in the dirt, a foot or so from the water's edge. The wind shrieked louder than ever – the door was open – and when I looked up Kay had gone.

It's all a bit hazy after that. It really is. I'm not trying to cover up – there's no point anyway. I know Martinez fell into the water. I may have shoved him. I probably did – my strength was failing by the second and I knew I couldn't last much longer. The little bastard pulled a knife on me – a switchblade. I kicked his knife arm as he came in low. He fell backwards and I kicked again. There was a hell of a splash but Faberge was beating me to pulp with that boat-hook by then. I was covered with blood and could hardly see straight. I found a length of rope from somewhere and was lashing out with that, trying to keep him at bay, but I was fighting a losing battle. And I passed out not long after that.

There was a very long silence when I finished. They were thinking over what I had told them. It was impossible to judge whether they believed me. Not so much as a flicker of an eyelid betrayed their emotions. Llewellyn sucked an empty pipe and turned the pages of a file. Kaufman sat staring at me, with his chin cupped in his hands. Bonello scratched his head and watched smoke drift upwards from his cigarette. They were the principal characters. I could see that now. Hewit and Richardson were merely assistants of some kind, and Henderson was probably somewhere in between.

Finally Llewellyn cleared his throat and said, 'The police arrived at the boat-house at twelve minutes past six that morning. You were unconscious. Martinez had drowned. And Faberge was dead, with a knife in his back.'

I nodded. There was nothing to add.

Kaufman slid his cigarettes down the table to me. He half smiled. 'Forget what you said in court, Sam – but just for the record – you never killed Faberge, did you?'

I had already told them so much more than had come out at the trial. I was beyond the point of no return. It was inconceivable to go back now – I had to go on. 'No,' I said quietly, 'I didn't kill Faberge.'

Kaufman almost sighed with relief. He smiled and said: 'And also just for the record – everyone in this room believes you.'

Various heads nodded, but Kaufman was already turning a page in his file. Without looking up he said, 'And the police autopsy says Martinez struck his head when he fell in the water. Drowned while concussed was their verdict. You go along with that?'

I shrugged. 'I know he fell into the water.'

Kaufman nodded. 'So with him gone that only left Faberge and you. At least so far as the police knew.'

'What's that supposed to mean?'

He smiled. 'Well, they never knew about the lovely Lady Kay, did they?'

'I told you – she left before I passed out.'

'Sure, Sam – but you did pass out. She could have come back.'

'No! She was terrified. Frightened out of her skull. Nothing would have—'

'Did you hear the automobile start up? Did you hear it drive away?'

'Don't be a complete fool – I couldn't hear anything above that wind. I was fighting two men, so much was happening—'

'Exactly,' he said quickly.

'Come off it, Kaufman – you know what happened to Kay.'

'I know she wrapped her automobile round a tree outside Didcot. I know she was concussed for three whole days. I know she lied her

163

head off to the police when she came round.' He paused, watching me carefully. 'What I don't know is whether she returned to the boat-house—'

'Well I'm telling you—'

'But you don't know. You can't know. Not for sure.'

'Yeah? What about the knife, Kaufman? How – where – would she have got a knife?'

'You said Martinez had one.'

'And you know what happened to it. You've read the files. The police found Martinez's knife in the water.'

'Perhaps Faberge had a knife?'

'He would have used it on me. Besides—' I stopped, caught by the sudden memory and wondering how to explain it. Wondering if I could explain it.

'Besides?' Kaufman repeated softly. 'Besides what, Sam?'

'Well, there was something else. At least I think there was . . .' I struggled with my memories. I was only half convinced. Even now I wondered if I had imagined it. Sometimes I thought it was an invention of my subconscious – convenient alibi for Kay. But I hadn't killed Faberge and if Kay hadn't – and I never thought she had – someone else had wielded that knife.

'Something else?' Kaufman persisted softly.

I took a deep breath and tried to explain. 'After Martinez went into the water, when I was fighting Faberge – well, I thought I saw something. I was backed up against the wall, trying to avoid his lunges with the boat-hook – lashing out with the rope and trying to keep him off – when I saw something behind him – at the other end of the boat-house.'

Every eye in the room was watching me. I could feel their scepticism. Their suspicion made me wish I hadn't started – but I had, so there was no alternative but to finish.

'There was a skiff,' I said. 'Very low in the water. Three men in it. The prow of the skiff nosed into the boat-house just as Faberge lunged with the boat-hook. I dodged and ducked away, and it was a moment or two before I had a chance to look again. One man was holding the skiff steady against the doors – and the man behind him stood up in the boat – he looked as if he were throwing something, or about to throw something. One hand was curled backwards over his shoulder. Then Faberge caught me across the face with that boat-hook and – and, well I don't remember much after that.'

Hewit inspected his fingernails. 'You say you thought you saw this – these men, this skiff?'

'That's right, Hewit, I thought I saw it. I was preoccupied at the time. Half blinded by blood leaking out of my head, fighting

Faberge for my life. Whatever I saw was for a split second – that's all – a split second in a bad light.'

Llewellyn murmured, 'I assume the light was too bad for you to give a positive description of these men?'

I looked at him sharply, sensing more of Hewit's sarcasm. But Llewellyn looked quite sincere. I said, 'The light was behind them – what light there was. All I saw were their silhouettes – black solids against the grey and white of the water. But the man standing up in the boat was a big man I think – bigger than the man holding the door. And . . .'

I can see him now. The man standing up. I'll always be able to see him. Just his shape, his outline. His left leg forward and his body half turned towards me. His right arm was bent, the hand half hidden behind his head – and his left arm was stretched out in front of him – to balance himself. Light glinted on something in his hand. His left hand, not his throwing hand. That's what caught my eye I think. That sudden glitter of light down by the river doors. That's all I remember, but it's a very sharp image – like a message flashed on a cinema screen in the middle of a film.

Kaufman rubbed his chin when I finished. 'Okay, Sam, we'll file it away for now. Unless you want to add anything?'

I shook my head miserably. They didn't believe me, I could see it in their eyes.

'And the man Brooks?' Kaufman asked. 'You never saw him?'

'No. But we all know what happened to Brooks, don't we?'

'We know what happened to him later,' Kaufman corrected. 'Not what happened to him that night.'

I nodded. There was nothing I could add. I had told them all I knew.

Kaufman bent his head over his papers, 'So let's go on from there, Sam. Six in the morning and that boat-house is swarming with cops. You're out cold and Faberge and Martinez are dead. Then what happened?'

I sighed. I had a very strong feeling that Kaufman knew what happened then. That he knew almost as much as I did. But another strong feeling said he would keep probing until there was no almost about it.

It's hard to explain what it's like to be arrested for murder. You have to live through it before you can understand. Like going to prison. You see pictures of prisons – all that institutionalised cleanliness, men swabbing the floors, washing down paintwork – and you would never think of the smell. But it hits you the moment you go in –

the smell of grease and dirt, and the all prevailing odour of degradation.

I was in hospital when they arrested me. I didn't know it but Kay was downstairs in the Special Care Unit. I awoke in a tiny white-washed room to find a policeman watching me through a glass-panelled door. It must have registered – but never enough to alarm me because I went straight back to sleep. My head throbbed and I was desperately tired, too exhausted to think. They let me sleep the clock round – and when I awoke the second time, they arrested me. I was taken to a tiny police station in the sticks somewhere, and charged with the murder of Marcelle Faberge. Too stunned to say much, I felt like death warmed up and must have looked it, dressed in the old sweater and clothes I had worn when they found me, torn and dirty and encrusted with blood. Then I collapsed.

I was in another hospital when I came round, this time in prison. A man sat watching me from the next bed. He grinned when I opened my eyes. 'It's all right, mate, there's only me 'ere.' He hopped across and sat on my bed. 'Dunno 'oo you are, but you've got 'em worried stiff. They bin in an' out of 'ere like a bull at a cow. Tryin' to get a statement.'

I learned a lot from that man. I never knew his name. We were only together for about twenty minutes. I must have told him a few things, I really don't remember but I remember his advice, 'Just say not guilty, mate. That's all you gotta say – not guilty. Don't let 'em verbal you – that's what they'll do – put words in your mouth an' read 'em out in court.' He drew a finger across his throat, 'All up then, ain't it? So don't forget – not a bloody word – 'cept not guilty. Got it?'

I nodded painfully and when the police came in a few minutes later that was all they got – 'not guilty' – until I was blue in the face. After that they went away and let me finish my sleep.

The following morning I was taken to Didcot Magistrates Court and remanded in custody. Lewis Collins was buzzing around by then. He made application for bail, but the police were protesting about that before Lewis even sat down. So bail was refused. Then Collins was on his feet again. This time explaining about Kay being in hospital and asking that I be given permission to visit her – under escort if necessary. But the police opposed that as well – so the magistrates handed down another refusal.

I was taken to Aylesbury Prison then. Collins arrived about two hours later and we were given privacy and a chance to discuss the charge levelled against me. I told him everything – well, almost. I told him about Faberge and the others being at Ashley Grange – but not what they had been doing. I just couldn't bring myself to talk about it. It made things damned awkward because like all deceptions it led to complications. For instance, Collins wanted to know how I got the bang on the head – the one which took nine stitches to fix it back together again. I waffled a bit, but in the end I had to admit I had been knocked cold in a fight before Faberge had left.

Collins fairly erupted with questions after that. 'Why had Kay left with them? What was the fight about? Why had they tried to make it look like a housebreaking?'

He knew I was being evasive and he got very angry about it. 'Listen, Sam. Not only are you charged with murder, but the police are very hostile towards you. Exceptionally so. What's got into you anyway? You've always been open with me before.'

I mumbled some sort of answer, but he was far from satisfied. He looked at his watch. 'I've got to get back to town now, but I'll be back tomorrow and I want to know exactly what happened. So sleep on it, eh?'

Life was a series of shocks after that. Some big, some not so big. Like breakfast the next morning – a rasher of greasy bacon and a mug of greasier cocoa. A screw yelling at me to make my bed. One lavatory for a hundred prisoners – with no door, no seat and no toilet paper. Prison clothing – stiff, discoloured underwear, worn thin by the laundry's efforts to cope with the results of incontinence – shoes worn by a hundred prisoners before me. And always that smell – that blend of excreta and urine and vomit which clings to your hair and flavours the food and settles deep in your pores.

Edgar Hardman came to see me the next morning. A prison guard stood by the door to take notes of everything we talked about. Edgar looked tired and haggard, and about ninety-nine years old. His normally straight back had bent a bit and he staggered slightly, like a man recovering from a stroke. He brought a couple of books and some newspapers with him, and obtained permission to leave them with me. They were searched of course, as if Lord Hardman were just the type to wrap a file or a Colt revolver in the pages of the *Financial Times*. I asked if he had seen Kay.

He nodded. 'Just left the hospital. She's still in intensive care. Multiple fractures of the skull, a broken leg, fractured pelvis. Still unconscious, of course.'

I groaned and felt very sick, even when Edgar said, 'She'll come out of it, Sam. The doctors are sure of it. In fact they aren't too worried about her being unconscious. Gave me a lecture on it being nature's way, all that stuff. I'm going back to the hospital from here.'

'Stay with her, Edgar. And – and give her my love – when she comes round.'

He nodded, but there was a deadness in his eyes, like a man in severe shock. He offered me a cigarette which I accepted. Then there was a bit of a pause, as if neither of us knew what to say. Edgar kept glancing nervously at the guard. Twice he started to say something, but he dried up both times. Finally he came right out with it, speaking quickly and fixing me with a look which said to keep quiet until he finished.

'The police have been to see me, Sam. About Kay being in town with me the other night. Silly misunderstanding when I called at your place earlier in the evening. I was on my way back from Bath, so I thought I'd give her a lift up to town. But, as you know, she had left already – she was actually waiting for me when I got to Lorimer's Walk.'

It was cold in that cell, but beads of sweat as big as raindrops stood out on Edgar's forehead. I was stunned at first. He had spoken so quickly that it took a second or two for his words to sink in. Then I was frightened. Frightened for him, not for me. Frightened at the risk he was taking to keep Kay out of it.

I was lost for words. The screw was standing there, writing everything down, glancing up curiously now and then. I could feel his suspicions. I was damn sure he would guess some kind of message was being passed between us.

Edgar's face twisted into a smile, but his eyes remained as dead as ever.

He said, 'Of course, as soon as I told her about the burglary at your place and you getting a knock on the head, she wanted to get back. Good job you 'phoned when you did I can tell you, otherwise she would have left there and then. As it was she left at crack of light in the morning you know. Before I was up. Of course I thought she had the Jaguar – not that little mini – didn't find that out till later.'

My brain meshed into gear. I marvelled at the way he had swept up all the loose ends. His statement to the police at Ashley Grange earlier that evening about Kay being at his place – even Edgar's own appearance at Ashley Grange had been explained. On his way back from Bath! What a story! And what more natural for Kay to have left at the crack of dawn to get back to an injured husband. It seemed foolproof to me. At least it did then.

Edgar stabbed his cigarette out in the tin lid which served as an ashtray. 'Anyway, all cleared up now, eh,' he said. 'Next thing I'll do is get onto this solicitor chap of yours – what's his name – Collins. Get you out of here. Dreadful misunderstanding – the whole business. Terrible mistake. Waste of public funds if you ask me.' He glared at the screw. 'Well, better get back to the hospital, Sam. I'll be in touch – try not to worry.'

When he left I was moved into the maximum security block, which is where I remained for my entire stay in Aylesbury. The Great Train Robbers had been held there in 1964 and the screws boasted they were the only people in the country to have held tight to Ronnie Biggs. I had no intention of escaping, but nobody believed me. In fact I was put onto special watch, which meant a screw sat outside my cell at all times, during the night as well. Even if I had been able to sleep he would have prevented it – he sat creaking his chair and rattling his thermos flask every five minutes, or rustling his newspaper, or clicking the peephole flap in the door. I was a bag of nerves by the morning.

I complained to Collins when he arrived, and he went off to see the governor about it. Things got better after that. As a remand prisoner awaiting trial I was allowed certain privileges. One of which was to have food and various other things sent in from outside. So Collins organised that and did his best to get the special watch removed. In fact he succeeded because they never posted a guard outside my door again, but they compensated for it with other things. Like just when I made a cell vaguely habitable they moved me to another one – generally in the middle of the night. And they were forever searching me, making me strip naked and bend over while they examined my backside. In short they threw the book at me and there was no doubt why – the place was full of rumours that I was going to escape, that people on the outside were going to spring me, things like that. Not a word of truth in them but once rumours like that start there's no way of stopping them.

I told Collins everything when he came back – everything – even that bit about Kay I kept back before, and about Edgar's visit and what had been said. We were talking in an empty cell, without a screw taking every word down. I suppose I'd got my second wind by then – despite the harassment. I was no longer in a state of shock. I was anxious to know how I stood, what sort of chance I had, how best to plan our defence.

Collins paced up and down, smoking cigarettes. 'You realise what's happened? Your aristocratic father-in-law has sold you down the river. He's—'

'Rubbish. He's just worried about Kay. And I want her kept out of it too. Edgar knows that – he's trying to protect both of us—'

'Funny way of showing it.'

'Suppose it all came out? What good would that do? Gives me an extra reason for being mad enough to kill Faberge, that's all.'

'And you didn't kill him?'

'Lewis, I just told you. That's exactly what happened. When I blacked out Faberge was only too alive—'

'Okay, okay – I had to ask, that's all.' He sat down and hitched up his trousers so not to spoil the creases. He avoided looking at me. I knew he thought I was lying. After a moment or two he scratched his head and said, 'It's a tough one, Sam, but what worries me as much as anything are the rumours flying around.'

'What rumours?'

'That you're a crook, a villain with your fingers in all sorts of pies, none of them legal.' He shrugged, 'It's bad, Sam. It's like someone's started a whispering campaign against you—'

'That's been going on for months. That Apex are going broke, that the tables are fixed at the casinos, Christ, I've had to live with that for—'

'But you're in here now and it looks even worse. Tell you what I've done. Commissioned a firm of private detectives to look into it – try to locate the source of the rumours. Naturally it's expensive but—'

'Forget the expense.'

He grinned. 'That's what I said. Winner Harris is in trouble. We've got to help out, no matter what it costs. Sort the money out later. So stay cool, Sam – we'll beat this yet.' He looked at his watch, 'I must go now, but I'll be back at the end of the week. And try not to worry – I'm working full time to get you out of this mess.'

I suppose his breezy optimism buoyed me up for a while, but by nine o'clock it had evaporated. Nine o'clock is when you're locked up for the night. I felt very depressed – really at the bottom of the pit. I tried to talk myself out of it by saying that things couldn't get worse. And that was a mistake. They got worse the very next day, when a receiver was appointed at Apex Holdings. We ran a bank overdraft like most other businesses, and the bankers had a charge on the assets of Apex as their security. The bank borrowing was well covered by assets and there was nothing to worry about in normal circumstances. But these weren't normal circumstances. The bank had panicked because of the bad publicity and had appointed a receiver over our heads. It was the beginning of the end for Apex. A receiver is a law unto himself. The directors automatically lose their authority when a receiver is appointed. Board meetings cease to have any validity and the sole charge of the business rests with the receiver – and he sets about turning assets into cash with which to repay the bank in double quick time. I had never dealt with a receiver before, but the man who came to see me that afternoon left me in no doubt as to what he was planning to do.

'Mr Harris, we're worried about these book debts. Generally that's the first thing we concentrate on – recovering money from debtors with which to pay the bank. In your view – are these debts good and recoverable?'

'Sure, you've seen the list of names. Some of the richest men in the country – in the world – use our clubs.'

The debts referred to related to restaurant bills, entertaining suites, car hire and a dozen other services which Apex provided for its clients.

'Some of these amounts go back a long time,' he shuffled through the pages in his file, 'in fact some are more than a year old.'

I shrugged. I knew what he was getting at, but he had made a statement, not asked a question. I was obliged to answer questions but statements might or might not warrant a comment from me. That statement, I decided, warranted total silence.

He frowned. 'Some of these debts go back over a year,' he said, 'and some are for very large amounts indeed.'

Another statement. I concentrated on looking attentive and prepared myself for when he would get down to asking questions. Gambling on credit is strictly forbidden under the law. However, there is no law which prohibits a casino from providing credit in other ways. Some of our clients lost half a million pounds at the tables. We were never going to worry about the twenty or thirty thousand they owed for our other services. As often as not we wrote the money off – at an appropriate moment of course – when we wanted to demonstrate our goodwill after a heavy night on the tables. Gamblers came to expect they could wine and dine on credit, with the added attraction that the debt might be wiped out by a sympathetic management. The casino business is a competitive one – every operator provides perks for his regulars. Some operators even accept cheques and then forget to bank the cheques for a year. If that isn't providing credit for gambling I don't know what is. Apex never did that, but we were undeniably generous with our hospitality.

'It seems to me,' the man said slowly, 'you are circumventing the law. Wouldn't you say you were providing credit for gambling – indirectly of course.'

At least it was a question. I said, 'No, I wouldn't say that.'

'But you would agree you give generous credit?'

'Not for gambling.'

'But on bills for wining and dining, and—'

'It's a custom of the trade. Everyone does it. If we stopped we would lose some valuable customers.'

'Because they think they can get something for nothing?'

I smiled. 'That's why they are there – remember?'

His lips tightened. 'Well not any more,' he said firmly, 'no credit will be given from now on. Even a drink at the bar will be paid for in cash.'

I stopped smiling. 'Look here,' I protested, 'the clubs make money—'

'By extending credit, Mr Harris. I am not prepared to do that. What's more I shall seek immediate settlement of all debts. I shall issue writs if necessary,' he flashed me a spiteful smile. 'Under the circumstances the drop at the tables may fall substantially – possibly to a level which makes the clubs no longer viable. If that happens we shall have no option but to close them down.'

I could hardly believe my ears. 'Lunacy,' I snapped, 'sheer bloody lunacy. Keep the clubs open – run them as they are now – and clientele will continue to gamble and you'll get your money—'

'You are talking about an on-going business, Mr Harris,' he said sharply, 'I'm talking about a receivership. The bank wants its money now—'

'You stupid bastard! Everyone gets their money if you tread carefully. Bulldoze things your way and—'

'That's entirely my decision. My view is all that counts—'

'I could get those book debts back in a month if – if I wasn't in here—'

'But you are in here,' he said spitefully. And shortly after that he left.

I seethed and stewed for days, but there was damn all I could do while incarcerated in Aylesbury Prison. I just hoped that Edgar and the other directors would close ranks and do what they could to save Apex. But in my heart I knew it was finished. The business I had given my life to was about to be destroyed.

When Kay emerged from her coma, Edgar kept the police at bay with a battery of physicians and lawyers. Then he moved her to a private nursing home. By the time she did make a statement it tallied with Edgar's exactly. I had already decided to keep Kay out of it, but her statement settled matters. Now I had no choice – or rather the only alternative was to call Edgar and Kay liars in open court, and I would never do that. Besides, who would believe me?

Meanwhile Lewis Collins was worrying about all sorts of things – but mainly about money. My income had ceased the moment the receiver walked into Apex, and although I was comfortably off I never kept much cash lying around. My money was tied up in Apex shares – now of dubious value – and in Ashley Grange and Rex Place (less their respective mortgages) and various possessions – motor-cars, antique furniture, paintings, that bloody boat, things like that. My bank statement showed a credit balance of thirty thousand pounds and I gave Collins a cheque for twenty thousand immediately – which seemed to keep him happy for the time being. But that was about all he was happy about.

'Only two people can vouch for your story,' he growled. 'One is your wife and we all know what she's saying. The other is this black guy, Brooks. And he's disappeared.'

'Disappeared?'

'Well my detectives can't find him. Sam, he's nowhere. Vanished from the face of the earth. Unless the police are holding him.'

'You mean in prison?'

'No, I mean under wraps. Holding him for the trial. To refute your evidence.'

'Can they do that?'

'Jesus, Sam – they'll do anything. I've never known them so prickly,' he scratched his head. 'And yet – it's not really the police. It's this guy Davis getting them all steamed up.'

'Inspector Davis? The Club Squad Davis?'

Collins nodded: 'Did you ever do anything to that man? Think carefully, it's important.'

I scowled. 'Davis is a pain in the arse. He's always on my back. I hate his guts.'

'It's mutual, Sam, believe me. Davis got at the local law even before we were in front of the magistrates. He fed them a tale about you being a bad influence in the West End. According to him you're an out and out villain. That's why the locals were so opposed to bail. That's why you are in maximum security. I tell you, Davis is making a career out of bad-mouthing you.'

'But if we know this we can stop him surely?'

'How? What we know was told me over a few drinks by the local law. A few drinks and—' Collins rubbed his thumb and index finger together, 'a half bent copper telling tales out of school is one thing. The same copper in court is a different animal. Besides the locals are convinced Davis is telling the truth. All these rumours prove his point – not ours.'

It was another gloomy meeting. They mostly were, at least with Collins. But a few other friends came to see me in Aylesbury. Jack, of course, but not Maria although she always sent her love and wrote at least once a week. (Remand prisoners are allowed extra mail. It's all censored of course, but a censored letter is better than no letter at all. Later it was different. A convicted prisoner is allowed only limited mail and no single letter can be more than four pages long.

Maria bought some extra large notepaper and wrote in the tiniest hand possible, putting down everything she could think of to cheer me up.) Edgar came to see me – but only twice after his first visit. Prison upset him and I can't say I blame him. But Kay never came. Nor did Charlie Weston, or old Darlington or Lew Douglas – or anyone else from Apex. Except the receiver – he came on a couple of occasions, ostensibly to discuss minor queries but mainly it seemed to gloat about the way he was ruining my business.

It took them five months to bring me to trial. Lewis Collins was as busy as a blue-arsed fly spending my money, but there was little to show for it. My detective had not discovered the source of the rumours, had not found Brooks, nor had he found out anything discrediting about Inspector Davis. About a month before the trial Collins engaged a QC for the defence and told me he was bringing them down for a conference three days later.

'Them?' I asked.

'The QC and his junior.'

I shrugged and waited for Collins to deliver the rest of the bad news. It was always bad news as far as I could see, but what came next was a real shock. 'Sam,' he said in little more than a whisper, 'this story of yours.'

'It's not a story—'

'I know, I know,' he raised his hands as if to fend off a blow, 'it's the truth—'

'The whole truth and nothing but the truth.'

He let that pass. For a while he smoked in silence. Then he said doubtfully, 'It's not a bad story – but it's not brilliant. And we certainly can't sell that story to the court. You know that, don't you?'

I took one of his cigarettes but when I put a match to it I noticed my hand was trembling. Then he surprised me by saying, 'Wouldn't amaze me too much if you got it wrong. What with that crack on the head and everything.'

I half rose to protest but he waved me down. 'Hear me out, will you? At least let me finish. It's Kay's account which screws us. Hers and her father's. On the other hand I can't help agreeing with you – if they told what really happened it would work against us as well. So suppose we use their story for our own ends. Suppose it happened like this. Ashley Grange was broken into, right? You got thumped on the head. Okay, let's stick to that because the police have accepted it. Your housekeeper goes to bed, you speak to Kay on the 'phone at her father's place – then you get to worrying. What were the burglars really after you ask yourself? Then you remember some important papers you left on the boat – say you were working

174

on them the previous weekend, something like that. In the end you worry so much that you get dressed and go over to fetch them. Then you run into Faberge and Martinez.'

'But – but what the hell were they doing there?'

He shrugged. 'Who knows – who cares? They had a grudge after that business at the club. We can bring witnesses to that. Maybe they found out where you kept your boat and were planning to scuttle it for spite. Hell, Sam, they're dead – they won't trouble us.'

I was sweating, but I tried to keep up with him while I searched for faults in his story. 'What about the car?' I asked. 'If Kay had the mini – how in God's name was I supposed to get there?'

'In the Jag. That was still at the boat-house when the police arrived.'

'But the police were at Ashley Grange earlier. They know the Jag wasn't there then.'

'Who says they know? Did they look for it? You never reported it missing. It could have been in the garage all the time. Anyway, a place as big as Ashley Grange – you could have parked it anywhere.'

I sat quietly thinking over what he said. I hated the thought of telling a pack of lies. On the other hand I was afraid to tell the truth.

Collins pressed on, 'Sam, don't you see – it's a much better story. Without Kay to rescue what motive did you have for going to the boat-house? There's only one answer to that – you went there to fix Faberge and Martinez once and for all. On the other hand if you remember it this way – you ran into them and they attacked you. Whatever happened then was self-defence. Got it?'

I smoked most of a cigarette before answering. Even then I'm not very proud of my answer because I simply asked, 'Will it work?'

'We're playing percentages, that's all,' he grinned, 'if you think this version gives you a better chance, my advice is give it to Malcolm Gerrard.'

'Gerrard?'

'The QC. He's a good man. Expensive of course, but—' he shrugged.

I signed another promissory note before he left. It was a practice started weeks before, when my money ran out. As Collins said, I was hardly in a position to negotiate a bank overdraft, so meanwhile promissory notes would do. 'We'll have a settle up when this is all over,' he said confidently as he went on his way. I was too punch-drunk to give the matter much thought. Collins appeared to be very busy on my account, and it was such a relief to have someone on my side.

Gerrard was a different kettle of fish. A gross, fat man with jowls like hams and the voice of a Shakespearean actor. I told him the story which Collins had suggested but Gerrard attacked it every inch of the way. I don't think he believed a word of it – and his junior sat in sneering silence throughout which unnerved me even more. I lost my temper eventually and we had a blazing row, but at least he stopped trying to browbeat me and offered an explanation. 'I'm trying to assess how you'll stand up in court,' he said, 'believe me what I've put you through is mild compared to what Gladwyn-Hughes will do to you.'

It was hardly a cheering prospect. He asked some questions about Kay which I fended off, and when he left he said: 'I think you'll go down, Mr Harris. I don't think I can save you. And if I can't there's not a man at the bar who can. Good afternoon. I'll see you in court.'

A week before the trial, Brooks turned up. I had been worried he might – especially after what Collins had said. In the event Collins was wrong but the manner of Brooks's re-appearance was almost as damning as far as I was concerned.

A farmer had been ploughing his fields, not far from the boat-house – and had unearthed a leg – a black human leg. Naturally he called the police and six hours later various other parts of a dismembered body were recovered from a series of shallow graves. They were the remains of Archie Brooks.

Of course the newspapers never actually said I was involved. In fact, with my trial less than a week away, they were careful about even mentioning my name. But they printed lots of stories about Brooks and the kind of life he had led. And photographs of Ashley Grange, where he had often stayed – 'as the guest of Sam "Winner" Harris, now awaiting trial, etc.' Collins was in despair about it and I wasn't exactly over the moon.

After that we went to trial. That was another shock because it was the first I had heard of plea-bargaining. Plea-bargaining is not supposed to happen in British courts, but according to Lewis Collins it happens all the time. The first inkling I got was at eleven o'clock, in my cell below the courtroom. Battle should have commenced at ten and I was wondering what the delay was about when Collins came to see me.

'Gerrard's had a long session with Gladwyn-Hughes. There's a chance of a deal,' he said excitedly. 'They'll drop the charge of murder and go for manslaughter – if we agree to plead guilty.'

'Guilty? But you've always said we'll fight all the way—'

'On a charge of murder. Listen, Sam, a murder conviction would get you life. That's about fifteen years realistically. Fifteen years, for Christ's sake! Manslaughter on the other hand—'

'But guilty! Lewis, I never killed him. I swear I didn't. Can't you get that into your head? I never killed the bastard—'

'Sam, listen a minute. Gerrard's convinced the most you'll get for manslaughter is six years. And six could mean three with remission. Sam, it's a breakthrough. Until now we've been fighting the possibility of life. It's one hell of a step forward—'

'Step forward? Lewis, I didn't kill him—'

'I've got to get back upstairs,' he said looking at his watch. 'Just thought you'd want to know what was happening. Sam – it's your first offence. The way Gerrard's dealing there's even a chance of a suspended sentence. You might not even go to jail.'

He left me to stew. Dammit, I was innocent. Why the hell should I plead guilty? And I was still asking myself that half an hour later, when Collins returned. 'They're in with the judge,' he said, 'both of them. Sam – there's a chance of a deal. A good chance—'

'Look, I don't know whether you believe me or not, but—'

'Be realistic, will you? If Gerrard agrees manslaughter they'll drop murder. On that deal alone Gerrard may have saved twelve years of your life!'

'But if we fight and win—'

'Percentages, Sam. Gerrard was doubtful of winning even before this Brooks thing. That's why he's wheeling and dealing. That's why he's in with the judge—'

'You mean the judge is part of this too?'

'Not officially – not part of the deal. But I'll tell you something, Sam. It will be a long and expensive trial if we fight, and if we lose the judge will take that into account. Not only will you be guilty of murder but you'll also be guilty of wasting public time and money. He'll throw the book at you for that.'

'A judge would want an innocent man to plead guilty?'

'Innocent – guilty – forget it, will you? Who gives a shit? The courts are overcrowded. They've got a backlog of cases a mile long. All they want is the case over and done with. Sam, we're dealing with practical men.'

'You mean Gerrard will get a decision now from the judge and then—'

'Not a decision. That would make the judge part of the deal. But an indication. Then you'll have to decide what to do. But my guess is you'll get a suspended sentence if you opt for manslaughter.'

'I have to decide? But I'm not a lawyer.'

'It's your trial, Sam. You instruct us.' He took another hurried look at his watch. 'Look, I must get upstairs. I'll be back as soon as I can – but Sam – you be ready with your instructions next time round – okay?'

And with that he was gone. It was a hell of a decision. Part of me wanted to fight all the way – try to prove my innocence once and for all – clear my name and salvage my reputation. But squaring that with keeping Kay out of it was becoming more and more difficult. And the prospect of freedom made me giddy. If I could get out *now* there was still a chance of saving Apex and of getting it back from the receiver.

Perhaps I thought of other things – other people, Kay, Edgar, friends like Jack and Maria – I think I did, but I'm not sure now. I had precious little time to think of anything, because Collins was back within fifteen minutes – wanting my answer. With a heavy heart I agreed to plead manslaughter. He looked pleased, patted my back and left me to wait in my cell.

You go up into court from the cells. A narrow passage leads to a small flight of stairs which ascend to the dock. One policeman walks in front, while another treads on your heels. The courtroom looked spick and span after the greasy dirtiness of the cells. I saw Gerrard in his wig and gown, laughing and joking with a man I took to be Gladwyn-Hughes. Lewis Collins was sprawled back in his chair, swapping stories with his articled clerks. Junior counsel were chatting happily together. They all looked so relaxed, so satisfied. Colleagues, not adversaries. A deal had been struck. Their professional reputations had been protected. Gladwyn-Hughes would chalk up another result. Gerrard would claim to have saved a client from life imprisonment. Both would have won in a way. There was only one loser. And he was sitting in my chair.

There was a movement, a scraping of chairs and clearing of throats as the judge arrived. Everyone stood up – and five minutes later my trial was under way.

It only lasted an hour. Gladwyn-Hughes had his say, and thirty minutes later Gerrard was on his feet, putting forward the mitigating circumstances. The stories they told bore little relationship to the truth – but then how could they? Anyway, as Collins so aptly put it – 'who gives a shit?' As long as it's over and done with and they all got their fees. Like court jesters telling two different tales to entertain their master – and at the end of the day their master was more taken with Gladwyn-Hughes's fairytale than the one told by Gerrard. As soon as the judge summed up I knew Collins had been over-optimistic. I knew I would be sent to prison. So I was prepared for the sentence when it came. Six years, the time already spent in Aylesbury to count as part of the term. The policemen motioned me to turn and go back downstairs to the cells, and just as I did so I looked up, to see Kay watching me from the public gallery.

I stopped dead in my tracks. The policeman behind me bumped into my back. Kay was in the front row, almost close enough to touch. I said her name aloud without realising it. She looked tanned and well, dressed in black, kid gloves holding a black handbag on her lap. She sat quite motionless, but her eyes were wet with tears.

'Kay!' I shouted.

The policeman behind pushed and I stumbled down the top two steps. I craned my neck, resisting the hands on my shoulders. I wanted to go back for a last look, a final word, ask how she was and where she had been. I was fighting the policeman now – he was shoving and I was struggling to stay on the stairs. I could see Kay's face, framed in the opening above me.

'Kay!' I shouted again.

Tears streamed down her cheeks and she fumbled into her handbag for her handkerchief. A man reached over to pat her shoulder. He stood behind her, resting both hands on her shoulders. I couldn't see his face – I was looking at Kay anyway. Then the policeman kicked my legs from under me and I fell down the rest of the stairs – and Kay had gone forever.

Collins arrived in my cell minutes later. Listening to him made me sick – anyone would have thought we had won. 'Sam, another judge and it would have been a suspended sentence. I swear it! But six years is a nothing. Six means three with remission – and that's before we go to work. We'll appeal, Sam, definitely appeal. Not against the verdict but certainly against the sentence. We'll cut it – mark my words.'

'Kay is upstairs. I saw her. Will you fix it for her to come down here? Just for a minute – can you fix that for me?'

He went away to try but Kay had left the court – or at least Collins was unable to find her. And when he came back he wanted to talk business. 'Sam, what's happening about your affairs in general? Someone has got to look after them. What are you doing—'

'Do I have to decide now – like this – here?'

'Sam. Be practical. Someone has to act for you. They'll need power of attorney. Think about it – bills to pay, expenses at Ashley Grange, this fight with the receiver. It was a full-time job for you, let alone anyone else. We must protect your interests, that's all – while we sort this mess out.'

I thought about Jack. He would look after things for me. But the comment about it being a full-time job stopped me suggesting him.

179

He had his own responsibilities. So I gave Collins the job and signed bits of paper there and then in the cell. Then a policeman arrived to take me to prison. I was handcuffed and led out to a Black Maria. We climbed into the back and it was driven away.

We went to the Old Bailey first. When we stopped, Davis climbed in. I was unhooked from the copper who was told to wait outside – then Davis gave me a real mouthful. 'Six years,' he said bitterly, 'should have been sixty. I'm still after you, Harris. I've got the Fraud Squad in at Apex, working alongside the receiver. They'll find something. And when they do you'll be back here on fraud charges.' He jerked a thumb at the Old Bailey. Then he got out and I was taken to Brixton Prison.

Kaufman stood up when I finished. He crossed to the windows. For a moment I expected him to draw the drapes for another film show. But instead he merely stood there, hitching up his trousers and staring out across the terrace. 'Well, well, well,' he growled to himself. 'What do you know? What do you know?'

'It all fits,' Richardson said, 'pieces of a jigsaw.'

'And how,' Kaufman said without turning round. Then he jerked his head in my direction. 'That poor schmuck never knew what hit him.'

I walked to the sideboard and poured myself a scotch. It was a relief to have finished, even though it left me feeling scratchy and on edge. I was still at a loss to understand what my life had to do with them – this house and being kidnapped. I took a long pull on the whisky, then said, 'Davis is bent. You say you're the law. Why don't you—'

'Sam,' Kaufman interrupted from the window, 'Davis is a nothing. If it's any consolation, the Fraud Squad business nailed him. He went too far. Sure the Fraud Squad investigated Apex, but there was nothing there and Davis kept badgering and that got reported. So people took a quiet look at him.'

'And?'

'Fifty thousand in three undeclared bank accounts – one in a false name. Davis earned a bundle making your life a misery—'

'He's still at it. He's still on the force. He's—'

'He's like Southampton, Hull – other bits and pieces in the Pipeline. We know them. Our men are onto them. You met Evans – he's our man. You'll get your revenge on Davis, but putting him away won't break the Pipeline. When we move we want the whole works – the Pipeline and the top man.'

I refilled my glass. The news about Davis was comforting but it was still a long way from an explanation. I said, 'And this top man – he's the one I'm supposed to know?'

'Oh, you know him all right,' Kaufman said, returning to the table. 'Like I told you, he's a friend of yours. That's why Corrao's orders were to take Apex without hurting you.'

'So you say.'

Llewellyn cleared his throat. 'Two men run the Pipeline – possibly three, but certainly two. Serracino is one, of course. He organises the procurement of heroin throughout the Middle East. The distribution end is run by a man known as the Ferryman, and we think a third man liaises between him and Serracino.'

'And the Ferryman is the man I'm supposed to know?'

'That's why we had to use you,' Kaufman stabbed a finger in my direction, 'you're the best chance we've ever had of penetrating the Pipeline. Tell him, Enrico, tell him about the man we had in Sicily.'

Bonello raised his sad eyes to mine. 'Two years ago,' he said, 'Fiore Serracino was seen back in Palermo. That's what put us onto it – the fact that the Pipeline might be controlled from Sicily. He vanished within a few hours of being sighted but our informant was a reliable man so we followed it up. The number of undercover men in the area was extended. We watched and waited. For months – nothing, for a year – nothing. Then one of our agents succeeded in confirming that part – if not all – of the Pipeline was organised from Sicily. He worked alone and took terrible risks, constantly in danger as he probed deeper. Then one day he overheard a name. How and where we never found out, but that the name was important was confirmed by events, because he was discovered and chased. He got as far as his hotel room in Palermo – got as far as reaching me on the telephone. Then they shot the lock off the door and murdered him – cut him to ribbons with their bullets. But not before he screamed a name down the line to me, Mr Harris, and we believe it was the name of the Ferryman.'

Kaufman swung back to me. 'We started digging after that. Tried to find out all we could about this man. On the face of it he was a respectable English businessman. Then we discovered his connection with you. Bear in mind that some months before we had learned Corrao's instructions – take Apex without hurting Winner Harris. So now we had another link. We watched this man, week in and week out. Nothing. So eventually we committed a little burglary at a house in Chelsea. His house. Still nothing – except for that photograph,' Kaufman pointed at the large brown envelope, 'so we ask ourselves – what's a man like that doing with a photograph like this?'

Warning bells rang in the back of my head. Very faintly. But I stifled my alarm – after all there are thousands of houses in Chelsea. A connection, a connection like that, was ridiculous.

Kaufman pointed a finger at me. 'Then we get your story. Your fight to save Apex. You fought your guts out, but you were always a step behind. Ever ask why? Because someone close to you was giving out inside information, that's why. And who was closer than anyone in Apex? Who was the man—'

'You're wrong!' I snapped. 'Absolutely – completely – up the bloody creek wrong. It can't possibly be true.'

'Yeah? You were framed and you know it. That half-arsed lawyer of yours didn't help – but who really bitched you? Come on, Sam, wake up! He knew you wouldn't contradict the story he gave the police. He knew it! And once you got suckered into that there was no way you could get out clean—'

'Rubbish! He was protecting Kay.'

'He was putting you away – that's what he was doing! Can't you see that you poor schmuck? You fought too hard. Maybe originally he wanted to give you a break for his daughter's sake, but when you left him no choice—'

'He was thinking of Kay – that's all – he had no other reason—'

'Like hell! With that photo in his safe? What sort of father is that for Chrissake? You think it was there for the family album or something?'

'You can't possibly be right.'

'I'm right, buddy boy. Some poor bastard agent screaming his last breath down a 'phone ain't telling lies. One name he got out – one lousy name – and that name was Hardman. That's the man running the Pipeline. That's the Ferryman. That's the man who ruined you! Your precious father-in-law.'

'I don't believe—'

'You don't want to believe. But you've got twelve hours to wise up because tomorrow you're going down the Pipeline. And the Ferryman is there waiting for you. He's already made contact—'

'Contact?'

'We got a girl answering your telephone at Rex Place. Edgar Hardman has called three times in the last two hours. Maybe he neglected you during the past couple of years, but by the sound of him he's damned keen on seeing you now.'

CHAPTER SEVEN

They drugged me when they took me from the big house. Oh, not the way they did before – there was no struggle this time, no mock heroics from me. After a meal they put something in my drink – at least I think they did because I was wide awake one moment and struggling to keep my eyes open the next. Kaufman was saying something, then his voice sounded far away and he was going out of focus. The next I knew was waking at Rex Place – bathed in sweat, with nightmares prancing over my bed.

My bed? That was a laugh. Nothing was *mine* any more. My whole life had been taken over by Llewellyn and Kaufman, with their crazy ideas about Edgar Hardman. It was madness. I raised myself off the pillow and reached for my cigarettes, then lay back and thought about the big house, remembering the endless questions, trying to make sense of it all. I shuddered. It was like a bad dream which needed daylight to drive it away. The clock next to me showed nine o'clock. Sunshine lay in strips across the carpet. Sounds of the rush hour traffic floated in from Park Lane just round the corner.

I showered and dried myself – then heard the noise downstairs – from the kitchen. Wrapped in a dressing gown I crept down the stairs. It was Jack, breaking eggs into a frying pan. He was whistling something half under his breath and concentrating so hard on the stove that he missed seeing me slide along the bench at the kitchen table. 'Are you the last?' I asked, 'or are there more surprises later?'

Not that I was really surprised. Something in the back of my mind said Jack was involved. He had to be. How else could they have bugged the place? How else could Lucia have been ready and waiting? Jack must have known – and so must Maria.

He was embarrassed at first, tensed up, nervous about my reaction – and bloody right, he got no sympathy from me. At least not to start with. But then I heard his side of it.

Maria told him about her background before they were married. Jack thought she was exaggerating at first, but then Enrico Bonello called to see him. Bonello confirmed everything. Not only that but Bonello filed a report with the Met. Police. 'Ever since then,' Jack said, 'we've had police protection. Nothing obvious, but they've kept an eye on Maria all right. They always thought Fiore might find out where she was and come looking for her – or send some of his friends.'

Suddenly the penny dropped. Now I knew why Jack always seemed to know just that little bit more about the police. All those years and he had never said a word about it to me. It hurt a bit, that he and Maria had never told me – we had been such good friends that for them to keep a secret like that was like not trusting me. But it was a selfish reaction and a moment later I regretted it. I tried to imagine living with the strain of something like that, forever wondering if the stranger at the bar had been sent by Fiore Serracino. It was a hell of a thought, even when Jack admitted that they had not been troubled.

'I never expected trouble,' he said. 'Not really. After all, we planned to stay in London. Italy seemed a long way off, a different world. On the other hand Enrico persuaded me to take some precautions. Like accept a degree of police protection and live life away from the bright lights, things like that.'

Another penny dropped. Suddenly I knew why he had pulled out of The Point of View. In fact he admitted it. 'You were getting all the international set there,' he said with an apologetic smile, 'London one week, Rome or Milan the next. Word might have got back. A chance remark, a good description, someone brighter than average putting two and two together. It never seemed worth the risk.'

Listening gave me a bad conscience. I called him all sorts of things when he pulled out of the club. I had been really sore. Of course I got over it, but I called him a few names at the time – said he was ungrateful, his business judgement was up the creek, things like that. Now it was like knowing him for most of my life, yet never really knowing him at all.

He read my mind because he said, 'It worked out fine, of course. Maria and I had fun with the The Dog's Home and I made a bundle on the antiques.'

I knew he was letting me off the hook but there was no point in pursuing it so I pressed him to go on with his explanation. 'Enrico came to see us about six months ago,' he said. 'We thought it was a social visit at first – but then he took us to meet Kaufman. Lucia was there too. It was the first time I'd met her. She and Maria never lost touch, letters and birthday cards and so on, but none of them posted – Enrico always delivers them when he's in London. We never even knew Lucia's address. She's even been to London before, but never to see us – Enrico forbade it. Enrico is the most cautious man I know.'

184

That shook me even more, knowing Jack had been involved for months.

Jack said, 'Kaufman needed my co-operation so he had to tell me what he was up to. About Serracino being involved, and old man Hardman running this end of it.'

It took self-control not to explode at that but I bit my tongue and remained silent. Jack shifted uneasily in his seat, probably guessing my reaction. 'The rumours started about you the day you went inside,' he said, 'a lot of people said you were taking the rap for someone else. That's what gave Kaufman his idea I think. He argued that the mob might come after you anyway, suspecting that you might know something. Well doing things Kaufman's way made sure – but, well he persuaded me that the benefits justified the risk—'

'Benefits?'

He stood up and crossed to the larder – a big, walk-in job on the back wall. I always thought it took up too much space but at least it was big enough to bung everything in. It was lined with shelves, hooks for pots and pans, things like that.

'You never asked how I let myself in,' Jack said. Then he pushed the back of the larder and it swung open. An entire section of wall moved open! I saw a short passage, with two doors at the end.

Jack grinned at my astonishment. 'You've even been through there as a matter of fact. You left that way the other night.'

Henderson and his mate! That was how they got into the cottage.

Jack closed the wall again and returned to the table. 'I'll leave Kaufman to show you round, but one door leads to a house in Wells Court and the other goes next door.'

'Wells Court?' I said weakly, trying to take it all in.

'It backs onto here. Kaufman's got a sort of field HQ there. Radio communications and all sorts of stuff. The point is they can come and go into here without anyone knowing – if the place is being watched I mean.'

'And is it – watched?'

'Kaufman knows if it is. The front bedroom next door is like a film studio. All the comings and goings of Rex Place are filmed. Twenty-four hours a day, infra-red equipment, the lot.'

I began to realise what Kaufman meant by watching over me like a baby.

Jack grinned. 'Of course the 'phone is tapped and the whole place is bugged. Even what we're saying now is being recorded at Wells Court. Kaufman is convinced that Hardman will attempt—'

'Edgar wouldn't hurt a fly. Kaufman's crazy—'

185

'Someone blew my car to pieces the other night. Someone—'

'Not Edgar Hardman.'

'How the hell do you know? I don't care tuppence about Hardman, if he's mixed up in this he deserves all that's coming to him. But if Serracino is after you your life's not worth a light. So wipe that look off your face and listen to me.'

I understood Jack's involvement then. Properly understood. Serracino in Sicily was one thing. Serracino in London was a different matter entirely, and the thought of him being that close to Maria was worrying Jack rigid.

He sighed and shook his head. 'I'm sorry, Sam, believe me. Keeping Maria's past a secret from you was fairly easy because once we re-arranged our lives we simply forgot about it. After all, we'd taken the precautions Enrico wanted us to take – there was no point in ruining every day by worrying. So after that—' he shrugged, 'but these last few months, boy, you wouldn't believe the worry.'

He sat there shaking his head in a mute appeal for me to see things from his point of view. I'm not sure I did, not completely, not when it came to deceiving me anyway. But then he said, 'Look, Sam, we made conditions. For instance Maria told Kaufman point blank that she would tell you everything that was happening unless he let you in on things within forty-eight hours of your release.'

I suppose that was something. It made me feel a bit better. I sipped my coffee and waited for him to continue.

'There's a whole bloody arsenal next door,' he burst out, 'you wouldn't believe the precautions taken to protect you. And another thing – Kaufman promised he'd get you out twelve months early. That was the thing that swung it. Maria and I kept thinking of you locked up in Brixton and, well, almost anything seemed better than that.'

So that was it. I had wondered about that. Even Collins had reckoned on three years. When it came to my release from Brixton I had assumed some extra remission had come my way – after all I bet they never had a more docile prisoner than me.

Jack said, 'Kaufman promised us this caper would only last a few days. A couple of weeks at the most. So when we set that against a year of your life—' he broke off helplessly and watched me with an anxious look.

I knew I would have made the same choice – either for him or for me. All the disappointment I had felt about him and Maria faded in that instant, and it was with a huge sense of relief that I reached over and punched his shoulder. 'Thanks, Jack, I'd have done the same for you.'

He brightened immediately, obviously sharing my relief. 'Thank

God for that. There's just one more thing, Sam – I dealt myself in. I stand right next to you in this deal.'

'But you can't get involved. What about Maria?'

'Gone away – staying with friends in the country – at Bath. She went last night.' He grinned from ear to ear, 'And The Dog's Home is closed – we bought the place next door and the builders are in extending the place. The pubs can run themselves for a while.'

I was telling him he was mad when the doorbell rang. It buzzed once, then twice, and ended with an extra long burst – like a snatch of morse code.

Jack's grin broadened. 'That's Lucia – you'd better let her in. She's our secretary – and maybe your girlfriend. The cover story is that you met her at our place and offered her a job. She's to work here for the time being.'

'Madness,' I said, standing up and pulling the cord around my dressing gown. 'Absolute bloody madness.'

Lucia kissed me when I opened the door. There were no preliminaries and it wasn't a peck on the cheek either. Both arms encircled my neck and her body pressed hard into mine. I was just relaxing into it when she pulled away. Two men stood a yard behind her, one with a raised camera and the other with a silly grin on his face.

The man with the camera said, 'Any statement this morning, Mr Harris?' while his mate asked, 'What about the new club? Got a name for it yet?'

Lucia snuggled into my side and answered before I got my breath back, 'No statement, boys, and before you ask, we're just good friends.'

'And how,' said the photographer, 'can I have another shot of two good friends saying good morning?'

'Why not?' Lucia grinned back at him. Her arms reached up again and her lips closed on mine. She smiled wickedly when she broke the clinch, winking a huge grey eye at me as she drew me across the threshold. As she closed the door she said, 'If we're going to do that every morning, can you shave first? You've got a chin like a pot scourer.'

'If I shave now can we try again?'

'I can wait,' she said drily, but she kissed me again as Jack came out of the kitchen. 'Keep the press happy?' he asked.

'No more than you did yesterday,' Lucia drew a folded newspaper from the pocket of her coat. And there I was again – on the inside page. This time Jack's photograph appeared as well, together with another one showing the premises at Baker Street. '*Winner Harris plans comeback*' read the headline, followed by Jack's optimistic assessment of the future. 'My name might be on the licences,' he was quoted as saying, 'but only Winner Harris can bring the glitter back to the West End.'

I went upstairs to dress and when I came down they were all in the kitchen. The larder door was open and Kaufman was at the table reading the newspapers. 'I'm going to retire from this racket,' he grinned, 'I'd make a fortune as a press agent.'

I blew up at that. For better or worse I've always run my own life – being Kaufman's robot didn't suit me at all, and I told him so. We had a bit of a row with me doing most of the shouting, but Kaufman seemed to have an answer for everything. Like when I raised the issue of Tomlinson who was making appointments with counsel and God knows who else on my behalf.

'Henderson's with Tomlinson now,' Kaufman said, 'he'll sort things out—'

'Don't you ever stop interfering?'

'Easy boy – easy,' he patted the air, 'it's benefit time, like your buddy said. Henderson's delivering a letter from the Home Office. The police will be instructed to withdraw their objections at the appropriate time. You'll get your licences back – when this is all over.'

Jack grinned and I didn't know what to say – and ten minutes later Tomlinson was on the telephone telling me about it. 'Quite amazing,' he said, 'I've had precious few dealings with the Home Office so I wouldn't know if there is a precedent or not – but it's very unusual.'

'But the letter is straightforward?'

'Oh perfectly – the police will not resist your application for licences. Couldn't be more explicit.'

'I wonder if Davis knows?'

Tomlinson appeared to share my malicious pleasure because he said, 'You know, I wondered that. Actually I doubt it. The second paragraph says the police will be instructed at the appropriate time. Rather implies they haven't been instructed yet, doesn't it?'

It really was beginning to look as if Kaufman had covered every angle. After I had spoken to Tomlinson I went back to the kitchen and Kaufman launched into his lecture on 'procedures' – what I was and was not to do. I was never to go out alone. Appointments would be cleared with Kaufman in advance. If anyone asked to meet me I would arrange to see them at Rex Place – or a public building, but never in a private house or somebody's business premises. It was quite a list and when he finished I said, 'There are more rules here than in Brixton.'

He grinned. 'Let's face it, Sam, they'll kill you if they want to

– no protection in the world can stop a sniper's bullet. But these people want to talk to you – at least they want to talk first.'

If it was meant to be reassuring the effect was spoiled by the look of concern in Lucia's eyes and the worried scowl on Jack's face. Kaufman tried again. 'Main job is to stop them snatching you,' he said, 'that's what they'll try to do. But don't worry, our people will be covering you every step of the way. Like I said, Sam, we're watching over you like a baby.'

Even so I jumped whenever the telephone rang. Lucia answered the calls in the sitting room but we could overhear every conversation. Most of them were with reporters asking about my plans for a comeback.

I ate the bacon and eggs which Jack had prepared earlier and drank some more coffee, but my digestion was spoiled by arguing with Kaufman about Edgar Hardman. Kaufman was so convinced he was right and I kept telling him that he was wrong by a mile that it was all a bit futile.

'Relax, Sam,' Kaufman kept saying, 'we've baited the trap. There's a small army next door,' he jerked a thumb towards Wells Court, 'all ready and waiting. Now we sweat it out. Waiting is ninety per cent of a job like this – but Hardman will call soon. Remember the procedure, that's all and leave the rest to us.'

Events proved him right. It was ten forty when the telephone rang again, and Lucia's face was flushed with excitement when it popped round the door. 'It's Lord Hardman,' she said, looking at me.

I avoided Kaufman's eye. I couldn't stomach his gloating satisfaction – or let him see the shock in my eyes. He could not possibly be right about Edgar . . . I told myself that over and over again. 'You're wrong,' I said bitterly. But even I could hear the doubt in my voice.

We followed Lucia into the sitting room. An extension had been fitted to the telephone on the desk, together with an inter-com of some kind. Kaufman reached for the extension and nodded to me. 'Procedure,' he hissed.

'Edgar?' I said into the telephone.

'Sam! I've been trying to reach you for days! Tried half a dozen times yesterday. Sam, how are you?'

I tried to analyse his voice, detect some difference. Crazy! Of course he sounded the same. Exactly as I remembered him. The same old Edgar. I said, 'Edgar, I'm fine – and you?'

'All the better for hearing you. Dammit, Sam, why haven't you called? I was hoping to hear, you know.'

I felt guilty. He was giving me the kind of welcome Jack and Maria had given me the day I came out – three days ago. *Only three!*

I said, 'Edgar, I'm sorry, I was planning to call you today – I meant to yesterday but I had meetings all day and—'

'Never mind that now – you're excused. Sam, it's simply splendid to hear you again. When can I see you? Are you free for lunch today?'

Kaufman was nodding and mouthing 'procedure' at the same time. I felt like a traitor but I said, 'Lunch is fine, Edgar.'

'Great! The Club then – about twelve thirty?'

The Club? Edgar's club! It even looked like a private house. Kaufman's lecture rang in my ears and I said, 'Edgar – I can't – not the club. I mean, I've another appointment—'

'But you just said—'

'No, no – I'm free for lunch – afterwards I meant, I've another appointment *afterwards.*' I knew I was making an awful mess of it. Kaufman stiffened with alarm. I gulped a deep breath, then said, 'Look, Edgar, do me a favour. Be my guest today will you? Problem is I must be in Hampstead at half past two for this wretched appointment. There's a good restaurant out there – really, The Hunter's Tower, you must know it. Could we meet there – any time – half twelve is fine—'

'Hampstead?'

'It's not far. Make a change from your club—'

'Hunter's Tower you say?'

'That's right. Edgar, if you wouldn't mind—'

'Mind? Why the hell should I? Just be great to see you again, that's all. Half past twelve then – all right?'

I was sweating when I replaced the receiver. Kaufman grinned and passed me the handkerchief from his top pocket. 'That was swell, Sam, handled it like a pro.'

I dabbed my face and returned the handkerchief. 'I still say you're wrong. Hardman would no more have a hand in the rackets than—' I stopped as the telephone rang again. It was Maria, for Jack.

Kaufman took my elbow, 'Come on, Sam, you gotta be briefed before you go to work.'

And we returned to the kitchen, where I received my instructions – just like any other spy.

Maria replaced the telephone just as Rosemary entered the drawing room carrying a coffee tray. 'Did you speak to Jack?' Rosemary asked.

Maria nodded and tried to hide her anxiety behind a smile. She crossed to the inglenook fireplace and sat on the chintz-covered armchair as Rosemary set the tray down and busied herself with the coffee things.

'And?' Rosemary persisted.

Maria shrugged. 'He sounds full of beans.'

'And how about your friend Sam?'

'Apparently he's forgiven us for deceiving him.'

'Well there you are then,' Rosemary smiled as if comforting a child, 'I told you there was nothing to worry about.'

Maria took a cigarette from her handbag – she was supposed to be giving up, or at least cutting down – but she knew that would go by the board for the next week or so. She would live on the edge of her nerves until this business was over. Her gaze wandered around the room, pausing at the collection of horse brasses next to a rather bad painting. Tat, Jack would call it, or at least some of it – but then Jack's taste in such things went beyond the ordinary. Still although the room lacked graciousness, it was at least comfortable. And very English. Like its owner, Maria thought, as she turned back to Rosemary.

Rosemary was a farmer's wife, at least for most of her time. Just as Charles her husband was a farmer for most of his time. It was what they did when not playing with their Somerset farm which had brought them into Maria's life. Rosemary had an uncle, a Brigadier Llewellyn, who was something or other in Whitehall. Maria had met him once at Wells Court when Enrico had taken her there to meet that man Kaufman.

'Cream?' Rosemary asked, with the jug poised over Maria's cup. Maria shook her head. She was remembering Rosemary's uncle, the man called Llewellyn – and the row they had had when they met. Llewellyn had insisted that Maria be removed to a safe place when Sam came out of Brixton. Maria had resisted – arguing that Jack was to stay in town, so was Lucia, so why not her? But that man Kaufman had joined in on Llewellyn's side. Maria had disliked Kaufman from the first moment. This whole scheme was his idea. It was all very well Enrico insisting that Kaufman knew what he was doing – but who was he to play God? What right had he to manipulate people's lives?

'Did you sleep well last night?' Rosemary asked.

Maria confirmed, for the second time, that she had slept well. It was a half truth. She had lain awake for hours, worrying about Jack and Sam and Lucia, and it was at least three o'clock before she dozed off. But she had slept soundly then.

Rosemary smiled. 'It's the country air. It takes most people a week to get used to it.'

Maria remembered the journey down. The two plain-clothed detectives collecting her from The Dog's Home, Jack coming to Paddington and kissing her goodbye on the platform. They hadn't been parted for years. It was strange to imagine Jack back at The Dog's Home while she ate dinner on the train with the detectives. 'Not like the food at your place,' one of them had grinned. He was nice that one, Peters he was called, Ray Peters. The other one was all right too, but Ray Peters fussed over her like a young man on his first date. He reminded her of Jack in some ways – Jack when he was younger – Jack when she first met him at that place she had taken the candlestick in Sloane Street. Mother had been alive then. Maria shuddered.

'Oh dear, is it cold in here?' Rosemary asked quickly. 'I can put the electric fire on if you like?'

Maria reassured her. She looked into the big hearth and remembered the log fire which had blazed there last night. Charles had met them at the station and brought them home to Rosemary, who had greeted them in the drawing room with the sparks from the fire dancing up the chimney behind her. 'I know it's unseasonal,' she had explained to Maria, 'but I thought you might be tired after your journey and I always think you feel the cold when you're tired.'

After that they had been taken on a tour of the farmhouse. It was a rambling old place, with about eight bedrooms and at least three baths. Immensely comfortable but lacking in style. Maria thought of the fun she and Jack could have doing it up. Her own room was well proportioned, the potential was there but masked by some awful wallpaper which clashed with the carpet and shrieked at the other furnishings. Ray Peters had tapped on the wall, 'I'm in that room and Harry's on the other side to you.'

'And Charles and I are just down the landing,' Rosemary added, while, not to be outdone, Harry Hall – the other detective – had said, 'And the security on the doors and windows is burglar proof. Place is more like a bank than a farmhouse.'

After which they had all trooped back down to the drawing room and talked for an hour or so before going to bed – with Charles busy at the drinks table and Rosemary serving a cold supper of chicken and pickles to Harry Hall and Ray Peters. Charles had explained about 'procedures' – Maria was never to go out alone, Rosemary would accompany her even on a walk round the garden, and Harry Hall was to know where she was every minute of the day and night.

Maria had protested, 'But this is ridiculous. I'm in no danger – it's Jack and Sam—'

'We know that, Mrs Green,' Ray Peters had cut in swiftly, 'but you're our responsibility now.' He grinned, 'Besides your husband might 'phone wanting to speak to you and he'll have my guts if I can't put you on the line right away.'

And they had gone to bed not long after that.

'Have some more coffee,' Rosemary said, interrupting her thoughts.

Maria shook her head. 'I'm sorry, I'm not behaving very well for a guest, am I?'

Rosemary smiled: 'You're behaving exactly like one of our guests.'

'Oh? You have others?'

'Not often. Perhaps once a year. Then Charles gets a 'phone call from London and we know someone wants a quiet place for a week or two.'

'And you just take them in? Anyone – I mean without knowing about them or—'

Rosemary lifted the lid of the coffeepot and peered inside. 'They're not anyone, otherwise my uncle wouldn't send them.'

'But who?' Maria stumbled, 'I mean – what sort of people—'

'I'm sorry,' Rosemary smiled as she poured herself another cup of coffee. 'Just say most of them are good people. Frightened people. Few of them English – Czechs, Poles—'

'I'm Italian,' Maria said, almost defensively.

'I know. You're our first one. You must teach me to cook – what was that marvellous dish we had when we came to The Dog's Home?'

Maria tried to remember the menu the night Rosemary and Charles had dined with them. It was a month ago. After Maria had lost her argument with that man Llewellyn. Well, they had all turned against her – not just Kaufman but Enrico – and even Jack had sided with them. 'I'm going to be with Sam,' he had said, 'and we all know there's a small army covering Sam. But we don't want another one camped here in The Dog's Home looking after you. Far better you go away until it's all over.'

She had teased him about it later, in bed, 'You just want me out of the way, while you and Sam paint the town. Be like the old days – every chorus girl in the West End will be fair game for you two.'

Jack had chuckled and pulled her towards him. 'You're afraid of missing your share, that's all. Come here and I'll give you something to remember me by.'

And he had.

Rosemary said, 'Something funny?'

'What? Oh, no – just thinking,' Maria shook her head to dispel the memory. But one thought leads to another and when she wasn't thinking about Jack she was worrying about Sam. It had always been like that – ever since she came to England. Jack first, then Sam. Sam was 'family' as perhaps only an Italian understands the closeness of that word.

'About what?' asked Rosemary.

'Oh – this and that – Sam mostly,' Maria stubbed the cigarette out and immediately opened the packet for another one. 'I wish I had spoken to him this morning. He, well he must feel so let down over this. That Jack and I have betrayed him—'

'I'm sure he feels no such thing,' Rosemary said smoothly.

'I should have spoken to him,' Maria said, biting her lip, 'I would have but Jack said that man Kaufman had taken him off to the kitchen.'

Rosemary said nothing. Past experience had taught her the art of listening. If she could get her guests talking – properly talking – within the first twenty-four hours all manner of things were possible.

Maria shuddered. 'We should never have listened to that man Kaufman. He's – oh I don't know – there's something about that man—'

'Bill Kaufman?' Rosemary sounded surprised. 'Oh he's all right. Really.' A shadow passed over her face. 'He's had his share of problems too, that's all.'

But Maria was not concerned with that. She had enough to worry about, with Jack and Sam and Lucia, and she was about to say so when the door opened and Ray Peters came in. Maria's eyes flew to his face. 'Any news?' she asked.

He smiled reassuringly, 'Only good news. Hardman made contact – they're meeting for lunch.'

'Oh that,' she said flatly, 'I know about that.' Jack had told her hours ago. She glanced at her watch and was amazed to realise it was not quite twelve thirty. Was that all? She groaned. She had to face days and days of this – just waiting. Waiting for news. God, she would go mad before it was all over.

The Hunter's Tower sits high up on Hampstead Heath, even above the Whitestone Pond. It's been there a long time, one way and another. Successive owners have added bits and changed others to make a bugger's muddle of the architecture. The car park has grown to the size of a football pitch – and a tiny, four-man lift has been installed inside to take the gentry up to the Turret Bar. The Old Bull and Bush is down the road, and beyond that lies Golders Green, where respectable Jewish families have replaced all the fish and chip shops with delicatessens.

But The Hunter's Tower rises above all that. I propped up the counter in the Turret Bar and looked out of the window. The three glass walls made the place like a goldfish bowl and let in more light than an artist's studio – but the view outside was a bit special. Across Hampstead to the bed-sit land of Belsize Park, then the West End, with the City office blocks on the skyline. Closer at hand the green of the Heath created an illusion of spaciousness – and of freedom. I smiled, illusion was right. Especially when I saw our taxi in the car park. Or rather, Kaufman's taxi. It may have plied for hire once but that was a long time ago. And I doubt our driver ever sat the exams taxi drivers go in for. He was downstairs now, in the other bar, but he wouldn't leave before me. No more than Henderson would. I turned slightly, the better to see him immersed in the *Financial Times* at his corner table. He had been there when we arrived. No acknowledgement had passed between us. A gin and tonic rested on the table in front of him, next to a menu. Not that he was ordering. He would wait for Hardman to arrive before doing that, to make sure his time in the dining room coincided with ours.

Jack looked across the room to where the two lovers held hands. Apart from us, and Henderson, and the man behind the bar, they had the place to themselves. Not that they cared, they were in a world of their own.

'Why this place?' Jack asked.

'Why not? It's never busy at lunchtimes. We can be sure of a quiet corner and we're unlikely to bump into any of Edgar's cronies this far out.'

'Quick thinking, Sam,' Jack mimicked Kaufman to perfection, 'handled like a pro, buddy boy.'

I grinned. 'He's wrong about Hardman you know – completely wrong. I felt bad earlier – about dragging Edgar into this ... this trap, but I feel okay now. It'll be worth it – just to put an end to Kaufman's senseless suspicions.'

Jack shrugged and carried his drink to the far window. To a casual observer he was admiring the view. Perhaps his back was turned on Henderson by coincidence, but somehow I doubted it. When I joined him he said, 'Don't underestimate Kaufman, or any of them – they're all professionals.'

'Including Lucia?'

He half smiled at that. 'Do yourself a favour and leave her alone. I saw the look you gave her this morning. Spend a week with the girls in Shepherd's Market when this is over – it'll be a damn sight less complicated.'

I watched three businessman types wander into the bar and take our place at the counter. They were arguing loudly about who was having what and whose expense account was treating whom to lunch.

Jack continued to gaze out of the window – and he was still talking about Lucia. 'She carries some sort of rank in the Carabinieri. Junior to Enrico but not by a lot,' he shrugged, 'I don't know much about her but her background includes Interpol and Christ knows what. She's tough, Sam – the only man who interests her is her brother Fiore – and not to kiss and make up either. Maria says she adored Franka. Everyone did but Lucia's devotion was a bit special.'

'Anything else I ought to know?'

He grinned. 'Plenty – but we'll find out together. You know as much as I do now.'

Even that was comforting. Ever since I left Brixton events had been shaping me rather than the other way round. Inexplicable things had happened; Jack's car being blown up; being kidnapped; the big house; Kaufman and his mob. Now at least I understood what was going on. And I was out and about again, able to act instead of reacting to the actions of others. It made me feel better. And having Jack around helped, made it like the old days with the two of us against the world. This was a rougher world but I would rather have Jack next to me than anyone I could think of. He was about to say something but I stopped him. Edgar Hardman stood in the doorway, blinking in the strong light flooding in through the windows. It was Edgar, but I had to look twice to recognise him. He had aged ten years since I last saw him – as if he had been to prison, not me. His once straight back had bent and his mane of grey hair had turned white – and he looked so frail that I half expected to see him walk with the aid of a stick.

'He's here,' I said softly, 'doesn't look like a killer, does he?'

'Neither did Crippen.'

I threw Jack a sour look and went forward to meet Edgar. His eyes lit up when he saw me and there was no mistaking the warmth of his greeting. It was every bit as cordial as I might have expected. I introduced Jack and told the story we had agreed upon – Jack was going on to a meeting with our architects 'just round the corner' and had stopped off for a quick drink. He was leaving now but would pick me up after lunch for us to go on to our important meeting together. Edgar was polite enough but seemed relieved when we were left alone. I ordered his dry martini and carried it to a corner table.

'This is fun,' he said with something of his old sparkle, 'lunch in the country no less.'

I chuckled. Edgar was a City man at heart. His office was less than three miles away but for him to leave the City during daylight hours called for a string of native bearers and a dozen packhorses. It was a hint of arrogance which reminded me of Kay.

Early conversation at reunions is always a bit stilted and ours was no exception. We reconnoitred old ground like soldiers in a minefield.

I suppose so much of the past had brought pain to both of us that we were anxious to avoid opening old wounds. And I was inhibited by Kaufman's warning – 'Let him make the running, Sam, find out what's on his mind.' It was completely ridiculous but I found it colouring everything I said. Especially when I remembered that photograph of Kay.

The head waiter collected our orders and we had another drink before going through to the dining room. It was very spacious, the other half of the top floor in fact, with the kitchens forming the central core. The furnishings were modern Italian – soft black leather with rosewood trim – but the cooking smells were decidedly French. Edgar sniffed with mild approval.

I was right about it being quiet. Of forty tables less than a third were occupied. From the corner of my eye I watched Henderson select a spot near the entrance before resuming his study of the share prices.

I tried to follow Kaufman's advice. I did try to make Edgar lead the conversation but apart from the occasional dry comment or amused observation, he was taciturn and ill at ease. Strain and nervousness showed in small mannerisms and he picked at his food with the appetite of a sparrow. It saddened, almost sickened, me to watch him. I remembered Edgar from the old days – full of life and authority – a quick, decisive man, a born decision-maker. Now he was a shadow of his former self. And just as he had changed, so too it seemed had our relationship. We had been good friends once, firm friends despite the difference in our ages. He could never have been my father with his background, but I had looked up to him as a sort of father figure. And he in turn had always supported me, encouraged me as a man might do with his son. I used to feel that we had so much in common – that Kay was only a part of it – but now that was all so far in the past that for the first hour we struggled to find things to say to each other.

Then, as we neared the end of the main course, Edgar raised his glass with obvious approval. I had ordered a Mouton Rothschild but then I never messed about with wine when Edgar was around – he knew more on the subject than anyone I ever met. He swallowed slowly and set his glass back on the table. 'It still exists,' he said, 'the quality trade. Only wish we still did it, but Charlie Weston moved us down market. Most of our stuff is what they call plonk these days. Rubbish shipped over in Charlie's tankers and bottled at Gravesend. Sold in supermarkets to poor devils who know it's good because they've seen it on the telly.'

I was more than surprised. 'Charlie Weston moved you down market?'

Edgar blinked. 'Didn't you know? Charlie Weston controls Hardman's Wine these days. Surely you knew that?'

'No,' I said, 'I didn't know that. How – why?'

He shrugged. 'That damn silly deal I did with Apex. Guaranteeing the share prices, remember? Seemed safe as houses at the time. But when the receiver sold it off – well, I had to settle with Weston and Douglas.'

I was stunned. Of course I had known Edgar would be hard pushed to raise that kind of money, but half of me had expected, had hoped, that Charlie and Lew Douglas might waive their rights under the deal – or at least settle for a lesser amount. Dammit – we had been partners, colleagues, we had worked together. When I recovered my voice I asked, 'You mean they called you – in full?'

Edgar sighed. 'Business is business. I don't blame them especially, but I could have done with more time. Might have sold Wyndham Hall you know, but it takes a while to find the right buyer for a place like that.'

'So what happened?' I felt helplessly angry. My blasted obsession with Apex had ruined us all. If only I had sold out! What wouldn't I give to put the clock back.

He was embarrassed. He must have guessed what I was thinking because he was trying to explain without laying the blame at my door. It was decent of him but it didn't make me feel any better.

'I settled with Douglas for cash,' he said. 'He's sold up here, you know – lives abroad – extended his hotels in the Mediterranean I think. Anyway, I haven't seen him since the beginning of the year, not since I settled with him. But, well, I owed Charlie Weston a million and a half. Takes some finding, Sam – especially in a hurry. The banks didn't want any part of it and I couldn't raise it without liquidating, so Charlie accepted shares in the wine business. He's been our bulk carrier for years you know, so he knows a fair bit about it. He was quite decent on the whole – the shares were transferred at a fair price, and that was that.'

'So what are you left with?' I asked grimly.

He reached across and patted my arm. 'Don't worry about me, Sam. I still own five per cent of the business. Of course, I'm only a figurehead these days, but they keep me on as chairman and provide me with a decent car.' He smiled in an effort to reassure me, 'I'm still rich, by some people's standards.'

A waiter cleared our plates away. I was about to say something but Edgar waved me down, 'Anyway, let's not waste time talking about my business. It's yours I want to talk about.'

I said 'yes' to the waiter about coffee and when I turned back Edgar was saying, 'This rubbish in the papers. About you going back into the club business. You can't possibly be serious, can you?'

I felt the first twinge of nervousness. 'Why not?' I asked uneasily, 'Jack Green and I are old pals – and I've got to start again somehow.'

'But for heaven's sake – *why* the club business?'

I remembered the arguments I had used on Tomlinson, about the club business being what I knew best – but when I started to replay them on Edgar he wouldn't listen. 'That's not the point, Sam,' he said hotly. 'They won't let you go back, surely you realise that?'

I froze. Kaufman could not – must not – be right. I had precious little faith left in anything but I would be shattered if Kaufman was right about Edgar.

'What do you mean? *They* won't let me?'

'The authorities,' Edgar waved a hand at the whole of London beneath the windows. 'That man who gave you so much trouble before – that policeman – Jones, or something.'

'He can't stop me. Not if the licences are in Jack's name—'

'Then *they* will stop you!' Edgar's agitation grew by the second.

I stared at him. I could not believe what I heard, what I saw in his face. The waiter arrived with a pot of coffee and Edgar fidgeted until the man went away. Then the wine waiter arrived with a brandy for Edgar and a scotch for me, so it seemed an eternity before I could repeat my question, 'Who are *they*, Edgar?'

Instead of answering he sat back in his chair and looked round the room. Only three tables remained occupied. The lovers still held hands, the three business types swapped stories, Henderson had put the *Financial Times* aside and was reading a paperback over his coffee. Looking at him reminded me of Kaufman saying, 'Ninety per cent of this job is waiting.' But it was only a vague thought – most of my mind was concentrating on Edgar's astonishing behaviour.

'Dammit, Sam, there must be something else. Another line of business—' he cursed as he fumbled with his cigarettes. He was actually trembling.

'You said *they* will stop me, Edgar. Who are *they*? I don't understand.'

He succeeded in removing the cellophane and managed to open the packet. He offered them to me. 'I don't understand either,' he said, 'not any more. There are lots of things I don't understand.'

As I flicked my lighter I saw the worry in his eyes. Worry – and something else. I tried to remember how old he was. I must have known once but had forgotten. Sixty perhaps, not more, but he looked much older. Old and sick, worried and – frightened! It came as a shock to realise it, but I knew I was right. Edgar Hardman was desperately afraid.

I stared at him quite openly. It was rude of me but I was just so astonished. He tried to smile but it was a shaky sketch of the real thing. 'An old man's whim, I expect, Sam. You get to my age and you realise how big a part luck plays in a man's life. I just think you would have better luck if you tried something else.'

I steeled myself to bully him. 'Luck's nothing to do with it – you said *they*. What was that supposed to mean?'

He squirmed in his chair. 'Sam – it's not I've anything against your friend Green – but – but, well I was rather hoping we might do something together. I know I'm not as well off as I was, but – well I would like to help you get started again.'

Was that all it was? Edgar rallying to help. The gesture of a friend.

'That's very nice of you Edgar but—'

'It would be fun,' he said quickly, 'start small and build up. Working together again. Any business you like except clubs—'

'Edgar, is something the matter?' I asked bluntly. He *was* frightened, I was sure of it. 'Something's worrying you,' I said, 'I can see that. Frightening you even—'

'Sssh Sam – *please*.' He looked round the room again, but we were too far away from the other occupied tables to be overheard.

I lied. It was a brutal, vicious lie of which I shall always be ashamed. 'Trouble is,' I said, 'I'm signing contracts on this new club tomorrow and—'

'*Tomorrow!* Sam no – for heaven's sake *no!*'

His fear was obvious now. It showed in his voice, eyes, mannerisms – I could almost smell it.

'But why no?' I asked. 'Edgar, just now you said *they* – who are they? Not Jack surely? Jack is my oldest friend—'

'Not here, Sam – we can't talk here.' He dabbed his face with his table napkin. More than once he glanced at Henderson but even that failed to prepare me for what came next. 'You see, I'm followed wherever I go.'

'*Followed?*'

'Sssh!' He wiped his hands on his napkin. Now his eyes were

everywhere – quick, darting looks round the room which gave a furtive cast to his expression. He said, 'I know it sounds ridiculous, an old man's imagination—'

I followed his look across to Henderson. 'You think *he* is following you?'

Edgar peered across the room. He frowned anxiously. 'I'm not sure. I think he is one of them. I've seen him before but—' he turned to watch the courting couple settle their bill, 'it gets you down after a while.'

'Edgar, you can tell me, surely?'

'I *must* tell you,' he said with sudden determination. 'Ever since January I've waited to tell you. But we can't talk here – and your friend will be back in a minute—'

'Jack? He can wait downstairs, get himself a drink at the bar—'

'They'll be closing – besides you have your appointment.' He swallowed the last drop of brandy. Some colour returned to his face and he seemed more in control of himself than a minute earlier. He checked his watch, 'And I ought to be going.'

I cursed under my breath. Jack's involvement had been Kaufman's idea – to provide an excuse in case Edgar suggested we went on elsewhere. Now I wanted to go on and Jack's presence prevented it.

'Why not come back to my place now?' I suggested. 'We could talk for a while longer, in privacy—'

'But your appointment—' he broke off, looking over my shoulder.

I turned and saw Jack in the doorway. He waved and began to thread his way between the tables to where we sat. I turned back to Edgar. 'Tonight then?' I said urgently. 'Come round for a drink—'

Jack arrived and grinned down at us, 'Sorry I'm late. Have I held you up?'

'Tonight, Edgar?' I repeated.

He crumpled his napkin into a ball and left it next to his coffee-cup. The waiter arrived with our bill. Damn and blast everything! There was so much I wanted to know. What had happened to reduce Edgar to this nervy hesitant ghost of himself? And what had become of the other person who had been with us ever since we sat down? Neither of us had acknowledged her. We had both avoided using her name, but Kay had been in our thoughts for at least some of the time.

'Tonight, Edgar,' I pleaded, 'any time to suit you.'

We stood up, I put some notes on the plate and indicated that the waiter should keep the change. Jack turned for the entrance, and then Edgar said, 'About eight then – will that be all right?'

I sighed with relief. 'We've a lot to talk about,' I said, with a hand on his elbow.

He knew I meant Kay. Or at least in part. There was a flash of pain in his eyes, followed by that haunted, worried expression. He nodded, and we followed Jack across to the lift. Henderson was settling his bill, folding his newspaper, marking a page in his book. The three businessmen called for another round of brandies.

We rode down in the lift and Edgar politely asked Jack about his meeting.

Jack shrugged, 'Oh, you know architects. Full of fancy words like ambiance and charisma to justify their fees.'

I thought how odd. These two are my closest friends, perhaps my only friends, yet they clearly dislike each other. Edgar was being cool and polite, but preserving his distance, while Jack was awkward, even a bit surly.

Edgar's chauffeur was waiting outside. We were offered a lift but Jack said he had a taxi waiting. Downstairs we turned towards the exit which opened onto the car park, then walked through the doors into the pale sunlight.

Once, when I was a kid, I was nearly run over. It all happened so quickly but every split second registered in my mind, everything froze in sharp focus, like a frame in a film. So it was then. At the bottom of the steps we started across the car park, our shoes crunching the gravel. Edgar's chauffeur climbed out from behind the wheel of the Rolls to open the rear door. The interior light cast a soft glow over magnolia upholstery and walnut woodwork. A flock of wood pigeons rose in a flurry of wings from a knot of trees thirty yards away. The air was quiet and still, like a churchyard. The sun struggled for life in a bruised sky which threatened rain. The car park was virtually empty. There was a dreamlike quality to the scene – as if I was involved, yet apart from it, watching it, like a play on the stage. Then I heard the shouting.

'*Down!* For Christ's sake – *get down!*'

I turned and saw Henderson ten yards away, standing close to a yellow car. His knees were bent and his right hand was thrust forward, supported by his left. He looked like a cop in a TV film. Especially as the gun in his hand was blazing away at the bushes under the elm trees. Jack shouted, and as I swung back I saw splashes of red on Edgar's coat. His eyes opened wide in some kind of appeal and his mouth worked convulsively without sound. His knees buckled and he fell backwards, while his gloved hands grasped his lapels, as if to pull the coat tighter against the cold. Then the slow motion camera inside my head stopped as Jack hurled me to the ground.

I heard a wildly revving engine, the squeal of brakes, felt my face cut by flying gravel, smelt scorched rubber, exhaust fumes. A taxi skidded to a halt in front of us. The driver screamed to get inside. We half crawled, half threw ourselves through the open door. The driver leapt out, crouched like Henderson, fired twice at the bushes, shouted something, threw himself back up behind his wheel, crashed into gear and almost stood the cab on its side as he swerved to avoid the Rolls. The door of the cab swung open. I saw Edgar's chauffeur face down on the gravel, the back of his head covered with blood, his uniform cap a yard away. Then I got a hand to the door and slammed it shut.

Jack was being sick on the floor and I was trembling like a leaf in a gale. The driver yelled something but he was shouting so much I missed most of it. Then I realised it was directed at his radio. He turned east at the exit, *away* from the West End, taking the road in the *opposite* direction – driving fast, dangerously, swerving the cab like a rugby player heading for a touch-down. We were in the back streets of Hampstead Garden Suburb within a minute, flying past smart houses and well tended lawns, braking hard to avoid a green VW as it emerged from a side road, then lurching on again at breakneck speed.

Jack wiped his mouth with a handkerchief. 'Where the hell are we?'

I clutched the seat and braced myself as we clipped a kerbstone at fifty miles an hour. Then we were back into the main road. I recognised Henley's Corner on the North Circular Road and panicked as I remembered Kaufman saying, 'Our hardest job will be to make sure they don't snatch you.'

Christ! Was this our driver?

More traffic about, we slowed down. The man shouted over his shoulder, 'You okay?'

I shouted back, 'Where are we going?'

'Procedure. Someone gets hit, you scatter. You see any sign of a tail?'

Jack craned his neck to the rear window, 'What am I looking for?'

'Could be anything. Anything keeping up with us?'

'Yeah? I'll tell you if I see a Formula One racing car.'

The driver chuckled and glanced over his shoulder. I got a better look at him. It *was* our driver! I sighed with relief. We crossed the North Circular and raced on towards Mill Hill. I still struggled to understand. 'Why aren't we going back to Rex Place?'

'We probably will, when I get word. But that might have been hit as well for all I know.'

Then it registered. Properly registered. They had killed Edgar! In broad daylight someone had killed Edgar! I groaned aloud and Jack gave me a sharp look, 'You okay?'

I nodded.

'Why should Hardman's chauffeur shoot him?' Jack asked.

'His chauffeur didn't,' I said, 'it was someone in the bushes.'

'But the chauffeur—'

'Got caught in the cross-fire I think. I dunno—'

The radio spluttered to life. Kaufman's voice shouted above the static, 'Oboe – oboe – report your position. Oboe – oboe – can you hear me?'

'This is oboe,' shouted the driver. 'We are on the outskirts of Mill Hill, heading north.'

Kaufman's voice boomed through a snowstorm of static, 'Where the fuck's Mill Hill?'

The driver told him. Then Kaufman asked, 'Your passengers okay?' The driver said we were. Even that failed to improve Kaufman's temper. He cursed bitterly, then said, 'Make sure you're clean, then get back to Sandringham. Use the back entrance. Okay?'

'Understood,' the driver said, 'may I have your closing RT procedure please.'

Not even the static masked Kaufman's fury. But he finally stopped swearing long enough to say, '*The Times* is a lousy newspaper.' Then the line went dead.

'He sounds hopping mad,' the driver said cheerfully.

'Where's Sandringham?' I asked.

'Rex Place,' he threw me a quick look in his mirror.

Jack grunted. 'What was that about *The Times*?'

'Safety code. He wouldn't have said it if someone was sitting there with a gun pushed in his ear.'

'I bet,' said Jack.

'We try to plan for everything.'

'Funny,' I said, 'Edgar Hardman used to say that.'

CHAPTER EIGHT

Rosemary Parker had long since learned that the best way of stopping her guests from dwelling on their problems was to give them something they could get their teeth into. The nature of the project varied with the guests. Most were men so as often as not Charles got them busy around the farm, but the women were Rosemary's responsibility and she decided that Maria Green was positively not the farming type. So what to do with her? She was to be at Glebe Farm for at least a week according to Bill Kaufman. She would worry herself to death left to her own resources. But Rosemary had decided upon Maria's project after that one visit to The Dog's Home – though she waited until after lunch before broaching the subject.

Charles had gone off to see his farm manager and the two women had adjourned to the drawing room, when Rosemary said, 'Maria my dear, you could do me the most enormous favour while you're here.'

Maria stopped worrying about Sam meeting Hardman long enough to say she would be delighted to help in any way possible.

'It's this room,' Rosemary said, waving a hand. 'The whole house really. Well, Charles's background is army and farming – mine too I suppose. We spent so much time abroad, then when we came here the farm itself took priority over everything else but, well I ask you, just *look* at this room.'

Maria looked. It was a big room, almost square, the fireplace wall all natural brick and horse brasses, the other walls painted a pale green. Blue carpet, yellow patterned curtains, red scatter cushions on the chintz-covered armchairs.

'It's a complete mess,' Rosemary announced. 'The whole house is a mess. But I thought if we did a room at a time?'

Maria looked at her.

'If you advised I mean,' Rosemary said hastily, 'colours, fabrics, what goes with what. Well, The Dog's Home is so exquisite. You've obviously got a wonderful eye—'

'Jack has—' Maria said quickly.

Rosemary shook her head, 'We could start with the wallpapers. If we went to Bristol and borrowed those pattern books they have we could then decide, room by room—'

'The whole house?' Maria exclaimed.

Rosemary threw her hands in the air. 'We've been here six years and done nothing. Oh, we've fixed the roof and renewed the wiring in some of the bedrooms, but nothing really ... and it's such a marvellous opportunity having you here.'

'But I'm not an interior decorator.'

'But you've got the eye,' Rosemary insisted, 'so I thought if we went to Bristol this afternoon and collected wallpaper books and carpet samples, and those little shade cards the paint makers give out – well, perhaps tomorrow we could decide on each room—'

'Jack's phoning at six,' Maria said quickly.

Rosemary checked her watch. 'It's not half past two yet. We could be in Bristol just after three. We've got plenty of time – don't worry, we'll be back here by six,' she paused, to smile appealingly at Maria, 'I really would be *so* grateful. Even Charles remarked upon the atmosphere at your place – and Charles could live in a barn without noticing his surroundings.'

Maria tried to quell her feelings of doubt long enough to return the smile. 'People's tastes vary – you've got to live here, not me. I would hate to suggest—'

'Then *I'll* suggest, you just stop me if I'm going wrong,' Rosemary persisted. 'Charles says I can have the whole house done. You can't imagine how long it's taken to get him to say that. And having you here . . .'

Maria laughed, caught up in the other woman's excitement. And it was exciting – to do an entire house from top to bottom.

'So if we could plan it this week,' Rosemary said, 'everything – carpets, drapes, everything—'

'You won't blame me – afterwards?'

'Only if you refuse to help,' Rosemary beamed.

Maria hesitated, taking another look at the room.

Rosemary said, 'There are some good shops in Bath, of course, but I thought we'd do Bristol today for samples and things.'

'The whole house?' Maria said, thinking aloud.

'We could do Bath later in the week,' Rosemary said.

Maria smiled. 'And we'll be back here by six?'

Rosemary nodded. 'Then we could look through the pattern books this evening . . .'

Maria laughed again as she warmed to the project: 'Right, you're on. But don't blame me—'

'I promised.' Rosemary jumped up. 'Oh this will be fun! Bristol it is then. Just as well Harry Hall and Ray Peters are here. They can carry the pattern books, they weigh a ton.'

It took us a long time to get back to Rex Place – but then it would, the way we went. Edgware, Harrow, across the Western Avenue at Hanger Lane and down into Ealing, then along the Uxbridge Road to Shepherds Bush and up the Bayswater Road. The driver wouldn't even stop for Jack to clean himself up properly. When we reached Marble Arch he made some adjustment to the fare meter and said, 'We're going in the back way. Wells Court. One of you pay me when we get there. Make a job of it – give me a fiver or something and I'll hand you some change. Then turn through the gate. The front door will open as you reach it. Go straight in, but don't run or do anything daft. You got that?'

I said yes. Then the driver said 'Park Lane' into his radio and someone answered 'Roger' above a noise like bacon sizzling in a frying pan.

Jack scowled out of the window. He had barely spoken for the last half hour. Being involved in a shooting is a frightening experience, but he looked more angry than scared. I was angry too – angry with Kaufman and his senseless suspicions about Edgar. And now Edgar was dead.

We turned into Mount Street and a minute later we were there – number fifteen Wells Court. I had been curious about the place earlier but I couldn't care less now – I was just too tensed up – too bloody anxious to get hold of Kaufman and tell him what I thought of his half baked ideas. But I stood at the kerb and handed the driver a fiver, with Jack looking up and down the street. The driver gave me two pounds and some silver. 'Right,' he said, almost under his breath. 'Turn now – and *don't run.*'

It was a very short path but it seemed a very long way. Any second I expected the crack of a rifle. My spine tingled where it would shatter under the impact of a bullet. But the door opened as we reached it and a second later I was inside, with Jack on my heels. The cab drew away as the door closed behind us.

'Down the end,' a man jerked his head and Jack brushed past me to lead the way. I heard raised voices, then a telephone rang and somebody snatched it up to bellow an answer. The room was at the back of the house, but even so the blinds were drawn and the lights switched on. It was quite large, bigger than the sitting room at Rex Place. Half a dozen easy chairs were set in a semi-circle facing a desk. Three reel-to-reel tape recorders were bracketed to one wall, and the long table against the far side was littered with telephones. Henderson was speaking into one, leaning against a grey filing cabinet and watching us as he talked. Kaufman rose from behind the desk as we entered. Llewellyn watched us from an armchair. Richardson greeted us with a sick smile from a coffee machine behind the door.

Jack covered the room with a couple of strides. 'You great, stupid bastard!' he roared at Kaufman. 'You said Sam would be safe. Promised me. So how *safe* was today, Kaufman? If I hadn't knocked him down he'd be dead now.'

'Back off will you!' Kaufman shouted back. 'Back off and get your head together. You know what was out there today? A professional hit man, right down to a Schneider 303 and telescopic sights. Don't kid yourself – if they had wanted Sam no fancy heroics from you would have saved him.'

'But—'

'But *nothing*!' Kaufman stormed out from behind his desk. He was shorter than Jack, but just as angry.

Henderson cupped the 'phone with one hand. 'For Christ's sake! Hang on will you – I can't hear a word he's saying.'

Kaufman bristled up at Jack, then swung back to his chair. Richardson closed the door behind me. Henderson resumed his telephone conversation.

Kaufman waved at an armchair. 'Sit down, Sam. You look white as a sheet. You want a coffee or something?'

'No,' I said, 'I don't want coffee.'

Henderson finished on the telephone and turned to Kaufman, 'Rossiter's blown a fuse about Hampstead. Says there'll be all sorts of repercussions. He wants you and the Brigadier up there at six o'clock.'

Kaufman scowled at Llewellyn. 'He's a pain in the ass. But unless we go his men with the pointed heads will trample over everything.'

Llewellyn nodded. 'Tricky situation,' he said mildly.

'Is that right?' Kaufman said aggressively. 'Well it's your end of things so I'm relying on you to keep him in line.'

'Quite,' Llewellyn nodded. He turned to me, 'Surprising turn of events, eh?'

'Not for me,' I said coldly, 'I never thought Edgar was your mysterious Ferryman.'

Kaufman flushed. 'So how many innocent men get whacked by hit men? Hardman being killed don't change a thing. He was in this up to his back teeth. Maybe someone down the line got ambitious. A struggle for power? Happens all the time.'

'That's your explanation is it?' I sneered.

'I don't have an explanation. You think this is little Miss Marples – saying the vicar done it in the study? Well it ain't that cosy. I told you what we got. A man ripped apart as he shouts Hardman's name down an open line. That fancy photo locked up in Hardman's safe.'

'He was frightened. Terrified! He was going to tell me—'

'Yeah? Well he ain't now,' Kaufman slapped the flat of his hand down on the desk. Then he sighed heavily, like a man trying not to lose his temper. 'Okay, Sam, cool down. Let's hear what you got on that recorder. You did switch it on I suppose?'

It was the most treacherous act of my life, but I opened my jacket and unbuttoned my shirt. The recorder taped to my chest was as slim as a cigarette case and about half the size. I winced as the plaster came off. Henderson proffered a hand and after giving him the recorder I fumbled with my cufflinks. They were the microphones but no wires connected them to the recorder so I had no idea how it worked. I placed the *cufflinks* on the desk just as Henderson slotted the recorder into a machine mounted on the wall. Then Edgar said, 'This *is* fun. Lunch in the country, no less.'

I felt sick as I listened. I had betrayed Edgar – led him to his death. Listening made it worse, hearing the fear in his voice, his warning, his obvious concern for me expressed only hours ago. And now he was dead. I couldn't stop telling myself that.

It was all there – right through to the gunshots in the car park – but nothing after that – either the tape had run out or the recorder switched itself off when Jack knocked me over. I chain-smoked my way through it and watched other people's reactions. Not that they gave much away. Richardson drank a gallon of black coffee, Llewellyn puffed on his pipe, Henderson fidgeted and Kaufman doodled on a scrap pad. It took an hour and a half to listen to the whole tape, maybe a bit longer, certainly long enough for me to get my nerves under control and for the temper to fade from Jack's expression.

When it was over Kaufman asked, 'What was that business about Charlie Weston and Lew Douglas? How come the old man owed them that much?'

I reminded him about the Apex deal, but his scowl deepened. 'Yeah, you mentioned something – but there's nothing in the Minute Book about it.'

'Why should there be? It wasn't really Apex business – more of a private arrangement between the directors.'

'You could have elaborated more than you did,' he said grudgingly.

'Oh, for God's sake! I answered your questions—'

'Sam,' he said heavily, 'it's not even a matter of questions. The point is us getting to know everything. Your story, remember? Somewhere there's a clue in your background. If we keep digging—'

Lewellyn interrupted, 'It's almost five thirty. I ought to be getting over to Rossiter's place.'

Kaufman sighed, 'Think you can handle him? By yourself I mean? It's not I'm chicken but—'

'Better without you,' Llewellyn smiled as he stood up. 'You'll be here, will you? If I need—'

'I'll be here,' Kaufman walked heavily to the table next to the coffee machine. 'I may not be sober but sure as Christ I'll be here.'

He picked up a bottle of Johnnie Walker. 'Want a slug before you go?'

Llewellyn shook his head. At the door he paused to look at me. 'He's quite right you know, Mr Harris. Corrao's instructions were to take Apex without hurting you. If we knew why I'm sure we'd know who. Don't you think?'

But he left before I could tell him what I thought. Richardson uncurled himself from his chair and followed him out.

'Drink, Sam?' Kaufman asked.

I accepted a whisky gratefully but Jack said, 'I could use a wash first.'

'Bring it with you,' Kaufman said handing him a glass. He sat on the edge of the desk and reached across to push a button on the inter-com. When Lucia answered he asked, 'Anything happening?'

'No visitors, but the 'phone's been busy. Press mainly – they've picked up the angle that Hardman was Sam's ex-father-in-law. They want Sam's comments.'

'And you said?'

'That Sam is shocked and very upset, and he's not taking any calls until tomorrow.'

Kaufman nodded approvingly. 'Nobody suggested Sam was there when it happened?'

'No, nobody,' Lucia confirmed.

I saw the look of relief on Henderson's face. I wondered how my name had been kept out of it. My face had appeared in the morning papers so one of the waiters might have recognised me.

'Anything else?' Kaufman asked.

'A man called Darmanin keeps calling. He sounds very upset and says he needs to speak to Sam urgently.' She hesitated, 'I would have buzzed through, but you said no interruptions.'

Kaufman looked at me. 'You know any Darmanin?' When I shook my head he said, 'Probably some lousy reporter. You ask what he wanted, Lucia?'

'Yes – but he'll only discuss it with Sam.'

Kaufman shrugged. 'Anyone watching the place?'

'Next door say nothing has moved in the last hour.'

'Okay – we're coming through,' Kaufman switched off and stood up. He looked at Henderson. 'Hang on for word from Llewellyn – see how he made out with Rossiter. Come on, Sam, let's go home.'

But I took a quick look at number fifteen Wells Court first, at least at the ground floor. The open door opposite revealed three men playing cards – tough, competent-looking men in their early thirties

210

who jumped up when Kaufman poked his head round the door. He said to relax and added something which escaped me. My attention was taken by the far wall, where a dozen guns were slotted into racks above enough ammunition boxes to support a small war.

Back in the corridor Kaufman said, 'House is divided vertically. From the front it's a three-storey house – from the back it's an army camp.'

He led the way into a passageway – and then we came out into the larder at Rex Place. The kitchen was full of light and warmth. Cooking smells closed round me like memories from another world – my world, Jack's world – the world of clubs and restaurants, of good food and mature wine.

Kaufman clapped a hand to his eyes and sniffed approval. 'Don't tell me – let me guess. Spaghetti bolognaise?'

Lucia turned from the stove. 'It's ossobuco – and it won't be ready for an hour yet.'

'Fine. Jack wants to brush up and Sam and I are going to bounce a few ideas around.'

Jack said, 'Smells good, Lucia.'

She pulled a face at his stained jacket. 'It did till you came in. Best put that on a hanger – I'll sponge it out later.'

Jack went upstairs while Kaufman and I went into the sitting room. The drapes were drawn and the room glowed softly in the light cast by the two table lamps. I noticed a neat stack of paper next to the telephones and remembered the notes Lucia had typed two days ago. Two days! Could it really be as little as that! I sat down and was reaching for my cigarettes when Lucia came in from the kitchen. 'Seeing you two with glasses in your hands makes a gal thirsty. Anyone going to pour me a drink?'

Kaufman did the honours. Lucia sat on the arm of a chair and I watched her watch him mix a Bloody Mary. I would have to get to know her all over again. She had seemed soft and feminine at dinner the other night, elegantly assured perhaps, but with that hint of vulnerability which men find attractive in women. But what had Jack said? 'She carries some sort of rank in the Carabinieri – junior to Enrico but not by much. She's tough, Sam.' She didn't look tough, sitting on the arm of that chair, her sleek legs crossed and the soft light painting shadows under her cheek bones. But appearances were deceptive. She had coped with the shock of what happened at Hampstead, fielded telephone calls from the press and no doubt dealt with a hundred other emergencies – and yet she still seemed cool, calm and collected. But the poise was deceptive too because her hand shook when she accepted the drink from Kaufman. 'You all right?' he asked quickly. She blushed faintly and nodded, just as the telephone rang and Jack came back from upstairs. Lucia rose and crossed to answer the telephone.

She gave the number, listened for a moment, then said, 'Yes – hello again Mr Darmanin – I'll check if he's in.'

But she looked to Kaufman for an answer. So did I. He shrugged and said, 'Why not?' We moved to the desk together. 'Remember the procedure,' he said softly. Then he switched on the loud-speaker extension.

'Hello – Sam Harris here.'

'Mr Harris – my name is Darmanin,' the voice paused as if to give me time to recognise the name. It meant nothing to me and when I remained silent the voice continued, 'My son is – my son *was* – Tony Darmanin.' I threw a puzzled look at Kaufman. Then the voice said, 'Tony worked for a friend of yours until – until this afternoon – in Hampstead.'

It took me a moment to realise what he meant. Then I blurted it out, 'The chauffeur?'

'Mr Harris, can you see me now – tonight?'

'Your son *was* the chauffeur?'

'Yes, yes—' the voice said impatiently, 'can we meet tonight?'

I wondered why. A bereaved father. A man I had never met. Nor had I known his son. It seemed such an unlikely request. I tried to think of the best thing to say – expressions of sympathy jostled questions in my mind. Kaufman was busy writing on a scratch pad and I was wondering how to answer, when Darmanin said, 'I – I *must* see you now. My courage will fail by the morning, or – or the Pipeline will kill me too.'

I heard Lucia's sudden intake of breath and saw Jack's shocked expression. Kaufman swore softly and wrote 'meet him' and 'procedure' on the pad. Procedure was underlined three times. As calmly as I could I asked, 'Where are you, Mr Darmanin?'

'Greek Street. Number fifty-one. I run a bar, The Lantern. It is closed tonight but I live upstairs—'

'Are you alone?'

'More – more—' he sounded close to tears, 'more alone than in the whole of my life.'

Kaufman wrote 'cab' in large letters, followed by something I couldn't make out. He wrote it again and added the name 'Ellis'.

I said, 'Look Mr Darmanin, I can't get over myself but I'll send someone in a cab. He'll be with you in ten minutes—'

'I must see *you*—'

'You will – I'm sending someone. He'll ring your doorbell and say he is looking for a Mr Ellis. Have you got that?'

'I don't understand—'

212

'Just remember – *Mr Ellis*. The man in the cab will bring you to me. Do it this way and nobody need know we've ever met. It is safer – understand?'

'Ellis? Yes – but—'

'I'll see you shortly,' I said and hung up. I looked anxiously at Kaufman. There was a grim smile on his face as he prodded a button on the inter-com. 'You get all that?' he asked, and Henderson said 'yes' from the operations room next door.

Kaufman said, 'Get down there. Take Watkins in the cab and have a back-up car behind you.'

'Understood. Which entrance when we come back?'

'He called *here* didn't he? If he's got this number he's got this address. Bring him to the front door.' Kaufman paused, as if struck by a sudden thought, 'Oh yeah – have Smithers look this place The Lantern over, *and* the apartment upstairs. Tell him we'll keep Darmanin here an hour – so he's to be in and out in fifty minutes.'

'Right,' Henderson said. There was a click as he switched off.

Kaufman flushed with sudden excitement. 'It's beginning to break. Didn't I tell you? Stir the pond up real good and all sorts of stuff floats to the surface. There're a lot of nervous people in this town right now.'

'I know,' I said, 'I'm one of them.'

'Stop worrying. You saw what we've got next door.'

'Very reassuring – but Edgar Hardman is dead and that man sounded *very* frightened.'

'He did, didn't he. *That* man – running a nothing special bar in Soho – whose son was employed by Hardman as a chauffeur. I wonder—'

'He's Maltese,' Jack said unexpectedly.

'He's *what*?' Kaufman snapped.

Jack shrugged. 'Darmanin. It's a Maltese name. I employed a Maltese waiter once. His name was Darmanin.'

As soon as he said it I knew he was right. It fitted. I said, 'Soho is full of Maltese. Mainly they run cheap bars, clip joints, the garbage end of the business—'

'And prostitutes,' Jack added. 'The Maltese are the biggest bloody pimps in the West End. Have been for years.'

I nodded and was about to add something when I saw the expression on Lucia's face. And when she spoke her voice was huskier than usual, 'My brother used Maltese papers to get into the UK at the end of the sixties.'

Fiore Serracino! That film – that cellar in Milan! Suddenly it seemed a hell of a lot closer. Even Kaufman's voice had an edge to

213

it when he spoke. 'Serracino pretended to be Maltese. That never made him one. This Darmanin—'

Lucia interrupted. 'Fiore lived in Cardiff amongst the Maltese. He would have made contacts—'

Kaufman snapped the button down on the inter-com, 'Henderson?'

'He's just left, Mr Kaufman. Hewit here.'

'You got anything on that chauffeur yet?'

'We're awaiting the police report now. It should—'

'Get onto Llewellyn. He's with Rossiter. Say we want everything on that chauffeur. *Now* – not next week for Christ's sake—'

'Yes sir!'

Kaufman looked at his watch: 'Henderson will be back soon. Meanwhile *think* Sam. You got any idea how long this chauffeur worked for Hardman?'

I shook my head. 'I wouldn't have recognised him. Put a man in a cap and uniform and he looks like any other—'

The squawk from the inter-com interrupted me. Kaufman answered and Hewit said, 'Sorry, Mr Kaufman. I just checked the info on the chauffeur. The prelims came across the teleprinter ten minutes ago. You want me to bring them over?'

Kaufman swore, then said, 'Just read 'em out.'

'There's not much,' Hewit apologised, 'just the preliminary details. Tony Darmanin, aged twenty-five. Single, lived with his father in Greek Street. Occupation chauffeur. Maltese nationality, been here about three years. No police record, clean driving licence, no record of any other employment.' He paused. 'That's all so far. You still want me to call the Brigadier?'

'You bet your sweet life,' Kaufman growled. When he switched off he gave Jack a grudging glance of admiration. 'You were right, Hardman *did* employ a Maltese driver.'

'That's not a crime,' I said.

'You heard his father,' Kaufman swung on me. 'So goddamned frightened he came out and said it – the Pipeline will kill me too.'

'Maybe they killed his son on purpose,' Jack queried, 'perhaps he wasn't caught in the cross-fire. Maybe they wanted to kill him?'

'Instead of Edgar?' I suggested helpfully. But even that failed to make sense. Edgar had been frightened of something. Something he might have told me about. Dammit, he had been going to tell me. What had he said – 'I must tell you ... ever since January ...'

'Something happened in January,' I said. 'You heard that tape. Something—'

'Okay Sam,' Kaufman waved a hand impatiently, 'we got men ripping Wyndham Hall apart right now. *And* Hardman's pad in Chelsea. Anything comes up and we'll know about it.'

But he looked at Lucia as he said it. And she caught that look. Kaufman was shutting me up. So was Lucia because she answered his look with one of her own. 'I'll make some coffee,' she said, moving towards the kitchen, 'I've a feeling it will be hours before we eat. Dinner will be ruined.'

Jack saw the look too because he said, 'What was that about?'

But instead of answering Kaufman listened at the window. 'That sound like a cab to you?'

'I asked what *that* was about?' Jack repeated pointedly.

'Sssh,' Kaufman cocked his head. Then he shrugged, 'Maybe not.' He crossed back to the desk and peered at his watch under the light from the table lamp. 'Christ, how far away is Greek Street anyway?'

I shrugged, 'Fifteen minutes – depends on the traffic. But that wasn't—'

'It's nearly seven,' Kaufman looked at me, 'what time did Henderson—'

'Nearly *seven*?' Jack checked his own watch, then raised it to his ear. 'Hell! I promised Maria I'd 'phone her at six. She'll be worried sick. Look, I'll just give her a quick call—'

'Make it upstairs, will you?' Kaufman nodded at the telephones on the desk. 'I want the outside line kept free here. We've installed another one upstairs. The green handset.'

Jack walked to the door. 'I'll keep it short,' he said casually, but he gave me a hard look as he passed. People swear we are telepathic. Perhaps they are right because I knew what he was thinking then. He was remembering Kaufman's look, fixing it in his mind. So was I. Kaufman was holding out on us. We both knew it – but right then Jack was telling me to wait until he came back before I made an issue of it.

I nodded and said, 'Give Maria my love.'

'Not likely. She talks about you too much as it is.'

He was still grinning as Lucia returned from the kitchen. 'Are you calling Maria?' she asked, and when Jack nodded she smiled and said, 'Give her my love.'

The pang of jealousy caught me by surprise as Jack left the room. 'Give her my love' was such an automatic thing to say about Maria. Everyone loved her, she was that kind of woman. Not that I was envious of Jack – I was glad for him, and Maria – if ever there were a perfect couple, they were it. But just at that moment I felt lonely for that closeness which sometimes grows up between a man and

215

a woman. Kay and I shared it once – a long time ago – another lifetime, when we were first married.

Kaufman jammed the button down on the inter-com: 'Hewit! Sound Watkins out in that cab of his. Find out where in hell they've got to.'

'Right away, Mr Kaufman.'

'Let's have another drink.' Kaufman carried his glass across the room. 'It's happening, Sam. I can feel it. We've rattled the bastards.'

I nodded. 'Like the Czechs rattled Hitler before the war. The next week he walked all over them.'

'Okay smartass. Got any suggestions?'

I shook my head. 'No suggestions,' I said, 'just premonitions.' And it was true. That secret look between Kaufman and Lucia had unsettled me. Suddenly I felt something was wrong, desperately, violently, dangerously, wrong. Watching Kaufman made me feel worse. Despite his confident assertions, he was obviously worried. Pacing the room, checking his watch every ten minutes, smoking like a chimney. Then the telephone rang. The outside line.

Lucia went white when she answered it. She stood perfectly still, holding her breath – catching her breath. And when she covered the mouthpiece she was trembling. 'It's Corrao,' she said, 'Pietro Corrao. At least he says he is.'

CORRAO! It might have been yesterday. Everything about him stood out in my mind. His sneering voice, that odd jerking motion of his head, his limp left hand – everything.

But Kaufman sounded relieved. 'Corrao,' he whispered – almost in awe, almost triumphant – as if something he had been hoping for but not quite believing had actually happened.

'They've made contact,' he said in a hoarse whisper, 'Jesus Christ – we're through to the Pipeline.'

We moved for the desk together, bumping into each other. He put a hand on my arm as I reached for the telephone, but I brushed him aside. My mind registered the quick film of sweat on his forehead, and then I was saying, 'Hello – Sam Harris speaking.'

And there it was. A jeering laugh burning a hole in my memory. 'Hello, Winner,' he said. 'How does it feel to be a free man again?'

Temper made my mouth go dry. Corrao! I hated him. Hated his name, his voice, mannerisms – hated everything about him. Hated him for the man I once was and the man he had turned me into.

'Winner? Still there, Winner?'

Even the use of the old nickname was a taunt.

'Yes, I'm here, Corrao. What do you want?'

Kaufman shot me a warning look, aware of my temper.

'Now Winner,' Corrao scolded, 'that's no way to greet an old friend – besides I thought you wanted to meet me. At least, that's what everyone's saying.'

'Then everyone's got it wrong,' I snapped. 'I want the organ grinder, not the monkey. What are you these days anyway? Still nine, ten, eleven in the line?'

He made a quick hissing noise. I even remembered that. Him hissing like a snake when he was really upset. But it made me feel better.

He said, 'You always were an arrogant bastard. Perhaps you need another lesson?'

I grinned spitefully, 'Listen, Corrao, I'll make it brief. I want a meeting with the Ferryman, and I want it fast. So fast that I'll blow one of your operations every day you delay. Starting tomorrow. You might not know it, but the name Forresters of Southampton is important to the people you work for. And it will mean a lot to the police tomorrow. You got that?'

'That's a big mistake—'

'Come off it, Corrao. Tell them it's Goodman's of Hull the next day. You want me to go on? I can you know – I've got a list as long as your arm.'

'I doubt that—'

'Do you? Well you explain it to your masters when the police hit Forresters tomorrow.'

Then I slammed the 'phone down. Kaufman never had a chance to stop me. It took him a second or two to catch his breath, then he went purple with temper. 'What the hell? You stupid bastard! Procedures I said—'

'I know what you said. You also said you weren't a gambler. Well, I ran casinos, remember? He'll 'phone back.'

'Do you realise next door were trying to trace that call? Do you understand what's riding on this? Now you get this straight—'

'No – *you* get it straight. You were wrong about Hardman. And you're holding out on me. Something happened in January and you know about it. You be straight with me and—'

The telephone rang. I was glad it did. Tracing Corrao's call had not occurred to me. I'm not even sure why I did hang up. Partly Corrao's manner – part instinct saying it was the best way to handle him. His voice was strangulated with temper. 'Listen Harris,' he snapped, 'you'll get your meeting but at a time and place of our choosing. And I'll guarantee you won't give a single name to the police.'

The open threat! Like three years ago. But there was no bluff then

– he had carried it out. I hesitated and he sensed my uncertainty because he laughed. 'Why not talk it over with your new partner?' he suggested, 'and I'll call back in an hour's time. Ciao, Harris.' Then he put the 'phone down.

I replaced the receiver and stared at Kaufman. 'He knows about you.'

'Like hell he does—' Kaufman scowled, interrupted by the inter-com.

'Trouble,' Hewit said breathlessly, 'Watkins reported in. Darmanin was shot as he answered the door to Henderson. It's a bit confused but under control. They're on their way back.'

'Shot? How?' Kaufman barked.

'Sniper fire. Watkins thinks it was the same man as at Hampstead. Darmanin opened the door with the light behind him, made a perfect target—'

'Is he dead?'

'I – I don't think he was killed instantly. But he's dead now.'

'Tell Watkins to get back to Wells Court. Wells Court – understand? Under no circumstances to use Rex Place.'

'Yes, Mr Kaufman.'

Kaufman turned from the desk and swore violently, just as the door opened and Jack came in. He looked vaguely troubled and preoccupied, but he managed a tired smile for Lucia as he slumped into an armchair.

But Lucia's face held my attention. She might have seen a ghost.

'How – how was Maria?' she asked. She tried to say it casually but her tone betrayed her. And she was dry washing her hands with anxiety as she waited for an answer.

Jack shrugged, 'She and Rosemary went shopping in Bristol. They weren't back. I'll call again – it's just I know she was worried and—'

'I'm going next door,' Kaufman said sharply, 'Sam, come with me. Jack, you stay with Lucia. Henderson's on his way back in, see him for me will you?'

'But you just told—' I began.

'You know what to do, Lucia,' Kaufman said as he took my elbow.

'Must I?' She was as white as paper. 'Must it always be me?'

But Kaufman didn't stay to answer. I was half led, half pushed into the kitchen. Then he crossed to the larder and was running down the passage with me on his heels. Hewit was in the big back room we had used earlier. Another man was at the long table against the far wall. He cradled a telephone under his chin and was writing furiously.

Kaufman snapped, 'Get Bath on the line.'

Hewit looked surprised. 'They just came on. About ten minutes ago. Johnny's talking to them—'

'Switch that loudspeaker on. No, don't bother, I'll do it myself,' Kaufman flung himself behind the desk and flicked a button on his telephone. 'Kaufman here – what in God's name has happened down there? Where's—'

'Cook here, Mr Kaufman. It's bad news I'm afraid. Very bad news—'

'Tell me,' Kaufman growled, staring at the telephone.

'Mrs Green and Mrs Parker went shopping for the afternoon in Bristol. They parked the car in an underground car park—'

'Parked the car? Who parked it? How many men did you have on this?'

'Ray Peters parked the car. He stayed with the car while Harry Hall accompanied the ladies shopping—'

'Just one man? Just one man went with them? Is that what you're handing me?'

The voice hesitated. 'Well, they were only going shopping—'

'Holy Christ!' Kaufman's head was in his hands. 'Go on – what happened?'

'They shopped – had tea out – Harry stayed with them all the time. Then, just before they returned to the car park, the ladies went to the loo. Harry positioned himself outside and waited. Well, nothing happened for a while – ten, fifteen minutes according to Harry. Then he got worried—'

'*Then* he got worried!' Kaufman's voice was muffled by his hands over his face. 'God in heaven! Two girls go to the can and he *lets* them go. Why weren't women assigned to this—'

'Harry went in after twenty minutes.' the voice said hurriedly. 'There – well, there was another entrance. It was one of those big stores – you know the sort of thing, public lavatories serve two floors, steps up and down—'

'What are you – a fucking architect?' Kaufman roared.

'Mrs Parker was out cold. Chloroform. But – well, there was no sign of Mrs Green.'

Kaufman groaned.

'Harry rushed down to the car park to fetch Ray Peters, but – but Peters wasn't there. At least not in the driver's seat. Mr Kaufman – a truly terrible thing happened. We only found the body minutes ago.'

'They killed her. You let them—'

219

'*Not* Mrs Green – Ray Peters. Garrotted with an elasticated cord. We just found his body in the boot, er trunk you'd call it. Harry never thought to look there—'

'Get on with it,' Kaufman implored in a voice cold with fury.

'Well, whoever did it left a message. A sort of message. We found a piece of zinc pipe on the front seat of the car. Makes it pretty clear—'

'Jesus!'

'Yes – well – exactly. Earlier, when Harry couldn't find Ray, he went back up into the store to phone in—'

'There was no RT?' Kaufman's astonishment threatened to render him speechless. 'There was no RT in the automobile?'

'It was Mrs Parker's own car. A Jaguar. We thought it would be less conspicuous. Ray 'phoned in from the store about an hour ago. They were just closing—'

'Mrs Green?' Kaufman's stubby fingers were doing terrible things to the flesh on his face.

'No sign of her yet, sir. But we've put out a full scale search – road blocks, the airport – it happened less than an hour ago – well about an hour—'

'Oh sweet Jesus Christ!' Kaufman moaned. His head was in his hands and he seemed intent on tugging great clumps of hair out of his scalp. Even as I watched he seemed to shrink. And when he lifted his eyes he made no effort to hide his despair.

'Listen Cook,' he said softly, 'you pass the word. Peters is the lucky one. Peters is dead. Maria Green got sucked down the Pipeline an hour ago. If anything happens, if they touch a hair of her head, I'll have you. *All of you!* Every single incompetent in that division. I'll come looking for you with my bare hands, I'll come after you with a public enquiry, I'll have you drummed out, I'll drag your reputations through so much shit you'll never smell clean again. Your own families will shun you! People will spit on you! May your miserable, useless souls rot in hell for what you have done today!'

The whispered response of 'yes, sir' came a second before Kaufman slammed the switch down on his telephone. He sat with his shoulders slumped, staring sightlessly across the room. Then he roused himself and crossed to the drinks tray. He moved with the purposeful clumsiness of a sleepwalker and spoke to me without turning round. 'You say a goddamn word, Sam,' he hissed, 'and I swear I'll kill you.'

CHAPTER NINE

Rosemary Parker still felt very shaky. She sat in the corner of the senior staff canteen and watched Harry Hall carry a tray across to her. The manager of the departmental store was talking to some uniformed policemen on the far side of the room, while half a dozen GPO engineers were unpacking telephone handsets on a nearby table. Then the door opened and Charles strode in, throwing anxious glances from side to side until he saw her. He hurried across, colliding with a policeman en route and almost falling over. Tears of relief sprang to Rosemary's eyes as she rose to greet him. But the strain made her dizzy and she clutched the back of the chair for support – then she was in his arms and he was holding her tight to comfort her.

'Maria . . .' she managed to say, stifling the sob.

'I know, I know,' he gave her an extra squeeze before lowering her back into the chair. Then he sat down next to her and took her hands in his.

Harry Hall set the tray down on the table. 'You'll feel better after a nice cup of tea. Drink it while it's hot.'

Charles lit a cigarette and gave her an anxious appraising look as he passed it to her. 'It's all right, it's all right Rosie,' he said gently, using the hated pet name, 'take your time.'

Harry Hall helped himself to a cigarette from the packet Charles had put on the table. His own hands were shaking as he put it to his mouth. Charles looked at him and said, 'I've got the gist of it but you had better tell me again.'

'No,' Rosemary interrupted. Her voice quivered slightly and she took a long pull on the cigarette before continuing. 'Let me tell you. It gives Harry another chance to check my story.'

Charles squeezed her hand. He was reassured – there was nothing much wrong with Rosemary if she could insist on something like that.

'Not that there's much to check,' she said quietly. 'We went to the loo. Maria was in such a happy mood. We really had taken her mind off – off what was happening in London. Really we had Charles – hadn't we Harry?'

Harry Hall nodded. 'She was very relaxed.'

Rosemary continued. 'We left most of the pattern books and stuff with Harry. He could see the entrance from where he sat.'

Harry Hall nodded again.

Rosemary sighed and shook her head. 'It was a typical ladies – cubicles, handbasins. Charles, two nurses were there, one was washing her hands I think. And I noticed a wheelchair just inside the entrance. Well I'd had three cups of tea and was dying to spend a penny ... anyway I went into one cubicle while Maria went into another. Then, when I unlocked the door to come out ... that's when it happened.'

Charles lit his own cigarette and listened carefully.

'That's when it happened,' Rosemary repeated. 'This nurse barged in with something in her hand ... the door banged back in my face, knocking me backwards – Charles she was so *quick*! One hand at the back of my neck while her other pressed something over my nose and mouth. The WC caught the back of my legs – I sat down and then ... then I was out like a light.' She shook her head, 'It was so quick ... I would never have believed ...'

Harry Hall sipped his tea and watched her over the rim of his cup.

'The next thing I knew,' Rosemary continued, 'was sitting on the floor with Harry squeezing a cold flannel down my neck. A wallpaper book was open near my feet and I remember wondering what a sample book was doing in the lavatory. Then Harry was wiping my face ... and some stupid woman was making a fuss about him being there.'

Charles stared at her, *willing* her to remember. She recognised the look for what it was but it just made her feel all the more helpless. 'I'm sorry, I'm not helping much ... I don't even know if the nurse was blonde or brunette ... all I really saw was her outstretched hand with this pad—'

'Sanitary towel,' Harry Hall corrected. 'It was a sanitary towel soaked in chloroform. The whole place reeked of it.'

'What kind of nurses' uniforms?' Charles asked. 'Any insignia—'

'None that I saw,' Rosemary bowed her head, 'a nurse is a nurse. Grey dress, white bib and apron ... and capes, black capes.' She paused, searching her memory, then added, 'But an ambulance man came in as it happened. Two nurses – one attacked me and I caught sight of the other one behind her – just as this ambulance man came through the entrance.'

Charles nodded: 'How did you know he was an ambulance man?'

'He wore that sort of uniform – dark blue, or it might have been black. Peaked cap. There was some insignia on his shoulder. St John's Ambulance Brigade perhaps?' She looked at Harry Hall, then turned back to her husband, 'I'm sorry, that's all I remember.'

Harry Hall opened his notebook. 'The entrance to the lavatory was on the fifth floor,' he told Charles. 'In fact it's a flight of steps down to the fourth. I found out since that you can obtain access to toilets on every floor – without negotiating a single step on even numbered floors. The manager says it's a boon to invalids.'

Charles made no comment.

'We've pieced together what happened,' Harry Hall continued grimly. 'Two men dressed as ambulance attendants commandeered a lift on the fourth floor. They held the doors open and refused access to public and staff alike, then two nurses arrived pushing a patient in a wheelchair. They went straight down to the basement car park where they wheeled the patient into the back of a white van.' He shrugged, 'Exit van, ambulance men, nurses and Uncle Tom Cobley an' all.'

'Any positive ID of the patient?'

'Only one witness so far. The patient was wrapped in a red blanket but not so well hidden to disguise the fact that she was female and a brunette.'

'It *was* Maria,' Rosemary whispered.

Charles grunted. 'And the white van?'

Harry Hall closed his notebook. 'Two witnesses so far, both of whom say it was just a plain white van – not an ambulance.'

'Make – registration number?'

Harry Hall pulled a face. 'What do you think?' Then his attention was drawn towards the door. A number of men were entering the room. He groaned. 'Here's Rossiter's crowd. I'd better go over and face them.'

Charles nodded. 'I don't want to make things even worse – but the Chief Constable is on his way over.'

'Nothing could make things "even worse",' Harry Hall said bleakly. He stubbed his cigarette out in the ashtray, then walked slowly across to greet the newcomers.

Rosemary clutched Charles's hand. 'You heard about . . . about Ray Peters?'

'I heard,' Charles said grimly.

'And . . . and Maria,' Rosemary whispered, pain showing on her face. 'She was the nicest person I've met for . . . oh, I don't know how long. Oh Charles!' Tears slid down her cheeks as she cried inside, noiselessly and helplessly.

Charles patted her hand. He turned away, watching the engineers unreel a cable drum down the far side of the room. But he watched sightlessly, his mind too full of another picture – Llewellyn's film of that cellar in Milan. It was a bad day's work all round, Charles reflected sourly, but he was damn glad Rosemary had never been shown that.

We were still in the big back room at Wells Court. Kaufman was half way down another drink and I had poured myself one with shaking hands. Hewit and the man Johnny had left, and Llewellyn had returned from meeting the man called Rossiter. Llewellyn knew what had happened. It was in his face. He slumped into an armchair without removing his overcoat, and gazed stonily across the desk at Kaufman. Nobody said a word. I'm not sure I trusted myself to speak – not right at that moment – and we were still sitting like that when the door opened. Watkins, the cab driver, stood in the opening. He glanced at the three of us – Kaufman rubbing his jaw, Llewellyn tight-lipped, and me with a glazed expression on my face – then he stepped back into the corridor and Henderson came in, looking like a refugee from a traffic accident. Blood spattered his shirt front and most of his jacket. He seemed shaken and tired, but more in control of himself than I would have expected after losing so much blood.

'It's not mine,' he said in answer to my unspoken question, 'it's Darmanin's.'

Kaufman looked up. His expression was no longer angry. Instead his face bore a bruised, beaten look and he quickly hooded his eyes, as if afraid of what they might reveal. 'Have a drink,' he growled, 'then tell me about it.'

Henderson was surprised – either by Kaufman's tone or the invitation itself. He looked from Llewellyn to me. I poured him a scotch. He downed half of it, set the glass on the desk, and collapsed into the chair next to mine.

'We found the place all right,' he said quickly to Kaufman, 'Darmanin must have been waiting because he came to the door immediately – wearing an overcoat, all ready to go. Then there was a shot and the poor bastard was knocked backwards down the hall. I flung myself after him and kicked the door shut behind me. It was just one shot. The old man caught it in the guts. Big shell, by the state of him. No point in calling a doctor. I said one was coming but I don't think he believed me – I don't think he cared—'

'Calm down. Finish your drink.'

Henderson had been speaking rapidly, *too* rapidly I suppose because Kaufman had stopped him. The sort of thing you would do to a man in shock – that, or slap his face. Henderson knew it too because he finished his drink then ran a hand through his hair. 'Oh shit,' he said, 'what a bloody awful day.'

Kaufman pushed his cigarettes across the desk. A telephone jangled with enough noise to make me jump. Kaufman hit a button and the ringing transferred itself across the hall. It stopped as someone answered it. A pulse twitched in Henderson's neck, jerking the vein like a fishing line. His eyes closed and I could almost feel him trying to relax. We looked away, embarrassed, as if we had caught him committing an indecent act. It went very quiet, for what seemed a long time.

Then Henderson resumed. 'We were in a heap at the bottom of the stairs,' he said, 'me and the old man. There was nothing I could do for him. I just cradled him in my arms, propped up on that step like a couple of drunks. I had my Walther on the floor next to me – just in case someone charged through the front door. But I never expected it. Watkins went on round the block, but the back-up boys were only fifty yards behind.'

He took another long pull on the cigarette. His hands stopped shaking and his voice steadied as he regained control. 'The old man kept calling me Mr Harris,' he nodded at me, 'obviously thought I was you. Said he had heard all sorts of rumours about me – Sam Harris that is – in his bar. Wanted to know if it were true about me having a score to settle with the Pipeline.'

His gaze shifted to Kaufman, as if anticipating a question, but when none came he continued. 'So I pretended to be Sam Harris. Yes, I told him, I had a score to settle, then I asked what he knew about the Pipeline. He kept shaking his head and saying he knew nothing but his son knew everything. It was all very garbled, just the odd word here and there. He was suffering a lot of pain. I'd got him turned to the wall because I didn't want him to see his guts hanging out – the smell was bad enough – and he was struggling a fair bit. I thought he was writhing with pain at first, then I realised he was trying to take a ring off his finger. He said I should take the ring to his son. His *other* son. He runs a bar too, called the Oyster. He kept saying the son knew everything – all there was to know about the Pipeline.'

Henderson paused to reach for the glass which I had re-charged. This time he merely took a sip and continued immediately. 'All this took four or five minutes,' he said, 'and then . . . then the poor devil died on me.'

The announcement was marked by another long silence. As long as a minute perhaps. A minute's silence. Respect for the dead. Like at the Cenotaph.

Henderson flicked his hair back with one hand and reached into his pocket with the other. 'Smithers never turned up,' he said to Kaufman, 'probably warned off by the back-up team. I remembered you wanted the place looked over, so I had a quick look through the flat upstairs. Not much – cheap tatty furniture, a few papers, bills, receipts, stuff for the bar downstairs – but nothing of value, nothing to link him with the Pipeline. Oh, there was one thing. I found his passport. Darmanin was Maltese. Maltese passport, with his photo in it. Then I heard someone ringing the doorbell like mad so I found a way out round the back. Watkins picked me up on the corner of Shaftesbury Avenue.' He withdrew his hand from his pocket. 'That's the ring. Diamond I think, but I'm no expert.'

It was diamond. A man's gold ring, with a square face in which small diamonds had been set in a Maltese Cross design. Not that I paid much attention. I was too appalled by Henderson's story, especially as it so swiftly followed the news about Maria, I was shocked to my core about that.

Kaufman used the stub of his cigarette to light another one. 'Where's this bar? What's it called – the Oyster?'

Henderson looked desperately tired. He had recovered his colour but he looked exhausted. He shook his head miserably. 'That's just it. I said it was garbled. The old man tried to tell me – God knows he tried – but it was right at the end and he was vomiting a lot of blood. I couldn't understand what he was saying. Then – like I said, the poor devil died. I never even got the son's name.'

A look of pain crossed Kaufman's face.

'I told Watkins,' Henderson said apologetically, 'he's trying to find the Oyster in the telephone directory.'

'And the sniper?' Kaufman asked.

Henderson shrugged. 'You'll have to ask Harvey and the back-up boys. All I know is he got away. He must have been on the roof opposite. I checked the angle, I reckon he could see into Darmanin's flat from there. That's what he was after – Darmanin coming to the door just made it easier.'

Llewellyn's growing impatience had been marked by a series of muffled curses. Suddenly he snapped, 'I can't imagine what Rossiter will say. He was bad enough about Hampstead. Then this Bristol thing sent him into hysterics – and now another shooting in London. Four killings in one day! I tell you quite frankly – as like or not he'll abandon the whole exercise.'

Kaufman lifted his head to stare, just as I found my voice. 'What's that supposed to mean?' I asked coldly.

Llewellyn shuffled a quick glance at Kaufman, then turned to me, 'Look, Mr Harris, some people take the view – I'm not saying I do, but there is a view which says this exercise was ill-conceived.

That you and ... um ... Jack Green for instance, ought never to have been involved. It seemed a justifiable risk at the time but—'

'Get to the point,' I said bluntly.

'Well, the view is you should be removed from the operation entirely. You said yourself – it was nothing to do with you. Naturally you would be required to sign certain papers—'

I began quietly – not until the end was I shouting, 'What's the matter, Llewellyn? You tired of playing God? Lost your bottle? You've messed my life about with the finesse of a back street abortionist – and now you want out. Is that it? Well you're too bloody late. What's happened to Maria? What about Jack for God's sake? I don't give a sod for the views of some people—'

'Sam,' Kaufman shouted, 'that's enough.'

'Screw you. You're as bad as he is. Smart as paint at that big house of yours. Now look at you. The first day of your bloody stupid scheme—'

'Shut up!' Kaufman pounded the desk. 'You think shouting helps? It's just so much happened so fast—'

'You bet it has. I remember fighting these bastards three years ago. They hit me every day, every night, every sodding hour until I didn't know my arse from my elbow. But that was just me – not knowing what I was up against. But you knew! That's what beats me – you knew, yet you still involved Maria and Jack and ...' I stopped in mid-sentence. Suddenly I realised it was an hour since we had left Rex Place. 'Where is Jack anyway? What's he doing over there?'

Kaufman avoided my eye. 'Lucia's with him. He's okay—'

'Okay?' I was on my feet and making for the door, 'I wouldn't take your word for the time of day. You're out of your depth. You're—'

The squawk from the inter-com stopped me. Kaufman touched a button and Lucia's voice sounded strained as she said, 'It's Corrao calling back – for Sam.'

Every eye in the room looked at me. One of the recorders switched itself on with a click like a whipcrack in the silence. I watched two ten inch spools share the tape out between them. Then I sprang across to the desk and grabbed the telephone. 'You little bastard! That's about your mark – kidnapping a woman. Well get this, Corrao, I'll murder you when I get my hands on you. By Christ—'

'Sam!' Kaufman grabbed my arm, 'you're not even through yet. Cool it for God's sake! Just get a grip on yourself.'

He was trembling with nerves and temper – or I was. 'Just keep him as long as you can,' he said, 'remember – shouting won't help

227

Maria.' He gave me a long hard look, took a deep breath, then touched a button on the inter-com.

I tried to stop shaking. 'Corrao – is that you?'

He laughed. The same remembered gloating sound. Then he said, 'Well, Winner? Did you have your little chat with Jack Green? How's his wife by the way? Did you ask him?'

Kaufman was making desperate signals. I gritted my teeth. 'Get ... get on with it, will you?'

Corrao chuckled, but he was just beginning to twist the knife. 'You won't learn, will you, Winner? Ask and you shall receive. Make demands and threats and ... well you see what happens?'

'Where's Maria? You listen to me, Corrao—'

'No! You listen. You wanted a meeting, well you've got it – but on our terms. Start understanding that and your partner's wife might stay alive.'

I bit my tongue until I tasted blood.

'You understood that?' he snapped.

'I hear what you say.'

'And you'll do as I say – just remember that.'

Kaufman had the loudspeakers turned on. Corrao's threat reverberated round the room until I thought my brain would explode. 'Listen, Corrao, I'll make a deal—'

'You haven't the cards,' he said contemptuously.

'Yes I have. Southampton, Hull, everything I know. That's why we're meeting, remember?'

'Go on.'

'Look – nothing happens to Maria, right? *Nothing*. I'll come to your meeting, bring the list, everything – but I want Maria back first—'

'*You* want? Making demands again, Winner?' he clicked his tongue. 'Forgetting your manners so soon. Ask remember, ask and you shall receive—'

'Dammit man – I *am* asking—'

'Begging?' he giggled. Then his voice hardened. 'Our terms, Winner, not yours. Now listen carefully because I'll only say it once. You are invited to a meeting in Alcamo in two days' time. Be at the Café Cordina in the Piazza Ciullo at eight o'clock in the evening. And Winner, make sure you bring that list—'

'Where? For God's sake – where did you say this meeting—'

'Alcamo. Don't say you don't know it, Winner. Alcamo is in Sicily. It's beautiful. Like Naples. What do you say? You'll die when you see it.'

Sicily? Fiore Serracino? The Sicilian connection out in the open? I put a hand to my forehead and it came away wet with sweat.

Kaufman signalled me to keep talking and somehow I stumbled on, 'Why two days?' I asked. 'Why not sooner? I want a meeting now—'

'Two days because we say so,' Corrao snapped. 'Goodbye, Winner. See you in the Piazza Ciullo—'

'Wait! Don't hang up. For heaven's sake – what about Maria?'

'She'll be there. Our terms, Winner. Your partner's wife in exchange for you. That's the deal. Talk it over . . . it should make an interesting discussion—'

'Where is she—'

'Quite safe. Bring your partner with you. His wife will be waiting for him at the Café Cordina. But one word in the wrong quarter—'

'No—'

'Yes. Just you and Jack Green – and the list of course.'

Then he hung up – just put the receiver down. The loudspeakers magnified the dialling tone to the noise level of a helicopter. I was so startled that I dropped the telephone . . . but the connection was broken already.

Kaufman jabbed the inter-com. 'Hewit—'

'Lost him, Mr Kaufman. Maybe another minute and—'

'Shit,' Kaufman cut him off. He looked at Llewellyn. 'Sicily,' he whispered, and I could see the fear in his eyes.

The scene in the staff canteen registered as soon as Bob Richardson stepped through the door. He saw Harry Hall seated with Charles and Rosemary Parker on the far side of the room. He would have words with them later – especially Harry Hall – first he must present himself to the senior officer.

'What's happening here?' he asked as soon as he had been introduced to Superintendent Roberts.

Roberts sighed. 'This – this *incident* – occurred just as the store was closing. The customers and most of the staff had left by the time we arrived.' He pointed to the GPO engineers, 'We're installing extra 'phones – then the store's personnel people and some of my officers will begin telephoning all members of the store's staff – asking if they saw anything unusual in the store this afternoon—'

'That's a hell of a job.'

'And that's an understatement,' Roberts said hotly. 'You know and I know what we should be doing. A television appeal – asking potential witnesses to come forward—'

'No,' Richardson shook his head, 'that's already been vetoed.'

'Then I want it known that we're working under a severe handicap,' Roberts snapped, trying to control his temper, 'something like two thousand customers and staff were in this store between five and six this afternoon. God knows how many of the employees are on the 'phone – probably less than a third—'

'I was asked to convey the Chief's apologies—'

Roberts snorted his disgust. 'Apologies will be worth nothing if we come up empty-handed. It will be my neck on the chopping board—'

'What about the white van?' Richardson interrupted.

'What about it? Every copper between here and Land's End is looking for it.'

'But nothing so far?'

Roberts didn't even bother to answer – the expression on his face was enough.

'The docks?' Richardson persisted. 'The airport—'

'All taken care of,' Roberts said grimly. 'Photographs of Mrs Green have been rushed to every emigration official, every customs man, every check-in desk—'

'I'm sorry,' Richardson backed off, 'nobody meant to imply—'

Roberts thrust a finger under his nose, 'The Charles Parkers and Harry Halls of this world do not come under my jurisdiction. But when they are involved in a job in my manor I should be told about it—'

'Quite,' Richardson nodded, wishing that he had been able to stay in London.

Roberts glowered. 'All right then, just so long as we understand each other.' He paused and when he resumed a note of sarcasm sounded in his voice. 'Now then – is there anything new you can tell me about this caper?'

Richardson hesitated. 'Well, we think we can guess where they're taking her.'

Roberts stared at him, 'Well, man, out with it.'

'Sicily.'

Roberts whistled softly. 'The Pipeline.' He shook his head sadly. 'That poor wee lassy – I wouldn't be in her shoes for all the tea in China. What do you rate her chances ... if we don't find her I mean?'

'I'm afraid we don't rate them at all,' Richardson lowered his gaze, unable to meet the other man's eye, 'our guess is that she will be put to death – unless we find her within the next forty-eight hours.'

It was the longest night of my life. Nobody got any sleep except Jack, and he was drugged. Lucia did it while we were all in the big back room, and she and Jack were waiting for us in Rex Place. I suppose she dropped something into his drink, the way they dealt with me the night before. I was blazing mad when I discovered it but Jack was out cold by then. Bonello appeared on the scene and deflected most of my temper away from Lucia. 'Jack can do nothing tonight,' he said, 'only suffer – or get in the way. Meanwhile we have work to do.'

And work we did. We split into groups in London whilst, from what I could hear, Bristol and elsewhere were being torn apart in an effort to find Maria. That worried me sick. Corrao had ordered my silence. What would happen if the Pipeline found out? What would happen to Maria then? Not that I had a chance to worry on that score ... I was too busy answering questions and trying to remember. Kaufman was obsessed with his theory that the best route to the Pipeline lay buried in my memory. If he could uncover that he might be able to reach Maria. So we picked up from where we left off yesterday – with the famous list of names. It was a continuation of the question and answer session started at the big house, but this time I tried so hard to remember that I thought my head would burst.

Kaufman's list seemed to include everyone I had ever known. He started with the old payroll records, people who had worked for me, everyone, right back to the days when I ran the sandwich bars. Then there were the employees at Winston's and Jennifer's and those at The Point of View. But his main list came from the membership records of the gaming clubs – he concentrated on those most of all. The police computer had processed them already so often Kaufman knew more about people than I did ... but still the questions came ... remember this, what about that, did you ever see these two people together? He was seeking a link, a pattern, a connection which would lead to the Pipeline, but with more than ten thousand names to examine it was like looking for a needle in a haystack.

Hour after hour, name after name. It seemed futile at times but we kept going. Working stopped me breaking out in a cold sweat at the thought of what might be happening to Maria. We smoked until our throats were parched, drank black coffee from the machine, then lit fresh cigarettes to start the cycle over again. Kaufman made lists and sub-lists, cross-checked and referenced, drew circles and lines on scraps of paper ... and was forever trying to link the lines back to Edgar Hardman.

'How often did Hardman visit the club? Was he a heavy gambler? Who were his friends? Did he take pains to avoid people?'

'You're wasting time. You're wrong – *really wrong*!'

'Yeah! Two things, Sam. That fancy photo in his safe at Chelsea—'

231

'Edgar was at his wits end. I know the man. He was a shadow—'

'He was giving a performance—'

'Rubbish! Why the hell should he pretend to me? You're so convinced he was guilty you won't even consider another explanation.'

'Such as?'

'Such as blackmail. Someone was blackmailing him. It's the only explanation—'

'With that photograph?'

'Why not with that photograph? What's wrong—'

'So why didn't he go to the police?'

'I don't know – people don't, not always – do they? I mean if—'

'People always go to the police – unless they're afraid of what the police will find out. What was Hardman afraid of?'

'Afraid of the photo being circulated—'

'Your wife wasn't doing anything illegal – not in that photograph. So the blackmailer couldn't threaten to send it to the police – and no newspaper would touch a shot like that—'

'But . . . Kay's circle of friends . . . her social life. It was important to her. Just that photo being shown around would be enough—'

'But Hardman had the photograph. And the negative. How in God's name could someone threaten him with what was already locked up in his safe?'

'Copies. Perhaps other people – someone – had copies—'

Kaufman shook his head. 'I don't buy that. Don't misunderstand – I've thought about it. But if you accept blackmail you must take what goes with it. Which is that Hardman knew something. If blackmail comes into this it's because someone found out Hardman's connection with the Pipeline. Now that would really give a blackmailer some leverage.'

I rubbed my eyes as if trying to get a clearer picture of what was in the back of his mind – or what might have been in the back of Edgar's mind.

'And another thing,' Kaufman drove on relentlessly, 'I got this little scene buzzing round my brain. A scruffy hotel room in Palermo. A man runs in, locks the door, grabs the 'phone, gives a number and hangs up to wait. He's sweating like a pig. He's frightened. Shaking too much to even light a cigarette. He's as good as dead and knows it. He knows they're onto him – knows he's only got a few minutes left. The 'phone rings – he hears footsteps running up the stairs – he's through to Bonello – someone starts kicking the door down – starts *shooting* the door down – armed men appear in

232

the opening – the man on the 'phone screams – shouts a name – then he's cut down in a hail of bullets.' Kaufman paused to ram the point home, 'And the name he shouts is Hardman. That's all – just one word – one name – and that name is Hardman.'

We came back to that every time. It was unanswerable. I shook my head as I walked over to the coffee machine. 'Okay,' I said. 'Let's have the next name.'

And so it went on – until midnight, when Kaufman called a break. 'Just for ten minutes, Sam,' he warned, 'to give your head a chance to stop buzzing.'

We went upstairs to find Henderson. He was in a room so small that the table and four upright chairs left little room for anything else. But Henderson had managed. For a start he had some sort of computer terminal, with a triple deck screen and a print-out unit. And a teleprinter. And maps on the wall – and an electric kettle, with a jar of Nescafé and half a pint of milk.

Another man occupied one of the chairs. He wore a blue shirt and black tie which might have been police issue. He stood up as Kaufman entered, then went back to checking names on a typewritten list. Henderson himself looked close to exhaustion. He had discarded his jacket, loosened his tie and was working in blood-stained shirtsleeves.

Kaufman took one chair and motioned me into the other. 'Well?' he said.

Henderson sighed as he reached for a handwritten list. 'A club in Fulham called The Pearl and Oyster. Three bars in the Greater London area called the Oyster Shell. Two pubs in East Anglia called the Oyster Catcher – a bar in a Birmingham hotel called the Oyster Room, and about fifteen fish restaurants.'

'And?' Kaufman offered his cigarettes.

'Nothing so far,' Henderson nodded at the computer screens, 'but the list gets longer all the time.'

'Anything else?'

'Immigration are checking their Maltese section. So far they've come up with forty-two Darmanins registered in London alone.' He smiled but not enough to dispel his air of weariness, 'Darmanin is beginning to seem like the Maltese equivalent of Smith.'

'What's happening to the names?' Kaufman asked.

'Being classified – given names, ages, occupations—' he broke off with a gesture of exasperation. 'If only I'd got his name! But the old man kept saying my son – my son. I thought he meant the chauffeur to begin with—'

'What about a list of licensees?' Kaufman interrupted. 'The old man said the boy ran a bar didn't he? Not worked in one—'

233

'It's being checked – or rather they are being checked. There is no central registrar. Each licensing authority maintains its own lists.'

'Shit,' Kaufman said quietly.

Henderson ran a hand through his hair. 'There's another complication. I discovered it earlier. Children of mixed British and Maltese parentage are allowed British *and* Maltese passports until their eighteenth birthday. Then they have to choose – British *or* Maltese.'

'So? You found a Maltese passport in Darmanin's apartment—'

'But his son might have a British one. In which case he won't be registered as an alien with Immigration—'

'Only if his old man had a British wife. You don't know he did.'

'I don't know he didn't.'

'Any sign of a woman in the apartment? Clothes, make-up, jewellery—'

'No, strictly a bachelor pad. My guess is the old man was a widower.'

Kaufman shook his head: 'I still don't see the problem. Get the Passport Office to run a check on all Darmanins holding a British passport.'

'It *is* midnight,' Henderson pointed out. 'The Foreign Office gave us a very frosty answer an hour ago. The Brigadier is sorting it out now.'

The Brigadier was Llewellyn – I had discovered that much.

Kaufman grunted as he stood up. 'Keep me posted, I'll be downstairs with Sam.'

Outside on the landing we bumped into Bonello and Lucia – quite literally because Bonello was struggling into his overcoat and not looking where he was going. Kaufman stopped him, 'You two taking a vacation?'

'We're going to a meeting with the Italian Ambassador,' Bonello said in a rush, 'at the Embassy.'

'At this hour?' Kaufman took an incredulous look at his watch.

Bonello pulled a face. 'We've already spoken on the telephone. He's not happy but he'll see us.'

'Mind telling me—'

'No time . . . just say there's a chance of putting forty armed men into Alcamo . . . armed to the teeth but totally invisible.' Then Bonello and Lucia were running down the stairs and Kaufman and I were left staring after them. Kaufman swore half under his breath, then he and I returned to the big back room, back to the lists, back to the questions, dates, places, names, relationships – and all the time Kaufman urging, 'Think, Sam, for Christ's sake think!'

It had turned two o'clock when Llewellyn came in, wearing a dinner jacket and smoking a cigar instead of the perennial pipe. He looked remarkably fresh, considering the hour and everything else. No black coffee for him either – he went directly to the bottles next to the coffee machine and poured himself a large brandy.

'You celebrating?' Kaufman enquired, 'or drowning your sorrows?'

Llewellyn took the chair next to mine. 'Hardly celebrating – an evening with Rossiter? God, what a bore he is. Insufferable.'

Kaufman glanced enviously at the cigar, 'Yeah – must have been rough.'

'No news from Bristol I suppose?' Llewellyn asked in a matter of fact voice.

'Bristol lose things,' Kaufman pronounced, 'finding them is something else.'

Llewellyn nodded and was about to add something when he stopped with an odd look at me. I had the impression very strongly that he wanted me out of the way, that he wanted a private word with Kaufman. But I settled deeper into my chair, as if to say I was staying, so he had no choice but to get on with it. Finally he pretended I wasn't there by turning his back on me and speaking directly to Kaufman. 'None the less,' he said as he withdrew an envelope from an inside pocket, 'Rossiter's people came up with something. They found this – at Wyndham Hall.'

Kaufman reached for the envelope and extracted a letter from the already unsealed flap. He raised his eyes to me in a curiously revealing gesture, as if he too would have preferred my absence. Then he turned his attention to the letter. He read quickly, and then – when I guessed him to be half way down the page – he gave a start of surprise. After which he turned to the second page and read more slowly – as if committing it to memory.

Their secretive attitude infuriated me. It reminded me of the earlier incident – the way in which Kaufman had shuffled away from my question about something happening to Edgar in January. Corrao's 'phone call had put it out of my mind, but it was back now – with a vengeance.

'You two make me sick,' I complained, 'you're quick enough asking questions but bloody slow in answering them.'

'Sure, Sam,' Kaufman said absent-mindedly. He was placating me rather than listening – and Llewellyn slid me a glance which said clearer than words that he hoped I wasn't about to create a scene.

'Something happened in January,' I said, 'and you two know about it.'

'In a minute, Sam,' Kaufman said softly. His full concentration was taken up by the letter in his hands.

'January?' Llewellyn murmured with polite interest.

I swore and wished Jack was around – it needed both of us. Then Kaufman whistled softly as he looked up, 'Where in God's name was this?'

'Hardman's desk at Wyndham Hall,' Llewellyn answered. 'It was stuffed at the back of a drawer – as if he'd forgotten it, or overlooked it.'

Kaufman rubbed the creases on his face. Then he placed the letter and envelope on the seat of his chair before crossing to the whisky bottle. He poured two drinks, added water to one, carried the glasses back to the desk and pushed one over to me. Carefully he reassembled the pages of the letter into their correct order. 'You got a copy of this?' he asked, and when Llewellyn nodded he persisted with another question. 'With you – you got a copy here?'

Llewellyn nodded again.

Kaufman held the letter in his hand, but he was no longer looking at it. He was looking at me. 'Read it, Sam. It's addressed to you anyway.'

My name and the Rex Place address were on the envelope in Edgar's spindly handwriting. It no longer angered me that other people had read what was intended for me, but Kaufman's attitude alarmed me. And when he spoke he avoided my eye. 'Look at the date first,' he said, 'it might help.' Then he turned to Llewellyn, 'Let's check on Henderson, bring your drink with you.'

But I doubted they were going to see Henderson. They wanted to discuss the letter, and perhaps leave me alone to read it. *It was dated January!* Even as I saw it I remembered Edgar in the restaurant – and Kaufman's reaction when I said – 'something happened in January'.

And on the twenty-eighth of January, Edgar had written:

My Dear Sam,
I doubt I'll ever send this. Hopefully I'll have the courage to tell you what I've done face to face, but if you ever read this you will know my courage has failed me – as it has more than once of late. I'm safe enough writing it now – I cannot post it anyway, not until you are released. The prison censorship officers would have a fine old time with it, even before it reached you – assuming it ever did. So I've a while yet to make up my mind about sending it – and a while longer to screw up my courage to talk to you about it.

So why write at all? Loneliness I suppose – and a troubled conscience.
An old man who can't sleep, with only a bottle for company.

Sam – Kay is dead. There, I've written it – even that helps. To set
it down in black and white. To say it aloud helps. Kay is dead. Not that
anyone knows – except a ruffian called Rogers and me, and now you
– and whoever murdered her.

I dropped the letter as if it had burst into flames. It had startled
Kaufman at exactly the same place – half way down the first page.
But he had read on, whereas I didn't want to – not that I could for
a moment – I was too stunned. *Kay was dead!* All that vitality, that
zest for life – gone, gone forever.

I drank the scotch which Kaufman had provided, helped myself
to another – lighted a cigarette and sat staring into space – thinking
of Kay – remembering her – mourning her. Oh Christ she was gone!
Kay was dead! I would never see her again. Never hear her laugh
– never get that funny feeling in the pit of my stomach when she
smiled at me. Never hold her in my arms, never make love to her
– never again. Never, *ever*.

And yet . . . and yet . . . hadn't I known? Hadn't some small voice
deep inside me whispered as much? Even in Brixton I had guessed
I would never see her again. Perhaps I had accepted it then – when
the divorce went through I wondered if I would ever see her again.
But dead?

For a few moments I was stunned by that shock alone. Then I
realised what Edgar had written. *Not that anyone knows – except a*
ruffian called Rogers and me, and now you – and whoever murdered
her.

Shock, the selfish pain of grief, the bitter empty sense of loss –
gave way to horror. Kay had been murdered! I pushed the whisky
aside and reached for the four pages of thick writing paper.

Kay never told me what happened that night – with Faberge and
Martinez – but I rather gather she was involved. All she would say was
it was all her fault – and that she would make it up to you, somehow.
It's important you know that, Sam – especially now.

She went to pieces after the trial you know – turned into a complete
nervous wreck. I never told you but the hospital diagnosed drugs when
she crashed the car that night. There were lots of questions, but nothing
came of it – nothing could I suppose, so long as Kay denied
everything.

I wanted her to go into a private clinic, but she wouldn't have it –
in fact she wouldn't have much to do with me either – spent her time with
that bloody awful crowd she'd got in with – either at Ashley Grange or

that place on the river. I tried to reach her – went down once a week to begin with, but she was jumpy as a tick with me and I couldn't stand the people she was with.

Anyway, next I heard she had money troubles. I gather she didn't see eye to eye with that fellow Collins who was looking after your affairs. I said I would help out if she was hard up, but I also pointed out that those leeches at Ashley Grange were sucking her dry. That didn't help – she went up like a sheet of flames and we had a hell of a row about it – then she came out and said it – that I wasn't welcome there any more. Well I took umbrage – damn silly but there it is – stormed out and told her she could stew in her own juice for all I cared.

I was cut up about it. I don't mind admitting. We're a rum lot us Hardmans – too damn proud by half I suppose – I felt she owed me an apology but it was more than that – I felt she owed herself. She was letting herself down, doing things unworthy of her, mixing with the wrong people. Of course I got no thanks for telling her, so things were a bit strained after that. I tried to get over it – after all, a man's only child means a damn sight more to him than a few unkind words. So I 'phoned her a few weeks later – and then she told me about the divorce. I was shocked. I tried to talk her out of it – reminded her of what she had said, that business about making it up to you – but she gave me a damn funny answer. At least I never understood it at the time. She said it was important for you both to be free when you met again – no ties, no obligations. If you went back together then it would be because you wanted to – not because you had to. I thought it was so much rubbish and said as much, and then she told me something else. That she needed money, cash, urgently – and a lot of it.

She said a divorce settlement was the only answer. Of course I asked why – what the money was for – but she went as tight as a clam and refused to say another word.

She rather avoided me after that. I tried to keep in touch, but I was having the devil's own fight with the receiver at Apex, trying to persuade him not to sell up, and I had the wine business to think of on top of that – so one way and another I was as busy as the proverbial fly. But I knew your divorce had gone through because there was a bit in the papers about it – and a couple of weeks later Ashley Grange was offered for sale in The Times. Then – it must have been about a month after that – Kay 'phoned me late at night. Her voice sounded weird and I knew she was in trouble. She was at Rex Place. It took me twenty minutes to get there and that wasn't a moment too soon. She had taken an overdose of something and was barely conscious. If the front door hadn't been unlocked I wouldn't have made it in time. As it was I roused her, got her on her feet, and walked her up and down and round and round until Bertie West arrived from his bed in New Cavendish Street.

It was a ghastly business, but it was a turning point. Bertie saved her life, and got her into some hush-hush clinic in Beaconsfield. We called it a nervous breakdown but of course it was nothing of the kind. Sam, I can't describe the hell she went through. It broke me up just watching her. I'll never know how she came through it – week after week, month after month – but I swear she was over it when she came out. Really over it! Whatever else you believe – I want you to know that.

She came to live with me then at Lorimer's Walk – or rather, in her old flat upstairs. I wanted to keep an eye on her and keep her away from her old crowd at The Fisherman. I expected trouble at first, but as she grew stronger she seemed to like living there. She became more her own self – more like the girl you married – as wilful as ever of course but perhaps not so headstrong. She got so clear eyed and glowing with health – eating properly – well I tell you Sam, you would have been proud of her.

We saw each other every day at Lorimer's Walk, and our roles reversed a bit as she got stronger I don't mind telling you. This fight with the receiver had worn me out. It was as good as lost and I was at my wits end, but a few weeks ago I got the old crowd together again to try to work out a salvage operation – a last ditch stand if you like. Old Darlington was in a blue funk and kept on about it being bad for the bank's reputation to be mixed up with receivers and Charlie Weston and Lew Douglas had washed their hands of it because of that damn fool undertaking of mine. Well, the meeting got a bit heated and in the end I lost my temper – especially with Charlie Weston – he really got under my skin. So I said if he wouldn't at least try to save Apex then I wanted nothing more to do with him. That brought him up with a start. He asked what I meant and I said the first thing that came into my head – that I would cancel my contract with his haulage firm for the shipment of our wines. A bit to my surprise it did the trick because he was much more helpful after that – and even Lew Douglas made a few constructive suggestions. It's all so much wasted effort now because I've just heard that the receiver has sold out over our heads – but I want you to know that I tried.

In point of fact I held the meeting at Lorimer's Walk, and Kay asked me the outcome after they left. Actually she asked if Apex could be held together until you came out. I had to say I was beginning to doubt it, but I told her how the meeting had gone, about me leaning on Charlie Weston and all the rest of it. We talked for about an hour, then she made some coffee and we went to bed.

She was up half the night I think. Certainly she was prowling about upstairs until gone two o'clock. Then in the morning she announced she was going on holiday. It must have been a sudden decision because there was no mention of it the night before. When I asked where she said anywhere in the Med. – just as long as she got some sunshine. Well, it was the usual bloody awful January in London and had I not been so busy I might have gone with her – wish to God I had now, but there it is.

Then something rather strange happened. She gave me a large brown envelope and asked me to look after it. She was very mysterious. I had to promise not to open the damn thing, just keep it in the safe until she returned. She said it really ought to be destroyed but it had cost too much for that – and just knowing it was there was enough to remind her of what she had lost. I couldn't make head nor tail of it, but I put the envelope in the safe for her – just to humour her. Then she went upstairs to pack and I left for the office, but she kissed me goodbye before I left and she said she would be away for a couple of weeks. Oh, and another thing, she told me to stop worrying about Apex because she felt sure it would turn out right in the end.

Well, Sam, now comes the hardest part of all. A week ago I had a 'phone call from a man called Rogers in Tunis. Damned mysterious. He wouldn't go into detail, other than to say it concerned my daughter and he was afraid it was bad news. Then he asked if I could get out there immediately? Well, I dropped everything and went. Devil of a job getting there – via Paris in the end, took me ten hours, but I was there the same day as the call. Not that it mattered – Kay was dead before Rogers picked up the telephone.

Rogers runs some kind of fishing business. He's English, but nothing to be proud about – a sly, ferret-faced man, as oily as a grease rag. His Arab fishermen had found Kay drifting in an open boat – somewhere in the Gulf of Hammeret. She was dead when they found her – and Sam – it's a horrible thing to have to tell you – but she had been badly beaten up, I won't go into detail but take my word for it – I saw her – though I wish to God I hadn't. She was dressed normally enough – shirt and jeans and sandals, and she had a handbag with her – but how she came to be in that boat is a mystery. Rogers found my name and address among her stuff, enough to know she was my daughter – so he 'phoned me instead of going to the police. That was his angle of course – he was no end impressed I was a Lord and not plain mister – and he kept nagging on about the scandal and the newspapers and that rubbish. I said to hell with that – I just wanted to get my hands on whoever had hurt Kay. I even suspected Rogers at first, but his fishermen all vouched for his story – I questioned them myself. And there was something else – Rogers found a hypodermic in her handbag – and some heroin. At least he said it was heroin – I wasn't sure one way or the other, but he seemed the type to know.

I wished to God you had been there, Sam, to share the decision. Even now I wonder if I did the right thing. But when I got over the shock of it I got to thinking, and it seemed to me that we've had enough of the bloody newspapers to last us a lifetime. I was thinking as a father naturally, but the thought of Kay's body being photographed and poked around by a lot of coroners – well, it turned my stomach. Even finding out what had happened, who had done these terrible things, well, none of it would bring her back to me – to us. Rogers offered to bury her at sea and keep his mouth shut. He wanted money naturally, but not a fortune. Sam – Kay loved the Mediterranean, you know that, she hardly missed a summer as a kid, and, well to my mind, it made as good a final resting place as any. Rogers made a kind of sleeping bag affair from white sail cloth – and in the early hours of the following morning we took a boat out, deep into the Med. and slipped her over the side.

It's taken the best part of a bottle of Remy to get this letter this far – so I may as well finish it even though the odds are against posting it. Sam, I did what I thought was best for Kay – please believe that. I thought of you too, and felt you would understand. It seemed almost logical out there – all that sea and sky, such a natural, simple, clean way to end it all – but back here in England, well I'm not so sure. Life is more complicated. For a start, Lorimer's Walk was broken into while I was away and that envelope has gone missing. I don't know what was in it, but Kay's words keep coming back to me – about it costing too much to be destroyed. This whole business has got me so confused I don't know if I'm coming or going – but is it too preposterous to imagine Kay being blackmailed? God alone knows what about – but her desperate need for money last year has to be explained some way.

Now something else has happened. A man from the Inland Revenue called yesterday. He wanted to talk to Kay about her tax affairs. I said she was away on holiday, but if it was a tax matter why not discuss it with her accountant? I gave him Forbes's address and telephone number and left it at that, but I was speaking to Forbes's this evening on another matter. Nobody has been to see him, and he couldn't think that the Inland Revenue would have a query large enough to warrant a personal interview.

It's all so odd! Twice lately I've had the feeling I'm being watched – that I'm followed even. Maybe I'm getting old and senile – but there it is.

You know, Sam, just writing this has made me feel better. As if we were talking it over. It eases the guilt and some of the loneliness – but I'm damned if I know what to do next. Kay can't be on holiday forever. All her old crowd seem to have dropped her but somebody is bound to ask sooner or later. What the hell do I say? That she's living abroad, I think – and hope nobody pursues it more than that. But it's a terrible worry.

Sam – try to remember all the good things about her. I know the pair *of you had troubles at the end – but she wasn't a bad girl – spoiled I know, but that was my fault not hers – irresponsible and selfish in some ways, but she sorted herself out in that clinic. She was settling down to wait for you, I'm sure of that, and now this terrible, terrible thing has happened.*

The letter ended abruptly. Without a signature. Perhaps he had intended to add more later? Or perhaps he had emptied the bottle of brandy? I whispered 'Poor Edgar' over and over again – and a lump filled my throat whenever I thought of Kay. I turned the letter over in my hands and read it again. Then I just sat staring into space. Minutes passed, I don't know how many – five, ten, fifteen – until the shock dulled to a steady pain like an aching tooth. Then I was angry. Suddenly I was shaking and trembling with temper. I stood up. Walked about the room – trying to get my nerves under control. None of it made sense. Kay, Edgar – dead – both dead – *murdered*! It was inconceivable. The very idea of Edgar being involved with gangsters had been laughable this morning. Now he was dead. And now Maria had been kidnapped.

All my life I've had a temper. It's cooled a bit with the years – Sam Harris at forty-two is less prone to fly off the handle than he was twenty years ago. But I have never felt so angry in the whole of my life as I did then. It took half an hour before I stopped twitching – and another ten minutes before my hands stopped shaking. I drank some coffee from the machine, smoked another cigarette, and something deep inside me turned to ice.

CHAPTER TEN

Richardson was drinking coffee with Superintendent Roberts at Bristol Police HQ. It was half past two in the morning. For the past hour Roberts had been hinting about getting some sleep, and Richardson's resistance was weakening. After all, not much was happening. Work at the department store had been abandoned at midnight. By then the police had spoken to most of those employees who possessed a private telephone. Very little had been added to the sum of knowledge. It seemed that nurses had been seen in all *three* public lavatories during the latter part of the afternoon. The local hospitals were being contacted but, so far, the nurses had not been identified. And that was all.

Richardson's thoughts wandered back to London. It all depended on Sam Harris, he was sure of that, somewhere in the recesses of Harris's memory lay a name, maybe more than one name, maybe an event, a combination of people and places ... get Harris to talk, Richardson assured himself, and this whole thing will make sense.

Roberts stifled a yawn. 'We'll have twenty men asking questions when the store opens at nine in the morning. Every employee will be shown photographs of Mrs Green and Mrs Parker. Everyone will be questioned—'

'Merely to confirm Harry Hall's story,' Richardson shrugged.

Roberts was about to make a sarcastic comment when the telephone rang ... after which all thoughts of turning in for the night were abandoned. 'They've found the white van,' Roberts said with his hand over the mouthpiece.

Richardson came to the edge of his seat, but Roberts was still listening to the voice on the telephone. He said 'yes' twice, then looked at his watch. 'We're on our way,' he said, then he hung up.

Richardson followed him to the door and was still asking questions when both men hurled themselves into the back of a squad car. The driver took off like a rally driver leaving a check-point.

'One of my brighter policemen found a nurse's cape thrown over a hedge,' Roberts said, 'it's our van all right ... abandoned in a hurry by the sound of it.'

They were there within twenty minutes, racing through the darkened streets like a bolting horse. The van was at the end of a cul-de-sac near open country, Richardson saw moonlit fields through a gap in the houses. Three other squad cars were there already, and a ring of arc lamps encircled the van. Other lights blinked on and off down the street, first at bedroom windows, then at front doors as people came to investigate.

Half an hour later two other nurses' capes were found in a dustbin. The van itself had been wiped clean of fingerprints, so no clues showed there ... and the forensic boys were still at their painstakingly slow business, an hour or more away from their report. But then came the discovery of the map. Tucked under the sun visor over the driver's seat in the van was a sheet of thin, cheap note-paper ... upon which had been drawn a sketch map. It showed the route from Cardiff, across the Severn Bridge, into Bath and out again to Glebe Farm, the 'safe house' to which Maria had been sent. And there was more ... another sketch of the route from Glebe Farm to Flitton Aerodrome on the other side of Bristol.

Roberts was positively optimistic. 'Flitton is little more than an airstrip. Ex-RAF, but used mostly by the local flying club these days, though some freight business goes through there as well, now that Lulsgate is so overloaded.'

'Export freight?' Richardson asked quickly.

'Aye, I've no doubt export as well. Laport Pharmaceuticals is just down the road – I'm told they use it . . .'

But Richardson was already hurrying back to the squad car.

Kaufman left me alone for a long time. Long enough to recover from the shock of Edgar's letter and the news of Kay's death, but never long enough to get used to the concept of murder. Before my trial murder had been something involving other people, headlines in a newspaper – now I was surrounded by it. Even for a loner like me, people – *some* people – were important. Kay, Edgar, Jack and Maria were . . . *had been* . . . the cornerstones of my life. Now two were dead and Maria was in mortal danger. And Jack would be too blinded by worry to think straight. Reminding myself of that helped me concentrate – made me think of other people – so that when Kaufman returned at three thirty I was ready for him.

He bustled into the room. His tie was loosened and he conveyed the air of a man who has been hectically busy. There was a determined set to his jaw and a look of subdued excitement in his eyes. He picked Darmanin's diamond ring up from the desk and tossed it from hand to hand as he looked at me.

I pointed to the letter. 'How much of that did you know?'

'Not much. We knew your ex-wife had disappeared. And we suspected Hardman of knowing a lot more than he was telling.'

'The man from the Inland Revenue – he was your man?'

Kaufman nodded. 'Old Hardman didn't miss much did he? He was even onto the surveillance team—'

'But he was never the Ferryman. Even you must admit—'

Kaufman flushed. 'Now hold on – that was rough, about your wife – a hell of a shock for you. And maybe I was less than completely right about Hardman, but that letter begs more questions than it answers.'

'Such as?'

'Such as what was your ex-wife doing in Tunis? Did you have friends there?'

'She was on holiday! For heaven's sake, you read the letter—'

'A sudden decision, made overnight? Come on, Sam, the Pipeline runs through Tunis. We're almost sure. It's the last leg of the journey to Sicily.'

'For Christ's sake! Don't you ever stop?'

'Listen knucklehead – your ex-wife is dead. So is your pal

Hardman and there's no telling what's happening to Maria. And in two days' time . . .' he ckecked his watch, 'correction – *tomorrow* – you go to Sicily with a fifty-fifty chance of getting your head blown off. You think now is a good time to stop?'

'But you'll find Maria . . . I mean, the search, there's still time—'

'You running a book on it? You want to know the chances of us finding Maria now?'

'But Llewellyn said every policeman this side of—'

'Forget it. I'll give you a thousand to one, unless . . .' he paused to jab his finger in my direction, 'unless you remember something real good in the next two hours.'

I made a gesture of hopelessness which was nothing to the frustration I felt. But then I had another idea. 'If you're right,' I said, 'if they get her out . . . if they get her to Sicily. Well, we know where she'll be. Corrao said—'

'So what? You think you can go in with a platoon of marines? You expecting an armed escort or something?'

I stared at him.

'Oh Jesus!' he threw his hands in the air. 'Do you imagine her sipping a campari while she waits for you? Then you waltz in, take her elbow and just lead her out of there?'

'I don't know . . .'

'Listen to me,' Kaufman said angrily, 'I'll tell you how these things *really* work. You and Jack arrive – sit in a conspicuous place, have a drink and smoke a few cigarettes while you watch the local colour. Meanwhile, you are being watched. Maybe you sit there half an hour – an hour – all night. If they smell a cop within a mile of you they'll let you sit there the rest of your life. You can rot there for all they care. But if they think you are clean, someone will join your table. "I can take you to your wife," he'll say to Jack. "Have you got the list?" he'll ask you. Then he will point at an automobile. "Just walk over and get into the back of that Ferrari," he will say.'

Kaufman paused to add emphasis. 'And you'll do whatever that man says, Sam. Nice and easy, without drawing attention to yourself.'

I rubbed my wrist with the palm of my other hand. A less observant man might have thought I was rubbing an itch, but Kaufman knew I was wiping the sweat from my palm.

Finally I said, 'That's when you move? When Jack and I get into that car?'

'Like hell! You think Maria will be in that automobile? Like she's picking you up on the way home from the beauty parlour?'

'So you follow the car?'

He sighed. 'I'll level with you, Sam. The way I see it – we won't even be there.'

'You mean ... Jack and I alone?' And I was still digesting that and trying to steady my nerves when Llewellyn arrived. He sat on the edge of the desk and tapped his knee with what was obviously a British passport. 'What do you know about Malta?' he asked me.

'Nothing, I've never been there—'

'That's where your ex-wife went. Not Tunis.' He handed the passport to Kaufman. 'Rossiter's people have finished at Wyndham. The place is clean, but they came across this. Hardman must have brought it back with him.'

Kaufman rifled the pages. 'Just her date of arrival. No departure ... no re-entry elsewhere.' He glanced at Llewellyn, 'This place she was found – how far is it from Malta? This Bay of something ...' he tossed the passport aside and reached for Edgar's letter.

'Gulf of Hammeret,' Llewellyn corrected. 'About two hundred miles. Sicily is even closer ...' He paused, struck by a sudden thought. 'That's an idea. Hardman employs a Maltese chauffeur and his daughter makes a sudden trip to Malta. Do you think there's a connection?'

Kaufman raised his clenched fist to within an inch of Llewellyn's chin. When he opened his fingers the diamond ring lay in the palm of his hand. 'Find Darmanin's son and you'll get your answer ... unless the Pipeline find him first.'

It went very quiet after that. I suppose we were all struggling to absorb this new piece of information. Malta? Kay had never mentioned the place to me. What on earth had sent her running to an island in the Mediterranean?

Finally Llewellyn sighed and asked, 'Is Enrico about?'

Kaufman explained about the dash to the Italian Embassy and the possibility of putting forty men into Alcamo – 'all armed to the teeth but totally invisible'. When he finished he grunted, 'Trust an Italian. Wasn't that an old Roman trick – that Trojan Horse business?'

'Greek actually,' Llewellyn had finished his cigar and was packing his pipe with tobacco, 'Odysseus and his crowd.'

Kaufman raised an eyebrow. 'Is that right?' he said doubtfully. 'Well, you would know – it was nearer your time.' He gave a tight little grin and tossed Darmanin's ring onto the desk. Then he rose and crossed to the coffee machine. 'Coffee, Sam?'

But I hardly heard him. I was thinking about Malta. A vague idea touched the corner of my mind, just the edge of an idea which slipped away before I could identify it. I picked the Maltese ring up from the desk. An inscription was engraved inside the gold band, very faint from years of wear. I had to screw my eyes up to read it. Even then only two initials were decipherable. P.D. P. Darmanin? I wondered what the P stood for.

'Sam?' Kaufman said from the coffee machine.

I concentrated on the ring in my hands. Was the idea something to do with that? Diamonds caught the light as I twisted it in my fingers. I told myself to do as Kaufman had earlier – draw a line from the ring . . . to what? The ring . . . Malta . . . Kay had gone to Malta? *FABERGE!* His name exploded in my mind. I could have sworn I said it aloud, but neither Kaufman nor Llewellyn showed any sign of hearing me. Kaufman returned to his chair. He was watching me intently.

I said, 'Look up Faberge on that list of yours. Let's hear the names of his associates again.'

Kaufman opened his folder, turned a page and began to read. I let him finish, then said, 'One name is missing.'

'Go on,' he said softly.

But I had already gone on, in my mind. My memory was picking up images like blips on a radar screen. I stared at the wall above Kaufman's head – afraid to look at him in case he distracted me. My brain clung like a limpet to those slender threads of memory.

I began slowly. 'When I was fighting Faberge that night. Martinez had gone into the water, Faberge was swinging that boat-hook like a claymore, and I was trying to hold him off with this length of rope . . . when this skiff appeared from the river. The man standing up threw something with his right hand, but his left arm was forward for balance. I thought he was holding something in his left hand at first. It caught the light. But it wasn't in his hand, it was on it. He wore a ring on his left hand . . . that's what sparkled.'

I lowered my gaze and met the scepticism in Kaufman's eyes, but I hurried on before he had a chance to interrupt me. I had the line now – in my mind if not on paper – and it stretched from Faberge to a ring which caught the light – and on to something else. 'The man in the skiff killed Faberge,' I said with slow conviction, 'and he wore a ring on his left hand. But it goes further than that. Kay was sitting behind the dock when I was sentenced at Oxford. I didn't know she was there till the last minute. She . . . she was crying and a man reached over to comfort her. He rested his hands on her shoulders. I couldn't see his face, but he wore a diamond ring on his left hand.' I tossed Darmanin's ring back onto the desk, 'I don't

247

say it had a Maltese Cross, but it caught the light – that's what reminded me.'

Kaufman massaged his jaw, as if he felt the need for a shave. 'Faberge knew someone who wore a ring like that? Is that what you're saying?'

Suddenly I was connecting people together . . . people I had never realised knew each other. Yet I must have known. Kay told me where Brooks had gone that night in the boat-house – but I was so thankful that he was out of the way that where he was seemed unimportant. Now it seemed vital. Although only to me apparently, because when I explained neither Kaufman nor Llewellyn appeared at all impressed. Kaufman's reaction was a blunt question. 'Are you saying Faberge knew Lew Douglas and that he was the man in the skiff?'

I hesitated. The man in the skiff might have been anyone, all I saw was his outline. I tried to calm down, to explain myself better. 'Kay said Brooks had gone to The Fisherman. Lew Douglas owns The Fisherman. He spends a lot of time there . . . so did Kay . . . you read Edgar's letter. What I'm saying is that Brooks met Lew Douglas that night. Douglas is a flashy dresser. I bet that was him in court that day with Kay and—'

'Okay, suppose you're right,' Kaufman interrupted. 'Suppose Brooks did meet Douglas at The Fisherman that night? So what?'

'Well, isn't it worth asking him? And another thing – if Brooks went there that night shouldn't Douglas have told the police afterwards? Why didn't he come forward?'

'You're reaching, buddy boy. Building one assumption on another—'

'It all fits,' I said excitedly. 'Listen, Edgar said Kay was spending a lot of time at The Fisherman. That's when she needed the money. That bastard Douglas was blackmailing her with that picture—'

Kaufman threw his hands in the air. 'Slow down, will you? You're getting carried away. You never liked Douglas. You and he had a row about Apex. Okay, but that doesn't make him—'

'Brooks must have taken the photograph to Douglas that night. He must have. They never had a chance to meet anyone else—'

'You don't know that. It was hours before you took that call from Kay—'

But I was trembling with excitement and frustration and anger all at the same time. I knew I was onto something, even though I was unable to define it precisely, even though I was having so much trouble in explaining myself that I was incoherent.

'Will you cool it?' Kaufman shouted at me. 'Now then, you say that photograph was taken that afternoon?'

'Of course it was taken then!'

'Did you see a camera? When you burst in—'

'For Christ's sake! I was hardly looking—'

'But you were there. And you didn't see—'

'It's the only explanation. They took the camera when they left.'

'Maybe it's one explanation.' Kaufman sighed heavily and slid a sideways glance at Llewellyn. 'But I can think of others—'

'Such as?' I challenged hotly.

Llewellyn cleared his throat impatiently. 'It's all assumption, Mr Harris. But ... um ... you are assuming that your wife only behaved that way on the one occasion. There may have been others.'

Blood rushed to my face. Of course he was right – it was possible – but I could never believe that. 'No,' I said stubbornly, 'that was the only time – and only then because she was spaced out—'

'Her boyfriends weren't,' Kaufman said sourly. 'Heroin turns men off like a cold shower. Makes them impotent.'

I avoided his eye and was trying to think of a counter argument when Llewellyn interrupted. 'I'm going to 'phone Bristol,' he said, rising to his feet. 'Then I'll look in on Henderson.' He paused at the door to look back at me. 'Maria Green's life might depend on your memory,' he said slowly. 'Time is running out, Mr Harris. Don't waste it trying to restore honour to your dead wife.'

I swore at him. I was confused and agitated but I knew what he was saying ... that there was no connection between Kay and Maria. But *I* was the connection, in a way which I could not define. And besides I had this picture of Lew Douglas in my mind. He was a great one for personal jewellery, always wearing diamond tie clips and fancy signet rings. It *could* have been him in court that day. In fact I thought that quite likely. And Kay had needed the money when she was thick with Douglas ... Edgar's letter said that ... so Douglas might have been blackmailing her. Then I remembered something else. 'You know Douglas has sold up here and left England?'

Kaufman shrugged. 'So what? Enough tax exiles leave this little island to populate Alaska.'

'He's not a tax exile. He's still in business. Edgar said he was expanding his hotels – somewhere in the Mediterranean.'

Kaufman went very still. His eyes narrowed. 'You trying to tell me something?'

'Tunis is in the Med. So is Malta, so is Sicily. And Kay was found murdered somewhere between the three of them. Why don't you find out where Douglas has his hotels?'

Kaufman stared at me. 'You're guessing Sam. Douglas is clean.'

'How come you're so sure?'

'How do you think? We investigated him.'

I sat there staring at him, willing him to tell me more than that. In the end he sighed and said, 'I told you about our informer – that guy who squealed about Corrao. Corrao had been told to buy Apex at almost any price. Nobody was to lose money. Make it a big pay day for Winner Harris.'

'That's what you meant by me being looked after?'

He nodded. 'You were in Brixton when this came out, and Apex was in receivership. But the finger had been pointed at you so we dug into your background, which included screening your business associates. They were all clean, Hardman as well at that stage. It wasn't until months later that Enrico's man in Palermo fingered Hardman.'

'Then you burgled Edgar's house in Lorimer's Walk?'

'That's right, in January. And we kept tabs on him, hoping for a break.'

'And Lew Douglas?'

Kaufman shrugged. 'His name's on a file somewhere – with a couple of hundred others.'

I can't really explain why I persisted – no single reason was so strong to warrant further investigation of Lew Douglas. But I had the damnedest feeling made up of all sorts of little things. I grabbed Edgar's letter from the desk. It took me a moment or two to find the place. Then I said, 'Edgar told Kay about meeting Darlington and the others. Then she spent the night pacing the floor and the following morning she took off—'

'To see Lew Douglas?' Kaufman said sarcastically.

'She went to see him about Apex. She tried to save it.'

'But why Douglas? Why not Darlington, or Charlie Weston – he was the biggest stockholder?' Kaufman stared at me then shook his head. 'Just now you had Douglas blackmailing her – now she's running to him like he's her big brother. You're jumping about like a flea on a hog's back.'

'But she might have gone to see Douglas. He was part of her crowd. Suppose he owns an hotel in Malta? That would clinch it surely?'

Kaufman swore and reached for the inter-com, 'Hewit?'

'Yes, Mr Kaufman.'

'You got the secondary PKX files with you?'

'No sir, they're at . . . at base.'

Kaufman flicked me a glance to see if Hewit's concealment of the location of 'base' had registered. It had, but I no longer cared about the big house. All I cared about was Lew Douglas at that moment, without really knowing why. Except the more I thought about him the more convinced I became that he had blackmailed Kay.

Kaufman said, 'Get onto Lawton, I want the Lew Douglas file. Especially I want to know where his hotels are.' He flipped the inter-com and looked hard at me. 'Satisfied?'

I don't think I answered. I was remembering something else . . . Kay telling me one day that Charlie Weston had called in and taken her out to lunch. 'We all went,' she had giggled, 'Brooksy and Marcelle – and Annie Crawford was down for the day so she came too. We went to The Fisherman and had quite a party.' So Brooks and Faberge went to The Fisherman that day too! It was yet another possible connection leading to Lew Douglas, and I was just about to tell Kaufman about it when the sqawk from the inter-com interrupted me.

Kaufman prodded a button and Hewit said, 'I've got the digest on Douglas's affairs if that's any help?'

'Skip the rags to riches bit, just tell me where he operates.'

'Some of this information is a bit dated,' Hewit began apologetically. 'For instance, it shows him still owning The Fisherman and two other hotels in England. He sold those, so that's wrong for a start—'

Kaufman scowled. 'You got any other wrong information I could use?'

'Lawton is updating things now,' Hewit said hurriedly. 'Meanwhile, from what I've got here – Douglas owns a part interest in an hotel at a place called Sousse. Then another in Salerno and a third somewhere called Gozo.'

'Sousse? Where's that?' Kaufman reached for a pencil. 'How's it spelled?'

Hewit spelled it out, then said, 'It's in Tunisia.'

Kaufman whistled softly. He set the pencil down, then spoke into the inter-com, 'You got any idea where this Sousse is? Like how far from Tunis?'

Hewit barely hesitated. 'About a hundred miles south, maybe a hundred and fifty by road, certainly no more than one eighty.'

'You sound like an automobile guide. Next you'll say it's a good road all the way and a view of the sea when you get there.'

'I don't know about the road, but the sea view is a safe bet. Sousse is on the Gulf of Hammeret.'

Kaufman had been about to light a cigarette. Now he stared at the lighter as if surprised to see a flame so close to his face.

Hewit said, 'Salerno is in Italy, just south of Naples.'

251

Kaufman put a light to his cigarette and blew a stream of smoke at the ceiling. 'And this other place? What's it called – Cozo?'

'Gozo,' Hewit corrected. 'It's an island next to Malta, part of Malta really.'

Kaufman stared at me. 'No wonder you ran casinos. Two out of three ain't bad.' He shook his head and was still shaking it when he turned back to the inter-com.

'You know these places, Hewit?'

'No, sir. I've never been at any of them.'

'So how come you're so accurate? Locations aren't filed in a digest.'

'I have an atlas open in front of me. I guessed you would—'

'Smartass,' Kaufman said softly. 'Okay – you want to tell me what comes next?'

'Activate Douglas's name from the PKX files to current operation?'

'And?'

'Establish Douglas's present whereabouts?'

'Right,' Kaufman agreed. 'But Hewit, quietly eh – very quietly.'

'Yes, Mr Kaufman. Anything else?'

Kaufman thought for a moment, then said, 'Well, you could send someone down with that atlas.' He scowled at me as he flicked off the inter-com. 'Wipe that look off your face. All we got is Douglas doing business in the Mediterranean. You make a Federal case out of it and you'll likely be disappointed.'

Which is what he said, but he sounded as excited as I felt. 'This hotel at Sousse,' I said quickly. 'Hewit said Douglas owns a part interest. Can we find out who owns the rest of it?'

Kaufman frowned. 'Maybe – it might be on the stuff Lawton's digging up. Alternatively . . .' he hesitated, as if wondering whether to confide in me, 'we got a man on his way to Tunis right now, to find this pal of Hardman's – maybe he could check locally—' he broke off as Henderson entered the room.

It was at least two hours since we had visited Henderson in his upstairs room, and there was a marked change in his appearance. He still wore the same stained shirt and was as much in need of a shave as I was, but his manner was totally different. The look of despair had vanished. Instead he grinned from ear to ear as he crossed to the drinks tray.

Kaufman's narrowed eyes followed him all the way, and when he spoke it was almost in a whisper. 'You've found him, haven't you?'

Henderson beamed and nodded.

'Thank Christ,' Kaufman whispered. 'So where is it ... this place, the Oyster Bar?'

'I've even got the telephone number,' Henderson poured himself a generous drink. 'His name is Salvio. Salvio Darmanin. And his bar is exactly where you would expect to find it.'

'In Soho?' I guessed.

'No,' Henderson grinned hugely, 'at a place called Rabat. In Malta.'

CHAPTER ELEVEN

Richardson listened to Superintendent Roberts take the man through his story again – or at least, he half listened. Mostly he heard the voices as background to the hubbub of his own thoughts. Soon, very soon, he would have to report back to Llewellyn. He dreaded that. And Llewellyn in turn would have his own nightmare when he reported to Rossiter. Then there was Kaufman to face. Richardson could imagine Kaufman's reaction. Kaufman had made his opinion abundantly clear when Maria was snatched ... the Pipeline had her and would keep her until it suited them ... an intercept was impossible and all efforts to find her would fail ... or so said Kaufman. Rossiter had disagreed, as had Llewellyn, even Richardson himself had felt sure that the police could prevent the Pipeline from smuggling Maria out of the country. But now he had changed his mind.

He looked at the clock above the door. Five thirty. Twelve hours since Maria had been snatched. Twelve bloody hours! He remembered that film of the cellar in Milan and shuddered.

Superintendent Roberts was grey with tiredness. He looked grey in the light cast by the single bulb and his voice sounded grey with strain.

There were five men in the Air Traffic Controller's office at Flitton. The Air Traffic Controller himself was an ex-RAF type called Batsby who had created no end of a fuss an hour ago when pulled from his bed and rushed from his home in a squad car. Next to him sat Murphy whose title was General Manager, though what that involved in a tiny place like Flitton was something the policeman had yet to identify. And next to him sat Higgins, the customs officer.

'Let's go through it again,' Roberts said wearily. 'Time of arrival of the Lear jet?'

Murphy stifled a yawn. 'Three thirty this afternoon. You've seen the log yourself—'

Roberts continued smoothly. 'A charter aircraft on hire to a French medical authority?'

'The Chief Medical Officer of Health for the Department of Mayenne,' Murphy said, consulting a file of papers and nodding confirmation of his own statement.

'What happened then?' asked Roberts.

Batsby, the Air Traffic Controller, answered. 'The pilot filed his return flight plan while the aircraft was refuelled.'

'Return flight to Le Mans?' Roberts checked.

Batsby nodded. 'Pilot's name was Mesurier – André Mesurier. It's all written down—'

'Had you met him before?'

Batsby shook his head.

'Then what?' Roberts persisted.

Batsby sighed. 'We had a chat about the charter business. He was telling me most of his time is spent flying businessmen and politicians around Europe. This was his first cargo flight and he'd had to take the seats out of the Lear jet to make room.'

Higgins, the customs officer, turned a page in his notes. 'The first of the medical supplies from Laport Pharmaceuticals arrived at four thirty and were checked through in the usual manner. But it was only part of the consignment – the rest was still en route from the factory in another van.'

'So the return flight had to be delayed,' Batsby cut in, 'Mesurier got all hot and bothered – typical bloody Frog – waving his hands about and saying the stuff was required urgently at the hospital at Le Mans.'

'We never held him up,' Higgins said quickly. 'The stuff was loaded onto the plane as soon as it arrived at the reception bay.'

'But you inspected it?' Roberts asked quietly.

'We opened two of the cartons. They were all non-restricted drugs – made at Laport's factory in Bristol. All in accordance with the manifest.'

Roberts nodded. 'So the goods were loaded onto the Lear jet. Then what happened?'

Murphy, the General Manager, took it up. 'Not much. Mesurier took a call from Laport's in my office. The rest of the stuff was definitely on its way and would arrive at about six. Mesurier went off to have a coffee, but he was in a hell of a state. Said people's lives were at risk in the hospital at Le Mans and every hour was vital. Dunno what he expected us to do. It wasn't our fault—'

'And the second consignment arrived at six thirty?'

'About then,' Higgins agreed. 'It may have been a few minutes later. I was bloody glad to see it I know that. That bloke Mesurier was a right pain – in and out every five minutes asking if it had turned up – telling me people were dying in France—'

'And it turned up at about six thirty?'

'That's right,' Higgins nodded. 'Just the one crate as I said before. Well, we rushed it straight through—'

'Without opening it?' Roberts queried yet again.

Higgins squirmed. 'It's standard practice. We don't open everything. The manifest was in order. We had spot-checked part of the rest of the cargo . . . anyway this Mesurier bloke was making such a fuss—'

'Laport's make regular use of our facilities,' Murphy said quickly. 'They are by far our best commercial customer—'

'Our only bloody commercial customer,' Batsby muttered, half under his breath.

But Roberts was still questioning Higgins. 'Can you describe this crate?'

'A crate is a crate. I dunno – maybe six feet long, about three wide and the same deep. Just a wooden crate, that's all.'

'Heavy?'

'Well, I didn't lift it myself. This bloke came in wearing Laport overalls and – well I sent the van straight out to the apron. The Laport boys loaded it directly into the plane. Mesurier was helping—'

'A white van?' Richardson joined in. 'They delivered the crate in a white van?'

Higgins flushed. 'Christ, if you'd had that poxy Frenchman flapping round your office all afternoon.'

'A crate like a coffin,' Roberts said quietly. He turned to Batsby. 'And departure time again was?'

Batsby checked his notes. 'Six fifty.'

Roberts was about to make a further observation when the telephone rang. He answered, gave his name and listened. Then he said, 'Thank you, Mr Samuels . . . yes I appreciate that . . . I know, but if you would accompany the policeman I would be most grateful . . . yes, at Flitton . . . that's right . . . no, I've no idea how long we shall be . . . but it could be quite a long time.'

Finally Roberts replaced the receiver. He looked at Richardson. 'That was Laport's export manager. He says no order was despatched from their factory for shipment via Flitton. And he has no knowledge of an urgent requirement from the Mayenne Department of Health.'

The Flitton officials gasped their astonishment, and although

255

Richardson took the news quietly his calm manner was deceptive. He felt sick. His confused mind buzzed with questions. Had Maria been in that crate? And if she had why had she been flown to France? France, and not Sicily? He checked his watch. Ten minutes to six. The Pipeline had maintained their twelve hour start. Not only that but there was now a greater distance than ever between quarry and pursuers. But France – of all places? None of it made sense. Richardson took a deep breath and rose to his feet. He would have to 'phone Llewellyn now. He couldn't delay any longer. He went to the next office to make the call. He just hoped Sam Harris had cracked, that's all. Crack Harris, or at least his memory, and maybe a short-cut would emerge. Something had to emerge, if they were ever to see Maria Green alive again.

All of the lights were out in the big back room at Wells Court. Kaufman hoisted the venetian blind. The small back yard was coloured grey by the pale light of dawn. Kaufman opened the window and sucked in a breath of chill air. 'You Brits kill me. This exercise is costing a million bucks but nobody can afford an extractor fan for this black hole of Calcutta.' He glanced at Henderson. 'By the way, I haven't seen Llewellyn's smiling face for a while.'

Henderson stifled a yawn. 'He went round to Rossiter's place.'

'He know about you finding Darmanin?'

Henderson nodded.

Kaufman blew a piece of tobacco off his lip with the explosive sound of Borg serving on the centre court. Shadows hung in pouches below his eyes and his need for a shave added to his villainous look. He closed the window and said, 'We need this Darmanin kid off the streets and under cover – like now.'

It was the third time he had said it, or something similar.

Henderson murmured, 'The Brigadier made exactly that point. He's hoping Rossiter might have local connections.'

'In Malta? Interpol or local police or what?'

Henderson shrugged.

'I better go round there,' Kaufman said anxiously. 'We don't know the local police. Look at Italy for Chrissakes. Half the Carabinieri were on Serracino's payroll.'

'Malta *was* a British colony,' Henderson pointed out mildly.

'Yeah? So was Chicago. It didn't bother Al Capone none.' The squawk box took Kaufman hurrying back to his desk, 'Yes, Hewit?'

'Lawton's been back on. He's updating the Lew Douglas material as best he can, but there is a complication. Well, not a complication exactly—'

'For Christ's sake!'

'Well it was news to me. Lawton says you are bound to know, but I thought I would check. You do know Douglas is dead, don't you?'

I felt my knees weaken with the shock. Kaufman slumped into his chair. Even in that poor light I could see the look of anguish on his face. Just as he could see my stunned expression. We stared at each other for a moment in mutual bitter disappointment, then Kaufman said, 'No, Hewit, I didn't know Douglas was dead – and why the hell didn't you tell me earlier?'

'I only had an old digest. I did say it wasn't up to date—'

'Does Lawton know when Douglas died?' Kaufman ironed the creases in his face. 'Or how he died?'

'Oh, nothing sinister. Natural causes apparently – heart attack, last February.'

I felt drained and exhausted. I had been concentrating for hours – all night in fact, linking names, events, times and places. True, I couldn't see where it was leading but I was beginning to feel that it was leading somewhere. Now it was like having a door slammed in my face. And from Kaufman's expression he felt the same way. 'Anything else known?' he was asking. 'Did he suffer a long illness? Anything like that?'

'Lawton seems to think it was quite sudden. Douglas died at his hotel in Gozo.'

Kaufman looked at me, inviting a question. I shrugged. What was there to ask now? What was the point?

Hewit said, 'Lawton wants to know shall he keep digging. I mean now that—'

'Keep at it,' Kaufman reached for the inter-com. 'Nothing has changed.'

But we both knew it had. What was worse was that it was almost morning and I had remembered nothing that was likely to help us find Maria.

By eight o'clock Richardson and Superintendent Roberts were back at Bristol Police Headquarters. By eight o'clock three people at Flitton had been shown the white van. All had said that it might be the vehicle which had made the Laport delivery yesterday. Yet Laport's were adamant – no goods had been exported to France. So what . . . or who . . . had been in the large wooden crate?

And by eight o'clock Richardson had spoken directly to the hospital at Le Mans, who confirmed that they had neither ordered nor received a supply of urgently needed drugs. Which was not the only mystery to have occurred at the hospital yesterday. At four in the afternoon a delivery van had been stolen ... the odd thing was that instead of stealing one of the hospital's four unmarked vans, the thieves had made off with a vehicle plastered with the hospital's name. Why, asked the hospital authorities in bewilderment, should thieves steal something so identifiable? Of course the matter had been reported to the Gendarmerie ... but so far the van had not been recovered.

But by half past eight Richardson had at least resolved that puzzle – by a telephone call to the tiny airstrip at Le Mans. *Oui*, they confirmed, a charter aircraft had arrived from England carrying an urgent supply of drugs for the Mayenne District medical authorities. The plane had landed at 2005 hours and been met by a Renault van belonging to the local hospital ... the van was clearly marked ... Besides someone from the hospital had telephoned an hour before, requesting that the cargo be dealt with expeditiously. Of course the customs staff had co-operated – didn't they always in matters of life and death? The cargo was rushed through without being examined and the van left the aerodrome within fifteen minutes of the aircraft's arrival. But where the van had gone *to* was a mystery.

What did any of it have to do with Maria Green, Richardson asked himself? She was being taken to Sicily according to Corrao. She would be produced at the Café Cordina tomorrow night. But perhaps Corrao said that to throw a possible pursuer off the scent? Perhaps Maria Green was to be held at a 'safe house' in France while negotiations were conducted at Alcamo? Perhaps ... perhaps?

'My people have left for the department store,' Roberts said. 'They'll start interviewing all staff the moment they arrive. Something might come of it.'

Richardson's scowl expressed his doubts.

Roberts sighed sympathetically. 'Rossiter was none too pleased I suppose?'

Richardson snorted. None too pleased was an understatement. Rossiter was out for blood. Llewellyn's blood ... Kaufman's blood ... even Richardson's blood if it would help.

'Come on man,' Roberts encouraged. 'Let's go down to the canteen for breakfast. They'll find us soon enough if something breaks.'

What can break now, Richardson asked himself? Jesus, the Pipeline have had Maria for fifteen hours. Maria will break ... she will be broken ... mutilated and destroyed. He shuddered. 'Harris,' he muttered. 'Bloody Winner Harris.'

'I beg your pardon?'

We're doing everything wrong, Richardson told himself bitterly. He's a tough sod that Harris, but he knows something. He knows more than he's telling. Llewellyn will pussyfoot around forever, but Kaufman is supposed to be damn ruthless. So make the bastard talk ... I would ... Jesus, I'd beat the bastard senseless, but by Christ I'd *make* him talk!

We had adjourned to the kitchen at Rex Place. Henderson brewed a cup of decent coffee instead of the muck out of the machine, while I messed about frying bacon and eggs. I remembered Jack yesterday morning, unveiling his surprises with the flourish of a magician. My God, how pleased he had been with everything. And now ... twenty-four hours later ... the Pipeline had snatched Maria ... Edgar was dead ... Jack was drugged on a bed next door in Wells Court ... and I was driving myself mad trying to remember things which had happened years ago.

My thinking had changed in all sorts of ways. For instance I had been furious with Lucia for putting Jack to sleep. Now it seemed the most merciful way of dealing with him. Nobody was looking forward to breaking the news to him. All night long we had prayed for the same miracle – that Maria would be *found* during the night. But now it was morning, and the news from Bristol was as bleak as ever.

I had changed in another way too. Kaufman was right – this *was* my story, at least in part. Too many of my friends and enemies were mixed up in it for me to be uninvolved. My mind kept going back to Lew Douglas and Kay and The Fisherman Hotel on the river. I was sure Douglas had blackmailed Kay. And Douglas had been mixed up with Faberge ... and Faberge had been involved in the Pipeline ... so why not Douglas too? Lew Douglas ... with an hotel in Malta ... Kay had gone to Malta ... Edgar's chauffeur had come from Malta. My head throbbed from the strain of stretching my memory and grappling with a succession of shocks.

Kaufman dabbed his mouth with paper torn from the kitchen roll. 'I'm going to see Rossiter,' he announced. 'You better stay here,' he said to Henderson. 'Answer the door – man the 'phone – the usual drill.'

I asked, 'What about me?'

He shrugged. 'Get some rest if you can. My guess is that we'll be moving out before midday.'

My stomach knotted into a ball. 'To Alcamo?'

He nodded and turned to Henderson. 'Get onto the Italian

Embassy and tell Enrico to get his tail over to Rossiter's place. Lucia too.'

I said, 'What happens when Jack comes round?'

Kaufman looked at his watch. 'He should be out cold for another hour. I'll be back by then. If not you'll have to break the news. It's a shit job but—'

'I'll tell him,' I said bitterly. I knew it would be me. But I would have volunteered anyway, rather than trust the job to anyone else.

Kaufman gave me a sharp look. 'Get Hewit or one of the other boys to stand by. Jack's too big to go berserk and—'

'Shove it,' I said angrily. 'No more knock out drops, Kaufman. From now on Jack and I are told everything, understand? And we make the decisions. Just the thought of you holding back makes me nervous.'

He flushed but took it without argument. Perhaps his mind was already elsewhere. He buttoned his shirt collar as he vanished into the larder like Alice going through the looking glass.

Henderson went into the sitting room to 'phone Bonello, and I had just finished drinking my coffee when the scuffling broke out behind the larder. The back wall opened and Jack came through, with Hewit at his heels. Nobody would have to tell Jack about Maria. One look at his face told me that. Jack knew.

'Where's Kaufman?' he snapped at me.

'You just missed him. He went out a couple of minutes ago.'

Jack swore savagely and clenched his fists so tightly that his knuckles shone white under the skin.

Hewit said, 'If only you'd sit down a minute—'

Jack only hit him once. He turned and punched all in one movement. Hewit's head snapped back as if his neck had broken. Both feet left the floor and he was still upright when he hit the pots and pans in the larder. He collapsed into a tangle of arms and legs and crockery cascaded over him with enough noise to rouse the dead. But Hewit never even twitched.

Henderson appeared in the doorway with a gun in his hand. Jack snarled and took a step towards him. I threw myself between them. 'All right, Jack—'

'Out the way, Sam. Out the way or so help me God I'll—'

'That won't help Maria,' I snapped.

That stopped him. He went very white, with that green tinge people get before they are sick. Even so I thought he would hit me. But then he lowered his fists and turned away. Henderson sighed his relief and pushed past me to get at Hewit. Jack stood over the sink, ran the cold tap and splashed water over his face. 'You know they drugged me?' he asked. He sucked his knuckles and stared at me carefully. 'Did you have any part of that?'

'No.' That was the truth, no matter what I felt afterwards. I took a deep breath. 'Maria is safe. Corrao's holding her, but he'll exchange her for me tomorrow night. She's safe, Jack – they won't harm her, I'm sure they won't . . .' I hadn't planned to tell him that way. God knows what I intended, but he had guessed about Maria and it seemed the fastest way of conveying some reassurance. Even so I would have given a lot not to have seen that terrible suffering in his face.

Henderson stepped out of the wreckage of the larder. 'He's out cold. His pulse is okay but—'

'He'll live,' I said, not caring much. I was still watching Jack, not daring to drop my eyes in case he thought I was telling a lie. 'She's safe,' I repeated. 'I've spoken to Corrao. They won't hurt her. They are just holding her hostage for me—'

'All right, Sam.' He took a few deep breaths and wiped the back of his neck with a wet hand. 'You'd better tell me about it.'

I was shocked by the murderous look in his eyes. I nodded and beckoned him to follow me into the sitting room, but Henderson objected. 'Use the back room next door,' he said, 'it's safer in there.'

I shrugged and changed direction. 'Did you get through to Bonello?'

He was too surprised to be evasive and said yes without realising it. I grunted and stepped over Hewit's legs. Jack followed and I led the way to the big back room in Wells Court. Despite the hour I splashed some brandy into hot coffee drawn from the machine and made him drink it. Then I told him what had happened during the night – more or less truthfully – even if I did exaggerate Corrao's promises to keep Maria safe. We smoked and talked – with me doing most of the talking – but now and then he asked a question or added a comment, like when I told him about Alcamo. 'Franka grew up there,' he said quietly. 'It's Fiore Serracino's town. Near Palermo. The heart of the Mafia country in Western Sicily.'

That gave me a nasty jolt but I hid my concern as best I could. I told him about Darmanin and Lew Douglas and Malta . . . and about Edgar's letter. He listened and was lucid enough, but now and then a look in his eye disturbed me. He was still in deep shock and I was damned if I knew what to do about it.

I had just about finished telling him all that had happened when the door opened. Kaufman entered, followed by Lucia and Llewellyn. Kaufman gave Jack a careful appraising look and received a baleful glare in return. Lucia immediately crossed the room to kiss Jack and take his hand in hers. She had behaved in a similar way with me at the big house. It was a touching gesture but I wished the reasons for it would stop happening.

'How was Rossiter?' I asked.

Kaufman looked at Jack. 'He's doing all he can to locate Maria. Try not to worry. She'll be all right – we're sure of that.'

'That's nice,' Jack said with chilling casualness.

Kaufman coloured slightly. He had shaved during his absence; now he looked more or less normal, if you discounted the dark circles under his eyes. And Llewellyn had changed out of his dinner jacket into a lounge suit.

'We're going to Malta,' Kaufman said to me. 'To make contact with this kid Darmanin. We'll cross to Sicily from there. There's a flight.'

'Who's we?'

'Me – you and Jack—'

'I'm not going anywhere. Neither is Jack,' I said as calmly as I could. 'You forgot. From now on we are told everything, then we'll decide—'

'Oh really!' Llewellyn snorted. 'There's hardly time—'

'So stop wasting it!' Suddenly I was sick and tired of Llewellyn. 'Listen you, whenever *you* make arrangements someone gets hurt. I followed your precious procedures when I met Edgar. Result? He was shot dead. And I arranged to meet Darmanin the way you wanted it, he was murdered too. Maria stays in the country on your say so – and she gets kidnapped.'

'What the devil are you implying?'

But he knew damn well what I was implying. I could see it in his face.

'Okay, Sam,' Kaufman interrupted. 'Back off. Rossiter's been singing the same song. I know it looks like a leak but I know the people we got working here. That cannot be the explanation. You'll just have to take my word for it—'

'I'm not taking your word for anything.'

Jack gave me an alarmed look. I knew what he was thinking. He was afraid I would refuse to go to Alcamo. He was damn near right too. Anyone else, *anyone* but Maria and I would have refused.

Kaufman watched me carefully. 'Okay, Sam, here's what we do. There are no scheduled direct flights to Sicily. Most people go to Rome and connect there. That's the obvious way and you bet the Pipeline will stake that route out. But another way is to fly to Malta and cross on the ferry to Siracuse, then drive across Sicily to Alcamo.'

'Why the performance?'

'Let me finish, will you?' Kaufman said heavily. 'Two people who look like you and Jack will be on today's noon flight to Rome. They will use your names and travel on your passports. Tonight they will stay in Salerno, hire an automobile and leave for Sicily first thing in the morning – all in plenty of time to reach Alcamo by eight tomorrow evening.'

I glanced at Jack but his face was expressionless. Kaufman followed my look but he was concentrating on me. He went on. 'We think our Rome party will be tailed. Henderson and a back-up team will be behind them anyway. Meanwhile we go to Malta on a charter flight and see Darmanin's boy.'

I stared at him, thinking about it, trying to take it all in.

Perhaps he thought I was about to object because he added, 'Remember what I said about Alcamo. How it *really* works. If this kid Darmanin knows as much as his old man claimed.'

'If.'

'Sam – we need something to trade.'

He stopped short of saying 'trade instead of you', but that's what he meant.

'What do we use for passports?'

He smiled. 'They're being prepared now. I work for a holiday tour business – and you and Lucia are a honeymoon couple.'

'Lucia! She's coming—?'

'You're going to Sicily, remember?' Kaufman pointed his finger at me, 'You know any languages?'

He had a point I suppose. I did know some Italian – restaurant Italian – picked up from waiters and kitchen staff. 'I used to know a little Italian.'

'Yeah? What was his name – Mussolini? Listen lame brain – it could happen fast out there. You won't have time for a phrase book.'

Lucia joined in. 'You and I will travel together, Sam. The Pipeline will be watching for you and Jack. It's better cover this way.'

I nodded. I could see the sense in that – even if I didn't like it.

'Jack comes with me,' Kaufman said, then in response to my look of surprise he added, 'don't worry, we'll all be on the same aircraft. I won't let him out of my sight.'

I glanced at Jack but he was staring at the floor with unseeing eyes. Something awful was happening to Jack, as if he were giving up hope. It would be up to me to make the decisions. I was racked with doubt and worry, trying to think objectively while fighting my own mounting panic. 'Why the decoys?' I asked eventually. 'After all, Corrao wants us in Alcamo—'

'You'll be there,' Kaufman nodded grimly. 'But it won't hurt for them to watch the front door as we come through the back window.'

I was unsure of what else to say. 'I suppose it's all right,' I admitted grudgingly, 'but I want to be armed.'

'Are you kidding? Like you're going through three sets of customs carrying a bazooka?'

'But they know surely? Who we really are I mean. The police in Malta.'

'Nobody knows,' Kaufman shook his head. 'We can't run the risk. Besides, if this Darmanin is in the clear, that's going to be part his decision – who to trust and who to tell. But we gotta reach him first.'

I squirmed, not liking it. Stubbornly I said, 'I'd feel better with a gun.'

'You got any experience? Hand guns, small arms?'

'No, but—' I was remembering that film – that cellar in Milan. If I could get Maria out I would take my chances after that . . . but whatever courage I had was not enough to face that cellar. I would kill myself rather than face that. 'I want to be armed in Sicily,' I said grimly.

Kaufman slid Llewellyn a quick glance. 'Okay Sam – we'll arrange that.'

I stared at him, wondering how much I could take on trust and what alternative I had. 'And I want that list,' I added slowly. 'The entire list – everything you've got on the Pipeline.'

'You'll have it,' Kaufman agreed. 'It's being prepared now.'

Jack raised his head then but I don't think he saw us. He had that blind look on his face again. I wondered how much of the conversation he had heard.

Lucia touched his arm. 'Come on, Jack. There's a fresh suit for you upstairs. I'll get someone to give you a hand.'

But instead of answering her Jack looked at me. 'All right, Sam?'

I took a deep breath. 'All right,' I said.

I hoped to God it would be.

CHAPTER TWELVE

I wish I had been at the early morning conference with Rossiter. The discussion must have ranged far and wide, but Kaufman was revealing the bare minimum to me. I knew it but there seemed damn all I could do about it – and so much happened so quickly that there was no time to go into the whys and the wherefores. But the travel arrangements went smoothly enough.

Lucia and I were taken by Watkins in his taxi to an office in Manchester Square. It was a large building and we were hurried in by a side entrance, so I had no chance to see whose name was over the door. I was separated from Lucia and photographed in a cubby hole of a place which served both as studio and darkroom. Another man was there. He was about my height and colouring, but the resemblance ended there. He gave me a curious look and smiled hello before being whisked off by somebody else. Then I was whisked away too. Wherever I went in that building I was accompanied – handed from one person to another like a parcel to be signed for – while the naked eyes of closed circuit television cameras followed me everywhere, even along the corridors.

My suitcase had been carried up from the taxi and I came across it ten minutes later in another office. The contents were taken out and examined one at a time. Then they were transferred to another case of similar size and colour. I had no chance to ask why. I was too busy answering questions and listening to endless complaints. The man behind the counter swore bitterly. 'Processing requires a minimum of three hours,' he grumbled. 'It's quite impossible to do these things quickly.'

I was saved the need to comment by answering his questions – How tall was I? What weight? What was the colour of my eyes? And did I have any distinguishing marks? He explained about scars and moles in case I misunderstood.

It reminded me of that first day in prison. The experience was the same. People made decisions about me as if I weren't there. They talked around me, as if I were deaf or daft, and expressed questions in such simple language that a misunderstanding was impossible.

In another room a different man complained about my clothes. 'The whole effect is wrong, much too formal,' he tut-tutted and walked behind me to look at the back view. 'Thank heavens you're a stock size, that's all.'

I submitted to being re-clothed in a safari suit and suede shoes. I don't think I said much. I answered when spoken to, but that was about all. Lack of sleep was taking its toll. Besides, items of clothing seemed of no importance compared to everything else. I kept worrying about Maria – wondering where she was, and what was happening to her – and when I wasn't fretting about her I tried to stop my mind wandering to a town in Sicily called Alcamo.

Lucia and I were married the previous day. At the Marylebone Registry Office. At least, that's what the marriage certificate said. Except my name was Samuel Howard and hers had been Lucia Portelli. Kaufman went through the documentation with me at ten fifteen, when I was shown into an office on the ground floor. He was dressed in a lightweight business suit, and wore a collar and tie instead of a cravat as I did.

'Passport,' he said, handing me one. 'Place and date of birth are the same as yours. Samuel Howard, right? No middle names. Both parents dead. Occupation, Sales Manager for F. Greenwood Limited. It's an office equipment business, okay?'

I nodded and flicked through the pages of the passport. According to that I had visited Paris the previous year, and Amsterdam the year before that. Those were the only entries. I turned back to where my photograph appeared opposite the name of Samuel Howard.

'You live in Fulham at that address,' Kaufman pointed at the passport. 'Here, let's go through the rest of this stuff.'

The documentation was extensive. I began to understand what the man meant by it normally taking three hours. Apart from the marriage certificate, there was a UK driving licence with one endorsement, a Diner's Club card, an Access card, and membership of both the AA and RAC. A bill from a garage in Fulham said they had serviced my car, a receipt from the Savoy Hotel confirmed that Mr and Mrs Howard had begun their honeymoon there, and a letter from my tailor complained that three hundred and eighty pounds should have been settled two months ago.

Kaufman tucked them into a worn pigskin wallet and turned to the rest of the items on the desk. Two torn ticket stubs from a West End theatre, a cloakroom receipt, airline tickets, a hotel reservation for Mr and Mrs Howard at the Grand Verdala Hotel, Rabat, traveller's cheques, and a little book which told me all about the trade-in values of typewriters.

'That's about it,' he said. 'It's not full cover, but it will do.' I was putting the stuff into my pockets when Jack came in. Except it wasn't Jack, not when I looked at him. But in a poor light or seen from the back, he could have passed for Jack.

Kaufman jerked his head. 'Next door, buddy.'

'Jack's decoy?' I guessed as the man went out.

Kaufman scowled. 'Don't say his hairline is different. What do you expect in a couple of hours?'

Then another door opened and Lucia entered, followed by the man who had dressed me up for a safari. Lucia looked cool and casual in a cream trouser suit. She carried a fawn handbag on a shoulder strap and wore a wisp of chiffon at her throat.

'You can kiss the bride,' Kaufman grinned.

Lucia smiled and stood next to me. Then the little tailor opened a packet of confetti and threw it all over us. 'It's in your luggage as well,' he said happily. 'It takes days to get rid of – pops up all over the place.'

I brushed confetti out of my hair.

'The car's ready,' the little man said to Kaufman.

Kaufman nodded and looked at Lucia. 'Stay in your hotel room until eight o'clock. Then make your way to the Oyster Bar. I'll meet you there. Okay?'

'Where's Jack?' I asked.

'Around,' Kaufman made a spiral with his hand. 'Getting kitted out. You'll see him on the aircraft – but don't acknowledge either of us – remember that.'

'I'll wait for him now—'

The little man frowned at his watch. 'The car is downstairs *now*.'

'I tell you Jack's okay,' Kaufman pleaded to me. 'Naturally he's upset, suffering from shock still, but—'

'I want to see him,' I said, leaving no doubt about what would happen if I didn't.

Kaufman threw his hands in the air. 'Whereabouts is he?' he asked the little man.

'Collier's office I think,' the man glanced at his watch. 'But there's no time—'

Kaufman pushed some buttons on a console set into the desk top. He nodded at a television screen in the corner. It flickered into immediate life and I saw Jack watching a man unpack a suitcase. I recognised the office I had visited earlier. Then the screen filled with a close-up of Jack's face. My stomach turned when I saw his expression, and the misery in his eyes provoked an involuntary gasp of sympathy from Lucia next to me.

Kaufman sighed. 'Best leave him alone for a while. I'll look after him.'

The door behind me opened and Henderson's head appeared. 'Congratulations,' he smiled at me, 'I'm sure you'll both be very happy.' Then he turned to Kaufman. 'The car is waiting—'

'For Christ's sake!' Kaufman punched a button and the screen went blank. 'Sam, you gotta go – don't worry about Jack. I'll take care of him.'

Lucia slipped her arm through mine. 'We must leave,' she

267

whispered urgently, taking a step towards the door. 'Jack will be all right, really he will be.'

I threw a final glance at the blank screen and followed Henderson into the corridor. Yesterday I had betrayed Edgar. Today I was doing the same to Jack. And tomorrow it would be Maria's turn – unless they found her in time.

Richardson was on the telephone to Llewellyn. 'Of course I can't swear it was Maria Green. But the Gendarmerie at Château la Vallière will swear that someone was transported in that crate.'

Llewellyn sighed. 'Go through it again – slowly this time, it's been a hell of a night.'

God grant me patience, Richardson pleaded under his breath. He cast his eyes heavenwards in a plea for divine intervention. Then he glanced at his watch. Ten fifty – ten fifty-*five* almost! Jesus – hours passed, minutes passed, seconds passed, and all the while Maria Green was being taken further away from them. His face screwed into an expression of concentration as he attempted to tell Llewellyn the story in as few words as possible.

'At eight o'clock this morning,' he began, 'the van stolen from the hospital at Le Mans was found abandoned in a country lane near Château la Vallière—'

'Where's that?'

Richardson consulted his notes. 'About twenty kilometres south-east of Le Mans. Near Tours on the Loire.'

'All right, go on.'

'It was full of medical supplies, wrapped in Laport packaging, everything was there as per the export documentation – everything that is, apart from the goods which should have been contained in a big crate. The crate itself was still there though – and that was empty.'

Richardson heard the scrape of a match at the other end and guessed that Llewellyn was lighting his pipe. 'Go on,' Llewellyn said, amidst a series of lip-smacking puffing noises.

'The crate was lined with foam rubber,' Richardson told him, 'and had holding straps inside. And air holes were drilled into two sides – about eighteen inches from one end.'

'And the Gendarmerie think—'

'They are sure someone travelled in the crate. They've found human hairs, black hairs—'

'But no positive proof that it was Maria Green?'

Richardson almost groaned aloud. 'Not yet they haven't but—'

'You're convinced,' Llewellyn said with faint sarcasm.

'She's not in Bristol,' Richardson said hotly, 'I'm convinced of that. And the rest of it fits – the white van at this end was definitely used in the snatch, almost certainly it went to Flitton.'

'But why France?'

Richardson bit back his frustration. France, Timbuktu – what did it matter? The scent was going cold on them – that's what mattered!

'And you want to go there,' Llewellyn mused.

'I'm doing no good here. Christ, it's a lead, it's the only bloody lead we've got!'

'I'll have to see Rossiter,' Llewellyn said gloomily. 'Interpol will become involved.'

'Well, are you getting anywhere?' Richardson demanded, his patience exhausted. 'I mean is Kaufman getting anywhere with Harris?'

Llewellyn paused a long time before answering. Then he said, 'Getting anywhere is difficult. They are certainly going somewhere. They're going to Malta, and then on to Sicily.'

A black limousine took us to Luton airport. The driver, a different man from Watkins, drove quickly but unspectacularly. When we arrived he found a porter for the luggage, who touched the peak of his cap. 'Have a pleasant journey, Mr Howard.' The girl at the check-in desk said something similar, 'Your flight will be called in fifteen minutes, Mr Howard.'

'This Howard business will take some getting used to,' I grumbled to Lucia as we turned away.

'Imagine what it's like for Mrs Howard. Come on, Sam, buy your wife a drink. And for heaven's sake, don't look so worried. We're on honeymoon, remember?'

The flight was crowded with holidaymakers. Lucia and I were among the first to board the aircraft. I found our seats in the section reserved for smokers, then kept a sharp look out for Kaufman and Jack. Ten, fifteen minutes passed without sign of them. Passengers wandered up and down the aisle, clutching boarding cards and examining seat numbers, bumping into each other and apologising with loud good humour. The aircraft seemed full to overflowing. I grew hot and sticky and even more worried. Then I saw Kaufman. He was leading a man by the elbow, a man who wore dark glasses and carried a white stick. JACK!

A stewardess ushered them into their seats. Jack staggered slightly, as if he was drunk – or drugged.

'Stop staring,' Lucia whispered, pretending to draw my attention to the in-flight magazine. 'It's good cover – that's all that matters.'

'Did you see him?' I hissed back. 'He could hardly walk straight—'

'They've probably given him a mild sedative, that's all. You saw the state he was in. Be reasonable, Sam, it's all for the best.'

All for the best! I remembered Henderson holding me down while his mate injected me, and Lucia saying 'It's all for the best' over and over again like a catechism. I turned to her, angry until I caught the look in her eye. She was afraid. Perhaps afraid I would create a scene and reveal our identities? Or afraid of the journey, afraid of what might happen in Malta, or what might befall us in Sicily. Afraid for Maria, for Jack, for all of us. I kissed her lightly on the lips. 'Poor Lucia, I wonder how often you've said that.'

We dozed for part of the journey. A private conversation was impossible anyway, and to close my eyes was at least some sort of rest, even if the events of the past twenty-four hours rushed round and round my head.

The cabin crew served a plastic airline meal. I ate some cheese, drank the coffee, asked for a second cup and smoked a cigarette. Kay had taken this flight, or at least one like it. In January. Alone. She must have gone somewhere when she landed in Malta. Booked into an hotel? Lew Douglas's hotel? And her last words to Edgar were to stop worrying about Apex. Why? Kaufman was right, had to be right – Kay had known something. But what? January? Douglas was still alive. Had Kay gone to plead with him, threaten him, make demands? What sort of demands? Perhaps they had argued . . . had a terrible row . . . Kay's temper . . . was that it? The argument boiled over, blows were struck, Douglas had beaten her . . . killed her . . . murdered her?

'Relax,' Lucia whispered. She unclenched my fist, finger by finger.

I gave her a brief smile and closed my eyes again. Kaufman's words rang in my ears. 'Corrao's orders . . . make it a big pay day for Winner Harris . . . the Ferryman knows you . . . he's a friend of yours . . . seen the show at The Point of View . . . visited Ashley Grange . . . gambled at The Derby . . . he knows you Sam and you know him.'

I sighed and opened my eyes just as the sign came on to extinguish cigarettes. Lucia and I were still holding hands. It was her left hand, the one with the wedding ring. She caught my look and squeezed back. It was a warming gesture – the impulse of a newly-married bride . . . or the gesture of a frightened girl who was glad to have a man around?

We landed at Malta's one and only commercial airport at three o'clock – or rather four o'clock local time. I adjusted my watch and craned my neck to catch a glimpse of Kaufman in conversation with the cabin staff. A stewardess peered across to the window seat where Jack was sitting, then a steward gave Kaufman a hand in hoisting Jack to his feet. He faced me for a second, but his eyes were masked by the dark glasses. All I saw was his fixed, immobile expression. Then he turned away, supported by Kaufman on one side and the steward on the other.

I half rose to my feet, but dropped back again as Lucia shifted her hand to my arm. Of course she was right, it would be senseless to interfere – but I couldn't help thinking that were our roles reversed Jack would do a better job of looking after me. I just hoped he understood, that's all.

People were ushered back to their seats to give Kaufman's party time to alight without being bumped by the crowd. I twisted my neck and peered through the window into the blistering sunshine. Heat shimmered in waves over the apron. Jack shuffled like an old man, held upright between Kaufman and the steward. Then something else caught my eye. Kaufman carried a burgundy-coloured briefcase in his left hand. Sunlight glinted on the silver security chain attached to his left wrist. The list? Was that the list? God Almighty . . . what with everything else I had forgotten about it. And tomorrow night my life could depend on it – my life, Maria's life and perhaps Jack's as well.

Walking out into that sunshine was like entering a furnace. The air was hot and my eyes were dazzled by the bright sunlight reflected from the white airport buildings. We collected our baggage and cleared customs – but by then Jack and Kaufman had vanished.

'Are they staying with us, I mean at the same hotel?'

Lucia was unsure. 'I don't think so. Anyway my guess is Bill Kaufman has arranged to meet someone else before going to the Oyster Bar. That's why we were told to stay at the hotel until eight.'

It was the only explanation available. I had to accept it.

We found a cab and fell into the back seats. My clothes were sticking to me in the heat. The road leading away from the airport made an English B road look like the M1. The countryside was parched, tinder dry with lots of yellow-brown grass and outcrops of rock. The road climbed slowly towards some old fortifications on a hillside. 'Mdina,' the driver pointed, 'built by the Arabs in the time of Christ.'

'Very interesting,' I said, 'but we want Rabat.'

'It's almost the same place these days,' he grumbled as the car bucked in a pothole. We joined another road and climbed slowly past white stone battlements. Pine trees dappled the badly surfaced road with patches of black shade. An old man went down the hill in the opposite direction, hunched in a cart pulled by a donkey. He lifted his walnut face and waved to our driver who shouted a reply. We entered a small town of narrow streets and I saw a sign to our hotel.

The Grand Verdala is set high up, on the edge of Rabat itself. It is a big, square modern hotel, and the air-conditioning was cold enough to chill beads of sweat into ice cubes. I signed us in as Mr and Mrs Howard and we were shown to our room. It was large, well furnished, with a huge double bed and an adjoining bathroom. Lucia studiously ignored the bed and crossed to the balcony. Half of Malta lay spread out below, with the sea shimmering a few miles away. It was a totally different view, but the panoramic effect reminded me of The Hunter's Tower and Edgar Hardman.

Lucia almost jumped when I offered her a cigarette. She accepted one and looked at me shyly as I flicked my cigarette lighter. During the flight we had held hands – but here, alone in this bedroom, I sensed her uncertainty. I remembered her embarrassment when Kaufman had so cruelly revealed her disfigurement. Perhaps the scars on her body, or the life she led, or simply old-fashioned values made the sharing of a bedroom with a man an uncommon experience for her – despite her worldly wise manner.

She looked out at the view. 'They say you can see Sicily from Malta – on a clear day.'

I smiled. 'Seeing it from here is fine – it's going there that worries me.'

She managed a faint smile in return. 'Try not to worry. Enrico is organising some help.'

Bonello! I had forgotten his cryptic comment about forty men in Alcamo, *and* about him and Lucia meeting the Italian Ambassador in London.

'You mean the cavalry arrive in the nick of time?'

A colossal explosion drowned her reply – as loud as the one that wrecked Jack's car in Dover Street. I grabbed her without thinking and pulled her away from the balcony. Then there was another explosion, and another – a whole series of them – like a military tattoo or big gun salute – followed by the chatter of machine gun fire and a screaming noise like the whistle of bombs. We had fallen backwards onto the bed and I was thinking about getting under it when I realised she was laughing. Lucia was actually laughing! Another deafening road split the air outside and Lucia clung to me as we rolled over.

'Sam, it's all right.' Her arms were around my neck and her hair was in my face. When she turned I saw tears in her eyes. Tears of laughter. 'It's a *festa*,' she giggled, then she kissed me.

We stayed on the bed while she explained. 'It's a feast day, to honour a saint. People celebrate with fireworks and firecrackers, and processions and bands – it's a festival. All the Mediterranean countries have them.'

Another series of *machine gun fire* rent the air outside and a whole series of bangs rocked the place. I propped myself up on an elbow and looked down at her. Fireworks? I had neither heard nor seen them in years. Not since I was a kid. Even then English fireworks were tame compared to the noise outside. And it was still daylight? Fireworks were a night-time thing – for kids gathered around bonfires on misty November evenings.

We listened to the thuds and bangs until the noise faded and died. Lucia's laughter had dispelled her shyness, and she kicked off her shoes to snuggle into my side. A feeling of tenderness existed between us, but not – for the moment – of passion. Perhaps because, despite her amusement minutes before, she was still frightened and worried. And we were both very tired. The shocks of last night and yesterday scratched our nerves like a rash on the skin. Neither of us wanted to make love, but her kiss said she was glad to be cradled in my arms, glad to rest, glad we were together. Which was how I felt before I dozed off.

The bedside telephone woke me. 'Finished your siesta?' Kaufman asked.

The bed beside me was empty. My watch said seven thirty.

'I'm down in the bar,' he said. 'You going to keep me waiting all night?'

'I thought we were supposed to meet at—'

'Changed my plans, and I don't want to interfere with yours . . .' he paused in case the subtlety of his point escaped me, 'but we *do* have an appointment.'

'I'll be right down. Is Jack with you?'

He hung up. I swore. The bathroom door opened and Lucia emerged. She was still wearing the suit she had travelled in, but she looked cool and refreshed. I guessed she had showered and I wished I had had time to do the same before going down to meet Kaufman. I grabbed my shoes. 'That bastard Kaufman has done something with Jack,' I said, 'I'll wring his neck before—'

'Where was he calling from?'

'Downstairs. He's in the bar. Let me have a quick wash first.'

The Verdala bar was even more reminiscent of The Hunter's Tower – except it was big enough to house the Palm Court Orchestra instead of the solitary pianist who played Chopin in one corner. The

273

plate glass windows displayed the same view as our balcony. The sky outside had turned a darker blue but pools of shadow testified to the continued glare of the sun. Kaufman sat on a sofa twenty yards away, talking to another man. But the man wasn't Jack.

'Ah – Mr and Mrs Howard,' Kaufman rose to his feet and extended a hand to indicate his companion, 'may I introduce Lino Cassar.'

I shook hands with a dark-haired man in his early thirties. He smiled and made a slight bow as he greeted Lucia. I glanced uncertainly at Kaufman. Meeting Cassar had thrown me off balance. I had expected Jack until Kaufman had hung up on me – then I knew he wouldn't be there.

Kaufman beckoned a waiter and ordered a Bloody Mary for Lucia and a scotch for me. 'Lino works for Enrico in Rome,' he murmured as the waiter departed, 'but he's Maltese by birth. He's come down here to help us out.'

Lucia had been right. Kaufman had arranged another meeting. But the explanation about Cassar was all I needed. 'Where's Jack?' I asked bluntly.

Kaufman shrugged. 'Tired after the journey. I left him sleeping—'

'Sleeping—'

'Save it, Sam. There're other things to talk about. Me and my buddy have had a busy time of it.'

Cassar smiled and brushed a hand through his hair in a gesture reminiscent of Henderson. He said, 'Enrico called me in the early hours of this morning. I was here before noon. I located Darmanin and left a man watching him, then I went to this hotel in Gozo. An examination of the register was most illuminating.'

I knew I was right! 'Kay, that's where she went in January.'

Lino Cassar nodded.

Kaufman said, 'And our man in Tunis found Rogers. Frightened him to death, but he stuck to the story he told Hardman – and tells it the same way afterwards – about the burial at sea and all the rest of it.'

I had never doubted that Edgar had written the truth, so I paid little attention. My mind was full of Lew Douglas – and what I might have done to him if the bastard was alive.

'We had to verify Hardman's letter, Sam,' Kaufman said. 'It checks out but that doesn't mean it's anything to do with ... with our immediate business.'

The blood rushed to my face. 'You mean you're disregarding it—'

'Ssh – cool it, will you?' Kaufman looked around the bar but his concern was unfounded. The pianist had moved into a Souza march and was playing as if the massed band of the Scots Guards was behind him.

'Look,' Kaufman pointed his finger at me, 'I told you not to make a Dreyfus case out of this. We checked it out because Hardman was involved, that's all. But your ex-wife and Lew Douglas were closer than fleas on a blanket. They could have fallen out about anything. There is no positive reason to suppose it concerns this investigation.'

'Investigation?' I scowled at him. 'You make it sound like we're dealing with a theft. Christ, even being here now – sitting around, having a drink . . . while every minute Maria's life is in danger—'

He flushed. 'You think we don't know that?'

'So what in God's name is happening? Is there any news . . . from Bristol . . .'

Kaufman slid Lucia a quick look, then he shook his head. 'Nothing positive yet. Our people are following up leads . . . maybe we'll have some news later tonight.'

I tried to take it all in. All sorts of things troubled me, but one was that it was eight o'clock. I would be in Alcamo in twenty-four hours' time. Meanwhile what the hell were we doing *here* – chasing round Malta, looking for a man who kept a bar. Even if we found him that would be of no help to me – not when I climbed into the back of that Ferrari.

A sudden explosion of sound rent the air outside as a battery of fireworks exploded.

'It's a feast,' Kaufman explained, dipping into a bowl of peanuts.

'I know,' I said, 'they have them in all the Mediterranean countries.'

He stood up and tossed some notes on the table. 'You know,' he said, 'I'm beginning to get a feeling about this place . . . this peanut-sized rock, sixty miles from Sicily. Seems like it could be another link in you know what. And I'll tell you something else. This guy Darmanin had better come across . . . we ain't got time for subtleties. Any holding back and I'll beat him to death.' He brushed a speck of dust from his lapel. 'Personally,' he added.

275

CHAPTER THIRTEEN

By eight o'clock Richardson and his two assistants were deep in France. A whole series of interviews lay behind them – the Gendarmerie at Château la Vallière, the hospital at Le Mans, the Medical Health Authorities – endless questions but very few answers.

It was clear that the stolen hospital van had rendezvoused with another vehicle in the quiet country lane at Château la Vallière, but at what time was difficult to say. Obviously during the night because the van had been located by eight in the morning. And now, at eight in the evening, Richardson reflected gloomily, the gap between quarry and pursuers seemed to lengthen all the time.

They were going to Lyons, for no other reason than a sharp-eyed gendarme had a hunch. Earlier in the day, just before noon, a minor traffic accident had occurred on the outskirts of Lyons. A black Citroen had collided with a farmer's lorry loaded with produce. Nobody had been hurt and the damage to the vehicles was slight – a bent off-side wing for the black Citroen and a damaged tailboard for the lorry. Under normal circumstances the police would not have been involved – but since the accident occurred within twenty yards of where gendarme Paul Maçon was standing, he had almost been compelled to intervene. The farmer had admitted liability and had offered there and then to pay for the damage – making a generous estimate of the cost of repairs and proffering a wad of bank notes which was promptly accepted by the driver of the Citroen. Paul Maçon had been surprised by the speed of the transaction – nobody in the Citroen had haggled for a better settlement – and that in itself was unusual in France. Indeed, the driver of the Citroen had seemed more anxious to resume his journey than to spend time extracting a better price from the farmer.

Maçon had cast an eye over the occupants of the Citroen. There were five of them, four men and a woman. The woman, an attractive brunette in her late twenties or early thirties, had remained in the car throughout, as had the two men either side of her in the back seat. Once, when Maçon's gaze had met the woman's eyes, he could have sworn that she was afraid of something. But of what? Of being involved in an accident? She had not been hurt, but shocked perhaps . . . frightened by the squeal of brakes, the jarring thump, the clash of metal on metal. Maçon had given her a second glance a moment later and caught her staring at him. Her eyes seemed to hold a message, a mute sort of appeal. But then the man on her right had distracted her by pointing at the old church, and Maçon's own attention had been diverted by the driver of the car accepting the money from the farmer. And less than five minutes later the Citroen had resumed its journey.

At four o'clock that afternoon Maçon had reported back to the police station at the end of his eight hour stint. A photograph was being pinned up on the notice board. The photograph of a young woman, an attractive brunette, English too, according to her name. Maria Green. Maçon knew at once he had seen her before. She had been the passenger in the Citroen.

Despite sharing a drink in the bar at the Verdala, Kaufman insisted on leaving before us. Presumably he felt that an observer might believe we had met by chance, just as it would be another coincidence for us to be in the Oyster Bar later. I saw the reasoning. He was anxious to preserve our cover as a honeymoon couple. So Lucia and I spent a few minutes browsing in the hotel bookshop, before following Kaufman and Lino Cassar through the revolving doors at the main entrance.

Night had fallen with surprising suddenness. The sun and the baked blue sky had given way to velvety darkness. A fat full moon shone amid a million stars. But it was still hot. Hot and noisy. The streets had been quietly slumbering when we arrived. Now they were alive with people. The cab driver outside claimed to know the Oyster Bar but was unable to take us there – most of Rabat's streets were now closed to traffic because of the feast. He shrugged. 'It's not much of a bar. I know other places, in Sliema or Birkirkara. The English like those much better.'

We walked – through streets blazing with colour and crowded with people. Street vendors shouted from stalls as elaborate as carnival floats, selling nougat and cheese cakes, while a man stood on the back of a cart and cut a huge swordfish into steaks with the aid of a saw. We passed two policemen in khaki uniforms with holsters on their hips. Coloured lights were strung across narrow streets little wider than alleyways. Flags and bunting hung from every window, plaster saints stood on wooden plinths at twenty yard intervals, the sound of church bells competed with the crackle of fireworks and the raucous blaring of a brass band.

Lucia clutched my hand like an affectionate tour guide. She put her mouth to my ear and shouted above the din, 'Once a year the statue of the saint is taken from the church and paraded around the streets.'

'These?' I pointed to one of the plaster figures on a nearby pillar.

She shook her head, laughing. 'No, they are the bit players – not the star of the show.'

Further explanation was impossible – the noise was overpowering. The atmosphere of carnival was everywhere on the warm night air. At the next street intersection a marching band was mobbed by a gang of kids, all shouting and singing lustily. Paper streamers showered down in matted clouds from balconies, like ticker tape from New York skyscrapers, to cover the band, the children, and everyone in the vicinity. A bandsman struggled to play while removing a tangled streamer from the slides of his trombone. The crowd surged on every side – mostly Maltese, but interspersed with a few tourists – whose paler skins were made white by the popping flashbulbs of their own cameras.

Lucia clung to my arm as we swept along on the tide of humanity. The Oyster Bar was in the square. So was the church. All we had to do was follow the crowd, or so the cab driver said back at the Verdala. I looked in vain for Kaufman and Lino Cassar. Finding them, finding anyone, would have been impossible in that crowd. The sky turned yellow and green and red as another cluster of fireworks soared high above the house tops. People sang and shouted and chanted 'St Paul, St Paul' with the fervour of a football crowd at a cup final.

The noise in the square was deafening. Another brass band played on a raised bandstand in one corner, but they need not have bothered – I doubt that even the musicians heard a note. Everything was drowned by the clamour of the bells and the roaring chant of the crowd – 'St Paul, St Paul'.

Lucia tugged my arm and pointed across the square to a neon sign which proclaimed the Oyster Bar to be open for business. I nodded and edged sideways, drawing her behind me, easing and shoving my way through a crowd packed more tightly than ever. The entire left hand side of the square was taken up by the brooding black bulk of the church. Every line of architecture was vividly outlined against the night sky by strings of coloured lights. Crowds swayed at the foot of the steps and the massive doors opened to reveal a brilliantly illuminated interior of purple and gold.

It took fifteen minutes to cross the square, though I doubt it was more than thirty yards wide. The sky changed colour, but the fireworks were no longer audible. Nothing could be heard above the bells and the roar of the crowd, but tracers of myriad colours arched endlessly upwards before bursting into balls of dazzling light. The effect was strangely dreamlike, people stood rooted to the spot, twice Lucia's hand slipped from my grasp, and twice I dived back into the mob to find her.

We arrived breathless, bruised from contact with people determined to stand their ground for fear of losing a vantage point. The only entrance to the bar appeared to be a hanging curtain of strings of beads. I glanced upwards, looking for the neon sign to check my whereabouts. Above me the Oyster Bar announced itself in letters two feet high, green one moment and red the next. I drew Lucia behind me and we passed through the screen to find ourselves at the top of a flight of stone steps.

'Is this it?' Lucia asked.

I shrugged. 'The cab driver said it wasn't much of a place.'

We descended. The steps curved in a spiral to reveal a cellar bar much larger than the entrance suggested. The main room accommodated at least a dozen tables, and archways opened on either side to reveal others – many occupied by men playing cards. A bar counter ran the length of the far wall, while giant fans overhead turned slowly enough to leave the flies undisturbed. Noise from the square faded to a buzz which murmured like surf on a distant beach.

Kaufman watched us from his stool at the bar. He turned away, disinterested, picking his teeth with a match as he listened to Lino Cassar next to him. I got the message, even without Lucia squeezing my arm. I steered her to the counter, where we sat far enough away from Kaufman not to be with him but close enough to hear his every word. An old woman glanced up from rinsing glasses in a sink, and a young barman in a grubby sweatshirt asked what we were drinking.

I ordered, then swivelled on my stool to take in the rest of the place. It was rough and ready; cheap furniture, white-washed walls, fly-blown mirrors and an Air Malta poster showing the Tower of London on a summer night. The lively Italian music coming from the jukebox seemed inappropriate for the clientele who were mainly middle-aged men, either talking or playing cards. They had looked up when Lucia arrived. Not just because she was a pretty girl, I realised that now, but because – discounting the old crone at the sink – she was the only woman there. The Oyster Bar, it seemed, was male territory, Maltese male territory, off limits to tourists and women alike. As if to emphasise the point the barman served my scotch warm and in a cracked glass.

A man laughed at a nearby table. I turned, sensing his laughter was directed at us, but all I saw were men playing cards. They argued volubly in Maltese, in a rough good-humoured fashion. Money lay in bundles amid the beer bottles, but that wasn't what caught my eye. What startled me was seeing a shotgun propped against the wall – and catching sight of another one leaning against a chair. And the fact that some of the men wore ammunition belts – and at least three bandoliers of cartridges were hooked over a broken chair. I counted seven shotguns in all. None of it would have suited the British Gaming Board, and right at that moment it worried me sick.

Lucia asked me to light her cigarette. I wondered if she had seen the guns. Especially I wondered if Kaufman had noticed them. What had he said? 'If Darmanin holds back I'll beat him to death – personally.' I took another look round at the Oyster Bar. It seemed a bad place to try.

Kaufman beat a tattoo on the counter with a coin. 'I'd like a word with the owner,' he told the barman, 'Salvio Darmanin. Is he around?'

The barman showed his surprise. 'You have a complaint?'

Kaufman's knowing smile conveyed the impression that he had taken inventory of every chipped glass and bottle of watered down scotch in the place. 'Nothing like that,' he said. 'It's a personal matter.'

The old woman raised her head from the sink. She stared at Kaufman, making no effort to conceal her interest. Finally she said, 'Salvio cannot be disturbed.' She withdrew her red hands from the water and dried them on a stained towel. 'He's had some very bad news.'

I stifled my gasp of surprise. Bad news! Darmanin knew. He knew about his father and brother. But of course he would – even if the police had not informed him as next of kin, somebody in the Maltese community in London would have contacted him. Bad news travels fast. But it had not occurred to me.

Kaufman, on the other hand, showed no sign of surprise. 'I know,' he said softly. 'That's what I want to see him about.'

The woman's lips tightened. She said something in Maltese to the barman, then they both stared at Kaufman. Eventually the barman shook his head. 'It is impossible,' he told Kaufman. He glanced at Lino Cassar with a look loaded with suspicion. Men who earn a living in bars learn to recognise trouble early.

Suddenly a man called from the steps. 'Buona sera Mario.'

I glanced over my shoulder. Several of the men with shotguns were leaving. In fact all of the men with shotguns were leaving.

'Ciao Tony – Grazie Phillip,' the barman called back. He waved casually, but a look in his eyes said he wished that his friends were staying. 'Ciao Joe, Vincent.'

Kaufman watched the men depart, then he tapped the counter

again – but not with a coin this time – Darmanin's diamond ring was in his hand. 'This was given me by a friend of mine,' he said, displaying the ring. 'The man who gave it him was dying – but he said to bring it to Salvio Darmanin.'

The old woman gasped and reached out a claw of a hand – but Kaufman avoided her. He slipped the ring onto his finger, closed his hand, then offered his fist for inspection. It was the woman, not the barman, who recognised the ring. She cried out, several words, a name perhaps? One of the card-players looked up from his game. He crossed to the bar, where he took Kaufman's fist in his hands to inspect the ring closely.

Lino Cassar slid down from his stool. He moved casually, as if stretching his legs, but I knew what he was doing. Counting the house, just as I was. Eight of them, including the man at the bar – but not counting the barman or the old woman. I breathed a sigh of relief. The younger men, the men with shotguns, had all left. Those who remained were older men, some in their sixties, some even older. Except for one, sitting alone, with a newspaper masking most of his face. Maybe it was the way he kept reading which gave me a clue, but something told me that he was the man Cassar had left to keep an eye on Darmanin's movements.

The man at the counter released Kaufman's fist. He spoke sharply in Maltese, turning from the barman to the old woman. She answered quickly, urgently. The man frowned, then turned to Kaufman. 'Is there an inscription? Inside the band?'

'Are you Salvio Darmanin?' Kaufman asked pleasantly.

The man shook his head.

Kaufman shrugged. 'Sorry – I'll tell Salvio Darmanin – nobody else.'

The barman stepped backwards towards the door behind the bar, but the old woman stopped him. She was mesmerised by the ring. Her fingers itched to touch it. I could almost feel the effort it cost her to wrench her eyes away. With a sigh she shuffled to the back of the bar and vanished behind the strips of plastic which screened the opening. I heard her climbing some stairs, a step at a time, pausing on each one to catch her breath.

'It's the heat,' the barman explained, 'her legs give her trouble in the heat.'

'That right?' Kaufman eyed the strips of plastic. 'Well, they're unlikely to trouble anyone else.'

The man who had inspected the ring returned to his table – but not to play cards. And the games ceased at the other tables. The music from the jukebox stopped, but nobody made a move to restart it. Every eye in the place watched Kaufman drop the ring back into his pocket. Lino Cassar climbed back onto his stool, but his action did little to relieve the sudden tension. The atmosphere, never welcoming, soured to a hostile silence.

Kaufman glanced down the counter and appeared to notice us for the first time. 'Well, if it isn't the honeymoon couple,' he beamed. 'Me and my buddy were so engrossed soaking up all this atmosphere that we never saw you. Have a drink with us.'

Lucia accepted prettily, while I had another warm scotch from a different cracked glass, and I was wondering why Kaufman had drawn us into things at that moment when the screen parted behind the bar. The young man who entered was dark-haired and brown-eyed, and wore an open-necked shirt over a pair of jeans – but that went for most other Maltese. What made this one different was being a cripple. He hopped along on a pair of aluminium crutches. I would have put him in his late twenties but for the silver threads in his hair. Maybe he was older – or perhaps had suffered more than his share of pain.

Some people are clumsy on crutches, but this one was as agile as a mountain goat. Crutches were an advantage to him, not a disability. He reached our side of the counter with surprising speed and as he passed I noticed his left leg was bent at the knee, and his left foot never touched the ground.

'Which one of you has the ring?' he demanded.

Now he was closer I could see the puffiness about his eyes. He had been weeping. I had little doubt that we had found Salvio Darmanin – and none at all that he knew about the deaths in his family.

Kaufman turned to face him. 'Are you Salvio Darmanin?'

'What if I am?' Darmanin's manner was petulant, like a frightened juvenile putting on a defiant act of courage. Everyone in the bar was watching. The men furthest away stood up to improve their view.

Kaufman regarded Darmanin steadily. 'Is there somewhere we can talk – in private?'

'So that you can kill me too?' Darmanin's voice rose to a scream. The onlookers gasped, shock registered on their faces and their voices combined into a growl of sympathy. Several stepped forward, to stand shoulder to shoulder with the young man.

'Nothing like that,' Kaufman said softly.

'Let me see the ring,' Darmanin demanded.

Kaufman reached into his pocket. Darmanin went white as he took the ring. He peered to read the inscription, holding it up to the light to see better. A half suppressed sob muffled his cry of pain.

Then the old woman started to shout. Nobody had noticed her return behind the bar. Not until she began to scream. She gesticulated wildly and pointed at Kaufman. Her shrieks galvanised Darmanin into action. He erupted into a torrent of Maltese – turning to his audience, shouting, indicating first the ring and then Kaufman, as if asking them to witness something. Other men appeared from an alcove, drawn by the noise. Three more emerged from the opposite side. The atmosphere was charged with the menace of suppressed violence. Now it would be fourteen against us – fifteen counting the barman – plus a cripple and an old woman – unless the man with the paper was Cassar's man.

Kaufman cocked his head attentively to Lino Cassar. I guessed Cassar was translating Darmanin's excited Maltese. Kaufman registered astonishment. He threw a quick glance at me, but I was too far away to hear Cassar's words. Everyone was talking at once. Darmanin and the old woman were shouting at the top of their voices. Not that I understood – it was all in Maltese – but one word, two perhaps, were repeated more than the rest – *Is-sajjied, Is-sajjied.*

'*Is-sajjied,*' Darmanin screamed, 'I *spit* on him!' He was looking at Kaufman but edging backwards at the same time – screening himself behind a protective line of onlookers. Kaufman stretched out a hand as if to correct a misunderstanding – but Darmanin misinterpreted. Planting his right foot firmly on the floor, he balanced his weight, and swung the right crutch upwards as an extension of his arm. The solid aluminium pole caught Kaufman across the face, knocking him sideways into Lino Cassar.

'And I spit on the messengers from *Is-sajjied!*' Darmanin shouted, while the old crone added cries of incitement from behind the bar. Men shouted on all sides, but expressions of shock were as numerous as angry looks. Only a few were willing to fight. Most were too old – the three or four who clustered around Kaufman were more intent on restraining than attacking him. Cassar called out to Darmanin, obviously disputing what had been said. Men shouted back – the old hag continued to scream and wave – and Darmanin started to hop towards the steps at the entrance.

Lucia and I were at the other end of the counter, a few yards clear of the main drama. Kaufman fought to free himself of restraining hands. 'Darmanin! Wait – you're wrong! Quite wrong—' But his words were drowned in a babble of noise.

Darmanin reached the foot of the steps.

'Sam,' Kaufman shouted, 'stop him. He knows something – he thinks we're from The Fisherman.'

Cassar shouted, '*Is-sajjied*. It means The Fisherman.'

283

My mind raced, but understood nothing. The Fisherman? Lew Douglas owned The Fisherman. Had owned The Fisherman. Kay had spent a lot of time there. But what on earth had that to do with Darmanin?

'Stop!' I shouted, but Darmanin was already mounting the curved steps with that curious hopping gait of his. The men from the nearby alcove turned towards me. I avoided outstretched hands and dodged round a table. Lucia was a pace behind me. Two more men blocked my path. I elbowed one, ground my heel into the other's instep. A third man lunged, Lucia knocked a chair across his path. Darmanin had already disappeared up the spiral staircase. At the other end of the bar Kaufman and Cassar were throwing punches to drive a path through the onlookers. The man with the newspaper joined in, intercepting the barman and throwing him to the floor. Lucia slipped neatly between two tables to reach the foot of the steps. It all happened so quickly. The clientele of the bar were more surprised than we were, and certainly less desperate. Lucia was already on the third step by the time I reached the bottom one. Kaufman was treading on my heels, while Lino Cassar was shaking off another man a yard behind. Then we were climbing and the old woman's screams were drowned by the roar of the crowd in the square – 'St Paul, St Paul'.

It took me a second or two to catch sight of Darmanin's head as he bobbed among the crowd. He was ten or twelve yards away. I shouted to Kaufman and plunged into the mob. Lucia was to my left. I tried to get a hand to her but she was too far away. She must have seen Darmanin too, because she was striking out in the same direction, squeezing and shoving her way through the packed throng. It should have been easy to catch him. I doubt he had more than a ten second start on us – he was a cripple and we were all reasonably fit. But although the crowd pressed on all sides, gaps seemed to open for Darmanin – perhaps because he was a cripple, or perhaps simply because he was a local whom everyone knew.

The noise was even more deafening. Massed batteries of fireworks lit the sky – the church bells pealed with unceasing clamour – and people shouted and screamed 'St Paul, St Paul' as if their very lives depended on it.

I risked a glance over my shoulder. Kaufman was perhaps eight yards behind, separated by a dozen or more people. His face was yellow in the glare from the fireworks. He shouted something, but should have saved his breath. I saw no sign of Lino Cassar, or his assistant. To my left Lucia was ahead of me, and further away than when we started – we were still swimming in the same direction, but no longer on a parallel course and more than fifty people stood between us. I looked ahead, craning my neck for that tell-tale hop which identified Darmanin – and cursed when I realised he was drawing away from me.

We were half way to the church when the firing started. Even so the sounds of gunshots were not immediately identifiable above the fireworks. But suddenly the unmistakable stench of cordite was everywhere, far too strong to have been caused by a solitary shot. Clouds of smoke as thick as mist rolled over our heads. The shouting ceased momentarily and above the ringing of the bells came a colossal salvo of shots. I flinched, expecting to hear screams all around me, bracing myself against a stampede of panic-stricken people, wondering if I could reach Lucia before she was trampled underfoot. But there were no screams. Not even when another salvo threatened to burst my eardrums. Then I saw the hunters – the men who had been in the Oyster earlier – flanked on either side of the church doors, perhaps twenty of them – firing round after round into the night sky. I heaved a sigh of relief. It was another feature of the feast – and as if in confirmation people on all sides shouted triumphantly – 'St Paul, St Paul'.

The thin khaki line of policemen sweated at their task of keeping people back from the church steps. But they broke ranks for Darmanin. I saw him scuttle up the steps, first to one hunter, then another, shouting and pointing back into the crowd. Men hesitated with their fingers on triggers, turning their heads, eyes searching the crowd. Then Darmanin was darting forward again, through the doors and into the church.

As I started up the steps I caught sight of Kaufman and Lino Cassar struggling furiously with policemen on the far side. Lucia was somewhere to my left, but I had no chance to find her. One of the policemen grabbed the tail of my jacket and heaved me back. I jinked sideways before turning and bringing both hands down on his wrist to break the grip. Then I was climbing again, side-stepping one of the hunters as he attempted to stop me. I reached the top of the steps and ran into the church.

It was packed tight. Every pew was occupied and extra chairs had been arranged just inside the doors. I collided with a brown-robed monk, cannoned into two nuns, one of whom lost her balance. There was no time to apologise. Children wandered aimlessly up and down the centre aisle, calling and waving to their friends. I caught a blurred glimpse of the spectacular richness of the interior and the blaze of tall candles – but it was only a fleeting impression. I searched for Darmanin. Then I saw him, hopping at speed towards a side door half way down the nave. I risked a glance over my shoulder. The police had given up but one of the hunters was bearing down on me, his shotgun under his arm and bandoliers of cartridges bouncing on his chest. And beyond him I saw Lucia – white-faced and breathless as she entered the church.

Bells tolled above, children got under my feet. I dodged and jinked, aware of the sacrilege, regretful of it – but over and above everything else I was terrified of losing Darmanin. I remembered his defiance in the bar. 'I spit on *Is-sajjied*,' he had shouted. The Fisherman? As if The Fisherman were a man, not a place. A man? What had Kay said, that night in the boat-house? Brooks had gone to The Fisherman. I thought she meant the hotel. But suppose it was a man? The man in the skiff perhaps? The man with the diamond ring? Had he been The Fisherman?

I gasped aloud as if in pain, vaguely aware of the shocked expressions on people's faces. Then Darmanin bobbed through the side door and back out into the night. I hurried after him, gaining on him, just as the hunter behind was gaining on me.

The door led to a courtyard. Benches were scattered over a widely paved area fringed by palm trees and decorated with coloured lights. The courtyard was built on the same level as the church, higher than the surrounding streets. Lamps spluttered on two diverging pathways, like flares flanking runways. The whole place was crowded with people, but not as tightly packed as the square at the front of the church. I could even run, if you count two steps forward and one sideways to avoid a collision, as running. But even so Darmanin managed to stay twenty yards ahead of me. He swung along on his crutches, throwing an occasional look backwards to mark my progress. The roar of the crowd reached us from the adjoining streets, fireworks still painted the sky and the bells tolled without let up. It was like a sequence from a dream – that running dream where you end up spinning through space.

Darmanin was descending some steps to the street. People blocked my path. I bumped and barged my way through. When I reached the top of the steps I was clutching my side with stitch. I had lost him. There was no sign of him in the street below. Instead it was crowded with a procession. Choirboys in white surplices carried a forest of candles, followed by men in scarlet robes trimmed with gold, and others dressed in blue, followed by yet more in yellow, all carrying richly embroidered banners and flags. And behind them a squad of twenty men heaved and strained under a huge gold statue of St Paul. Ticker tape streamed from balconies, people reached out to touch the statue, leaning from windows and hanging from the railings – and all the time, the great roaring cry of 'St Paul, St Paul.'

Then I saw Darmanin. He had crossed the street and was on the opposite corner, looking up at the balustrade which flanked the steps. We saw each other in the same instant. A flicker of recognition crossed his face. He turned and scuttled down a side street.

When I looked back there was no sign of Lucia – or Kaufman or Lino Cassar. But to delay – to wait for them – would mean losing Darmanin. His knowledge was of vital importance. I barely hesitated. I was down the steps and waiting for a break in the procession, dodging church officials in ornate costumes to cross the street. The side road was no more than an alleyway. I could almost reach out and touch the shuttered houses on either side. It was dark, lacking the coloured lights which decorated the main thoroughfare. Tall houses, built so closely together that the light from the night sky was muted and filtered in the alleyway. It was quiet, empty of people, full of dark shadow. I cursed aloud. I had no flashlight, no gun, no weapon – and I was alone. The alley made a sharp turn to the right. I eased round the corner, pressed tight against the wall. My eyes adjusted to the darkness. Already the crackle of fireworks sounded a long way off, the roar of the crowd no more than a murmur. The alleyway was empty! But Darmanin had to be here. I heard footsteps behind me – turned quickly, but saw no one – hurried onwards, walking on tip-toe, following the old stone walls as they twisted right and left. It was like a maze. Suddenly – twelve yards ahead – a door opened on a latch. A shaft of light splashed across the cobblestones – for a split second – but long enough to see the splinter of light reflected down the length of an aluminium crutch. Then the door closed softly and the latch dropped back into place.

It took me a minute to make up my mind. I left the door open behind me. It seemed the sensible thing to do – if Kaufman and Lino Cassar were following down the alley, they would see it. I stripped off the safari jacket and dropped it across the threshold. Then I stepped over it and into the tiny walled garden. Lemon trees flanked a narrow path. The dense black bulk of a building loomed up in front of me, its shuttered windows clearly visible in the moonlight. I crept forward, step by step along the path. A cricket started up in a nearby bush, other insects rustled in the foliage of the lemon trees. Cracks of light made an outline around the shutters on the ground floor. I wondered if I could edge close enough to hear what was going on inside. That was as far as I would go – that would be enough – Darmanin's voice would be enough – then I could wait for Kaufman to arrive – Kaufman and the bloody army he was supposed to have looking after me. But I was still a yard from the house when the twig snapped behind me. I turned quickly, spinning

287

in my tracks – quickly enough to see one of the hunters behind me, quickly enough to see his shotgun swinging towards me – but not quickly enough to avoid it. The stock smashed into the side of my face with enough force to break my jaw. I remember crying out, remember the coppery taste of blood, remember thinking that half my jaw had been taken away – and falling. But that's all I remember ... until some time later.

CHAPTER FOURTEEN

Richardson was impressed. Not only the Gendarmerie but also the Sûreté Nationale had been pressed into service in the search for Maria Green, and by the time Richardson arrived in Lyons the local top brass were assembled to greet him.

His two assistants were sent off to a local café, but Richardson himself was made comfortable in the Chief Inspector's office and up-dated over a glass of cognac. Paul Maçon's report had been acted on long since, and a nationwide alert was out for the black Citroen. Maçon himself was summoned, introduced, questioned, congratulated and then dismissed. And just after that the telephone rang on the Chief Inspector's desk.

The Frenchman listened patiently, asked some questions, checked his watch and replaced the receiver. He smiled thinly at Richardson across the desk. 'The Citroen has been located,' he said, then shrugged, 'but alas not Madame Green.'

Richardson felt sick with disappointment. He set the cognac aside, unable to finish it.

But the Chief Inspector was far from finished. With the thin smile still at the edge of his lips he said, 'Two men were picked up with the car. They made an unsuccessful attempt to escape. I'm quite sure they are implicated.'

Richardson waited, not daring to interrupt. He thought of Bonello in Rome, Kaufman in Malta, Llewellyn in London – all searching desperately, all worried sick by the passing of time.

'Both men have criminal records,' the Chief Inspector continued, 'and not surprisingly perhaps, one is known to have links with the Mafia.'

Richardson found his voice. 'Why not surprisingly?'

'Because they were picked up in Marseilles, my friend. The rat hole of France. The only place in the country where the Mafia have real power.'

When I recovered I was in a room with a very high ceiling. It was the first thing I noticed. Even so it took time to work out what it was. It was so far away – a creamy white background with thick black tramlines drawn across it. Then I realised it was white-washed plaster, supported by heavy timbers, like oak beams in a Tudor tea shop. Just opening my eyes made my head spin. I closed them again, but not before Lucia said, 'Oh thank God – he's come round.'

Sounds came and went. The murmur of voices, angry at times, shouts – threats – someone pleading, close to tears. Kaufman was there – I could hear him in the background. My jaw throbbed painfully. I explored my teeth with the tip of my tongue. An upper tooth had been loosened, but that seemed the extent of the damage. Except that my bottom lip was split and swollen to twice normal size. Speech would be difficult. Not that I contemplated saying anything. I just lay there, with my head in Lucia's lap while she bathed the side of my face. Gradually my strength returned. My brain shook itself free of cotton wool, and tried to make sense of the immediate past. The flight to Malta. The Oyster Bar. *Darmanin!* Chasing him – through the church – the alley – *the hunter with the upraised shotgun!*

My eyes opened in alarm. The room turned over as I tried to sit up. Lucia restrained me with gentle hands, I brushed her aside to prop myself upright. My surroundings came into focus. The hunter who had knocked me senseless was almost next to me – no more than a couple of yards away. Next to another man who had been in the Oyster Bar. Darmanin sat beside them; awkwardly, with his chin crooked at a strange angle and an expression of pure terror on his face. Then I saw why. A necktie had been knotted round his throat. The other end was attached to the trigger guard of a shotgun . . . and Kaufman held the shotgun. Both barrels were pressed into Darmanin's neck and Kaufman's fingers rested across the triggers. A sharp movement – almost *any* movement – and Darmanin's head would be blown off his shoulders.

Kaufman glanced my way. 'Easy boy – everything's under control.'

Beyond him heavy bolts were rammed into place across a big wooden door. The shutters were closed. Below them a man lounged in a chair, with another shotgun cradled in his lap. It was Cassar's man, the one who had read the newspaper in the Oyster Bar.

Lucia dabbed the side of my face with a flannel. 'It's stopped bleeding, but you could do with a stitch in that lip.'

Darmanin and his friends were arranged in a semi-circle on one side of a coffee table, opposite Lino Cassar. Kaufman sat alongside, resting the butt of the shotgun on the table, allowing the barrels to press into Darmanin's neck. Various documents were laid out on the table.

Lino Cassar was talking. He had never stopped, I realised that now. Even with my eyes closed I had registered his voice in the background talking softly in Maltese. Kaufman had been the one doing the shouting.

'What's happening?' I asked. My split bottom lip distorted my voice.

Kaufman's gaze remained fixed on Darmanin's face. 'Lino's laying our credentials on the line,' he said grimly. 'Telling them what happened to the kid's old man – and what will happen to him unless he co-operates.' He jerked the shotgun to emphasise his meaning – Darmanin winced and looked more frightened than ever.

I swung my feet off the sofa and lowered them slowly to the floor.

Lucia whispered, 'We were only a few minutes behind you.' She sounded suitably apologetic.

I worked my jaw left and right, and up and down. It hurt like hell.

Suddenly Darmanin screamed, '*Is-sajjied* will kill me if I tell you.'

'He'll kill you anyway,' Kaufman snapped brutally. 'He's already murdered the rest of your family. What more proof—'

'But I kept quiet,' Darmanin protested. 'We *all* kept quiet. Don't you understand? Why did he do it? Why—'

Kaufman jerked the gun again. The skin beneath Darmanin's chin was already chafed sore with red blotches. He looked on the verge of collapse, licking his lips and demanding querulously, 'I *must* have protection—'

'You ain't got none now,' Kaufman pointed out spitefully. 'You are dead unless you co-operate. Your chances of being alive this time tomorrow—'

'I *am* co-operating. I *will* co-operate,' Darmanin pleaded, trembling. 'But you must help me.'

Kaufman's shrug conveyed his indifference. He was deliberately frightening Darmanin, I realised that – the kind of trick a trained interrogator would use. I remembered the bad time Kaufman had given me at the big house. But now the murderous look in his eye made me wonder how much was for effect and how much was genuine.

'Listen, you gutless little creep,' he hissed, 'they wasted your family on your account. Right now I'm treating you as a hostile witness in the murder of—'

'*NO!*' Darmanin twisted his head to escape the gun. 'No ... no ...'

Lino Cassar cut in with a burst of Maltese, but his voice was persuasive rather than angry. I guessed he was playing good guy to Kaufman's heavy – another interrogator's trick. He spoke to the hunters as much as to Darmanin – perhaps appealing to their judgement, their common sense. One of the men answered, then turned to Darmanin, obviously pleading with him to co-operate. God knows what he said but it certainly helped because a moment later Darmanin embarked on his story. His head moved back so that the gun no longer pressed into his skin, and he swallowed compulsively from nervousness.

'Start with *Is-sajjied*,' Kaufman ordered.

'He came to see us, three years ago. We ... we ran a garage then, in Balzan. My father, my brother and me. Repair work, panel-beating, the usual things.'

Kaufman eased the shotgun back a few inches and Darmanin's voice was less strangulated than before. 'My brother ... my brother was the best mechanic in Malta. And I was the best panel-beater ... trained by the British REME. Everyone said I was the best, you can ask—'

'I'll take your word for it,' Kaufman said with studied indifference.

'He wanted some work done ... in Sicily. It was unusual ... to be asked to work in Sicily, but he explained they lacked the skills—'

'Panel-beating?' Kaufman sounded doubtful.

'And welding ... welding to very high standards. Seams had to be invisible. *Is-sajjied* was very exacting. He even gave me a test piece before he would employ me.'

'Go on,' Kaufman grunted.

Darmanin's white face strained into a faint smile. 'I was to take a team of four men to Sicily. For three weeks. I was in charge, you understand. The pay was good, very good – we were to get half before we left Malta and the rest when we returned.'

Kaufman nodded but made no comment.

'We went over on the ferry – to Siracuse.' Darmanin's speech was almost normal now – now the shotgun was no longer pressed into his windpipe. But he was still very frightened. 'A Transit van collected us at Siracuse and took us to where we were working. It was hard work – difficult, tiring, long hours. We worked non-stop, never went out, stayed at a farmhouse next to the garage, had our meals there, slept there, everything. Twenty days hard labour it was – but none of us minded because—'

'The money was good,' Kaufman said drily.

Darmanin bobbed his head. Perhaps his continued shrugs and head nodding helped his super-human effort to stop trembling. 'The day we finished he came to inspect our work. It—'

'He? You mean this fisherman?'

'*Is-sajjied*. *The* Fisherman. It is the only name we know him by. None of us know his real name.'

Kaufman scowled in evident disbelief. 'You're doing all this work and you don't even know the man's name?' He fingered the bruise on his face but the fingers of his other hand never strayed from the trigger guard of the shotgun.

Darmanin swallowed. 'It is not necessary to know a man's name to take his money.'

'Is that right?' Kaufman sounded bored. 'Okay, so he inspected the work – then what?'

'It was all good. He passed it. We might have gone out that night to celebrate but it was late when the inspection finished and we were tired. Besides there was plenty of wine in the farmhouse. And next morning we returned to Siracuse, to catch the ferry home.'

I exchanged a quick glance with Lucia. Spots of my blood stained her crumpled suit and a damp patch showed on her thigh where she had cradled my head.

Darmanin slid a sideways look at the hunters. An expression of pain flickered in his toffee brown eyes. And when he spoke he addressed his friends, not Kaufman. 'Joey Grech drove on the way back to Siracuse. Just the five of us in the Transit. *Is-sajjied* told us to follow his Mercedes – one of his drivers would bring the Transit back later. Well, we set off, but he drove the Merc. too fast. Joey had trouble keeping up with him – through the mountains, all twists and turns, hairpin bends – *Is-sajjied* only had one passenger in the Merc., there were five of us in the Transit. Not that it mattered – a van could never have kept pace.'

He seemed to be apologising, and even more strangely, now seemed as frightened of his friends as of Kaufman. He kept throwing them timorous looks as if he were about to reveal something they wouldn't like. Kaufman sensed it as well because he brought the muzzle of the shotgun up to Darmanin's ear and growled a warning for him to continue.

Darmanin shuddered. 'It wasn't Joey's fault. He was trying to catch the Mercedes. But ... we took this tight bend, high in the mountains ... and, and there was this truck – parked right across the road. Joey never had a chance. We were going too fast. The road was very narrow and ... and we crashed through the railings at the side—'

One of the hunters swore. 'Shut up,' Kaufman snapped. He looked at Darmanin, 'Go on.'

Darmanin would have preferred not to, that was clear from his face. He wanted to explain something to the hunters, but the shotgun changed his mind.

'It was a very long drop,' he said. 'Six hundred – seven hundred feet. The van hit the mountainside on the way down. I don't know ... I don't remember much. The passenger door next to me buckled and burst open ... and I was thrown out. Then ... then the van blew up. It just disintegrated, like ... like a bomb. Flames as hot as hell, flying metal, screams for a moment ...' He put his hands to his ears as if to shut out the noise.

Kaufman shifted the gun until the muzzle rested on the lobe of Darmanin's left ear.

Darmanin hastened to finish. 'We fell near a road ... the same road really, just lower down. A man and a woman were running towards us. My leg was all twisted up. I was on the verge of passing out. Then *Is-sajjied* drew up in the Merc. He and the man with him came across ... they were arguing with the man and woman about what to do with me ... at least I think they were. But the woman was a doctor, an American doctor, on holiday with her husband. She insisted on her husband driving to the hospital in Palermo, while she nursed me in the back of their car. I think *Is-sajjied* wanted to take me elsewhere, but the woman insisted. I am a cripple today, but without her I would have lost my leg—'

'You would have lost your life,' Kaufman sneered. '*Is-sajjied* and his buddy would have finished you off. Didn't you ever figure that out?'

Darmanin stared, but said nothing.

'What about the others – your workmates?'

'All dead,' Darmanin whispered.

Kaufman rolled his eyes. 'Would you believe. Go on – what happened then?'

Darmanin's voice remained a whisper. 'I was in hospital for weeks. *Is-sajjied* paid for everything. He was very good. He gave the money the men had earned to their families in Balzan – and more, in compensation, even though it hadn't been his fault. And he came to see me every day in hospital.'

'With grapes,' Kaufman grunted sarcastically.

'He ... he did want a favour,' Darmanin admitted, throwing an anxious look at his friends. 'I ... I was to forget about the work we did ... and, and forget about the truck across the road. I didn't want to ... not at first ... it would reflect discredit on Joey, and it wasn't his fault. But *Is-sajjied* said the truck belonged to some friends of his who would get into trouble ... and them being in trouble wouldn't help Joey anyway. If I forgot everything *Is-sajjied* would look after Joey's widow. With money, you understand?'

'I know about money,' Kaufman sighed. 'So you forgot about the truck?'

Darmanin nodded. He turned to the hunter next to him and said something in Maltese. The man still had a sour look on his face, but he grunted some kind of answer – perhaps to indicate that he understood the reason for the lie. Darmanin turned back to Kaufman. 'I told everyone a tyre had blown out. *Is-sajjied* was very pleased—'

'I bet.'

'Joey's widow got five thousand pounds,' Darmanin shot back with rare spirit.

'And it wasn't even Christmas,' Kaufman said sarcastically. 'Okay, and what did Santa Claus bring you?'

Darmanin looked uncomfortable. 'He ... he promised to look after me ... me and my family. We were to work for him occasionally and be protected ... as long as I kept quiet.' He flicked another nervous glance at the shotgun inches from his face. 'We sold the garage ... the work was too heavy anyway, what with this leg and everything – so I bought the Oyster Bar and this villa.'

'And your pa and brother – what did they get out of all this?'

'Tony always wanted to go to London. So *Is-sajjied* got him a job there. And he bought my father a little bar in Soho.'

I stiffened. '*Is-sajjied* got your brother his job?'

The words were out before I realised how painful it was to speak – but I was stunned to hear that a Maltese fisherman had recruited Edgar's chauffeur.

Darmanin shifted his gaze to me. 'With his partner – Lord Hardman.'

I went cold. I couldn't believe it. It could not be true! Not another link to Edgar. Edgar was innocent! Dammit, even Kaufman had been half way to believing that last night.

I was about to say something else but Kaufman interrupted. 'This work in Sicily,' he said to Darmanin, 'tell me about it.'

Darmanin looked terrified. '*No!* Nobody was to know. *Is-sajjied* said—'

Kaufman's open left hand cracked across Darmanin's cheek, knocking his head backwards until the tie looped round his throat jerked it forward again. One of the hunters swore and jumped to his feet, but the man by the windows shouted and pointed his shotgun. A pistol appeared in Lino Cassar's hand. Nobody moved for a second – the hunter looked hard at Lino Cassar – then slumped back into his chair.

Kaufman snapped, 'Forget what *Is-sajjied* said. He said he'd look after you, didn't he? He murdered your family—'

Darmanin screamed, 'How do I know that? How do I *know* who you are—'

Kaufman hit him again, harder this time. A trickle of blood ran down Darmanin's chin. His face was a picture of misery – doubt, fear, shock, grief, confusion – he was shaking violently – on the verge of tears – then he *was* in tears, both hands flying to his face as he broke down and sobbed uncontrollably.

The two hunters started talking at once, casting anxious glances at Kaufman while gesturing sympathetically towards Darmanin. It was obvious what they were saying. They wanted Kaufman to take the shotgun away. So did I – until I remembered Maria.

Cassar turned to Kaufman and nodded at the shotgun: 'We might do better if you took that away.'

'No dice,' Kaufman shook his head. He bristled at Darmanin. 'Listen dummy, the hit man who killed your Pa could be an hour behind us. He could be in town now – looking for you. You got that?'

Darmanin shuddered into silence, then he nodded shakily. Some of the colour returned to his face, but he still twitched badly. Clearly he was terrified of Kaufman.

'This job in Sicily,' Kaufman growled. 'You going to tell me about it?'

Darmanin looked on the verge of passing out – his eyes had an almost glazed look to them. But then he cleared his throat and said, 'We . . . we worked on the wine tankers. We fitted a second skin.'

'How's that? How's that again?'

'The wine tankers. Hardman's Wine. They all have a second skin. Inside the main body. Each tanker carries two separate loads at the same time.'

It went very quiet. Perhaps we were trying to understand his meaning – or perhaps we understood and were working out the implications.

'You know what a road tanker looks like?' Darmanin added shakily, by way of further explanation. 'A big metal tube, right? Well, Hardman's tankers have a tube within a tube.'

Kaufman stared at him. We all did. Darmanin permitted himself a little smirk of professional pride. 'It's more complicated than that of course,' he said. 'The inside container carries most of the volume and is directly accessible through the two filler caps on top. That's because English customs men use dip sticks to check the load – they take the filler caps off and lower a stick until it reaches bottom. They can still do that with Hardman's tankers – what they don't know is all they are measuring is the inner tank. There's a two inch gap between that and the outside shell. An extra cargo can be carried within that gap.'

Kaufman frowned. 'Can't you see the gap – with the filler caps off?'

Darmanin shook his head. 'It's a sealed unit at the top. You need different filler caps. Put one filler cap on and you pump out the main tank. Put another filler cap on and you pump out the cavity between the walls. If you give me a pencil I could draw it for you.'

We had discovered the Pipeline!

I knew it – the instant Darmanin finished. We didn't need a diagram. I tried to calculate the volumetric capacity of a two inch gap the length and circumference of a tanker lorry. A tanker with cavity walls. But a sum like that would have defeated me on the best of days – let alone when I had taken a crack on the head.

The frown stayed on Kaufman's face. 'You're telling me that even if a tanker was impounded and pumped dry – all you would get would be the contents of the inner tank?'

Darmanin nodded. 'That's all you *could* get – without the special filler caps.'

Kaufman picked his teeth. Nothing in his expression betrayed his excitement. All was quiet for a moment, then he said, 'Nobody goes to that kind of trouble for nothing. You must have known your work had an illegal purpose?'

Darmanin hesitated. 'There is a saying in Sicily. See nothing, hear nothing, say nothing – and you live to be a hundred.'

'Is that right?' Kaufman looked at him coldly. 'Pity the four kids who worked with you can't hear you say that. Or your Pa and brother.'

'*Is-sajjied* promised!' Darmanin said indignantly. 'We would be unharmed if we kept quiet. We *did* keep quiet. I swear we did! We did everything—'

'We? We did?' Kaufman echoed. 'What did your Pa and brother have to do with this cosy little arrangement?'

'Not much. My father's bar was used as a pick-up point for parcels, that's all. And Tony kept tabs on Lord Hardman.'

'Yeah? How?'

'He kept a diary of Hardman's movements. If Hardman went anywhere out of the ordinary . . . Tony phoned my father to let him know.'

'What did your father do?'

'He just passed the information on, that's all. Oh Madonna! Why kill a man for doing what he is asked to do?'

I might have missed it but for Lucia. She squeezed my arm so hard that her nails threatened to pierce the fabric of my shirt. I concentrated on Darmanin's words. Was that it? The chauffeur had passed the word about Edgar meeting me at The Hunter's Tower? Both sides had been watching Edgar? Poor frightened, lonely Edgar.

'This man,' Kaufman was saying, '*Is-sajjied*. Why was he called that? Was he a fisherman?'

Frightened though he was, Darmanin couldn't hold back a smile. 'With his money? You should have seen the villa behind the farmhouse in Sicily. Enormous. Swimming pools, servants – everything.'

'And it belonged to him?'

Darmanin shrugged. 'He stayed there.'

'But he doesn't live there?'

'No, he lives in Gozo.'

I sat bolt upright. Lucia gripped my arm, Kaufman shot me a warning look – but I got my question in first. 'He was English?' I asked with sudden understanding. 'He was English – not Maltese? This – *Is-sajjied*?'

Darmanin seemed surprised. 'Yes, an Englishman. Very rich – I told you, partners with Lord Hardman.'

'Did he wear a big ring on his left hand? A diamond ring?'

'You know him!' Darmanin's face contorted with fear. 'It's a trick – all these questions. *Is-sajjied* sent you to trick me—'

'No,' I protested. 'He's dead. His name was Lew Douglas and he died—'

'LIAR!' Darmanin spat at me. 'Liar! Filthy bloody liar! I saw him a week ago—'

Suddenly there was a noise at the door. And at the shuttered windows. A slap, then a slopping sound, as if someone had thrown a bucket of water over the outside of the house. And the sound of breaking glass. Cassar's man jumped up. We all swung round – even Kaufman. Lucia cried out in alarm. Lino Cassar rushed across to the door and even before he reached it the automatic pistol was back in his hand. Then he slipped. His feet skidded and he lost balance. There was a gap beneath the door. Water was coming through, covering the tiles like a flood tide.

'Jesus!' Kaufman used both hands to untie the necktie at Darmanin's throat. 'Back off. Hit the deck!'

Then there was a whoomph and the water caught fire.

'Gasoline!' Kaufman shouted.

Darmanin screamed and hopped towards the far wall, knocking Lucia aside. Kaufman shouted at the hunters. Cassar's man was pulling them to their feet. I turned away and pulled on my jacket, just as Darmanin wrenched open the door on the inside wall. Cassar stumbled into my back, beating flames out on his trouser leg. The smell of petrol was everywhere, and smoke seemed to pour from the outside wall.

'Get those bolts drawn back!' Kaufman roared, but nobody took any notice. Cassar's man pushed the two hunters towards the inside door. Lucia was regaining her feet after being knocked down by Darmanin. Kaufman yelled, 'For Christ's sake – they'll be too hot to touch in another minute!'

Everyone was coughing in the smoke. My eyes were streaming, making it difficult to see what I was doing. Kaufman threw himself at the big wooden door and started to attack the three bolts. The shutters to the right of the door suddenly burst into flame. Kaufman was bent double, dragging at the bottom bolt, coughing and swearing in equal measure. I couldn't understand why he wanted the bolts drawn back but something prompted me to go to his aid. But first I turned to push Lucia through the door behind me, just as Darmanin came in from the passage. He was moving awkwardly on his crutches, hampered by a blue plastic bowl which he carried in one hand.

'Lino,' Kaufman shouted from the door. 'Get upstairs – see what you can see from an upper window.'

And it was just as Lino Cassar pushed past into the hall that Darmanin threw the bowl of water. There may be faster ways to spread a petrol fire than to throw water around, but if there are I don't know them. Darmanin's bowl of water carried the flames and smoke everywhere. Kaufman was engulfed in a cloud of hissing steam. Flames licked the drapes at the other window. We were all spluttering, but Kaufman was almost totally overcome by a fit of coughing. By the time I reached him he was convulsed, gasping for breath, quite unable to deal with the flames on his sleeve. I dragged him back to the other side of the room. Lucia came to help, she took Kaufman's full weight as he collapsed into her arms. Darmanin was screaming with terror – perhaps it was the final shock – the one which pushed him over the edge. I shoved him back and went to help Lucia with Kaufman. Kaufman gripped my arm. Green mucus ran down from his nose. 'Don't open the door,' he panted. 'But get those bolts drawn back. Quick Sam – *quick.*'

We helped Kaufman into the hall first, and I was about to turn back into the room when Lucia stopped me. An open door opposite revealed the kitchen. Three paces took her to the sink. Dirty dishes were stacked on the draining board. She filled a saucepan while tugging the scarf loose from her throat. Then she turned and threw the pan of water all over me. She thrust the scarf into my hands: 'Put that over your face.'

I ran back into the room. Smoke is the biggest killer in fires – you can't breathe. The wet scarf at my nose dried in an instant. My clothes steamed. I stumbled into the sofa, bumped into a chair, knocked over the coffee table. God, it was hopeless! Even before I reached the bolted door the heat was overpowering. Hairs scorched on my hands. I backed off, half turned and retreated – but Kaufman's words rang in my ears – I knew it was important without knowing why. I was sobbing, trying to make each breath last as long as three normal ones, ducking my head away from the heat as I reached for the middle bolt. It was already half clear – Kaufman had managed that much. And the bottom one was *completely* clear. I yelped with pain as my fingers touched scorching metal. It was *impossible* – without gloves, without something to hold it with – but a split second later I was hacking away with my shoe – using the heel as a hammer. The middle bolt came free! Only the top one to do. Shift you bastard, SHIFT! Half way there – one good hit – missed the bloody thing. God, I can't breathe – I can't breathe! One more blow – hit it, hit it again. Thank God! Knock the latch up, don't open the door, just knock the latch upwards. God! I'm on fire!

I turned away, blinded, knocking into furniture until I pitched onto my knees. Then Lino Cassar was dragging me through the smoke and into the hall. I was spluttering, nose running, eyes streaming, gasping for air.

'Stop!' Kaufman roared. 'For Christ's sake stop!'

My vision cleared just in time to see Darmanin hop through the door at the end of the passage. I could see the street outside. Cobblestones lit by moonlight. Cassar's man dived after him, trying to pull Darmanin back by his jacket – but Darmanin twisted away. He was screaming as he ran into the street. I could see him quite clearly. He half turned to look back at us. Then his head split open. Blood and pieces of bone spattered over his shirt and sprayed everywhere. For a fraction of a second he looked like a dandelion gone to seed – except his puffball head was red, not white. I never even heard the shot. All I heard was Kaufman shouting, 'Stupid bastard! Goddamn stupid bastard!'

Then Cassar's man kicked the door shut.

'Oldest trick in the world,' Kaufman was sprawled on the floor next to me, an anguished expression on his face. 'Bomb one entrance with molotov cocktails and they run out the other way. Oldest trick ... Jesus, I tried to stop him—'

Cassar dashed into the hall. 'The garden at the back is empty,' he shouted, pulling Kaufman upright. Then he shouted at his man in Maltese.

Kaufman was doubled up by another bout of coughing. Lucia was saying to me, 'Keep still while I get your shoe back on.'

Lino Cassar swung back to me. 'We're leaving – same way we came in. Come on.'

I was coughing as badly as Kaufman, but Cassar pulled me upright as Lucia ran into the kitchen. She was back within seconds with another pan of water. I was ready for it this time but Kaufman gasped and shook himself like a dog. Cassar pushed me to the door of the room. I flinched as the heat hit me. The wall opposite was a solid barrier of flame and smoke. Wooden beams crackled overhead and sparks showered down everywhere. Lucia returned with more water and doused Cassar and herself. 'Scarves,' she shouted, 'we need scarves.'

Cassar screamed, 'No time – follow me.' Then he hurled himself into the room, ducking as the heat hit him. Bent double, he reached for the sofa and gave it an almighty shove towards the unbolted door. It slid easily on the tiled floor, with Cassar staying right behind it until another heave sent it crashing through the door. The air was full of the noise of splitting wood, the wall of flame parted, smoke swirled everywhere – billowing into our faces more furiously than ever with the draught. But Cassar was through to the garden; rolling into a ball and coming to rest beneath a lemon tree, his automatic already in his hand as his eyes scanned the surrounding walls. I landed beside him and Lucia fell over me, while Kaufman staggered to a halt a yard away. Behind us the flames leapt upwards to the bedroom windows and the glare from the house lit the garden as had the fireworks earlier.

'He's gone,' Cassar panted, craning his neck and swivelling round to look up at the flat rooftops.

'He got what he came for,' Kaufman grunted between another fit of coughing.

'What about the others?' I asked, looking back at the house.

'My man will take care of them,' Cassar said. 'Come on – hurry.'

I heard bells in the distance. Not church bells this time. Someone had raised the alarm; the fire brigade was on its way. I helped Lucia to her feet.

'Get to the automobile,' Kaufman gasped, and a moment later we were in the alleyway behind the row of villas. Children ran past us towards the fire. We hurried, running at times, wanting to flee the scene as quickly as possible. My clothes were torn and scorched – all of us were dirty, stained and grimed with dust. The alley twisted and turned towards Mdina.

'Goddamn idiot,' Kaufman hissed, 'Darmanin. He could have taken us there. This farmhouse, next to a garage—'

'Save your breath,' Lucia panted. 'Are we nearly there?' She clutched her side.

Moonlight lit the middle of the path but doorways were pools of black shadow.

'Next corner,' Cassar said over his shoulder.

The alleyway opened into a small square. The moonlight seemed brighter, no longer obstructed by tall houses crowded together. We found the inevitable church – cars rested their bumpers on its steps. Cassar had his keys out and a moment later Lucia and I were clambering into the back of a Toyota saloon. Cassar gunned the engine and Kaufman said, 'Get back to the boat – like fast.'

I felt safer in the car. Less vulnerable to a sniper's bullet. And just sitting down gave me a chance to catch my breath.

'Our clothes are at the hotel,' Lucia said.

'Well we daren't go back there now,' Kaufman turned, his arm along the back of his seat. 'Lino's boy will have his work cut out explaining that lot to the cops.'

'Where's Jack?' I asked.

'On the boat, don't worry,' Kaufman looked out of the window.

Jack was on a boat! It was the first I'd heard of it. Kaufman and his bloody secrets! I swore aloud and Lucia reached across for my hand.

Cassar took his eyes off the road to glance at Kaufman. 'You going over on the boat?'

'How long will it take?'

'Depends on the weather. If you're lucky less than four hours to Siracuse, but Enrico might want to land further round the coast.'

'Is Enrico here?' Lucia asked in surprise.

'Arrived from Rome at eight o'clock.' Kaufman shook his head, 'No way we can use the ferry now anyway.'

'The *Miranda* was always a better bet,' Cassar told him.

I looked out of the window. Stone walls flashed past, a few crabbed trees, terraces of cultivated land. We were already out of the town and into the country. Sea glistened a couple of miles away, glimpsed between a gap in the landscape. Kaufman swivelled round to Lucia. 'What about that? Narcotics men all over the world train tracker dogs to sniff the stuff out and Hardman brings it through in sealed tankers. Wait till Enrico hears that.'

When Lucia failed to reply Kaufman twisted back again and looked out of the front window. 'Say, we didn't come up this road. The yacht marina is the other way. You moved the boat?'

Cassar nodded. 'Had to, the harbour police restrict movement at night. You need special permits and they ask too many questions.'

'So where now?'

'A fishing village on the other side of the island. It's very quiet.'

'Any trouble – if we move out tonight?'

Cassar shook his head. 'Malta's entire navy consists of six coastal patrol boats. The *Miranda* can outrun them. But it won't be necessary, Alexis will know when to put out.'

But Kaufman was only half listening. 'Damn stupid kid, Darmanin. He could have taken us there. Proved Rossiter wrong though with all that crap about a leak. That's how they knew where Hardman was meeting you, Sam. The chauffeur told them and got killed for his pains.'

'The chauffeur didn't know about Maria,' I said bitterly. 'And the chauffeur was dead when I arranged to meet his old man. But that's not important – did you hear what Darmanin *said*? Douglas is still alive – *he's still alive*—'

'*Is-sajjied* is alive! That's all we know.'

'Rubbish! He set Tony Darmanin up to spy on Edgar. Of course it's Douglas—'

Lucia interrupted. '*Is-sajjied* couldn't be the Ferryman, could he?'

Kaufman shook his head. 'Living in this Gozo place? No way. The Ferryman is based in London.'

'The third man,' I said softly. 'You said three of them were running it. Serracino in Sicily, the Ferryman in London, and a third liaising in between. *Is-sajjied* is the third man, and *Is-sajjied* is Lew Douglas!'

Kaufman was looking to the front, so his face was hidden from me, but when he spoke it was in pursuit of his own theories. 'Yeah, that's how they knew you were meeting Hardman all right. And as for Maria – well the papers were full of you and Jack going back into business, so they picked it up from the papers. Then they tailed Maria, slipped those incompetents at Bristol, then zap!'

'But why kill the chauffeur?' Lucia asked. 'And his father?'

'They didn't kill the chauffeur,' Kaufman said, still peering out of the front window, 'Henderson did.'

Lucia caught her breath.

'He asked me to keep it quiet,' Kaufman shrugged. 'It'll be on his record, of course. He caught the chauffeur in the cross-fire. He wasn't sure, but they identified the slug later. That's why he was so upset about the kid's old man. Once the kid was killed his family had to be wasted. The Pipeline couldn't risk them staying quiet.'

My mouth started to bleed again and I dabbed it with my handkerchief. Through the windows the moonlight showed a narrow road bumping downhill to a tiny harbour. The open doors of a café splashed yellow blotches of light across the waterfront. It was only ten o'clock but I was desperately tired.

The *Miranda* was a very large boat. I remembered *Aphrodite* as Kay had christened our boat on the Thames. The *Miranda* was much bigger. She was moored right at the end of the quay, well away from the handful of fishing boats. Lino Cassar drove right up to her. I saw Bonello standing at the rails, with Jack next to him. I breathed a sigh of relief – even when I saw the look on Jack's face.

We said a hurried goodbye to Lino Cassar, and scrambled up the walkway. I ached all over. Alexis, the skipper, introduced himself before instructing one of the crew to show me to my cabin. I looked longingly at the narrow bunk and fought the urge to stretch out for five minutes. Instead I stripped out of my clothes and had a stand-up wash in front of the handbasin – and I was just towelling myself down when Jack came in. I've never seen so much misery in a man's face.

'Maria is in Corsica,' he said. 'They're almost certain.'

'Corsica?' I sat down quickly on the bunk.

'They reckon she was taken to France in a crate. A crate, Sam! Like a coffin. Jesus – can you believe it?'

I found my cigarettes and lit one for each of us – and I made Jack sit down before he fell down. He buried his head in his hands. 'After that they got her to Marseilles, or an airstrip just outside, Bonello knows the name, I've forgotten it. Anyway they had a light aircraft there . . . and . . . well they think they've flown her to Corsica.'

'But why? I mean Corsica . . . I don't understand—'

'Alexis reckons they'll take her across to Sicily tonight – by boat.'

I was silent at first. I was relieved in a way, once I recovered from the initial shock. Ever since Llewellyn had told me about the search I had been worried sick that the kidnappers might be panicked into killing Maria. But putting my thoughts into words was difficult. Jack rocked back and forth with misery, running a hand through his hair as if he wanted to pull it out by the roots. 'A coffin, Sam . . . a coffin—'

'*Not* a coffin,' I said as firmly as I could. 'Jack, it proves she's still alive and unharmed. They said they'd produce her tomorrow night to swap for me – they *said* they would—'

'Oh Jesus, I don't know what to think . . .'

After that I talked non-stop. God knows where I found the strength. But I drew on every last ounce of energy to persuade him that Maria would be unharmed. And I think he believed me in the end, even though he was still ashen with worry.

I was so busy talking that I hardly noticed the throb of the turbines and the motion of the deck beneath our feet. Not until I stood up and crossed to the port did I realise we had put out to sea. I stared into the night and watched the lights of Malta recede on the starboard bow. The next land we would sight would be Sicily. I thought of Maria and Kay and Edgar Hardman . . . and of walking into a town called Alcamo at eight o'clock tomorrow night.

CHAPTER FIFTEEN

Gozo lies between Malta and Sicily, but all that lies between Gozo and Sicily is fifty miles of open sea. It was rougher than I imagined, but then I've been brainwashed by the travel brochures which show the Mediterranean as a continuous expanse of blue water linking one golden beach to another. The bright boys at Saatchi and Saatchi should see it late at night – twenty miles from land when the wind blows up. The surface of the sea boiled like a witch's cauldron and smashed tons of black water over the bows of the *Miranda*. Life was snug and warm in the salon below, but I was glad not to be spending the night on the open deck.

'As treacherous as a Sicilian,' Bonello said, forgetting where he was born. 'Calm one moment, dangerous the next – such a sea can take the lives of the unwary like that,' he flicked his fingers.

'You trying to frighten us?' Kaufman raised an eyebrow. 'Like it's been a lulu of a day and we've got to man the pumps all night?'

Bonello smiled. 'We are in good hands. Alexis and his crew have spent their lives on the Mediterranean.'

Kaufman grunted and sipped *rapitala* from his glass. The heavy-knit sweater with *Miranda* picked out in white across his chest was too bulky to fit smoothly under his shoulder holster. He had eased the leather straps a notch but the result was hardly elegant. Whereas Lucia brought a certain *chic* to her outfit, even if the sweater was too large and the rollneck gaped like the latest fashion in plunging necklines. All three of us looked like walk-on parts in *HMS Pinafore* dressed as we were in identical sweaters, jeans and rope-soled sandals.

The remains of a meal of *lampuki* littered the table in the mahogany-panelled dining salon. I had eaten well, despite the difficulty with my bruised lip. We drank *rapitala* and strong black coffee and I fought the urge to go to sleep. Kaufman had done most of the talking, telling Bonello about Rabat, now he asked, 'Are we clear of the Maltese Navy?'

Jack glanced at his watch. 'Alexis said the first half hour was the tricky part. We've been underway an hour and a half. We're well clear now.'

I was reassured by his manner, but I never stopped worrying. He was more distant than usual, cooler, sullen when he spoke to Kaufman – but at least the dazed look had vanished from his eyes. The shock had worn off. Now he was like a coiled spring.

Kaufman turned to Bonello. 'Anyone else likely to interfere? Sicilian coastguard – anyone like that?'

Bonello showed his surprise. '*La Finanza*? We are bound for Castellamare. The untouchable coast. *La Finanza* never interfere with boats there.'

Jack said, 'Alexis reckons there'll be plenty of fishing boats about.'

'But not fishing,' Bonello smiled, 'not at night. Castellamare has the most spectacular coastline in the world. It makes the French Riviera look second rate. But it has never been developed. And why? Because Castellamare is the bridge my friends – the bridge between North Africa and the States. The boats land at night – unloading in the creeks, behind hidden rocks – landing their cargo of drugs, arms, diamonds—'

'And victims?' Jack asked bitterly. 'Is that where they'll land Maria?'

Bonello looked at him. 'Perhaps,' he said sadly.

'Well, if we know that—' Jack's frustration boiled over.

'Knowing it doesn't help,' Bonello countered sharply. 'This is Sicily. The FBI call it the aircraft carrier of drugs—'

'Forget the FBI. I'm talking about Maria. If you know—'

'We don't,' Kaufman interrupted. 'Not for sure.'

'Besides, who would help us?' Bonello asked. 'Sicilians? Sicilian police? *Carabinieri*? *La Finanza*? The *publica sicurezza*? Those who are not owned by the Mafia are afraid of them—'

'There must be someone! Some way—'

'I'll tell you a story,' Bonello leaned across the table. 'Last year a young man from *La Finanza* – the financial police – stayed overnight in Castellamare. The following morning he was found hanged from a tree – the way farmers treat vermin – to frighten others of the same kind. Kill a policeman in other countries and you'll run for the rest of your life. But in Sicily,' he shrugged, 'a few questions, no answers, and that's an end to it.'

Jack said nothing. His quick glance at me was enough. If the police wouldn't help, who would?

'The police are controlled by the politicians,' Bonello explained. 'And politicians have many links with the Mafia. The Christian Democrats could never hold power in Italy without the Mafia organising their vote in the south. Each accommodates the other. Ask who owns whom and nobody can tell you – because nobody knows any more.'

Kaufman sighed. 'Okay Enrico – you told us before. You're the only true born Sicilian not in the Mafia – right?'

'Wait a minute,' Jack persisted. 'If the drugs are landed at this place we're going to – this Castellamare—'

'There's no chance of an intercept now,' Kaufman said firmly, 'I'm sorry Jack, it's got to be said—'

'So you're going to let it happen? Let them get away with it?'

'Jack! Will you listen to me? We don't even know where she is—'

'On a boat. Coming from Corsica—'

'It's a theory – that's all. Even if it's right—'

'Oh for God's sake!' Jack thumped the table.

Kaufman was about to add something but Lucia stopped him. She reached across and placed her hands on Jack's clenched fist. 'Maria will be at the meeting tomorrow night. That's what it's all about. They won't harm her and we'll get her out – you'll see.'

He brushed her aside and stood up. 'I'm going on deck for a breath of air,' he glared at Kaufman as he crossed to the door. 'You come up with some constructive ideas or I'll beat the hell out of you!' Then he stepped into the corridor and slammed the door behind him.

Kaufman rubbed the mark on his face made by the aluminium crutch. It would turn to a bruise tomorrow. 'Poor bastard,' he said softly.

'Constructive ideas,' Bonello sighed. 'Does he think we're not trying?'

'He's worried out of his mind,' I said.

'We've found out a hell of a lot,' Kaufman looked round the table. 'Added to what we already knew – we'll work something out by morning.'

'It's midnight now,' I pointed out. I felt exhausted, but I was worried sick about the passing of time. We had so little left. I said, 'Maybe Jack's right – if we know where the drugs are landed—'

'Forget it,' Kaufman shook his head. 'It's a terrible thing to say, but forget Maria too. They'll produce her tomorrow night—'

'But this place – Castellamare—'

Bonello shrugged. 'Drugs have been going into Sicily for years. Without local co-operation there's not much we can do about it – just concentrate on spotting them coming out. It's hard, but we've had some successes – like the marble from Castellamare.'

Kaufman managed a tired smile. 'Sicilian marble is the best in the world – red and green, and some veined like malachite. The trick in the early seventies was to ship it out via Genoa. But before it left Castellamare the blocks were cut into slabs and numbered. And holes were cut into the slabs, and in the holes – heroin. Pounds and pounds of it, worth millions at street prices.'

'You'll see the marble factory tomorrow,' Bonello told me, 'Mafia interests still own it – even today.'

Kaufman rubbed his face again. 'Now they're shipping liquid heroin out in tankers. Holy Christ – what next?'

Bonello frowned. 'Do you think there's a connection with the wine rackets?'

'Who knows? Every racket overlaps another in Sicily. Every cellar is its own chemical plant in Alcamo.'

Bonello explained to me. 'Wine doctoring is big business. Very big, worth a hundred billion liras annually. Every year Sicily exports more wine than can possibly be produced from the grape harvest. It is very successful. The English, Germans, American, Swiss – all drink more wine – and anyone who is a wine drinker has drunk doctored wine without knowing it.' He shrugged, 'It does you no harm. It can cause a slight headache which real wine will not give you, but nothing more than that.'

I remembered something Edgar said over lunch at The Hunter's Tower, but it was only a passing thought and Bonello continued before I could pursue it.

'Doctored wine is made from hot water, sugar and enzymes,' he said. 'Add a little colouring and the wine will become red or white. Total cost? Maybe 130 liras a litre – half the cost of the cheapest real wine. There are expenses naturally – bribes, forging EEC documentation, things like that – but it leaves a good margin of profit.'

Kaufman pointed a finger at me. 'And where you're going – Alcamo – is the centre of the wine rackets. Like I said, come harvest time and every cellar becomes a . . .' He dried up, in mid-sentence, as if struck by a sudden thought. Then, very slowly, in an almost awe-struck voice, he said, 'Every cellar becomes a chemical plant. *That's it!* By God – that's the cover!'

We stared at him. Nobody spoke. The hum of the engines below decks and the sighing of the wind and sea were the only sounds.

He swung round to Bonello. 'Don't you see? They've gone into the manufacturing business. They're actually *making* the stuff. They're making heroin in a winery. Shipping latex into Sicily and processing there. That's what they're doing – I'll stake my life on it.'

His look of excitement was reflected in Bonello's eyes, who said nothing at first, just stared at Kaufman, then at Lucia and me.

'Do you know anything about making heroin?' Kaufman asked me.

I shook my head.

He had looked tired earlier, now he was wide awake. 'I'll simplify it, but pay attention. I know you're exhausted, we all are – but this is important.'

I did my best to rouse myself, but the food and the wine, lack of sleep and my aching body all conspired to make me drowsy.

'The base is opium of course,' Kaufman said. 'Poppy. Not the oriental or common poppy, but PSL. Papvar Somniferum Linnaeus. You cut an incision into the green seed capsules of a PSL poppy before they ripen. White latex appears – like on a rubber tree. It hardens and turns brown after about fifteen hours. Cut a field of PSL and you can smell the aroma for miles.'

'Wouldn't that give you away?' I asked.

'They're not *growing* it in Sicily,' Kaufman snapped.

Bonello explained. 'PSL is grown quite legally in many countries. Greece, Turkey, Bulgaria, even Russia. It can be grown anywhere up to a latitude of 56 degrees. It's an all the year round crop, sown in May for August, and in August for April.'

'Someone,' Kaufman interrupted, 'the Pipeline – now imports the latex into Sicily and processes it there.'

'In a winery?' I asked blankly.

He nodded. 'The latex is just the first step. That has to be made into a morphine base, which in turn is made into diacetyl-morphine. And *that* is called heroin by those without a degree in chemistry.'

'Is it difficult – making the stuff?'

'You need a pulveriser – some types of wine press might do – vacuum pumps, a drying room – but the real difficulty is acetic acid. Know what that is?'

I shook my head.

'It smells like vinegar. Processing diacetyl-morphine creates a

308

tremendous amount of acetic acid. Two problems – one, the smell while you're making it, and two, getting rid of it.'

'But not in Sicily?'

He turned to Bonello. 'What do you think?'

Bonello took his time answering, 'The smell would certainly be disguised in a winery. Many have a vinegary smell. Not as strong, of course—'

'But enough for a cover?' Kaufman persisted.

Bonello agreed. 'And as for getting rid of it – as you said, every cellar in Alcamo is a chemical plant. The smells from the drains are notorious. Besides,' a slow smile spread over his face, 'you might even disguise it as wine vinegar and export it in tankers – if you had the transport of course.'

They stared at each other. Despite aching with fatigue I shared their excitement. I said, 'That's why the chemistry lesson? You think Jack and I will be taken somewhere – if we smell vinegar we'll be at the head of the Pipeline. Is that it?'

Kaufman enjoyed his moment of triumph. Another piece of the jigsaw. His excitement buoyed us all up for a while – stopped us worrying about Maria and took my mind off what might happen to me tomorrow night. I listened to their technical discussion on heroin but after half an hour of it I had to admit defeat – I was just too tired to absorb any more.

Kaufman poured himself more coffee. 'You bring those photographs?' he asked Bonello. He waited for an answering nod, then asked, 'And is this film crowd all organised?'

Bonello nodded again. I wondered what they were talking about, and might have asked had not Kaufman suggested I turn in. I guessed he was getting rid of me but I was beyond caring. My jaw throbbed painfully and my eyes were gummy with tiredness. 'What about Jack?' I asked.

'Enrico will look after him.'

I said my goodnights and dragged my aching body back to the tiny cabin. Undressing was painful – blisters had appeared down the entire length of my left arm. I swore, rolled onto the bunk, and pulled a sheet over me. And I was about to switch off the light when there was a tap at the door, and Lucia came in.

A bathtowel covered her nakedness. She wore it like a sarong, knotted beneath her arms and reaching down to her knees. She leant against the door for a moment, looking at me with her wide grey eyes. Then she said, 'Tonight was to have been our honeymoon night.'

I remembered the huge bed back at the Verdala, and Lucia's expression when we were shown into that bedroom. Fleeting apprehension. But there was nothing apprehensive about her now, she came into my arms as if she had spent her life there. 'I was looking forward to it,' she whispered, 'I wanted you to know that. I still am – but not now, like this – when I feel bruised and tired and—'

I kissed her, stifling her words, holding her close. But a moment later she was gone, a fleeting vision at the door. I think she was crying but I'm not sure. I wondered about following her, comforting her, perhaps making love after all. But the weight of my limbs drew me down onto the bunk like a magnet. She was right. I wanted her, but not there – like that. Not when we were tired and bruised. But soon – if I lived long enough.

I slept so soundly that Alexis had difficulty waking me the next morning. The coffee was scalding hot. It burned the fur off my tongue and almost warmed the icy emptiness deep inside me. Almost, but not quite. I sat staring into space. Something nagged at the back of my mind. A thought which had come to me during the night? It lay too deeply buried in my sub-conscious to uncover, but it was there, nagging away in some dark recess. The effort of searching for it left me feeling keyed up, as if I was on the verge of a discovery. It was eight o'clock. I shuddered at the thought of what might happen to me in twelve hours' time.

My arm was sore, but at least my lip was less swollen. Speech would be easier. I washed and dressed – then went up on deck.

It was Saatchi and Saatchi's Mediterranean again. Calm, turquoise waters beneath a cloudless sky, the sun already warm with the promise of a hot day. We were running parallel to the shore, about two miles out. I've never been to the French Riviera so I've no comparison, but Bonello was right about his spectacular coastline.

The others had started breakfast, though without much enthusiasm. The atmosphere in the salon was strained enough for me to wonder if I had interrupted an argument. It had that tense, edgy feel about it. Bonello said good morning, but with an unsmiling frown on his face – and Lucia looked washed-out and ill. She was staring at a slice of toast when I came in. She glanced up, hesitated, then kissed me – but without a word of greeting. And Jack looked like death – gaunt and drawn and decidedly shaky. He managed a brave grin, but the bleak look stayed on his face and he avoided my eye. Only Kaufman was eating a cooked breakfast and even he was playing with it. 'Want something to eat?' he asked.

'Just coffee,' I helped myself.

Kaufman had the air of a man who had stopped in the middle of his work rather than someone starting the day – and Bonello looked too tired to have seen much of his bunk. Neither had shaved and I wondered if they had worked through the night. Kaufman interpreted my look. 'Sorry about waking you, but we've plenty to talk about – and Jack was getting anxious.'

I went cold. 'What's happened? You've heard something about Maria?'

Kaufman shook his head, but the atmosphere still puzzled me. I looked at Jack. 'Did you get any sleep – *any* at all?'

He bit his lip and avoided my eye. 'Something's happened all right,' he said bitterly. 'Kaufman's been telling us his plan – that's what has happened.'

'Can you think of a better one?' Kaufman demanded angrily. 'It will work I tell you—'

'Tell him,' Jack jerked his head at me. 'He's the poor sod you're condemning to death.'

It went deadly quiet. The engines vibrated the deck enough to tingle my feet through the soles of the sandals – but not enough to cause the shiver which ran down my spine.

Kaufman pushed his plate away and reached for his cigarettes. 'Cut it out, Jack. The waiting is getting you down. I always said it was the worst—'

'Oh for Christ's sake! Get on with it.'

I sat down slowly, on the bench next to Lucia. They all avoided my eye now, not only Jack. I took a cigarette from Kaufman's packet. 'I'm sorry to have kept you waiting,' I said, 'perhaps we had better get started.'

But the steward arrived at that moment to collect the breakfast things. Kaufman told him to leave the coffee, then watched while the rest of the stuff was loaded onto a tray. Some of the tension faded, but not much.

As the man closed the door Bonello started to spread maps over the table and Kaufman cleared his throat. 'Hardest thing about these jobs is deploying the troops,' he said.

'Troops,' Jack sneered, 'I told you before, there can be no question—'

'Will you *listen*!' Kaufman snapped. 'An expression that's all. Shut up for a while – let Sam judge for himself.'

They swapped angry stares until Jack lapsed into silence. Kaufman sighed and looked at me. 'The trouble with a place like Alcamo is that newcomers stand out like a hand of sore thumbs. The locals suspect all strangers. Part of the mentality, right Enrico?'

Bonello nodded. 'It was the first thing to worry us.'

Kaufman continued. 'For the past five weeks a film company has

311

been working in the hills around Alcamo. Location shots for a spaghetti western – the place is supposed to be Mexico. Enrico found out about it in London. The point is people have become accustomed to seeing this film crowd around the place – dressed as Mexican soldiers, cowboys, that sort of thing. And technicians of course. Camera men, sound engineers – all rushing about in jeeps loaded with equipment.'

He paused to look at his watch. 'At eleven this morning a charter flight arrives from Rome with more men and equipment. Except these are *our* men and *our* equipment. We can put forty armed men on the ground without exciting local suspicion. Better than that – the kind of surveillance stuff we need – parabolic mikes, radio gear, all that garbage can be used openly.' He gave me a quick look of satisfaction. 'Make you feel better? Didn't I say we'd have an army of people looking after you?'

I said it was a bit much to call forty men an army, but Kaufman was already turning to Bonello. 'Those four undercover men – how long they been in the area?'

'Over six months. Marius has been there nearly a year.'

'So they've got good local knowledge,' Kaufman turned back to me. 'The leader of the film unit meets up with the undercover men at noon. Enrico will join them. That gives us eight hours to pin-point the place—'

'Maria will be there,' Jack interrupted furiously. 'It's too dangerous. If these people even *suspect*—'

'We're trying to locate the place, that's all! We'll be lucky to come up with a dozen possibles—'

'We daren't mount a search!' Jack gripped the metal rail at the edge of the table so hard that it came loose of its fixings. 'You said so yourself last night. It's too dangerous. Stick to what we're supposed to do. Sam and I will go to this meeting—'

'Then what?' Kaufman challenged, and when there was no answer he repeated what he had told me in London – about how these things really work – about the man with the Ferrari and us climbing into the back seat. I had heard it before and it would never be my favourite story, but it put ten years on Jack. His feeling of utter hopelessness was reflected in his face. 'God keep her safe,' he whispered, shaking his head.

'Who knows this film crew idea?' I asked.

Bonello answered. 'Six people outside of ourselves. The Italian Ambassador in London, two government officials in Rome, the president of the film company – also in Rome, and the director and producer – both in Sicily.'

'What about the real film crew? What will they say when your mob turns up?'

He smiled. 'The charter flight bringing our people in will take the real crew out. Filming has been transferred to Italy.' He rubbed his thumb and forefinger together. 'Everyone gets a bonus from the Italian government. Don't worry, they'll be very happy.'

'I'm glad someone is,' I said, looking at Kaufman. 'So what happens then? If your men start this afternoon they've got damn all time. Besides, what are they looking for? Corrao could take us anywhere.'

'Some places are more likely than others. That farm Darmanin went to for instance – a farm next to a garage.'

'A garage could be a barn. Most farms have a barn.'

'*And* a big house in the background – a villa, with swimming pools—'

'We don't know where Darmanin was taken,' Bonello said, pouring himself more coffee. 'And even around Alcamo there are many large properties. Fifty, sixty—'

'So find one next to a winery,' Kaufman pointed his finger at Bonello and looked down it like the barrel of a gun. 'Find that and I'll find you Maria.'

'I don't like it,' Jack muttered.

'You can't be sure—' I began.

'Who's sure?' Kaufman asked. 'Are you *sure*? Am I? Christ, we've got to start somewhere.' He shook his head, 'Don't worry, nothing much depends on it – it would just save time, that's all, if we knew where we were heading before they take you there.' He stood up and crossed to the door. I thought he was leaving for a moment, but instead he opened a cupboard and dipped inside. When he turned round he was holding the wine-coloured briefcase I had seen him with at the airport in Malta. 'The list, Sam,' he announced, bringing it to the table. 'Or at least a disguised list.'

'Disguised? You promised the lot – everything you had on the Pipeline.'

'It is the lot – but the pages are numbered to give the appearance that every second and third one is missing. It reads one, four, seven and so on. This way it looks like you're only delivering a third of what you know.'

I sucked my sore lip while I thought about it.

He said, 'Your first job is to trade that list for Maria's release—'

'Trade it! How the hell can I do that? They'll take it by force—'

'So what have they got? Pages one, four, seven—'

'You mean I bluff them?'

'You ran casinos, didn't you? You're quite some poker player. So you negotiate. Tell them that if they want the rest of the list they'll have to release Maria. Jack will bring her back to the *Miranda* she stays on board, Jack collects the rest of the list from the safe and returns to your cosy little meeting. That way they get the whole list, Maria is removed from danger and you start talking—'

Jack almost exploded with temper. 'But there is no more list. What happens—'

'We know that but they don't,' Kaufman said grimly.

'They'll never agree to it.'

'Why not? They've still got Sam. If you don't return they'll kill him.'

'You bastard!' Jack lunged across the table but Kaufman was too quick. He ducked away as Bonello sprang across to hold Jack down in his seat.

'Sam's got another ace,' Kaufman added hurriedly. He looked at me. 'Say you've left another copy of the list in London. Unless you contact your associates every two hours your organisation will take over—'

'They'll never fall for that!' Jack roared. 'You know bloody well they won't—'

'They'll play for time,' Kaufman lashed back angrily. 'That's what they'll do. They want to find out how much Sam knows. They've heard the rumours – they need to know what sort of organisation he's got—'

'They'll find out from *him*' Jack snapped, pointing to me. 'They'll nail the poor devil to the floor finding out.'

'Not to begin with they won't,' Kaufman flatly contradicted. Then he looked at me. 'The first priority is to get Maria out. If you're convincing enough—'

'No chance,' Jack said angrily.

'Sam?' Kaufman said, and everyone looked at me.

It took some thinking about. Especially when I remembered that cellar. But I would have some cards to play – I wouldn't be going in empty-handed. Doctoring the list sounded a clever idea, and if I could make them believe there was more to come – that was the crux of it. Which would they rather have? Maria, or the full list? After all, as Kaufman had said, they would still have me – and they could kill me.

It took me a long time to say it, but eventually I said, 'I think you're wrong, Jack. I think they will release Maria – after all, she'll have served her purpose.'

Kaufman sighed with relief, but Jack just stared at me. 'Ask him what happens next,' he said.

I looked at Kaufman but Bonello spoke first. 'Don't rush it,' he cautioned.

Kaufman nodded. 'Let's go through the sequence of events,' he said to me. 'One – Corrao makes contact with you and Jack, then takes you to this meeting. Hopefully that will verify Maria's whereabouts. Two – you negotiate her release with Jack. Three – they both return to the *Miranda*. All right so far?'

I nodded.

'We'll be tailing you all the way,' he said, 'I'll explain how in a minute. Let's say they take you to this farmhouse. Maria and Jack come out—'

Jack groaned and beat the table with his clenched fist.

I looked at Kaufman. 'Okay, I've got that. What happens then?'

He took a deep breath. 'Fifty minutes after they leave – we storm the place.' He saw the look on my face. 'Sam, we'll get you out of there—'

'Dead!' Jack shouted. 'He'll come out dead. They'll murder him first!'

'Will you shut up?' Kaufman snapped. He swung back to me. 'Sam, we've got forty highly trained men. Well equipped with stun grenades—'

'There must be another way,' Jack said desperately, 'there's got to be.'

'Not if you want to see your wife alive,' Kaufman said brutally.

I knew he was right. It was the only way. We spent the next half hour pretending to look for alternatives, but I was only half concentrating. My mind was still reeling under the shock of Kaufman's plan. I knew it would come back to that in the end . . . and it did.

Kaufman was summing up an hour later. 'Don't forget. You park the VW then go and sit in the Café Cordina. Then you wait. Whatever happens just sit there – understand? Don't ask questions, don't do a goddamn thing – just wait. *Someone* will make contact, and you'll do whatever they say.'

My mouth was dry. I sipped coffee as I listened.

'You'll be under surveillance from the minute you step into the Piazza Ciullo. Them and us – we'll both be watching.'

The coffee was cold.

'Any questions?' Bonello asked.

They were all looking at me. Lucia threaded a handkerchief in and out of her fingers. Kaufman massaged the bruise on his face.

315

Bonello peered at me from behind the spiral of smoke rising from his cigarette.

'What about a gun?' I asked. 'You agreed we would be armed.'

Kaufman shrugged. 'If you insist, but there's no point. You'll be searched long before you get near the Ferryman. A gun would be no protection. It might even add to your risk.'

I thought it would be hard to do that – add to my risk – but I stayed quiet. Perhaps it made sense. After all, I had never fired a handgun in my life.

We all fell quiet for a while, then Jack cleared his throat. 'I suppose there is a chance,' he said grudgingly. 'Maria *might* get clear.' He continued to avoid my eye. I knew why. A chance for Maria, not much for me – that's what he meant. Even then Jack was afraid that I would pull out.

I reached over and patted his shoulder. 'More than a chance, Jack. Maria is as good as back at The Dog's Home.' I looked at Kaufman. 'It's a good plan. I think it will work.'

'I'm *sure* it will,' he said with obvious relief.

I hoped he was right.

The atmosphere was a bit strained after that. We each reacted differently. The plan was made, a decision taken – perhaps we all knew that our lives would never be the same again. We tried to cope in different ways. Kaufman and I pretended it was a business deal. He kept reminding me of things to say. 'Don't forget,' he said, wagging his finger, 'you called this meeting. They think you've got a list of names big enough to wrap them up for good. They *believe* that. They're afraid of you, Sam – don't forget that.'

Bonello reacted differently. He talked a lot, much more than usual. The rest of the meeting was his anyway, so he disguised his nervousness with a lot of words. He showed us photographs of Alcamo and Castellamare – picking out features here and there – told us to remember this and that. The same with the maps – roads, landmarks, churches. After an hour of it I had a good idea of what to expect.

And Jack stopped objecting to the plan. I suppose he had no alternative, once I accepted it. He listened carefully to Bonello. The geography lesson was mainly for him anyway. I would never have a chance to use it – but Jack might, if he got lucky. So he concentrated and stopped bickering with Kaufman, which helped – we had enough on our plate without fighting each other.

But Lucia never said a word. She held my hand without shyness, staying close beside me – lighting my cigarettes, pouring my coffee, ministering to my needs like a nurse in a sick bay.

The *Miranda* dropped anchor at eleven o'clock and Bonello went ashore. He had changed his clothes and shaved. We wished each other luck and I waved him goodbye from the rails – a lightly built, narrow shouldered little man, sitting bolt upright in the prow of the tender as it spluttered across the bay. Lucia had been on the verge of tears when she kissed him goodbye and Bonello had trembled himself.

We ate a light lunch, served under a canopy on deck. Conversation was minimal and what there was sounded stilted and false. Kaufman discussed the list of names but eventually he gave up and went off to check the radio equipment. Perhaps Jack thought he was playing gooseberry too, because he took himself off for a nap in his cabin, or so he said, though I doubted he would sleep. I made no attempt to stop him. The truth was we felt awkward with each other, our Englishness got in the way of words – so we said nothing and hoped the other understood.

It should have been soothing sitting there, watching the sunlight play on the water – just Lucia and me. We smoked a couple of cigarettes and pretended not to have a care in the world – but finding the right thing to say was a strain. We had no shared past to remember and neither of us dared talk about the future. Finally I went to my cabin – saying I needed to change into the clothes I would wear ashore – but it was an excuse and we both knew it.

Oddly enough I wasn't afraid. At least not of death. Perhaps I couldn't envisage it – nobody thinks he is going to die. But I wished to God I had never seen that film. I could imagine that cellar only too well – and I *was* afraid of that.

I sat there for an hour, hoping to find a way out – a way to save Maria and Jack, and me as well. But Kaufman was right – we had to do it his way, and I was reconciling myself to the fact when the door opened and Kaufman came in. He clutched a sheaf of radio messages in one hand and wore an excited look on his face.

'We found out the name of Douglas's partner,' he said, 'the one in the hotel business.' He sat on the end of the bunk and offered his cigarettes. 'Are you sure you never knew?'

I shook my head and wondered why he was so excited.

'You were the one to suggest we find out,' he said, watching me carefully.

I accepted a light and waited for him to get on with it.

'Are you still saying you never knew?' he asked sarcastically.

'I don't know. I said so, didn't I?'

'Come on Sam – quit stalling—'

'What the hell are you talking about?'

'You knew all along.'

'That's rubbish and you know it.'

He shook his head. 'I said you knew – I always said it was your story.'

'What the hell are you on about?'

'Douglas's partner – that's what I'm on about.'

I stared at him. Clearly he expected me to know. The shadowy idea which had come to me in the middle of the night haunted the back of my mind. I hadn't been able to crystallise it – maybe that's why I came back to the cabin – not just to think about Kaufman's plan but to mull it all over – the whole damn business, everything, all that had happened.

I took another look at his expression and said, 'It's someone we know, isn't it?'

'It's someone you know. You know who he is – you know who the Ferryman is.'

A shudder ran up my spine. I think I did know – *then* – in that split second. I had never believed Edgar guilty – never, not once – but if not Edgar, who? I had thought non-stop about that, ever since Kaufman put it to me at the big house.

'You damn well know,' Kaufman hissed.

Suddenly the words just spilled out. 'I know what Bonello's agent was trying to say,' I said, 'when he was shot down in that hotel room. He was trying to tell Bonello about the tankers. Hardman's Wine is what he would have said – if he had time.'

Kaufman nodded excitedly.

'The tankers never belonged to Hardman,' I said in a rush. 'He subcontracted transport to his haulage contractor.'

Kaufman's agitation was infectious. Now I was shaking – suddenly I was certain, but I laughed aloud, but the sound rang sour – like the taste in my mouth. 'My God! Of course – even the name – the *Ferryman*!'

'Douglas's partner—'

'Christ! They set me up, didn't they? Way back. All those years ago. And I thought I was my own man – Sam Harris doing his own thing.'

'Easy boy—'

'Easy!' I boiled over with temper. 'What a blind, stupid bastard I've been. Kay said I was – but even she couldn't know *how* blind, *how* stupid—'

'Sam—'

'What a schmuck! That's what you called me, isn't it? Sam Harris – being what he always wanted to be – someone important in London. Bloody agony—'

'Take it easy, will you?'

'Take it easy! Christ Almighty!' I was trembling all over. Every nerve in my body twitched. Kaufman mistook it for fear but he was wrong. It was anger. Like the fit of shakes I had after reading Edgar's letter. Finally I said, 'That's why Corrao was told to pay almost any price – I understand now. They must have laughed their heads off. Make it a good pay day for Winner Harris. That's what they said – right? A good day for me – but a bloody sight better one for them.'

'Wait a minute—'

'Don't you see? We had a chance until poor old Edgar played right into their hands. Once he guaranteed a price for their shares they were safe. They could send the heavy mob in then. It even saved them money. All they had to do was wreck Apex and pick up the pieces from the receiver, for sweet damn all. They didn't have to pay Edgar – or me – or old Darlington's bank—'

'You're reaching, Sam.'

'Like hell.'

'And Lew Douglas?'

'Sold off the hotels and pulled out of the UK.' I was sure I was right. Suddenly it all made sense. I said, 'Once they'd got the night-clubs and casinos from the receiver, they no longer needed places like The Fisherman. They had far better outlets—'

'And Douglas didn't die.'

'That's what I'm saying. It was a smokescreen. Your boys were nosing around by then so Douglas fakes a heart attack—'

'Your ex-wife must have guessed,' he said. 'Maybe when Hardman told her about that meeting of his – when he put the squeeze on Charlie Weston and threatened to cancel the wine shipping contracts—'

I laughed bitterly. 'Christ, I bet that frightened them. Remember Edgar's letter? That bit where he said even Lew Douglas tried to think of ways to save Apex.'

'That's why she went to Malta,' Kaufman said quickly. 'She guessed something. She must have known Douglas was in the drugs racket. Maybe she issued an ultimatum – either Douglas supported her Pa against the receiver or she blew the whistle—'

'She did it for me,' I said bleakly. 'And that bastard Douglas murdered her.'

'And this Tusker crowd in Cardiff—'

'Charlie Weston actually started in Cardiff. And Tuskers started in Cardiff. Serracino hid out in Cardiff. I bet they met there and . . .' I clasped my hands together in an effort to stop trembling. I swear to God that I would have killed with my bare hands at that moment. I couldn't get over it – but I knew I was right. Kaufman knew too – he knew when he came into the cabin – he must have

– and after that the floodgates opened in his mind just as they did in mine. I sat shivering on the edge of the bunk, swearing over and over again, until Kaufman passed me another cigarette.

He lit it first. 'Stay here,' he said, then he went out, shutting the door after him.

I looked at the radio messages he had left on the bunk. The top one read:

'The Rif Hotel at Sousse – owned by Solus Investments, registered office, Republic Street, Valletta, Malta. Majority shareholders Onyx Securities, registered in the Bahamas. Onyx Securities jointly owned by Charles Wesley Weston and Lewis Arthur Douglas – both British citizens.'

'Charlie Fucking Weston,' I said aloud, 'alias the Ferryman. You prize bastard.'

And I was saying that over and over again when Kaufman came back with a large brandy. 'Here – drink this.'

'I'd rather have a scotch.'

'Drink it – don't enjoy it. Lucia's organising some coffee.'

I took a sip and handed the glass back. I kept seeing my past life in my mind's eye. I remembered so much. For instance, having dinner with Jack and Maria years ago, with a girl named Ziggi who had moved in with me. It was the day Charlie Weston had called with the proposition to merge our businesses. The day he set me up. Jack thought I was mad even to consider it. 'What's in it for you?' he wanted to know. 'You've already got everything you want – your own business – money – the good life. What more do you want?' And I had answered, 'I've got to think about it. This could be big – the biggest there is.' *And it had all led to this!*

Kaufman cleared his throat. 'Charlie Weston's not at his London office, or his home – or his office in Cardiff.'

'Charlie Weston is in Alcamo,' I said positively, 'with Lew Douglas and Serracino – waiting for me.'

'With Maria,' he said quietly.

'Sure, with Maria. They're good at hurting women. Serracino with Maria's mother and Lucia. Douglas with Kay.'

The excitement had returned to his voice. 'We've cracked it, Sam. We've cracked the Pipeline. We know who runs it – how they shift the H – everything.'

But I was hardly listening. It was as if part of my mind had seized up. 'They set it up right at the start,' I said, to myself as much as to him, 'when Charlie Weston came to see me. He knew everyone – he proposed the board of directors and the other investors – it was all planned out then. I was to be the front man – the fall guy – me and Edgar. Talk about lambs to the slaughter.'

'Knock it off, Sam.'

'What a fool – what a blind, stupid fool! It's all thanks to me – all this. You realise that, don't you? Kay, Edgar, Maria—'

'Crap! You can't make a martyr of yourself.'

'I might have saved them—'

'Rubbish! Will you stop that. The point is we've cracked the Pipeline. We've cracked it from here – that's what I'm saying. Will you listen to me?'

I looked at him.

'We can smash the Pipeline without you even setting foot in Sicily.'

I stared until the colour crept up his neck and into his face. 'What about Maria?' I asked.

He avoided my eye. 'All I'm saying is – well, most people would say you've done enough. Understand? Nobody would blame you if—'

I had my hands at his throat before he could move. Not too tightly, but hard enough to be uncomfortable. 'Listen, Kaufman, I won't give you all that it's a far, far better thing crap – because it's not like that. I *want* those bastards. So bad it hurts. I want Maria out of there, then wham! Understand? Forget taking them to trial – you get Maria out, then put a gun in my hands because—'

'Okay, Sam, I've got my own score to settle. But I'll make you a promise . . . Serracino will never see the inside of a courtroom.'

There was a lot of pain in his eyes, but not because of my hands around his throat. The pain was still there five minutes later, when Lucia arrived with the coffee and I was wondering what Kaufman meant about his own score.

CHAPTER SIXTEEN

It was almost six o'clock when the tender took us ashore – Jack and me in the middle of the boat, Alexis's man at the tiller. Bonello was right – Castellamare was like a picture postcard. The full sweep of the bay was revealed as the outboard carried us across the wide expanse of sheltered water towards the shoreline – spits of sand set against a background of lush green vegetation topped by purple mountain peaks. The pink and white houses at the foot of Monte Bonifata looked like a pile of gambling chips faded by the sun.

The *Miranda* fell astern, Castellamare drew nearer. I picked out the wine warehouses on the far side of town. Nearer at hand a few fishing boats bobbed at rest. Fishermen sat repairing nets on the cobbled quayside. Apart from them and a solitary dog nosing through the lobster pots the place looked deserted. The end of siesta time. Soon the shops would re-open, traffic would flow, people would take the air, fill the cafés and spill into the streets. I remembered Malta. How quiet when we arrived ... how noisy later.

There was air on the water, but it would be humid and sticky inland. A man could breathe out here and enjoy the sun on his face – whereas he might suffocate ashore, or meet death in any number of ways.

We reached the steps at the end of the quay – there were more a hundred yards away, wider than these and easier to climb – but they were close to the fishermen so this was as far as we went. The man cut the engine and slid the boat smoothly alongside old stones. I scrambled ashore just as Alexis's man spoke to Jack, 'I'll wait here for you later. Fix this spot in your mind. It will be dark when you return.'

Jack nodded. I watched in silence, doubting I would return, not caring much – only one thing mattered – to get Maria out before taking my revenge on Weston and Douglas. Serracino could be left for others, Weston and Douglas were mine.

Jack leapt onto the steps. The man pull-started the engine. He shouted good luck over the noise, avoiding my eye. He didn't expect me to return either.

We turned right at the top of the steps, away from the town. The road climbed gently, parallel to the shoreline – but only for a mile, then it turned inland – at least it did on the map.

Jack eased the pack on his shoulders. We were dressed alike: strong shoes, faded blue trousers, white shirts – makeshift outfits scrounged from the *Miranda* designed to disguise us as hikers. We each carried a backpack – mine had a red blanket strapped to the top, Jack's dangled a tin mug. We were both uncomfortable in the role – twenty years too old for it and even in our youth the open air life had never appealed.

'Bloody Kaufman,' Jack grumbled, 'right little boy scout – I half expected him to tell us to start a fire with two sticks of wood.'

'It's not for long. Come on, walk in the shade.'

The road was flanked with trees on the inland side – olives and pines twisted into bizarre shapes by the wind. The olive trees were stunted but the pines provided some shade.

'You've changed your mind, haven't you,' Jack asked, 'about Kaufman?'

I shrugged. It was true in a way. Kaufman had done all he could – now it was up to me – and Jack of course.

Climbing that hill was like crossing a chess board – black shade one moment, blazing white heat the next. The sun was still high in the sky. A cricket startled me by its sudden noise, there were a lot of flies about and a bird rose from a thicket with a flurry of wings.

'Suppose he's wrong?' Jack demanded. 'Suppose there is no farmhouse? Suppose Maria is in the café after all?'

'Then you take her hand and get the hell out of there,' I said. But Jack was whistling in the dark. Kaufman would not be wrong. Maria would not be in the café.

We paused to look back after two hundred yards. The bay shimmered blue and white and the place looked as quiet as a ghost town. But I suddenly stiffened when I saw the fishermen. Three had watched us come ashore – now there were two!

'So what?' Jack said. 'He's probably gone for a leak or something.'

I squinted into the sunshine. No movement – not even under the trees. What had Kaufman said – 'Assume everyone's Mafia – you won't be far wrong!' I cursed and stepped up the pace, so that we breasted the hill like soldiers on a forced march. But then I slowed down. Kaufman had warned us not to travel too fast – 'Don't arrive early ... you'll have to hang around ... that would look suspicious.'

So much to remember!

The trees thinned out, there was less shade, my shirt clung to my back. I wiped sweat out of my eyes, sucked my sore lip and resisted the impulse to light a cigarette.

'We should be armed,' Jack grumbled, 'Kaufman carries a gun all the time. See that shoulder holster? He's armed, and we're out here with fuck all.'

The track dragged inland, stumbling from one pot-hole to the next, less than a couple of yards wide in places. Our breath rasped as our feet scuffed the dirt. Then I heard the bells, the air was suddenly full of them. Not church bells, a thin tinkling sound, like chinese chimes jangling in the wind. But there was no wind! Then we rounded the bend and goats were everywhere – all over the track. They gave ground grudgingly, pushing their snouts against us, staring with flat, malevolent eyes. There were a lot of them – at least a couple of dozen. I wondered why someone wasn't tending them – a goatherd? Then I saw him. Brown-faced, sharp-eyed, a man in his middle years – watching us with the same unblinking gaze as his animals. He sat on an outcrop of rock thirty yards away and never even raised a hand in greeting. I wondered how long he had been there? It was high ground – he could see for miles – perhaps he had seen us come ashore? Perhaps he had watched the tender return to the *Miranda*?

We pushed the goats from our path and continued on. I could *feel* the goatherd's eyes on my back, but I said nothing to Jack. What was the point?

We reached the cemetery early. We wandered around, pretending to be interested in the tombstones – so many stark blocks of marble, the shimmering blue sea in the background. Many headstones were split down the middle like decayed teeth – the customary way to mark the grave of a murdered man. No need to speak Italian to read the inscriptions – even I understood *Da maso assassina*. Some graves bore faded photographs – sad-eyed young men sporting thin moustaches grown with the first hair on their upper lip – the first and the last. Many men were murdered in Alcamo. Jack counted six in one year.

Ten minutes later came the sound of the engine, in low gear, protesting a bit. Then the VW poptop lurched into sight, swaying from side to side as it wheezed towards us. Jack stepped into the track and waved it down.

'Where you heading?' a man asked from the passenger's window. His accent sounded faintly Australian. Maria would never mistake him for Jack, neither would I, but a stranger might.

'Alcamo.' Jack looked round, but nobody was watching our game of charades.

The man jumped down. 'Get in quick.'

We heaved the packs from our shoulders. My back felt sore where the straps had rubbed. Jack and I squeezed into the back of the camper and sat on padded benches opposite each other. The man climbed back in and slammed the door. 'Anything about?'

I told him about the fishermen and the goatherd. He shrugged, 'Forget it. We've not even been tailed since we got here. I reckon they stopped worrying – once we reached Sicily.'

The driver resembled me slightly. I had seen him before, in the little room in Manchester Square. He re-started the engine. 'Cases are under the benches,' he said over his shoulder. 'Hurry up and get changed.'

It was difficult, undressing in that confined space. Jack and I bumped each other, cursing the unpredictable motion of the van. My suitcase contained my clothes – they really were *my* clothes, the ones I had worn when I left Rex Place.

The driver glanced at me in his mirror. 'Papers are in the glove compartment. It's a rented van, rented in Salerno. Everything's in order. If you're asked why you didn't get a car say the hire firm didn't have one – height of the season and all the rest of it. The VW was all you could get.'

I looked around for the microphones. Everything we said could be heard in one of the film company's jeeps. And the van was bugged in another way – with an electronic locating device which transmitted a signal not only to the jeep but to the radio room on board the *Miranda*.

The man who looked like Jack was watching me. 'You'll never find it.'

'Don't you have to press a button, switch something on—'

'No, just talk – they can hear everything.'

'Can they call us?'

He shook his head. 'They've only got a receiver – they can't transmit. Want to run through the procedure again?'

Jack finished tying his shoes and said, 'If the plan works and Sam sweet talks them into releasing Maria, I'm to drive her back to Castellamare in this. If we're alone I get her to talk about everything she's seen – how many men they've got, where they are, security systems, everything.'

The man nodded. 'And if they send someone with you just do the best you can.'

The driver interrupted, 'Hurry up. You've only got four minutes – then it's our turn. Get ready to swap places.'

At least he stopped the van for that, pulling off the road into the shade of an olive grove. But we dealt with the wine-coloured briefcase before we did anything else. I took it out of my knapsack and the man who looked like Jack handcuffed it to my left wrist. 'You won't need a key,' he told me, 'that way you can't take it off and they can't take it away from you. The locating bug in there has the same range as the one on the van – twenty kilometres. It's well hidden but a real search *might* find it – so don't let them inspect the case too thoroughly. Just keep it padlocked to your wrist and that way we'll follow you wherever you go.'

Then we all exchanged places. Jack pulled himself up behind the wheel, I slammed the passenger door, and we were off again. The man who had been driving said, 'Move it – we're two minutes down on schedule.'

Jack made up the time, he drove well, as if the VW was his Rolls.

'Don't forget, Sam,' said the man like Jack, 'we allow half an hour for the first part. That's for you to talk them into swapping Jack and Maria for the rest of the list. But an hour after you go in we're coming in after you – whatever happens. One hour, got that?'

I said yes. I knew the plan by heart. Even the reduction in time between my arrival and the troops coming in after me. We were all getting nervous.

'And Jack,' he said, 'don't worry if they send you and Maria back to Castellamare in a different vehicle. We'll be ready for that. If they let you use this it will be a bonus, that's all.'

The parched countryside gave way to a built-up area as we approached Alcamo Marina – a noisy, steamy jungle of clapboard summer houses sandwiched between the road and the railway – built by Mafia money, hugely profitable for the owners and hell on earth to live in. And when we passed the marble factory I remembered another of Bonello's stories.

'It's *still* owned by Mafia,' said the man who looked like Jack, '*everything* is owned by the bloody Mafia.'

'Don't forget,' said the other man, 'parking in the Piazza Ciullo is a right cow. It's always crowded. So we've got a car there waiting for you. A blue Datsun. He'll pull out as you drive into the square. Park in his place, lock up, then walk across to the Café Cordina.'

We set them down on the outskirts of Alcamo. They stood at the roadside and waved goodbye – two hikers, with packs on their backs, calling thanks for the lift we had given them. I glanced over my shoulder. The clothes they had worn earlier – suits similar to the ones we now wore – were in their backpacks, and behind me the suitcases were under the benches and everything was neat and tidy. The change of identities had been completed in minutes.

'No more decoys,' Jack grunted, 'we're the hunted now.'

'Wrong, we're the *hunters* and don't you forget it. This is *my* meeting, Jack. I called it. They snatched Maria to level the odds, that's all. But it's still my meeting and by Christ we'll run it that way.'

'Kaufman never had a better pupil,' he said, shaking his head, 'but that sounds like the old Winner Harris.'

'You'd better believe it,' I said grimly, sounding more confident than I felt.

We passed some wine tankers. Italian markings, not Hardman's Wine. Probably not even wine, even though *vino* was painted on the side. Sugar and water and enzymes. A racket worth millions a year. Christ – what a place!

Then we were there. The main square – the Piazzo Ciullo. Cars were parked in front of the Jesuit Church. Cars and motorcycles. About 45,000 people live in Alcamo. Maybe they don't all own a motorbike – but it sounded like it.

The blue Datsun waited until we were a few yards away, then

reversed at speed, spinning its wheels and burning tyres. Jack slotted the VW into the space a second ahead of a battered Volvo.

I took a deep breath. Alcamo. Forty-eight hours ago I had never heard of it. Since then I had thought of little else. Everything fell into place. The extent of my knowledge surprised me. There was the church – with the Bank of Sicily next to it. The bank was run by the mayor.

The mayor was a Christian Democrat – and the Mafia organised his vote. Wheels within wheels. Next to the bank was a café with tables spilling out over the pavement. The Café Filipi, the café of the peasantry. The Café Cordina was opposite. I could see it in the wing mirror. The Café Cordina was the café for the better off, the wine doctorers, the small traders, the *petty* Mafia, and the messengers of the Mafia itself.

'Ready?'

I nodded.

Jack reached across to shake hands, a clumsily embarrassed gesture. 'Good luck, Sam,' he said. 'If . . . if we get Maria out I'll be straight back. Whatever happens. You know that—'

I punched his arm. 'Who else would lend me a hundred grand?'

He smiled and opened the door.

The Café Cordina was crowded, but so was the whole of the Piazza Ciullo. Crossing it reminded me of the square in Rabat. Not quite so bad but there were plenty of people about. People and cars, and the ubiquitous motorcycles. Half a dozen youths straddled Hondas outside the Café Filipi, revving their engines while shouting to a boy on a balcony. Street vendors called from the fish market fifty yards away. Rubbish littered the pavements, dumped there by the owners of shops and cafés. The warm evening air was scented with cooking smells, and the sky began to turn that shade of blue-black velvet I was beginning to recognise as Mediterranean. It was exactly eight o'clock.

Most of the tables were occupied, but we found one eventually against the back inside wall. It suited us. From where we sat we could see not only the entrance but most of the café. We ordered pizzas and lemon *granita* with *ice pile* and settled back to wait for the man in the Ferrari.

Maria was not there. Nor was any other woman. Like the Oyster Bar, the Café Cordina was strictly men only. And they were a mixed bunch. Some played cards at a nearby table, and beyond them four men in black suits talked earnestly over a meal of charcoal grilled fish. Near the door four men draped their jackets over the backs of their chairs. One of them passed our table on his way to the gents. A light-meter hung on a strap around his neck. I watched him return to his table and strained my hearing to eavesdrop on the conversation. Two of the men were American. Brief snatches of their talk reached me – some in English and some in Italian – all about camera angles and shooting schedules and problems with the light. They talked loudly, unworried about being overheard. They were good, I had to admit that.

We ate our food, drank our wine and watched the clock. Eating was difficult with the case chained to my wrist. I tried putting it on the floor next to me, but that made me sit all lopsided – so in the end I rested it in my lap.

Nine o'clock came and went. Quarter past. Jack's face creased with worry. We ordered more wine and fresh coffee. I mixed water with the wine, determined to keep a clear head. People came and went – but many stayed to drink and talk, as obviously was their habit at the end of the day. Time and again I felt we were being watched – but I never caught anyone looking when I glanced up.

Then, when I was as sick with worry and fear as Jack, it happened – at nine twenty. Jack went to relieve himself and as soon as he vacated his chair a man sat down. 'Give me the case,' he said softly.

He spoke English with an American accent. I recognised him. He was one of the fish supper crowd – but when I looked their table was empty.

'The case,' he repeated.

I eased back to show him the chain connecting the case to my wrist.

'Take it off.'

I shook my head. 'I don't have a key,' I said. I remembered Kaufman's pep talk about taking the initiative, so I added, 'I came here for an important meeting. Don't waste my time—'

'You'll do as you're told,' he snapped, breaking off as he realised that his voice was rising.

Then Jack came out of the gents. I knew something was wrong as soon as I saw him. He walked straight past me, towards the door. Two men stayed very close behind him. I pushed my chair back but the man at the table restrained me. 'One moment,' he said, 'we don't want to attract attention.'

Kaufman's words – they rang in my ears – '*Do whatever the man says, Sam – nice and easy, without attracting attention.*' I stared at the man. He had used the same words. It was uncanny – as if he had been briefed by Kaufman too.

He smiled. 'Your bill has been taken care of – just get up and walk outside – slowly.'

'We've got a van in the square,' I said stupidly. 'A VW camper.'

'I know. It's being looked after. Your friend had the keys.'

We passed the film crowd on the way out. One of them told a joke and they all roared with laughter. Another beckoned a waiter for some more wine, they looked like making a night of it.

It was warm outside. Fans had created a draught in the café, but outside the air was heavy and oppressive. I wondered what would happen to the VW. We needed that – it was part of the plan.

Kaufman was wrong about the Ferrari, but then Kaufman was wrong about a lot of things. Jack was climbing into an Audi ten yards away. I turned towards it but the man at my side put a hand on my arm. A Mercedes pulled away from the church steps opposite and slid towards us. I panicked. Jack and I were being separated. Holy Christ, *we had been separated*!

'Jack – wait a minute. I'm coming with you—'

'With us,' said the man angrily, pulling my arm.

'Jack!' I shouted.

He turned towards me, but then he was bundled into the car. Two men leapt out of the Mercedes and a second later I was in the back seat with a man either side of me. The man from Cordina's jumped into the front as the driver gunned the engine.

There were plenty of people about. Sixty, eighty, a hundred perhaps – but nobody spared us as much as a glance. I twisted my face to the side window, just in time to see a figure emerge from the Audi and run across to the VW. I was sweating like a pig. *Christ, it had all gone wrong!* Right at the outset. Jack and I had been separated! We had lost the VW! And Kaufman's bloody army were still in the Café Cordina drinking themselves silly.

'Were's Corrao?' I demanded.

The man on my right hammered his elbow into my ribs. I jerked forward but not before I glimpsed the VW swing out behind us. I tried to sit up, but the man grabbed my hair and yanked so hard that I jackknifed in the seat. Then he wrenched my right arm so far up my back that my head touched my knees.

I spent the next twenty minutes like that. I tried to follow our route – when we swayed right it meant a left turn – things like that. It sounds easy but it isn't. I gave up and relied on the bug in the briefcase. I was worried sick about being parted from Jack. Kaufman had never allowed for that. Our plan *depended* on us staying together. Keep the initiative Kaufman had said – *Christ, what bloody initiative*?

329

Then the gunfire broke out and so many things happened at once that events kaleidoscoped. We had been climbing – the tilt of the car told me that. I guessed we were making for the farm in the hills. Suddenly all hell broke loose. The driver screamed. Shots rang in my ears. The man on my left collapsed over me; warm, sticky blood seeped down my arm. The man to my right leapt out of the door. The car was out of control. Then we hit a stone wall . . . head-on . . . I saw it in the headlights. The driver was impaled on the steering wheel, the man from Cordina's went through the windscreen – I damn near dug my eye out with that case, then my head cracked on the door pillar and I was being pulled out of the wreckage. It took me a few moments to recognise my rescuer. It was Henderson.

'It's all gone wrong!' he shouted, 'they've got Bonello. For God's sake keep down!'

He had to repeat it – even then it only half registered. We were crouched behind a low wall, next to some men dressed as Mexican soldiers. Beyond them were some arc lamps and a searchlight was being swivelled on the back of a jeep.

Henderson shouted, 'Bonello went off with one of the undercover men at two thirty—'

A flat crack of sound made him throw an arm over my shoulder to pin me to the ground. He cupped his hands to my ear, 'Marius, the agent, thought he could guess which farmhouse. They went to scout it out – then they were jumped. They've got Bonello in there somewhere.'

There was the farmhouse. At least I assumed it was. Various buildings were about thirty yards from where we crouched. Away to my right the Audi was on its side in flames. Bodies littered the ground like a newsreel clip of a traffic accident. I saw Jack in the flickering glare, blood ran down his face and he clutched his right shoulder with his left hand.

'What's happening?' I shouted.

Henderson grabbed my shoulders and shook me, 'Dammit, I just said – I just told you. For God's sake keep down!'

Then Kaufman arrived. He raced across the open ground to the stone wall, ducking and weaving as he ran, to throw himself into the dirt beside me. 'They knew we were coming,' he gasped. 'Fuck everything! They knew it!'

'What's happening?' I repeated.

'Marius took Enrico off to scout possible locations. They were jumped. Marius must have blown cover—'

'Where's Bonello now?'

'In there goddamnit! They've had him six hours. Marius escaped and hid out till he could get back to us. We came immediately—'

My head began to clear. 'You mean you've changed the plan—'

'Changed it? What are you – *stupid*? They've had Enrico *six* hours. Don't you know what that means?'

When I rubbed my head my hand came away sticky with blood. 'He'll have talked? Is that what you're saying?'

But Kaufman was no longer listening. Instead he was shouting at a man who emerged from behind the blazing Audi. But Henderson was still trying to make me understand. 'Sam, they *know*! They know Enrico. Who he is, what he does – they'll have worked him over.'

I felt sick as I remembered that cellar. Poor devil – poor, helpless, forsaken devil. But even as I reeled from that shock I thought of Maria. 'My God, what's happened to Maria?' My question was drowned by a screech of brakes as a jeep skidded to a halt behind me. Kaufman was across to it in a flash and instinct took me with him. Then I got another shock as I recognised the Mexican in the passenger seat. It was Lucia. She steadied herself against the dashboard while clutching a microphone in her other hand.

'They've pulled back from the farmhouse,' she told Kaufman breathlessly, 'we've got most of them trapped on the back road—'

'Most of them?' Kaufman snapped.

'Some got across to the villa. At least four. They've got Maria . . . she's *alive* . . . she's in the villa—'

Kaufman snatched the microphone. 'Murphy, you hear me?'

A man's voice boomed across the static, 'Receiving you.'

'Did you see the girl? Was she with them? *Definitely?*'

'Positively. Two of them dragged her between them. We identified Serracino—'

'You got *that* close! Without stopping them—'

'They had a gun at her head. But they've bought a one-way ticket. They can't get out. We've got the back of the villa covered. Johnson's rigging up floodlights—'

'Any sign of Enrico?'

'No, sir, we searched the farmhouse—'

'Shit! All right, this is what you do. Just stay put. Don't try to flush them out. We'll do that from here. You got that?'

'Yes, sir.'

Lucia was in my arms. 'Oh, Sam, thank God you're safe. Sam – Maria's alive, she's still *alive*—'

Kaufman was shouting into the microphone, 'What about the others? Those on the back road?'

'They're trapped in a gulley with the mountain behind them, solid rock. To get out they've got to walk down a track ten yards wide. The four men I've got covering it could stop an army—'

'Okay,' Kaufman sucked in a giant breath of air, 'okay, Murphy, I'll get back to you.'

Suddenly I realised that Jack was next to me and must have heard everything. His first words confirmed it. 'She's alive,' he whispered, then gripped my arm. 'Sam, she's *alive*!' Then he and Lucia were embracing each other and she was in tears. I hoped my shaky grin concealed what I was thinking – which was to wonder how much longer Maria could *stay* alive with this circus camped outside the door. But I was only half concentrating – the rest of me was getting my bearings. We were huddled next to the jeep alongside the stone wall. Ten yards to the left was the track which led up to the farmhouse. Away to the right the wall was much higher, and beyond the flames belching from the wrecked Audi were the biggest pair of wrought iron gates I ever saw in my life.

'That's the front entrance to the villa,' Kaufman said. 'This wall runs right round it. We had the place surrounded and were about to move when somebody opened fire. Then you arrived.'

I took in the rest of the scene. Two more jeeps were parked yards to the right. A searchlight was trained through the iron gates towards the villa. Mexican soldiers were everywhere, some at the entrance to the farmhouse, but most near the big gates, crouched low, all armed with rifles. When I looked back at our jeep I recognised the driver. It was the man who looked like Jack – the man I had seen in Manchester Square, the man in the VW.

'We found the manufacturing plant,' Kaufman was telling Henderson, 'big barn back of the farmhouse. Smell of vinegar knocks your head off—'

'What about my wife? To hell with—'

'All right, Jack,' Kaufman said quickly. 'She's alive – just hang onto that will you?'

He spoke with crisp authority but he looked desperately tired. I suppose we all did. Lucia's face was so drained that her flesh seemed translucent. Jack was grey except for the blood at his forehead, and the lines on Henderson's face might have been chipped from granite.

'No sign of Enrico – no sign of the poor bastard anywhere,' Kaufman was saying miserably to nobody in particular.

Suddenly a shout drew our attention to the gates. Kaufman set off at a run, the rest of us on his heels. I stumbled as my foot twisted on something soft. It was the man who had collected me from Cordina's. He was quite dead.

The villa was about fifty yards away, at the end of the drive. It was big, only two storeys high but long and rambling, bathed in brilliant white light – and now that I was at the gates I realised that both jeeps were equipped with searchlights. The house was fronted by a wide terrace, at least twenty yards deep, with a sweep of steps rising to a central front door, flanked either side by a series of shuttered windows. The swimming pool set into the right hand side of the terrace was fed by fountains from the far edge. A drive ran directly up to the left hand side of the house and stopped at some big doors which I assumed to be an integral garage.

Someone was saying to Kaufman, 'The front door opened, but it closed again, almost immediately.'

The man who looked like Jack had followed us in the jeep. Kaufman snatched the microphone, 'Murphy?'

'Receiving you.'

'Okay at the back?'

'Nothing's moved.'

'You got floodlights on? Can you see *everything*?'

'Even the cracks in the walls.'

'What about the sides?'

'I got men posted. There's a door on the left hand side, your right. We've got lights on it and men covering. There's no door the other side, not even ground floor windows, but I've got two men on the wall over there, just in case.'

Kaufman was nodding, his eyes closed, visualising the other flanks of the house. He drew a deep breath, 'Okay Murphy, I'm ready to start.'

'Good luck.'

Jack grabbed Kaufman's arm. 'You're not going to rush the house. There's *no way* we can storm that place without Maria getting killed—'

Kaufman hurled him away. 'For Chrissake take hold of yourself!'

Both Kaufman and Jack were trembling, so were the rest of us. We stood grouped in a little tableau, clustered around that jeep just outside the gates, the other two vehicles pressed up to the entrance and every Mexican rifle trained on the house. It fell so quiet that I heard water splashing into the swimming pool from the fountains. Then Kaufman's breath rasped as he struggled to control his temper. 'Now you listen, Jack. I'm going to *try* to talk them out. I'm going to *try* to persuade them to give themselves up. But I don't want another outburst from you until this is all over. You better understand that or else I'll—'

'Jack,' I said, a pack of cigarettes in my hand, 'here, light these for us, will you?'

Jack's gaze fell from Kaufman's face to my outstretched hand. My movements were clumsy, hampered by that wretched briefcase

333

clamped to my left wrist. Lucia reached across and took the packet, then offered it to Jack. The moment passed, I breathed a small sigh of relief.

Kaufman turned and walked away, passing between the two jeeps, going right up to the gates, in full view of the house. He pushed one gate, it swung open a yard. He made no attempt to go further, instead he stood like a general surveying the field of battle. Beyond him every window in the villa was shuttered, the door firmly closed, no threatening movement came from the house, yet the atmosphere tingled with danger. Lucia trembled beside me. I squeezed her arm. Jack coughed nervously. We all expected a shot to ring out and Kaufman to fall to the ground. But nothing happened. A soft wind rustled the warm air. One of the Mexicans shifted his position, scraping his boots on the ground. Henderson gestured for silence. But it was silent already – my God, it was quiet as the grave.

A minute passed, though it seemed longer. Then Kaufman turned to the jeep on his right and lifted a megaphone from the seat. 'Serracino,' he shouted. Lucia jumped, though she must have expected it. 'Serracino.' The name boomed from the megaphone, amplified, bringing an echo – 'Serracino . . . cino . . . no.'

'You are surrounded . . . rounded . . . ded. Come on out . . . on out . . . out.'

It brought no response.

'Come out with your hands up . . . hands up . . . up.'

Water plopped into the pool. The soft breeze shivered the twisted branches of the olive trees. We held our breath.

Kaufman replaced the megaphone in the jeep and returned to us. He looked at Jack: 'I'm going to send two men in. Just half way up the drive, that's all, just as a probe. When they're in place I'll try again.'

I knew why Jack was looking at me. He was waiting for me to say no. But what alternative was there?

Kaufman called two men over. 'I'll douse those lights for twenty seconds. When I do I want you up that drive. See those statues – take cover there. And keep your heads down when the lights go back on. Got that?'

The statues were about twenty yards in, almost half way to the villa, not far from the edge of the terrace. Both men gauged the distance, then glanced at each other before nodding. 'We'll make it,' one said, and they walked back to the gate.

'Maybe if *I* spoke to them,' Jack was saying desperately, 'if I *appealed* to them—'

'Okay – when I've positioned the men you can try,' Kaufman said with surprising reasonableness. He walked back to the gates and spoke to the men manning the searchlights.

I wondered what response an appeal from Jack would bring – none I could imagine. Nor did I believe Kaufman expected one. Events had moved too far for that. I tried to visualise the happenings inside the villa. If Serracino was there so were Weston and Douglas, I felt sure of that.

'Count down from ten,' Kaufman was saying to the two men by the gates. 'Ten ... nine ...'

What a catalogue of killing had brought me to this place, almost face to face with my enemies. Charlie Weston who set me up ... Lew Douglas who almost certainly murdered Kay ...

'six ... five ... four ...'

Poor tormented Edgar ... poor terrified Maria with that bastard Serracino ... who had butchered her parents and disfigured Lucia for life.

'two ... one ... NOW!'

My fists bunched as the lights went out. Blindness. I felt a great surge of hatred for the men up at the house, and exaltation at the thought of their capture, what I would do to them. *Then came the explosions!* Followed by a man's scream ... another scream, high-pitched, terrifying! Lucia cried out beside me. Henderson shouted. The lights came back on and we all gasped at the sight confronting us.

'Mined!' Henderson was saying incredulously. 'The bloody place is mined!'

Neither of the two men had reached the statues. Both were only about fifteen yards from the gates. One screamed piercingly into the night, clutching the bloodied stump of his right leg where it ended at the knee. The other man lay motionless.

'Get me a rope,' Kaufman was shouting, 'get me a rope for God's sake!'

Henderson snatched a coiled line from the back of the jeep and ran to the gates. Lucia buried her head in her hands. Jack groaned with despair. I tore my gaze away from the injured man – my heart sinking at the prospect of ever seeing Maria alive again. Then she was there ... *Maria was at the top of the steps, by the open front door.* I could hardly believe my eyes. It *was* Maria. One arm twisted behind her, the other shielding her eyes from the glare of the lights. But it *was* Maria! She was held firmly from behind, her feet were hobbled, she was too far away for me to tell if she was bruised or hurt, but at least she could stand upright. And that was Lew Douglas behind her, I was *sure* it was.

'Harris!' he shouted. 'Harris!'

It *was* Douglas.

I came to life and dashed to the gates, side by side with Jack. 'Maria!' he roared, and might have run up the drive but for Henderson holding him. '*Maria!*'

Kaufman had snaked a rope out to the injured man who was groaning pitifully but holding on desperately as inch by inch the rope drew him towards us.

'I'm here,' I shouted at the top of my voice, 'I'm here. This is Sam Harris.'

Maria had seen Jack. She screamed his name and started to struggle. Then Douglas got a hand over her mouth and dragged her back across the threshold. He shouted from just inside the open door, 'We'll negotiate with you, Harris. You hear that. We'll negotiate with you. Stay there until you read our terms.'

Then the door banged shut just as another opened, the garage door, at the top of the drive. It only opened a fraction, then a shade wider, but nowhere near wide enough for a car. Instead a donkey came out. A donkey! It had a sack thrown across its back. The animal blinked nervously at the strong lights, backing away, but someone in the garage must have hit it because it turned again and started towards us.

'*Maria!*' Jack shouted into the night, freeing himself from Henderson. But Maria was gone. Two of the Mexicans started to lift the injured man past me towards one of the jeeps. He cried out in pain through clenched teeth.

Kaufman was watching the donkey. The animal walked deliberately towards us, keeping to the centre of the drive, the lumpy sack on its back swaying from side to side.

'No way,' Kaufman was whispering to himself, 'no way that animal can walk through a minefield, unless—'

Suddenly Lucia screamed, '*No!* Oh God, please *no* . . .'

It was Bonello. *The sack* was Bonello. His fingertips trailed in the dust on the near side of the donkey, his head bounced on the animal's flanks.

'Get her out of here,' Kaufman snapped at me, his eyes still fixed on the approaching donkey. I took Lucia's arm and tried to pull her back from the gates, but she was determined to stay.

The donkey passed the statues and reached the dead Mexican. It paused a moment, nuzzling the man's head. He did not move. Then the animal resumed its slow advance towards us.

Bonello was roped to its back. Looking down at his mutilated body I was reminded of his own words when he described cutting Vito's body down from that scaffolding in Milan all those years ago . . . '*barely recognisable as a man – as a human being – a thing of dignity*

. . .' And I remembered Jack telling me that Bonello was the most cautious man he had ever met. But I was most conscious of my rising nausea and an incredulous revulsion that men were alive who could bear to do such things to another human being.

Lucia turned her head away and sobbed helplessly in my arms as Kaufman untied the ropes. The note was pinned to Bonello's chest. Kaufman read it quickly, then passed it to me without a word.

Maria had written – *'The grounds are mined electronically. They control them from in here. They say they will switch the mines off long enough for Sam to come up to the house. They want to negotiate. They say unless Sam comes in ten minutes they will kill me.'*

CHAPTER SEVENTEEN

Some experiences are never forgotten. That memory will haunt me forever . . . that little group of us clustered by those gates . . . Kaufman's frustration . . . Jack's misery . . . Lucia weeping over Bonello's body . . . the injured Mexican groaning pitifully as someone tended the remains of his leg. I felt too angry to be afraid. My hands kept bunching as if to clasp a throat and throttle someone.

But the shocks were far from over. Kaufman was saying something when his words were lost in the noise – a *new*, unexpected noise which took us all by surprise . . . a clattering sound on the night air. Suddenly a searchlight came out of the sky, red and green navigation lights appeared, and a second later the whirling rotor blades of a helicopter cleared the ridge behind the villa to swoop over us. We scattered instinctively, hands clapped to our ears against the terrifying noise. For an instant the machine hovered directly above us, then it moved nearer the house, to dip down by the pool and come to rest on the terrace.

Its arrival was so sudden, so completely without warning that we were all knocked off balance. The ridge was little more than a hundred yards away – I suppose the land and the direction of the breeze had masked the sound of the machine's approach. But there it was – on the terrace, rotor blades still spinning, the pilot clearly visible. We stood mesmerised for a moment, then I was running back towards the other jeep, not of my own volition, Kaufman was dragging me and shouting at the same time. 'That's how they plan to get out. That's their escape route.'

337

Ten minutes had been allocated, ten precious minutes before I was to walk up the drive and into that house to *negotiate*. Kaufman and the man who looked like Jack worked like demons. The radio-transmission equipment was wrenched from the jeep with feverish haste, then Kaufman hugged it in his arms and ran down towards the olive grove. His voice came clearly over the receiver. 'Can you hear me?' he kept shouting, 'can you hear me?' The man who looked like Jack was waving and shouting back – then Kaufman returned in a rush, gasping for breath. 'This is going in that case, Sam. Then we'll know what's going on. We'll hear every damn word said in there.'

They unlocked the briefcase, removed the precious list, reams and reams of it bound in a folder, and inserted the transmitter. Positioning the microphone took most of the time. Then Kaufman spiked holes into the top of the case before locking it again. It felt heavy on my wrist, much heavier than before, but not unmanageable. He hurried me back to the gates. 'Sam, we'll be listening in on *everything*. Just you remember that. It's our best chance, Sam. It's our *only* chance.'

I glanced at my watch. Ten twenty-five. The ten minutes were up. Looking up the drive I saw the pilot still inside the helicopter.

'I'm going with him,' Jack was telling Kaufman, 'I'm going and you won't stop me.'

Henderson interrupted. 'The door's opening – *look*, look at the villa.'

Every eye focused on the house. Maria stood at the top of the steps, held from behind as before, her feet still hobbled.

'Harris?' came a shout.

I stood between those huge gates and waved. 'I'm ready.'

'I'm coming too,' Jack said behind me.

There was no time to argue. I shouted, 'Jack Green is with me. We're coming in now.'

Then I started to walk. A delay might have brought a refusal from the house – might have cost me my nerve – might have been wiser. But I was in no mood for wisdom. Not even the sight of the dead Mexican deterred me. I drew level with his twisted body without even knowing if Jack was with me or not. He was, but I don't think I cared. Kaufman had been right all along. This *was* my story. Mine and everyone close to me – Kay, Edgar, Maria, Jack . . . and now Lucia too.

I passed the statues. The helicopter's blades had stopped spinning but the motor was still running – I could hear it. The pilot watched me every step of the way – dark glasses shielding his eyes from the glare, an automatic rifle cradled in his arms. I reached the edge of the terrace before it occurred to me that I had walked through a minefield. The shock of that took the edge off my temper, calmed me down a bit – even so every ounce of concentration was keyed up for what lay waiting for me in the house. I passed the helicopter and skirted the edge of the swimming pool – stepped over a diving board – then I was there. At the foot of the steps. I looked up, expecting to see Douglas holding Maria. But the entrance was empty. Just an open door.

Jack caught me up. We climbed the steps shoulder to shoulder. The deserted lobby was full of menacing shadow, empty of light – and the smell of petrol was everywhere – the place reeked of it, with a stench so overpowering that Darmanin flashed into my mind. Poor, frightened Darmanin – another victim, another helpless . . .

'Stop! That's far enough.'

A man's voice. A voice I knew. *Charlie Weston!* Here . . . waiting for me.

'Shut the door behind you.'

He was in a room ahead of us, on the right hand side, light escaped through a half open door, I saw his shadow on the far wall, a gun in his hand.

I did as I was told. The searchlights at the bottom of the drive were shut out as I closed the door. The gloom in the lobby intensified to total darkness. Then lights came on above us. But Weston remained in the room up ahead. 'You're not armed I take it?'

'Of course I'm bloody well not armed,' I snapped. 'For God's sake—'

'What's that you're carrying?'

'The list. I've brought the list. Part of the deal, remember?'

'I can't imagine it tells us anything Bonello left out,' he chuckled.

Jack swore and took a step towards the door.

'Stay where you are,' Weston snapped. 'Face the wall and put your hands above your heads. Both of you.'

I nodded to Jack and we turned together, resting our hands on the wall above our heads. The case on my arm weighed a ton. Soft footsteps sounded behind us. A hand patted my jacket, then each trouser leg . . . one-handed . . . as if whoever it was held a gun in the other. But I was mistaken. When I turned I saw the explanation was simpler than that. The man only had *one* effective hand. *It was Corrao*. Pietro Corrao. Our eyes met his as dead as ever behind dark glasses . . . mine blazing with hate. And beyond him stood Charlie Weston, sneering at me.

He hadn't changed. Exactly as I remembered him. Except for the gun in his hand. He stepped into the hall and jerked his head towards the room. 'Walk slowly,' he said, 'and Mr Green – remember that another gun is pointing at your wife's head.'

'You prize bastard,' I said as I walked. I passed within a yard of him. I could have touched him, struck him, launched an attack – a *real* hero would have – instead I turned into the room and saw Maria. She sat at a table, chalk white, rigid with tension, terrified eyes casting a mute appeal to Jack to do as he was told. A useless appeal. He was across the room as soon as he saw her, ignoring Weston's shouted warning, oblivious of the gun Douglas levelled at Maria. But nobody pulled a trigger. Jack swept her into his arms. She clung to him then, sobbing uncontrollably, whimpering with fear or released tension. I wanted to go to her too, just to rest my hand on her shoulder, just to tell her everything would work out. But how the hell could I do that?

'For Christ's sake!' Douglas snarled. 'Shut her up.'

It was my first close look at him. Douglas had changed. He looked twenty years older. The spoiled little rich boy had grown into a raddled old man.

Suddenly someone brushed past me to wrench Jack and Maria apart. A big man, shirt-sleeved, bull-necked, broad-shouldered, moving quick as light. A back-handed slap across Maria's face sent her staggering backwards. Jack roared but the man chopped him so fast that I doubt Jack even saw the blows – two, three, even four stiff arm jabs into the throat as the man's knee came up. Jack buckled and was half way to the floor by the time I leapt forward. Maria screamed. Douglas had his gun at her head. And I hesitated just long enough to be hit in the face. The room turned over. Weston had his gun in my neck. Then the man in front of me sank his fist into my stomach.

'We haven't got time for games,' he shouted furiously when I straightened up. 'You should be grateful for that.' He looked beyond me to Weston. 'Get on with it. Every minute is crucial.'

'Okay, Fiore,' Weston said as the man left the room.

So *that* was Serracino. Even in my dazed state I recognised a psychopath, a sadist – inflicting pain gave him real pleasure, and all three of us had been hurt. Jack coughed and spluttered to his feet, then helped Maria into a chair, her movements hampered by the rope around her ankles. I fought back my nausea and turned to find that Weston had backed off and was a couple of yards away. 'This place is surrounded—' I began.

'By mines,' he interrupted with a smile. 'Every yard of ground beyond the edge of the terrace is mined. We control it from over

340

there.' He jerked his head. For the first time I spared a glance for the rest of the room. Corrao had followed us in from the hall and now sat at some kind of console which housed three video screens and a radio-transmitter, beyond which was another box which presumably activated the minefield. All three of the television screens showed pictures of the grounds. I even saw Henderson down by the front gates amidst the blaze from the arc lamps. The sophistication of their defences sickened me when I remembered Kaufman's plan to rush the place with stun-grenades. None of his men stood a chance in that minefield – but then he already had one dead and another crippled to prove that.

'Twenty-five minutes left,' Douglas said from his side of the room, his gun still pointing at Maria.

Weston turned to me. 'This is what you are going to do. Go back out to Kaufman and tell him to withdraw his men to the other side of the olive grove. That's almost a thousand yards. We want them there by eleven o'clock – *all* of his men, and their bloody searchlights.' He smiled grimly, 'No lone sniper left to take a shot at us when we lift off in the helicopter.'

I don't know what surprised me the most. Finally I blurted out, 'So you know Kaufman too?'

'Bonello was stubborn, but after three hours with Fiore . . .' he shrugged. 'The word's out. We've alerted most of the Pipeline by radio. And we'll be away ourselves in a minute.'

'But we'll take that list,' Douglas smirked, 'as you've been kind enough to bring it.'

'An exchange,' I parried, 'I'll take Jack and Maria—'

'Don't be a bloody fool. They stay here until we lift off. Then they'd better move – this whole place will be ablaze within minutes.'

Petrol! Suddenly the smell made sense. *That* was the plan. To set a torch to the villa as they left. But even as I grappled with that thought another one struck me. 'But what about the minefield? How will they get past the minefield—'

Weston shot Douglas a quick glance. 'We'll switch it off. *If* Kaufman pulls back.'

He was lying – as plain as day he was lying. 'What if Kaufman stays put?'

'Then we shall kill our hostages and take our chances.'

They would kill Jack and Maria anyway – one way or the other, I felt sure of it. But I wondered what Kaufman was thinking. If the radio was working he was listening to every word. *What would he do?* Immobilise the helicopter where it stood? But good God, if he did that . . .

341

'The case,' Douglas was saying, 'we'll take the case now.'

It was hard not to panic. 'It's locked,' I said quickly. 'And locked to my wrist. I didn't bring the keys. Kaufman's still got them. You only gave me ten minutes . . .'

Nobody believed me – it was clear from their faces. Weston raised his revolver until it was level with my eyes.

'I forgot the bloody keys I tell you. For God's sake . . .'

'Then you'll come back,' Weston decided. 'You'll deliver the message to Kaufman and come back – and Sam, bring the keys this time, there's a good chap, otherwise your friends—'

I tried one last gambit. 'Send Maria. It makes no difference to you. She can tell Kaufman—'

But he shook his head. 'She's served us well. Why part with a lucky mascot?'

Every avenue was covered. Every line of escape, every hope, every possible plan. I was at my wits end. There seemed nothing left – *nothing*! I glanced at Douglas, his gun only inches from Maria's head. Weston's gun was pointing at me. He sensed my desperation because he said, 'Maria will be dead before you get half way here.'

'Let Jack untie her,' I said. 'If she's to run out of here . . .'

'It's almost ten forty,' Douglas interrupted.

'Untie her, Jack,' I said, watching Weston's eyes. I don't know what I thought, but if Weston was trying to read my mind he stood no chance, it was a mess of discarded ideas, one thought racing in pursuit of another, nothing which could be described as a plan. Meanwhile our eyes locked in a battle of wills. I heard a slight scuffle behind me, then Jack said, 'Right, Sam.'

'It *is* ten forty,' Douglas said.

'Walk,' Weston jerked his gun. 'You've got twenty minutes to save their lives.'

I threw Jack a quick look. 'I'll be back,' I promised. Serracino appeared in the doorway, wearing a jacket and carrying a suitcase. 'Put this in the helicopter on the way past,' he ordered. He was so *in control*, they all were, so sure, so confident.

I carried the case down the hall. The lights died as I reached the door. Then I stood at the top of the steps, squinting into the shafts of light which flooded up the drive. I think I expected them to shoot me then . . . in the back as I started down the steps . . . I don't know why exactly, but that's what I thought. But no shots were fired. I reached the helicopter, needlessly ducking my head – the pilot stretched a hand for the case. The cockpit was small, a squeeze for four passengers I thought, but I supposed they would manage. Then I skirted the swimming pool and crossed to the edge of the terrace. I wondered if Corrao had switched that bloody minefield off. I knew I had let Jack and Maria down. I told myself that bitterly, angrily ashamed of myself. But what else could I have done? One wrong move and Maria would have been killed there and then. That bastard Douglas would have shot her for sure ... but I should have done *something*!

I passed the statues – almost stumbled over the dead Mexican – raised my right arm to shield my eyes from the glare. Then I was at the gates and Henderson was pulling me behind the wall, out of sight of the house.

Kaufman pounced on me. 'Great, Sam, you did great,' he was saying as he unlocked the chain on my wrist. 'You did marvels in there—'

'They'll kill them both! You stupid bastard, don't you realise that?'

'Easy boy,' Kaufman handed the briefcase to the man who looked like Jack, who rushed away with it. 'Just catch your breath,' Kaufman said. He turned away to shout at Henderson, 'Okay, start now. Make it look good.'

Henderson called some of the Mexicans over to a jeep.

Kaufman sounded like a bloody doctor – no, that's wrong, more like a fighter's manager when the poor dumb boxer reels back to his corner at the end of a rough round. But gradually what he was saying got through to me. I thought he was mad at first. Why not, his other plans had failed. Some of the remaining Mexicans were working furiously behind the wall, either side of the big gates, burying something beneath the pillars, but burying what escaped me. Anyway I was too busy concentrating on Kaufman. 'I'll go through it again,' he said, and he did. I stopped arguing then. What he said made sense – *if* it worked right – if it didn't I would be dead ... so would Jack and Maria.

'Sam, it will *work*,' he insisted. 'What else can they do? You heard them – they're leaving on the dot of eleven. They've *got* to leave then by the sound of it.'

The man who looked like Jack arrived back with the briefcase. He carried it carefully, but then so did I when he handed it to me. 'It's fixed,' was all he said grimly to Kaufman.

Henderson ran over. 'We've finished at the gates. It's five to eleven.'

Behind him one of the jeeps lurched into gear and trundled past us to bounce down the track towards the olive grove.

Kaufman was saying, 'Okay, give it a minute. I want Sam cutting it as fine as possible when he goes back.'

The last arc lamp was dismantled. Suddenly the night seemed

very dark. The headlights of the remaining jeeps sliced through the blackness as they backed up and prepared to depart. Mexicans clambered aboard. Kaufman was still giving me last-minute instructions as we walked back to the gates. Then he slapped me across the shoulder and scrambled up into the nearest vehicle. 'You can do it, Sam. *You can do it!* Good luck.'

And then I was alone – standing there, watching their red tail-lights bounce down the hill, the noise of their engines already fading. I turned to face the house. A single lantern shone above the front door. Navigation lights glowed red and green on the helicopter. The cockpit was unlit but the pilot was still aboard because he revved his engines impatiently. There was no light on the swimming pool, I told myself that *at least* there was no light on the swimming pool – we had a chance whilst that remained in darkness. Some chance.

My watch showed two minutes to eleven. I shouted and waved my left hand, gripping the case tightly in my right. 'Weston! They've gone. Weston – can you hear me? Okay to come back now?'

For answer the helicopter flashed its lights.

I shouted again, 'I'm coming up now. Switch those blasted mines off for God's sake!'

Then I drew a deep breath and started to walk. It seemed twice as far as before. Strangely the case felt less heavy though, which was odd because I would have expected a bomb to weigh more than a radio transmitter. Kaufman's chuckle echoed in my ears, 'Two can play with radio detonated bombs.' I repeated his instructions under my breath. And I prayed. I prayed for Maria, I prayed for Jack, and I prayed for me. The statues loomed out of the darkness. I passed them, my eyes straight ahead. The white paved edge of the terrace showed twenty yards away. The noise from the helicopter was deafening, engine howling, wind screaming as the rotors gathered momentum. I reached the edge of the terrace. Then the front door opened and Jack and Maria stood framed in the entrance, exactly as Kaufman had forecast. 'They'll use Jack and Maria as a screen when they come out,' he had said. 'They won't trust me not leaving a sniper.'

I ducked away from the rotor blades and skirted the swimming pool. 'Water is the best shield there is against a bullet,' Kaufman had said. 'Water deflects a modern high velocity bullet better than anything I know. Hit the bottom of that pool Sam and stay there.' There had seemed no point in saying I couldn't swim – even Kaufman could not have coped with that.

Jack and Maria were already half way down the steps. I clambered

344

over the low diving board. Serracino was behind Jack. Douglas and Weston were further back, only partially shielded by Maria. I glimpsed a gun in Douglas's hand. Suddenly a huge flash of flame filled the entire lobby. Corrao ran out and started down the steps. Black smoke billowed from the door behind him. They were all out now, moving cautiously to the bottom step, using Jack and Maria as a screen.

Kaufman had promised a diversion – *when, where, how?* Weston was armed too, I saw that now – he would shoot Jack as soon as he reached the helicopter. Douglas would shoot Maria, then me, once he got the case. I had my back to the pool, the open door of the helicopter less than two yards to my left. The noise was deafening – the screaming slip-stream of wind tore at Maria's hair as she crossed towards me. I held the case up high for Douglas to see. *God, where was Kaufman's bloody diversion?* Suddenly Serracino shoved Jack aside and made a run for the helicopter – he was there, climbing on board, almost in. Weston was close behind, his gun arm swivelling towards me. Douglas grabbed the case and swung it aboard the machine, using the same hand to pull himself in after it, his gun already turning back for Maria. *He was going to shoot!* Weston's gun was on me. Then Corrao jogged everyone as he heaved himself upwards. '*JUMP!*' I screamed, dragging Maria over the edge of the pool, 'Jack, *jump!*'

Then Kaufman's landmines exploded under the front gates. The flash turned the night sky into daylight. I was falling backwards, Maria's hand still clasped in mine, both in mid-air. I glimpsed the shocked alarm on Weston's face as he twisted towards the explosion. Then my left arm went numb as I hit the water.

When I surfaced the helicopter was almost on top of me, skimming the pool, Douglas leaning out, his gun flashing as I went under again.

Jack came from nowhere to carry me spluttering to the surface. He kept shouting, 'Sam, you're hit,' but I was watching the helicopter. It was almost over the ridge. I saw the red navigation light quite clearly. Then the machine was surrounded by a ball of fire. For the tiniest fraction of a second its entire structure stood out like so many black lines in the centre of this huge orange glow. Then it blew apart, just as I sank beneath the surface.

Something was wrong with my left side. My arm was useless. Maria got her hands under my chin and dragged me kicking upwards. Jack was splashing wildly on the other side of me. I heard Maria crying, 'Jack, your leg, your leg.' Then I went under again.

We reached the side eventually. I clung onto the rail with my right hand. Jack was shouting, 'Thank God, Maria, thank God!' and she was sounding hysterical about his leg. I swallowed a gallon of water. Every time I shouted I seemed to slip below the water line. I was like Jack, I think, needing to tell them it was all over and wanting to hear it from them simultaneously. We were all shouting at once, Maria was crying and laughing and kissing us both at the same time, nearly drowning me in the process. I remember shouting that I couldn't swim and all of us roaring with laughter as if that was the funniest joke we had heard in the whole of our lives.

The explosion stopped us laughing. Kaufman was coming through the gates – except the gates weren't there any more – his *diversion* had ripped them from the walls. Now they were chained to the front of the jeeps, sticking out like cow-catchers on old-fashioned locomotives, but brushing the ground in front. The first driver-less vehicle, jammed into gear, with its steering locked, made twenty yards before being blown up. That was the noise we had heard. And by the time we were peering over the edge of the pool the Mexicans had advanced up the drive to clear the debris. Then came the second jeep, similarly equipped with a huge wrought iron gate bouncing along in front of it as it bucked and lurched towards the terrace. It almost made it too. Then came another explosion and the jeep was upended – but the leading edge of the gate had reached the terrace. They had breached the minefield!

Jack was out of the pool by now, reaching down for me, Maria shoving from behind. Jack's leg was a mess. Even as he stood there blood pumped out from below his knee. I banged my arm on the way out, my left arm – the knock made me so sick and giddy that I damn near passed out. Then Jack was lifting me clear and stretching me out on the terrace – and a moment later Maria was trying to get me out of my sodden jacket. Behind her flames from the villa's shuttered windows licked up into the sky, but I was barely conscious of them – all I really saw was Maria. I kept asking her if she was all right, but she was crying and laughing and kissing me too much to answer.

The funny thing was that I wasn't in pain – even when they got my shirt off and wiped enough of the blood away to see the two bullet holes, one in my shoulder and another in my upper arm. I ached and felt dizzy and numb, and suddenly desperately tired, but the pain wasn't unbearable.

Suddenly there was a rush of running footsteps and Lucia arrived with Henderson and some of the Mexicans. I was made to sit up while a tourniquet was applied to my arm, then my head was in Lucia's lap and she was smothering me with her tears. 'Serracino is dead,' I was assuring her. 'It's all over. The nightmare is over.

You needn't be afraid any more.' It brought a smile through her tears. 'We won,' I kept saying. 'Lucia, we beat the bastards in the end. We won, didn't we?'

Behind her Kaufman was hugging Jack and beaming down on me. Henderson was shouting for a stretcher, while grinning from ear to ear and giving me thumbs up signals. Maria wrapped her arms round Jack's neck and Lucia kissed me.

'Will you look at that,' Kaufman said from a long way away, 'I ask you – is it any wonder they call him *Winner* Harris?'

THE KILLING ANNIVERSARY

'Ian St James has the gift of storytelling'
The Times

'Irresistible' *New York Times*

'A compulsive entertaining read'
Daily Mirror

'A definite narrative gift . . . places him
with Jeffrey Archer . . . without doubt one
of the potential best sellers of the year'
Irish Times

'A sweeping yarn by a born story-teller'
Anne Macaffrey, *Success Magazine*

COLD NEW DAWN

'The fascinated reader cannot put the book
down'
Des Hickey, *Irish Sunday Independent*

'Page-turning potential to pull in the
punters' John Nicholson, *The Times*

THE MONEY STONES

'Extremely impressive . . . crisp writing, strongly escalating plot and whiff of mystery and menace'   *Observer*

'A plot that in complexity and ingenuity matches those of Paul Erdman'
          New York Times Book Review

'Excellent and unusual thriller'
          Sydney Morning Herald

'St James has done a top notch job . . . an intelligent, engrossing thriller'
          Publishers Weekly

THE BALFOUR CONSPIRACY

'Ian St James has the gift of storytelling. You always want to read the next page'
          The Times

'The authentic stamp of a born storyteller'
          Observer

'St James writes in the Deighton style – fast, clean and hard-hitting'
          Nelson De Mille

Gerald Seymour

writes internationally best-selling thrillers

'Not since Le Carré has the emergence of an international suspense writer been as stunning as that of Gerald Seymour.' *Los Angeles Times*

HARRY'S GAME
KINGFISHER
RED FOX
THE CONTRACT
ARCHANGEL
IN HONOUR BOUND
FIELD OF BLOOD
THE GLORY BOYS
A SONG IN THE MORNING
AT CLOSE QUARTERS

FONTANA PAPERBACKS

Duncan Kyle

'One of the modern masters of the high adventure story.' *Daily Telegraph*

GREEN RIVER HIGH
BLACK CAMELOT
A CAGE OF ICE
FLIGHT INTO FEAR
TERROR'S CRADLE
A RAFT OF SWORDS
WHITEOUT!
STALKING POINT
THE SEMONOV IMPULSE

FONTANA PAPERBACKS

Fontana Paperbacks: Fiction

Fontana is a leading paperback publisher of fiction.
Below are some recent titles.

- ☐ THE GATES OF EXQUISITE VIEW John Trenhaile £3.95
- ☐ LOTUS LAND Monica Highland £3.95
- ☐ THE MOUSE GOD Susan Curran £3.95
- ☐ SHADOWLIGHT Mike Jefferies £3.95
- ☐ THE SILK VENDETTA Victoria Holt £3.50
- ☐ THE HEARTS AND LIVES OF MEN Fay Weldon £3.95
- ☐ EDDIE BLACK Walter Shapiro £2.95
- ☐ THE POOL OF ST. BRANOK Philippa Carr £3.50
- ☐ FORTUNE'S DAUGHTER Connie Monk £3.50
- ☐ AMAZING FAITH Leslie Waller £3.50
- ☐ THE CORNELIUS CHRONICLES BK 1 Michael Moorcock £4.95
- ☐ THE CORNELIUS CHRONICLES BK 2 Michael Moorcock £4.95

You can buy Fontana paperbacks at your local bookshop or
newsagent. Or you can order them from Fontana Paperbacks,
Cash Sales Department, Box 29, Douglas, Isle of Man. Please
send a cheque, postal or money order (not currency) worth the
purchase price plus 22p per book for postage (maximum postage
required is £3.00 for orders within the UK).

NAME (Block letters) _____

ADDRESS _____

_____